FOLLOWING THE SUCCESS of his first rambunctious volume of memoirs, *Puttees And A Pinstripe,* covering his wartime childhood, teen years in the pre-Permissive Age and National Service in Korea and Gibraltar, now - with *All Wind And Pips* - Mike George resumes the chronicle of his unconventional life from 21 to 40. Military manoeuvres, civilian courtships and literary landslips are recounted in his inimitable style, which one critic described as "somewhere between Flashman and David Niven".

Twice widowed, currently he lives with his partner in Eastbourne, staving off senility and prolapsed kneecaps, while croaking off-key grand opera in the bath, awash on a pain-numbing sea of export-strength Plymouth gin.

By the same author

Puttees And A Pinstripe

Clive James,
Bill Bryson and a liberal
dash of *Flashman* meet as one
in **Mike George**

David Gee
Author *Shaikh- Down*

ALL WIND AND PIPS

by

Mike George

Published by New Generation Publishing

British Library C.I.P.

Author: mag@mikegeorge.co.uk

A MOTH-EATEN RAG on a worm-eaten pole,
It doesn't look likely to stir a man's soul;
'Tis the deeds that were done 'neath the moth-eaten rag,
When the pole was a staff and the rag was a flag

Sir E.B. Hamley

YEARS AGO on a TV chat show Peter Ustinov described a bellicose old colonel as being 'all wind and pips . . .'

I rather liked it!

For Rachel – Tali and Lex

ONE

BRIGHTON'S FIRST EVER NEWSPAPER was published on 6 September 1806.

I wasn't born then, so it wasn't going to be for another 150 years – fast forward to a chill morning in January 1959 - that I would become its newest staff member.

The Herald - for that was the newspaper's name - soon became rapidly established as one of Britain's leading provincial weeklies.

It was the first newspaper, for example, to report Napoleon Bonaparte's escape from Elba in 1815; the start of France's 'July Revolution' of 1830 - and in March, 1848, the story about the abdication of France's last Bourbon King, Louis Phillipe.

Didn't know any of that, did you?

Hey – so even as belatedly as this, it's still news to you; see?

That's the power of the (even provincial) press.

Mindful of the fate of Louis XVI and Marie Antoinette, his unfortunately guillotined forbears, and thus understandably fearful for his own life, Louis Phillipe had fled from Paris by coach (incognito, of course, and actually – no, *really* - disguised as one *'Mr Smith'*) eventually to touch safe landfall eastward along the coast from Brighton, at today's funnily enough stinky little French-owned Gateway to Britain, the rather insalubrious port of Newhaven.

As Michael Caine would have said: 'Not a lot of people know that.'

(See, you're not alone.)

The dear old paper was to enjoy many more equally exciting scoops as these, until on 4 November 1922 it became renamed *The Brighton and Hove Herald*, and in 1934 had grand new offices opened in Pavilion Buildings, just off Brighton's Old Steine, in the attractive architectural adjunct to the Prince Regent's famous Taj-Mahal-style palace.

After 165 years in circulation, its final edition (number 8,621) was produced on 30 September 1971, when it then became absorbed by the *Brighton and Hove Gazette*.

Since the paper's demise the ground floor of its erstwhile offices has long since become an eaterie called the *Ha! Ha! Bar and Kitchen*, but although a very nice place, shades of the last Bourbon king (and his chef) do not necessarily stalk its premises.

Aged twenty, I had just finished my National Service with The Royal Sussex Regiment in Korea and Gibraltar, and come back to live *pro tem* with my now divorced bank manager father in his bungalow at number 21, Stoney Lane, in Southwick.

Unless one was a member of some London criminal gang, people weren't looking to hire too many trained killers up the home-counties' high streets of Britain in those days, so necessity dictated that I should now embark upon a different career path to the one for which at great expense my country had already trained me.

From the age of twelve some of us know with absolute certainty that we have been put on earth by God to become a dentist, a doctor or an accountant, and with undeflected dedication we pursue that path, single-mindedly overcoming all hardship and obstacles in order to achieve our goal.

As for the rest of us, it would seem to be an incontrovertible fact that as our education system has been dumbed down so disastrously in recent decades, and our Establishment and society have slithered further and further into the trough of moral despair, if we have not become the acknowledged clog dancers of Europe by the time you are reading this, then it's long overdue and we pretty soon will be.

There was recently a TV advert for something - I don't know what, because half the time these days I can't grasp what they're advertising anyway, but it featured newly graduated university leavers clutching their all but worthless rolled scrolls and preening for the photographer in their hired mortar boards and gowns. The star turn, a cheerful young chappie in the centre with a pearly grin, was treating us to the Walter Mitty-like flashes of some of the many career options that were now open to him. First we saw him imagining himself a green masked and gowned surgeon gorily delving into a patient's stomach cavity; next he's conducting a thousand-strong orchestra; then bedazzling a packed courtroom with the power of his oratory - in short, poised at the threshold of an inevitably exciting and rewarding life. More or less able to read and write, the whole world apparently was now his oyster.

Would that it were so.

The majority of twenty-year olds (and at the time of which I write, I was one of them) don't have a clue what to do with themselves, and in the absence of wise parental guidance, which they would probably rail against anyway, those other than the already mentioned pre-ordained dentists, doctors and accountants, either set off down a wrong path completely, or else, surprised, hurt, non-comprehending and resentful, find themselves smacked up against the brick wall of reality and spend the rest of their lives on benefits.

What to do?

It was cold that mid-January of 1959.

Most of the time I spent sleeping on the drawing room floor beside the dying embers of the fire.

Unshaven and unkempt I don't think I undressed more than once a week, and then only to scratch.

Dad had no shower – people didn't, so much, in those days - just a luke warm avocado coloured bath, with dodgy grouting and inadequate heating.

I was twenty, unskilled, unqualified, unpolished, penniless and wheel-less. The garden was frozen solid so I couldn't mow the lawn for a work-out. I had no friends. I had only one civilian shirt, a pair of brown shoes and grey flannel trousers, a Harris Tweed jacket and a tie; no overcoat or gloves. I craved the warmth of Gibraltar and my erstwhile 'family', my buddies in the Royal Sussex Regiment who were still serving there and whom I had just left behind – but more than anything I longed to be back again with Rachel, my recently acquired Gibraltarian fiancée. Only a few weeks before I had left her waiting there trustingly for me on The Rock, while I 'established' myself in England quickly, so that I could return to get married and bring her back with me to start our life together.

Each morning when dad had gone off to work to manage his bank, I sat on the mat inside the front door awaiting the postman. More often than not he would delight in teasing me, saying there was nothing but a gas bill, but then turning at the end of the drive and seeing the tears in my eyes and an expression not unlike that of a dog whose bowl's been removed, he would take compassion: "Oh, look; there *are* a couple for you here I seem to have overlooked," he'd announce with a grin, holding aloft the familiar blue airmail envelopes as I lolloped eagerly up the drive to snatch them from his hand.

"Now look here, son," dad said to me one rainy Sunday afternoon, putting down his newspaper while I was sitting on the drawing room floor desultorily picking holes in the soles of my feet, "don't you think it's about time you started to sort yourself out a bit? It's not that I dislike that record you keep playing over and over again, nor do I really mind your room looking like a sodbuster's shack in the outback, and - believe me - I did appreciate your kind gesture in making my bed for me the other morning, although I would remind you that this *is* my home and not a barrack block: it's years since I've had my bedding and pyjamas 'boxed', and I'd really rather not have them boxed now. By the same token, I'd rather not have my slippers and shaving mug laid out for kit inspection either. I understand your position, but I'm afraid I can't afford to keep you for the rest of your life, mooning about here like a lovesick wossname. It's disturbing. You'll turn into a recluse soon, or else go doolally or something. Now - what do you say? How about a concerted effort? Clean yourself up tomorrow and go out and find a yourself a job properly."

Jeez.

He meant it.

A warning shot across my bows.

A salutary nudge in the right direction.

It was a crisp, clear day. The sun shone. But it was still cold.

Now that I was out in the fresh air I knew I would have to find a job soon, just so that I could buy an overcoat.

I had taken a long overdue bath earlier that morning, spruced myself up as best I could, and caught the bus from Southwick along the coast to Brighton. Wandering about, bereft of ideas, although I wasn't to know it until later, something nevertheless seemed to be drawing me inexorably towards the offices of Brighton's oldest newspaper.

I had just had a warm up cup of coffee and a Bath bun in Joe Lyons and was walking down North Street.

Rounding the windswept corner at the bottom and turning left into Pavilion Buildings, I glanced up to see a distinctive black clock mounted proudly outside some impressive looking offices, and that was when I discovered for the first time the existence of the *Brighton and Hove Herald.*

Once through the brass, glass and wooden revolving door, its tiled lobby led me across to a beautiful, highly polished, wrap-around wooden counter, behind which a clutch of attractive girls was industriously beavering away answering telephone enquiries, processing classified advertisements and buffing their nails.

As I approached one section of this vast semicircular counter, a more mature lady got up from her desk and came across to greet me with a nice warm smile.

"Good afternoon," I said. "I wonder if you have a job?"

"Yes, thank you," she replied. "Quite a nice one as a matter of fact, and I'm very happy doing it. May I enquire why?"

"Er - no; what I mean is. . . I was rather thinking of - well, a job for *me*, actually."

5

"Yes, I thought that's probably what you meant." She laughed. "What sort of 'job' do you have in mind, exactly?"

"Any job, really" I replied. "Well, you know - something nice, of course; if you have one."

"Why do you need a job, particularly?"

"To buy an overcoat. I mean, I haven't got one. A job, I mean. Nor an overcoat."

"Yes, those would seem to be good enough reasons. What were you doing before?"

"Before what?"

"Before you came in here."

"Having lunch."

"I mean what sort of work were you doing?"

"I was a trained killer - guarding things."

"*Course* you were; silly old me. I should have known."

"Actually, they haven't let me kill anyone for simply ages," I told her. "In fact, I've been . . . 'laid off', so to speak."

"How *dreadful,*" she sympathised, and suddenly I had the feeling that she might be about to press one of those little emergency buzzer things beneath the counter with her foot.

"I've just finished my National Service," I blurted.

"I thought it might be something like that." She smiled. "I'm not in a position to offer you anything personally, you understand . . ." I nodded my head, to show that I did - "but I do believe that Mister King is looking for a young man upstairs at the moment."

"And you'd like me to help try to find him?"

"No, not exactly: I thought you might *be* him. If you'd care to wait a moment I'll go and find out if he can see you, shall I?"

Harold King, the Managing Director of the *Brighton and Hove Herald* was a blue-suited, bespectacled, crisply moustached, brusque and businesslike little newspaperman who smoked cigarettes and smothered his waistcoat with ash. He had been in the army himself at some stage and agreed to see me because apparently he liked my initiative in just polling up at his front office on the off-chance – besides which, it saved him having to advertise.

Hard as they still were, things must have been somehow easier in those days. This had been my first ever approach at finding a job, and just by opening a door and walking in . . . here I was being interviewed for one already.

"Sold space before, have you young man?"

I had not yet developed much interview technique, though. I gaped.

"Space," he repeated. "It just so happens that you have appeared here rather fortuitously this afternoon. I'm looking for someone to fill a vacancy in our advertising department, to sell newspaper advertisement space to local tradespeople. Think you could do that?"

"I'm quite sure I could."

"Is it the sort of thing you had in mind?"

"Not exactly, no; I've always rather fancied the editorial side of things more, to be honest."

"Ever had any experience at that sort of thing?"

"Not yet, no."

"You see, my editorial staff are fully up to strength at the moment, so I couldn't slot you in there I'm afraid. That's not to say you wouldn't get the opportunity to write the occasional piece if you felt like it, and if it was good enough I'm sure we'd be able to print it, but in the meantime the vacancy in the advertising department is open if you'd like it. It's up to you."

"Very well. Thank you. I'd like to take it."

"You will? Oh, good. We'd better discuss your salary then, hadn't we."

It wasn't so much a salary. More a wage.

£9 a week. About £8,000 p.a. today.

I was asked to start next morning.

Dad was so delighted when I rang him at his office to tell him the news that he left early, to come and finance the purchase of a seven-guinea suit for me from the popular high street tailor, Montagu Burton.

Next morning, my first day in my new job, I was leaning against an oil heater sipping tea and getting to know my new colleagues when the door was flung open and in strode Harold King himself. Thinking I was still in the army I leapt to my feet as a prelude to saluting him, but then remembering where I was I pretended I had burned myself on the heater.

"Nice suit," Harold King said, smiling.

"Nice to see you too, sir," I replied.

Robin Turrell was our manager; Freddie Bowers, Alan Klein and I were the reps, and Mavis King (the boss's daughter) was 'the girl'. We shared an office, and a green and yellow *Herald* van which we took it in turns to use.

I was to work there for a year.

Robin left to start his own printing business; Alan lived with his mother but then left to get married; Freddie became married to Mavis (just for a little while, mind) - and in June of that year I flew back out to Gibraltar to marry my Rachel.

By then I had vacated my bedspace on dad's drawing room carpet and found myself a one-room bedsit at number-nine Farman Street, in Hove. It was the top floor of a town house owned by a senile old vicar, his lesbian daughter and her butch girlfriend. I had a kitchenette the size of a coracle's galley, and use of the communal bathroom.

It was agreed that I could remove and store the existing single bed and replace it with a cast iron Put-U-Up sofa-bed, which I purchased for a fiver at some local flea market for my new wife and me to become better acquainted upon. Robin, Alan and Freddie helped me deliver this beast in a van one day and manhandle it (the Put-U-Up, not my new wife) up the narrow stairs and into place against the wall of our two-by-four room in that insalubrious little Hove backstreet. For the transplantation and accommodation of one rare and exotic 19-year old Mediterranean bloom, here was I, Michael George, who had spent the last three years since I was seventeen sleeping in barrack rooms, aboard troopships and in snow-filled Korean ditches, now eagerly preparing his own little nuptial pad over which no parent, sergeant or CSM would have jurisdiction.

I was surprised that Rachel's mother hadn't intervened.

Subsequently I learned that she had of course, understandably so, and in no mean fashion, but apparently my betrothed really did fancy me and was determined to see the whole thing through to completion - so everything was now set for 22 June 1959.

Tea chests of feminine apparel from Gibraltar began to arrive at Brighton Station for collection, containing several years' accumulation of bottom drawer goodies and other indescribably frilly and seemingly impractical feminine items that made my pulse race in anticipation. Rachel and her family must have been under the mistaken impression that I was a young man of means, with capacious quarters in which to house her. Nothing was further from the truth. Exciting as they were, these incoming dowry shipments of hers packed the single room so tightly that I could scarcely open up the sofa-bed to sleep on at night.

As an indication of how low down there on the first rung of self-sufficiency I was, I used to shop only once a week. My purchases were always the same and consisted of seven tins of oxtail soup; seven pints of milk; seven instant-whip type 'Angel Delights'; coffee, bread, butter and strawberry jam so that I had my fruit intake. These ingredients comprised my regular daily diet for my six months of civilianised bachelorhood, and the preparation of even these limited comestibles was sufficient to tax the outer resources of my culinary abilities.

All I possessed to offer this marriage, was myself on a tin plate.

Jim was to be my best man.

My best buddy in Korea and Gibraltar was a chap called Jim Davidson. I had left him behind soldiering-on in Gibraltar when I'd come home the previous December. It was now June, and just a few weeks earlier he had been demobbed himself, as I was to discover to my embarrassment one day.

Jim's father owned *The Cambridge* pub in Hastings, in which he was to work and would one day inherit, so he had no need to acquire or retain any other gainful life's employment.

Like those doctors we spoke about earlier, Jim's career path as a professional dispenser of alcohol had been mapped out since birth.

Harold King was having a conference upstairs on that afternoon when Jim burst into the vestibule of the front office below.

He was going through his own uncouth rehabilitative period of adjustment, when he neither washed nor shaved and had time on his hands.

He had also taken to smoking a misshapen and foul smelling pipe.

Clad in beaten up old beige cavalry twill trousers, a pair of suede chukka boots, navy blue Guernsey sweater and his grease and mud-stained green Korean parka, he had stood in the middle of the lobby while the outraged revolving door he'd just swept through hissed behind him like a trio of freshly violated spinsters tugging down their skirts - and bellowed: "Where's that bastard George, then?"

Down in the basement the thundering press faltered. The older female employees all went "Oh," and shied away, while the younger ones sat up to pay attention and lean forward with mounting interest. Weaker chinned members of the male staff back-pedalled swiftly up the stairs as if scorched, while Jim - who had only ever been jungle-trained so was oblivious to the consternation his appearance had caused - stood happily grinning, legs apart, hands on hips, emitting pungent puffs of pipe smoke through his nostrils, waiting for something to happen.

It was our sterling Mrs Kessler, the sweetheart who'd greeted me so nicely and got me my first interview with Harold King, who now peered cautiously above the counter-top like Chad, to ask if she could be of assistance.

"Yup," said Jim, turning his head like a heavy animal to face her and focus. Shifting his body round he clumped across to the counter. "I understand Mike George works here."

"Er . . . that's right, yes, he does," Mrs Kessler nodded. "Have you come to get him," she asked, momentarily forgetting she was fronting a provincial south coast weekly, not the *Chicago Blaze*.

"Just to say 'Hallo'," Jim beamed . . . "and to let him know I'm home again. We're buddies, you see. In Korea together," and he whipped round to mock machine-gun the still attentive row of startled typists. My stock was either going rapidly up, or else down, out there in the front office. Jim was coming on like a beneficent Genghis Khan besieging a castle whose only defence was loyal but ill prepared hand maidens, while the good Prince, whom Genghis had befriended and come to see, dined on unawares up in the Keep.

"I'll see if he's in for you, shall I?" Mrs Kessler croaked, fearfully groping for the voice pipe up to our advertising office.

"There's a . . . there's a . . . some sort of a person down here to see you in the front office," I heard her voice whisper up the pipe into my ear. "Says he's an army acquaintance of yours." There was a pause; and then as an even more fearfully added afterthought, she asked: "Do you think perhaps I should call the police?"

"Wassisname, Mrs K?" I asked through a mouthful of hot buttered muffin Mavis had just thrust into my hand to accompany my tea.

"Er . . . a Mister . . . he says it's Jim."

"JIM" I shrieked in joyful disbelief. *"Bless* you, Mrs K. I'll be right down."

I flung my half eaten muffin onto the blotter and dashed from the office to clatter down the stone stairs and out into the front office.

"JIM" I roared.

"MIKE,' he thundered reciprocally.

We crashed into an instant bear hug and shoulder pummelling session and the front office was stunned to learn that their nice, quiet, polite and unassuming young Mr George had this other, darker side to his character, and, obviously, something of an extremely questionable background.

What had happened?

My buddy Jim had come home, that's what had happened.

They were very nice people, civilians, but they hadn't been with Jim and me and the rest of the good old Royal Sussex Regiment out in the frozen wastes of Korea, so although it wasn't *their* fault, in *our* puerile minds they lacked something at that time. All a load of simulated post adolescent cobblers of course, but to us it meant an awful lot.

"So what about this wedding of mine out in Gib then, Jim?" I asked him.

We were strolling along Brighton seafront together, and had reminisced and updated to exhaustion. I was now fully apprised of the latest Battalion scandals, the new personalities within it, and its proposed future moves. Jim had already met Rachel in Gibraltar of course, and was not in the least averse to me marrying her.

"Why on earth can't you have it over here?" he grumbled. "Why do you have to go all the way out to Gib to do it?"

"Because that's where she lives, and all her family and friends are out there," I said, always having taken it as read that the ceremony would take place on The Rock. "The bride's family usually makes all the arrangements, doesn't it - the scoff, and invites and things? My mother and younger brother Anthony are out in South Africa, and my father's busy that afternoon, so if we had it over here there'd be no one to attend. It's much easier for me to fly out there.

"Yeah, but not for me," Jim groaned, trying to conceal some sort of embarrassment.

"Why?" I asked. "All you do's get on a plane this end, and three hours later I meet you in Gib."

"Truth is, Mike, I've spent all my money. I've no longer got the air fare to get there."

"Christ," I said. After all, *I* was not in a position to pay his fare for him, and it hadn't even begun to occur to me until then that perhaps I should have done. "What do we do now then?"

We walked some more and chatted some more and in my youth and eagerness I still didn't hoist in that Jim's reluctance to undertake his previously agreed role as my best man, was a thinly veiled endeavour to withdraw from the commitment completely. Upon reflection I fully understood Jim's reticence to get himself all the way back down to Gib just to stand at my side as a token gesture for half-an-hour, when he had already paid-his-dues in Korea, in far more harrowing ordeals. But there on Brighton seafront that day his reticence still hadn't registered, so I persevered.

"Tell you what, Jim," I said excitedly, as the thought came to me. "You could hitch-hike down. The wedding's not for another three weeks. You'd have plenty of time to get there . . . *and* see France and Spain on the way. It's summer. You could sleep in ditches and have all *sorts* of adventures. I could take your suit out with me on the plane."

"Suit? What suit? I haven't got a suit. No one said anything about a suit."

"Oh." I was still being obtuse. "Well, it doesn't really matter Jim."

Who was I to condemn a man, just because he had no suit?

I hadn't had a suit myself until a few months back.

Nor an overcoat.

But I thought he might have made a bit of effort to get one for my wedding. After all, it would always come in useful later.

"So whaddya say, Jim?" I prompted, still puzzled by his seeming lack of enthusiasm.

"About what?" He kicked a pebble which went skidding along the promenade ahead of him.

"Hitch-hiking down to Gib," I persisted.

"Well, I suppose I could," he grinned, probably realising that to agree was the only way to shut me up.

"*Good* man," I enthused, thumping him on the back. "Now, I really must dash back to the office, I'm afraid: I've got a newspaper to run."

(Get *me*.)

My regiment had recently been relieved in Gibraltar by the freshly amalgamated - and thence only recently formed - Prince of Wales's Own Regiment of Yorkshire, just in from Aden, and . . .

. . . when I say 'my' regiment (the thousand-strong 1st Battalion The Royal Sussex Regiment {whereas in WWI we had fielded not just one, but *23* battalions}) it sounds most pretentious: almost as though I owned it. Commanding officers have always legitimately and proudly referred to it during their tenure of office as CO, as being 'my' regiment, and Colonels of regiments (usually generals, who assume avuncular roles as watchkeepers of 'their' respective regiments' interests) also do so - but then quite legitimately so does everyone else who's ever served in a regiment and worn its cap badge.

Whether one is a family patriarch or just a junior member of it, it is still 'my' family.

So it is with a regiment.

My regiment was at this time almost 300 years old, and I had done nothing especially spectacular, noteworthy or memorable whilst serving within it, except 'serving', and thereby 'paying my dues' and acquiring lifelong 'membership', along with the many, many, *many* thousands of others who had done so before me (although not quite so many since . . .)

But it was still 'my' regiment and since its return from The Rock was now stationed at Hobbs Barracks, at Lingfield in Sussex.

The Battle of Quebec had been fought on 13 September 1759.

We were there.

Not Jim and me; we would have been too young - but our regimental forbears were there.

It was at the Battle of Quebec that they had plucked the glorious white plumes from the headdress of the defeated French Roussillon Regiment, and afterwards incorporated them into our own regimental cap badge. The plume resembled a single Prince of Wales's type feather, and miniaturised in silver looked most well curling from behind our badge's Garter Star and Scroll. We are very proud and fond of our Roussillon plume, which today - since the regiments's sad demise - has been further incorporated into the more recently amalgamated Princess of Wales Royal Regimental regalia.

In 1959 the Royal Tournament was being held as usual in London's Earl's Court, and to celebrate the 200th anniversary of the Battle of Quebec that year, The Royal Sussex Regiment was to take part in the tournament, performing a historical re-enactment of its role in that great and decisive battle.

It was Friday 2 June.

With his rucksack on his back and stout boots, Jim had set out by foot a week earlier for his mammoth *schlepp* down to Gib, and I was flying out during the early hours of the 3rd - the very next morning, so as I had to be in London that evening anyway, it had seemed like a pleasant stag-night send-off to take myself along to watch the boys perform at the Royal Tournament. It would be the first contact I'd had with the regiment since I'd left them six months before.

Standing in a small queue at one of the Earl's Court ticket offices waiting my turn to shuffle forward, I noticed that one of the figures up front looked distinctly familiar.

"Jim?" I called anxiously, in a husky croak.

He had just reached the kiosk window to buy his ticket. Hearing my voice he tried to sink his head into his shoulders, dropped his change, scrabbled to retrieve it amongst the fag packets and then shuffled back sheepishly to where I stood.

"Jim," I spluttered.

"Sorry, Mike," he said. "It was all too difficult."

"What was?" I gasped.

"The whole bloody thing, dammit man. I set out full of good intentions, with a freshly laundered plume in my helmet, spear held aloft, but then I got blisters. I looked at the map and was daunted by the distance, so I turned round and came home again, spear snapped, plume bent . . ."

"How far did you get?" I asked.

"Folkestone," he said.

The Royal Tournament was fabulous. The regiment's re-enactment of the Battle of Quebec was *formidable*. A myriad of memories were evoked where Jim and I had supported and helped each other out in the past, and I wallowed afresh in that wonderful atmosphere of raillery and chiding camaraderie peculiar to the armed forces. Some years later I was to hitch-hike down to Gibraltar myself, and it was then that I appreciated how justified Jim's reluctance to do so had been.

After the show many old faces appeared and thronged round us, and later twenty or more willing hands packed me off into London Air Terminal.

I was on my way back out to Gibraltar - to be married.

TWO

"LADIES AND GENTLEMEN, YOU ARE ASKED to extinguish all cigarettes and fasten your seat belts, please. We shall be landing at Gibraltar in just a few minutes."

The southern sun glared hotly through the window, adding to the discomfort of the previous night's alcoholic send off from London. The plane circled the dear old Rock and touched down gently (so I was told) before taxiing to a standstill about fifty yards from the main terminal building. The iconic North Face soared away 1,400-feet above us as it had done for millennia , tall, straight, sentinel-like and proud, and at ground level porters and airport officials rushed slowly about the place.

I was back once more on the southernmost tip of *mañana*-land.

Filing into the plane's open doorway I glanced at the waving, smiling crowd of lightly clad people expectantly gathered up on the airport roof. They were each of us passengers' respective personal reception committees.

Rachel and her family were somewhere up there amongst them too, waiting with pensive anxiety . . . wondering.

It was her 19th birthday.

Carrying a copy of that day's *Daily Express* beneath my arm I tripped at the top of the ladder and went crashing headlong through the rest of my elegantly alighting fellow passengers. Coming to rest on the tarmac at the bottom, all shook up, I was helped to my feet by two burly airport policemen who set me off in the right direction, but then had to retrieve me again when I went veering at a tangent towards the nearby Spanish frontier, right in the path of an incoming Viscount. A couple of alert photographers snapped off a few quick ones just in case they were unwittingly witnessing some sort of political defection, and then a customs official pointed me back towards the proper channel.

Up on the roof Rachel and her folk experienced a sinking feeling.

There is nothing more frustrating than hanging about in suspended animation in a customs hall, seeing the people you have flown half way round the world to see standing plainly visible and well behaved, but incommunicado, behind a plate glass window. At best you can give wan little smiles and funny little waves and reassuring nods to each other, while mouthing inane and incomprehensible absurdities whenever your eyes chance to meet, so it is best to try to ignore each other, until customs have finished with you and you can then fall into each other's arms properly.

On this occasion I was spared such a scenario on account of being unable to focus much beyond the barrier anyway. But everyone else saw Rachel, patiently standing there, serenely elegant, and I am sure they sympathised with her.

"Yes, my dear; that dreadfully hung-over young man who fell down the gang-plank. I mean, just look at him there now, tap dancing like a loon, waving his newspaper about and kissing that poor customs man. Why, look Cynthia, he's squinting at you. No - he's not, he's actually winking. Well, really . . . Cynthia? Why are you smiling like that . . .?"

And so it came to pass that after a six months separation our romantic reunion consisted of a very unsure peck on a reticently proffered left cheek, a formal handshake from Rachel's parents, and a slightly strained walk out to the car.

Driving through Gibraltar's 11.00 a.m. streets Rachel assured me that she had been keeping very well thank you.

Even the family car sensed the atmosphere.

It stalled twice in sympathy for one faction or the other.

I suspect mine, because on the second occasion it did so to allow a ravishing specimen of Gibraltarian pulchritude to smoulder her hip-swinging way across the road in front of us, whereupon Rachel saw fit to pinch me good and hard.

I yelped and rubbed my thigh.

The thaw had set in.

By the time we reached the family home at 64, Kingsway House, all were smiles once more. The mantle of reserve had been lifted and there emerged all the people, places and things just as I'd remembered them six months before. By lunchtime it was as if I had never been away.

My prospective mother in law was something of a gourmet and received with pleasure the delicacies I had procured for her from a London delicatessen the previous day.

But it was Rachel who came off best.

Shoes from Bond Street's Russell & Bromley, a myriad of odds and ends - and . . . *a pink bikini.*

There descended an ominous silence.

When the offending item was withdrawn from the depths of my suitcase, even the curious goldfish on the bookcase looked more goggle-eyed than usual, and back pedalled so fast that it buckled its rear fin on the far side of its bowl.

The sun clouded over, a sudden frost crackled, and the happy grin froze and faded on my stupid face.

Over the ensuing years Rachel would happily and healthily come to romp in the brinies of the world with her deliciously tanned boobs a go-go and bare bum flashing in the breeze, but perhaps I should have known that to produce a bikini in Gibraltar's constrained 1959 society would cause even more consternation than at the court of Queen Victoria.

My fiancée's parents blanched and shuddered.

Whatever was going to befall their beautiful daughter - about to be plucked from the bosom of her family and dragged off to that licentious northern land in the hands of this debauched reprobate who seemed intent on displaying her young body on the beaches of the world clad in nothing but that . . . that disgusting . . . *thing?*

Heaven forfend.

(All this rattled off in quick-fire Spanish, of course).

Rachel winked me a mischievous wink, which suggested "perhaps not tonight, Joseph, but give me time and I'll think about it . . ." and we poured a tot for her little old Spanish granny, who was also present, now prostrate on the floor with the simulated shock that decorum decreed.

When she'd fully revived a few days later, I caught the old dear secretly cadging a sly glance at the expensive frippery, fondling it saucily and chuckling to herself, lost in some reverie of her own, although I couldn't imagine that she recalled bikinis much. In her day it had all been *strappados; tourniquets; conquistadores* and *inquisitores.*

That little pink bikini never saw the light of day in Gib again, or in Spain.

My vain attempt to enlighten those moral-bound and pious places through the medium of my (not entirely unwilling) fiancée did not go down in history.

Today it is a different story entirely of course, when it is possible - even the norm - to romp naked on most Spanish beaches, but in 1959 just the sight of a bikini would have been cause for the *Guardia Civil* to fix bayonets and charge, so for the rest of that summer Rachel and I had to baste in our conventional one-pieces.

We brought our honeymoon forward and enjoyed three weeks holiday together *before* our wedding, sunbathing, swimming in the turquoise depths, drinking and merrymaking in Spain, watching the bulls fight, sailing, arguing and loving.

Then dawned the day of reckoning.

Monday 22 June 1959.

We were to be married.

I was awakened in the spare room that morning by Rachel jumping onto my bed to festoon me with clutches of coloured telegrams that had arrived from family and well wishers at home and around the globe.

For traditionalists I should explain that accommodation in the two-square miles that constitute Gibraltar, has always been at a premium. This was the height of the summer season. Hotels were packed. It was only practical for me to stay at Rachel's home. The previous night had been spent until 3.00

a.m. anyway, with Tito and Danny, two of Rachel's brothers, at the Panama Night Club on Eastern Beach savouring the delights of what, for me, were to pass next day for evermore (!), so at 3.30 a.m. on Monday 22 June I didn't feel much like sleeping on a park bench just to comply with outmoded tradition.

In the event, immediately after breakfast I was hustled out of the place completely, and told to go and sit on the beach or something, until called.

Feeling like the least wanted person in the whole world, I sat on a rock lobbing small boulders at the Med., contemplating the shores of Africa opposite, thinking *shall I?* but just as I decided that yes, I probably would, I was collected by a fraternal deputation, taken home and led through a bustle of unfamiliar faces to the bathroom where I was unceremoniously dumped into the bath and told to prepare myself.

Scrubbed, dried and dressed up in my new charcoal grey suit, I was then thrown to the vultures again and told to go and sit over in Alameda Gardens, the park opposite, and not let myself get dirty. I would be called for when needed, so should not wander too far.

I realised a wedding is the bride's day, and that I was merely an accessory.

At 5.00 o-clock I was whistled back in again, and this time got to stay.

It was the real thing at last.

I was ushered through a sea of Goya-esque faces.

A flashlight popped.

I felt like the key witness arriving at a People's Court.

Then I saw our wedding cake.

It stood 4-feet high in the centre of a sumptuously decorated table.

I didn't half miss my mum.

Rachel and I being of different religions had posed a slight problem. She did not wish to marry into my church, nor I to hers. Neither of us was especially orthodox, but was content enough in our respective camp not to want to rock the boat.

The outcome was to be a delightful old style Spanish wedding held on the balcony of her home, overlooking the Bay of Gibraltar, with the Iberian peninsula beyond.

General Sir Charles Keightley, the then Governor of Gibraltar, had had to issue a special licence to allow the ceremony to be performed in this manner, a ceremony which was conducted by Gibraltar's registrar, the appropriately named Mr Norton Amor.

When I leaned forward to sign my name in the open register, a great *Olé* just chanced to come ringing out across the Bay, from the bull ring, over in nearby Algeciras.

A moment of truth indeed.

"Ladies and gentlemen," the registrar intoned: "in the course of my duties, as you can imagine, mine is the pleasure to kiss thousands of brides. On some occasions, I confess, it is something of a dubious pleasure and more in the nature of an occupational hazard, but I can quite honestly say that for a long time I have not looked forward to claiming my privilege quite so much as I do this afternoon."

He probably said this to most of the brides, but we didn't mind.

A short while later he bade his farewells and nipped back to City Hall, and by then Rachel had returned in her grey and white going away suit, with red accessories.

It seemed as if the whole of Gibraltar had turned out for our send-off. Rachel's apartment block was eight stories high. People hung from windows, thronged the passageways and threw rice from the rooftop, which rattled like buckshot on the car. They sprinkled bags of confetti over our heads and shoulders. They waved. They cheered. They dabbed their eyes. I felt like a prince for the day, and gained some inkling of what it must be like to be someone popular making a public appearance.

The beribboned car pulled out onto the main road and sped us to the airport.

We were off to spend two days in London, prior to my returning to resume my duties at Brighton's oldest newspaper once more.

Our two-day London honeymoon was not a memorable one. The Strand Palace Hotel had seemed like a good idea at the time, and sufficed as a base for a compressed sight-seeing tour of the capital for Rachel, who at that stage of her young life had only ever been as far afield as Tangier and Malaga.

We arrived at the hotel at midnight.

Innocents on the threshold of our new marriage, we were aware that certain things were expected of us, but were both too tired and weary to want to try too hard at any of them. Hell - with fair weather and a tail wind, sixty years lay ahead of us - why rush to conform to an expected pattern?

Besides which - I was ill.

Was I ever!

Nerves? Exhaustion? Anti-climactic disillusionment?

I didn't know what it was, but no sooner had I tipped the porter and closed the door than I started to sweat, shake, and come on with a runny nose. It seemed that I must be allergic to my new wife all of a sudden, or the thought of her, or the officially sanctioned close proximity to her. Instead of cracking our nuptials I opened our bottle of duty free Scotch. It seemed like an acceptable and manly enough thing to do in the circumstances, even out of a plastic mug. It was the sort of thing men would have done in other like plights, such as sweating out a bout of malaria on a charpoy in some far flung hell-hole of a colonial outpost.

Rachel said she understood.

She even seemed slightly relieved.

We slept.

Next day I was fine again.

After breakfast we saw London by taxi, watched *South Pacific* in cinemascope, fell asleep quickly again that night, and then the following morning caught the train back home to Brighton.

Home?

There was no line-up of family retainers waiting to greet their new lady on the steps of my Dickensian bedsit in Farnham Street. All that awaited us there was a gas bill and a small pile of mail and wedding presents, delivered during my three weeks away in Gib and strewn neatly across the Put-U-Up by our lesbian landlady.

Because of Gibraltar's perennial housing shortage, Rachel had become so conditioned to the accommodation plight of many of her recently married friends, that this attic love nest I had secured for us seemed even classier than *The Ritz*. Mind, it was fortunate that we had few possessions, and no cat.

The doorbell rang.

Footsteps trod the narrow stairway up to our heavenly eyrie.

It was my father, by pre-arrangement hot footing it round to satisfy his curiosity.

"Olé," cried Rachel, snapping her fingers and striking a dramatic flamenco pose on the mini-landing at the top of our stairs.

"How do you do?" said dad, rather like Captain Mainwaring in an embarrassing situation.

I smiled approvingly, and let them get on with impressing each other. They seemed to do this quite well, because a week later dad stole my young bride away to Glyndebourne for the evening, to assess her cultural adaptability - and also to be seen accompanied by a stunning piece of skirt on his arm.

"I'm afraid I was only able to get tickets for two," he explained to me placatingly.

Me? Married? It was ridiculous.

Whether it was post-matrimonial nerves, or what, but I still didn't really know why I'd done it. It must have had something to do with my parents' divorce when I was sixteen, my mother and 17-year old brother having emigrated to Cape Town (Mum to fulfil a long held girlhood dream to see the Dark Continent), my having left the Army, and/or Dad's bungalow being too small for the two of us.

I was twenty-one, and although now gainfully employed selling advertising space for Brighton's oldest newspaper, I knew I was still basically directionless and seeking a proper calling, and the thought of a nest of my own with an attractive and cuddly inmate to person it, wash shirts, sow buttons, and tickle my fancy had seemed like a good idea at the time. Accordingly, I had allowed myself to go with the flow.

I was a lately vacated army number - 23463195, just for the record - who was now inhabiting an empty shell. I knew there were a good few years of heavy forging and personal development still ahead of me before I could stand up and be counted as a proper person, so it was encouraging to think that Rachel must have seen some promising potential, to have latched on to me as she did. Oh, I was a pleasant enough, clean cut young fellow who didn't drop his aitches or pick nostrils in public or swear in front of the vicar, and I suppose I gave some impression of being reasonably ambitious, although what it was I might eventually succeed in might have been difficult to foresee. What had helped decide her to uproot from her native Mediterranean shore and relocate to the alien soil of Sussex, I never knew. When I asked her about it years later, she still didn't know herself, either, but smiled with enigmatic resignation.

So there we were, the two of us, back there in the late '50s on the brink of married life with not much going for either of us except our youth and beauty. The former we associated with gaucheness and found to be a drawback; the latter quality we were unaware of, but even if we hadn't been we wouldn't have known how to market it as a profitable commodity - at least not legally . . . or nicely. If Rachel had been some Romany mystic into tarot cards it might have been easier to see what she was up to. Our new found connubial arrangement would have been fate having cast me as her soul mate, and not for the likes of mere mortal underlings to say her nea. If she had been an opportunist young Gibraltarian go-getter who wanted access to England, I could have seen what she hoped she might have been up to as well - but she was neither of these. She was an ordinary, attractive, gentle natured and principled young woman with a gorgeous figure and lovely skin who had agreed to try out becoming a Mrs George.

In recognition of my new responsibility, the oldest newspaper in Brighton generously increased my salary/wage from £9 a week, to £10. Rachel decided that seven tins of oxtail soup and Angel Delights for pudding were insufficient for two people to live on each week, so in order to supplement the contents of our kitchenette shelf she agreed that she would have to start work as well.

When I'd first met her in Gibraltar Rachel had been a secretary for Lewis Stagnetto, the A.F. Gomez BMC (British Motor Corporation) Concessionaires.

Back in those days the Rock was enjoying a wave of popularity as a film location. Although they're 'history' today, some of those movies still spring readily to mind. Alec Guinness's *The Captain's Paradise* made there in 1953 was the story of the skipper of the Mons Calpe ferry that plied the strait between Gibraltar and Tangier. He had a staid English wife (Celia Johnson) at home in Gibraltar, and another (Yvonne de Carlo) who played a more exotic number, at his other home in Tangier.

In 1957 the singer/entertainer Frankie Vaughan came out to make *Wonderful Things* on the Rock, where he played a Gibraltarian fisherman caught in a love triangle. While he was there he befriended a popular local roué called Levy Attias, and encouraged him to leave Gibraltar to try his hand in show business in UK. Levy took his advice. Resembling a latter day Gilbert Roland and renaming himself Ricardo Montez, Levy made several TV commercials and then had a successful run playing the part of Pedro in TV's *Mind Your Language.* Years afterwards Rachel's big brother, Joshua, was staying with friends in Kingston (Surrey; not Jamaica) when one of his friends' children, playing with the telephone, inadvertently dialled a random number and roused an irate subscriber. Leaning forward quickly to retrieve the sticky handset and apologise to whoever had been troubled at the other end of the line, Joshua was delighted by the amazing coincidence of discovering that it was none other than fellow Gibraltarian, Levy Attias, whom he had not seen for years.

Everyone is familiar with the traditional tale that if ever the apes leave Gibraltar, the Rock will be lost to Great Britain. *Operation Snatch,* filmed there in 1962, starred Terry Thomas as Lt 'Piggy' Wigg, the fictional wartime custodian of the apes - who loses one, so then has to venture behind enemy lines to capture another as a replacement.

In 1987 Piers Brosnan (007) was parachuted onto Gibraltar, and then had a hair raising race down the Rock in a Range Rover in *The Living Daylights* - but it was two films made there in 1958 that interested me the most.

The first of these was *I was Monty's Double.*

In order to fool the Axis powers into believing that General Montgomery was planning to mount the Allied invasion of Europe from somewhere other than Normandy, in 1944 a real life Lt-Col David Niven unearthed an obscure Royal Army Pay Corps lieutenant called Clifton James, who a) fortuitously was an amateur actor, and b) just happened to bear a striking resemblance to General Montgomery. While Monty himself was engaged elsewhere on affairs of import and high purpose, Clifton James appeared with great panoply out in Gibraltar in Monty's rig. His presence there hoodwinked the German spies into reporting back to Berlin that that was where Monty was, thereby adding to the jigsaw of their frightful dilemma regarding the location of the anticipated Allied invasion.

In 1954 (when I was still at school) my father and I went to a lecture at the Winter Garden in Eastbourne one evening, given by Clifton James, at which he told his incredible story. I still have the autographed copy of his book from that evening. Then four years later, when I'd come back from Korea, we were to meet again, in Gibraltar when he was there, playing himself, playing Monty, in the film of his book - *I was Monty's Double* . . .

. . . in which 'my' regiment was heavily involved.

The 'extras' we provided were impressive.

When 'Monty' landed in Gib 'that day in 1944', for the benefit of the German spies, he was conspicuously introduced to the Fortress's officers and dignitaries drawn up at North Front airfield to meet him. Captain Peter Calver (our OC 'C'

Coy) became a full wartime colonel for the day. CSM Mutter, fully garbed in breeches and a kepi, played a French general. Lt Brian Goring was a kilted Jock - and so on.

John Mills played a brigadier in the film.

To gain access to the set each morning, this well known actor had to be driven past Four Corners Guard Room down on the Spanish frontier, next to Gibraltar airport, already kitted out in his brigadier's uniform for that day's filming. As the Guard Commander there, bereft of instruction, I had been left to my own devices. Imbued with the adage that it was not the man inside the uniform, but his 'commission' that one saluted, we happily turfed out the guard each time to Present Arms to John Mills's slightly outdated King's thespian commission as he went past. He was amused by and appreciated our gesture enormously, which was always rewarded with a cheery wave from the car's window, and him crying out: "Morning chaps; please carry on."

Rachel had got to play a veiled Arab girl holding a tethered camel beside a Moroccan oasis in *I was Monty's Double*. One of her aunts was responsible for the Gibraltar end of many of the stars' wardrobes. During one fitting Rachel walked in and bumped into Dawn Adams. They became good friends and went off on a shopping spree together in Spain. On another occasion she went to a bullfight there with John Mills and Leslie Phillips.

The other film made there in 1958 was even more fun.

BMC had recently introduced the radically designed MGA sports car. Conveniently combining an MGA promotion with a travelogue of Gibraltar, a small unit of Columbia Pictures had shipped one of these red open-top phallic symbols out to the Rock, and were looking for an attractive girl to drive it round the place. There are many attractive girls in Gibraltar, but the local BMC concessionaire's secretary - Rachel - was there on the spot and as attractive as any, which is why she was invited to 'take the role'. As her fiancé I went along for the ride; riding shotgun. It never won an Oscar, but was a fun little flick to make, and at least we got an end of filming dinner at The Rock Hotel out of it.

THREE

THE PRINCIPAL PROBLEM WE HAD TO DEAL WITH at the start of our marriage was the unusual intensity of Rachel's homesickness. Latins are an emotional lot at the best of times. If they feel like it they'll burst into tears even if you just say "Good morning."

Pining for her family back in Gibraltar, Rachel cried herself to sleep every night for two years.

The first year - before I became used to it - was the worst. I used to think it must have been something I'd said. She was like a leaky tap that came on each night, which I assumed might get fixed one day. In order to allay this homesickness she stated categorically that she would have to visit her family each summer - or die. She was working as secretary to Lionel Chopin (no relation) the Managing Director of the Plummer-Roddis department store (later taken over by Debenhams) in Brighton's Western Road, and although her salary from there helped boost our kitchen(ette) shelf stock, it wasn't enough to finance a Mediterranean sabbatical each year, so to pay for the trip (and stave off her death) she took a supplementary evening job in a coffee bar in Church Road, Hove, called *The Cordoba*. She was hard working and popular, so when I went there for my supper each evening the various echelons of staff turned a blind eye to my choice veal cut and second coffee and strudel, when the bill was only for an egg mayonnaise sandwich.

It was at *The Cordoba* that we met and befriended Claire, Rachel's co-waitress for the duration.

Claire Walker was a handsome, personable, and strapping 22-year old blonde New Zealander in the process of working

29

her way round the world with a brunette Australian sidekick, called Alice.

Alice was soft, gentle, silly, sexy, and nice, and we loved her to bits: but Claire we adored.

She was a powerful woman, the likes of which one encounters only a few times in life. She would hate to have her femininity assailed, but she was a big, trail-blazing pioneer gal who could push back frontiers with a 32-foot buffalo-hide bullwhip and curl lesser mortals to a crisp with a twanging cut of her tongue. I harboured secret fantasies of making it with Claire, but doubted I was man enough even to tingle her little finger. She was awash with humour and warmth, a gutsy girl who could have powered her way unaided to the moon if needs be.

After six months living in a flat in Brighton, and keeping us on tenterhooks with their antics, and what they might get up to next, while daily grasping life by the throat and consuming it, she and Alice upped sticks and moved on to Europe - to Italy; then to South Africa, and North America, working their way the while, renting accommodation, whooping it up at parties and gathering about themselves loads of lifelong friends and admirers, all of whom were bowled over, enraptured and utterly captivated by this concentrated duo of lovable and dynamic, larger than life antipodean sunshines, and hyperbolical as this description might sound it is still insufficient to do their personae justice.

Then Alice married an Italian, and the team split up.

Claire, in due course, returned to New Zealand, married Stas Koes, an American psychologist she'd met working there, produced Katya, broke her leg in eight places skiing, divorced Stas, returned to the States and in the summer of 1977 married a heavily bearded Barry Simpson of Prickly Mountain, Vermont. She and Barry then produced a daughter, Sarah. Communication was never Rachel's strong forté, but Claire was much too good to lose touch with, so she and I gleefully maintained a correspondence for many years, during the course of which she has heaped fuel on the fire of my desire to write

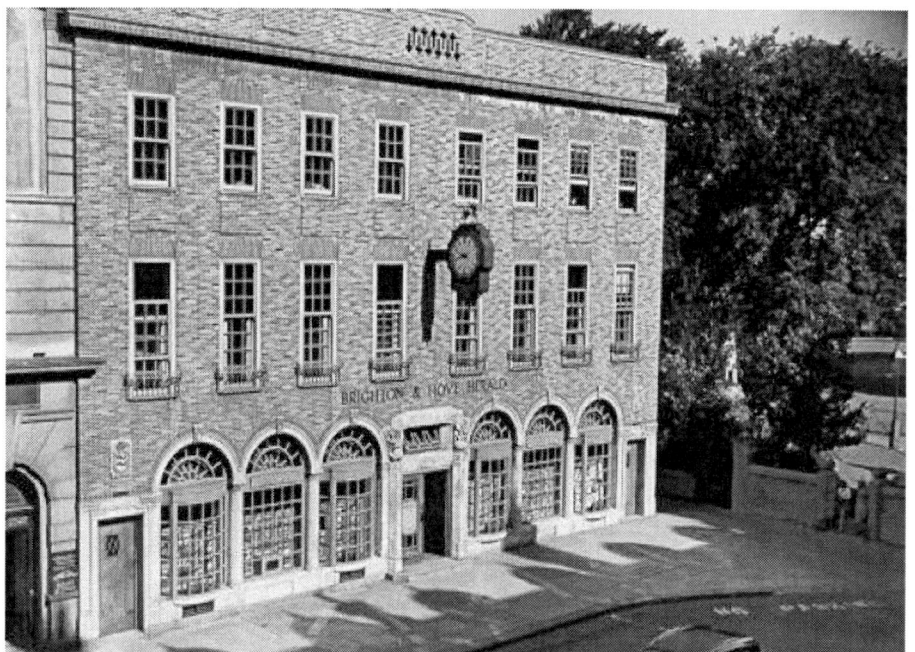

The Brighton & Hove Herald building: author's office 5th from left, first floor

An early love affair: another of the author's myriad of follies

Mr & Mrs Michael Aston
George –
Alameda Gardens, Gibraltar –
22 June 1959

**FATHER
& SON**

Mr & Mrs Heilyn Aston
George – honeymoon, Hove,
1937

Mr & Mrs Michael Aston George
– honeymoon, Hove, 1959: times
was 'ard: note the groom wearing
his father's same hand-me-down
sports jacket!

CLAIRE

ALICE

this book. Thanks Claire. You're priceless. One in a million. Treasured and much adored.

Coming from Gibraltar, Rachel had never seen snow.

We were married in June 1959.

In April 1960 we were having tea one afternoon with friends in Hove. It had been quite a warm, sunny day an hour earlier when we arrived. Now, as I opened the front door to leave, it looked as though God was emptying sacks of pretty little cotton wool balls all over the town.

I glanced up and down the road for the film crew, who must have been artificially generating the stuff.

It was still too warm to have been anything else.

Great billowing white flakes were whooshing down from the sky, like an accelerated quadruplication of the Arnhem landings. It was a gorgeous little prolonged freak flurry and didn't settle, but was memorable for the expression it caused to cross Rachel's face when she came to the door, saw it, and then with wonderment realised what it was.

"SNOW," she shrieked, gleefully, clapping her hands, jumping up and down like a three-year old, and doing a little jig in her summer dress and high-heel sandals as the joyful realisation of what she was seeing assailed her. "Oh, *do* please look everyone . . . *real snow*. Oh, how *lovely."* She flung out her arms to try to catch some of it in her outstretched fingers, grimacing and turning her face away as it settled on her eyelids and hair, and around her lips. Quickly she knelt to scoop and retrieve some from the lawn, but to her disappointment, with contact each flake instantly dissolved. She was beside herself with the experience, and that night babbled on *so* excitedly about it for fifteen minutes on the telephone, to her mother in Gibraltar.

For my part I knew that the expression of wonderment I had seen on her face that afternoon would stay with me the rest of my life.

Then we got the car.

Out of the £250 I had saved in the Army (£4,000 today) £100 of it had gone on air fares, the honeymoon, and setting up our bedsit.

The remaining £150 still lay nestling in a bank deposit account, waiting to make me rich.

Meanwhile, the desire for my first car and the possibility of actually being able to acquire one, grew a pace within me.

Some men seem not to be aware of or too bothered about personal grooming.

Others attach no importance to the interior of their car looking like a mobile ashtray; to them it is nothing more than a work horse, to be hammered, getting them from A to B.

Assuming the psychologists are right and that a man's car is a phallic representation of his imagined virility and persona, well, I'll go along with that. I know I would not be content driving around in a Morris Minor, or any other middle piece family saloon. As with women, in a car I go for good lines, reliability, and performance. There is nothing more satisfying than having a sun tan, a smart rig, and a gleaming pedigree automobile at one's command, in which either to hit-the-town or set out on a long journey. Over the years I have spent a lot of time in cars, and like to feel right in them.

By inclination a fastback coupé was to become my favoured marque.

Ideally, in metallic silver: *Pwhoarrrr.*

Intuitively, in 1959 I set out as I hoped to continue.

Michael George had espied and fallen in love with a second-hand MG, on a Hove garage forecourt..

LPJ 649 was a white 1949 'Y'- type, going for the then princely sum of £349.

£150 down and £9 a month for two years.

I bought it.

Rachel was not impressed.

I was stunned.

I thought any girl would be tickled pink to have such a car at such a time. *And* it had leather upholstery and a wooden dashboard.

"Think what else we could have done with all that money," she wailed.

"I did," I said, "and couldn't. What else could we have done with it that would possibly have been a better and more enjoyable investment than this?"

"*Any*thing," she cried. "Stocked the larder! Bought some furniture! Gone to Gibraltar . . .!"

Without yet having read about it in magazines, it was at that moment I learned that women are wired differently to men.

It was six-o'clock on a lovely summer evening. Hurt and in high dudgeon I took my beautiful new car out for its first test drive.

We purred proudly out of Brighton together on the A23. Putting my foot down we gradually reached 65 mph, and that's when its oil seals spontaneously burst. The brakes locked solid and boiling water and steam spouted like a geyser from the radiator cap.

My young heart was sorely hurt.

Feeling almost terminally dispirited by this momentous setback, I hitch-hiked home with tears in my eyes, and was very late for supper.

I told Rachel I'd parked round the corner.

Three days later I had to borrow £20 from a friend, to pay the backstreet garage's repair bill.

After one further prang, and my inability to sustain its maintenance costs any longer, I sold it a year later for £200. Would that I'd possessed keener foresight, money, and a long term garage for storage. That same model, refurbished, today couldn't be got for ten-grand!

And so - allied with other minor occurrences - we passed our first year of marriage together.

One night a good looking, 37-year old South African habitué at *The Cordoba* who drove a great big shiny Jaguar, suggested to Rachel that for certain considerations other than just frothy coffee, smiling, and flicking his table top for him, he might be prepared to consider financing her first trip back to Gibraltar for her, to see her mum. She must innocently have

36

mentioned to him once the reason why a nice girl like her was working in a place like that, and he, understandably, assumed that she had been giving him a pitch. As far as I am aware Rachel did not ever take him up on his offer, and having anyway by now saved enough for her trip, she left *The Cordoba* and flew back down to Gib for three weeks.

Thus the pressure of her homesickness was alleviated for a little while.

Number 9 Farnham Street's bedsit had now unquestionably become too small for us, so when Rachel returned from Gib refreshed, deliciously suntanned, smiling and ready to start again, we found ourselves another flat, and I changed jobs.

Number 74 Goldstone Villas was going to look good on a letterhead.

It, too, was no more than one room, a kitchen and a bathroom, above Jean's Hairdressing Salon, just outside Hove Railway Station, but its one room was larger than the one room we'd had in Farnham Street.

Moving there enabled us to ditch our ghastly green Put-U-Up, and buy our first proper bed, which in those far off, halcyon, destitute days of our early 20s - being young and beautiful, remember - was the centrepiece of our existence.

Now long since defunct as such, and absorbed by other companies, Ronuk was a firm that used to make the most highly acclaimed floor polish of its time.

Their head office and manufacturing complex were located at Portslade, near Brighton.

They had advertised in the local press for a Marketing Assistant.

Image-wise, I thought this sounded a bit like me, so I applied, was successfully interviewed, short listed, and was offered the job.

£40 a month.

Wow!

The big time at last.

Salaried with prospects.

The Marketing Manager, my master, was an able, dedicated, nail-nibbling, rotund little moustached ex RAF pilot-officer, with a keen sense of humour, called Pat Honan.

As I was soon to learn, Ronuk not only sold its domestic products to the housewife, but also operated a Contracts Department, which undertook the cleaning, preparation and preservation of large industrial floor spaces. Part of the Marketing Department's remit in pushing the whole RONUK concept was to give lectures, when invited to do so, to various groups such as the Womens' Institute, and Wives' Clubs. This was Pat Honan's task and one which, as his assistant, I could see him angling to dispose of in my direction. Towards this thinly disguised end he took me along with him on a couple of occasions, for me to learn the ropes and to see how good he was. Conveniently, he then got 'flu one day, and I was on my own.

My debut mission that evening was to talk to some obscure womens' group or other, in Horsham. They met at a local girls' school each week to discuss each other's cakes and good works, and to enjoy a guest lecturer.

Me.

I arrived at 7.30 for 8.00 p.m.

Busting to go to the loo.

Big loo. (First night nerves, y'see.)

Of course, there was only a Ladies, but there seemed to be no one else around, and my need was great, so I had no option but to use it.

Because it was a junior school, it had a low slung pan.

Squatting there like a legless Buddha, scanning the teenaged graffiti, my breeks crumpled round my ankles in waterlogged newsprint on the floor, I started . . . as an outer door crashed open and the surrounding cubicles swiftly began filling up with a never ending horde of women - my audience - eagerly chattering, and evacuating.

"Oo they got talkin' to us tonight then, Glad?" *(Snap; snap.)*

"Dunno, Marion." *(Flush; flush.)*

38

"Summatadowivwoodworkinnit." *(Rustle; twang-twang, rustle.)*

Then suddenly: "'Oo's that in there, then?"

One of them was standing immediately outside *my* door, rattling its handle, behind which I sat chewing a knuckle, quaking. I wasn't at all *au fait* with procedures in ladies' loos. For all I knew she might be going to jump up to have a look over the top. It was going to be daunting enough as it was for me to get through the evening; I didn't need this. I had never lectured in my life before. For my debut to be launched so inauspiciously was a dreadful omen. I was an embarrassing incident waiting to happen. I knew that somehow I was going to have to pre-empt my imminent dreadful dénouement.

"C'mon in there," persisted the harridan outside, testily rattling the handle again, seeming to think that she had greater claim to my sanctum sanctorum than I. "There's other people want a leak as well, you know, so shake a leg in there, whoever you are."

"I assure you that what I am endeavouring to shake in here, Madam, is considerably more than my leg," I boomed courageously.

The effect was electrifying.

Like the silence that suddenly pervades a flock of flamingos before they take terrified flight.

Were they suddenly about to be confronted by the butchest lesbian in all the world?

Next there came a startled little flurry of gentle *"Oh's"*, a flurry of activity as they collectively adjusted all their underpinnings as fast as they could, a lot of giggles and subdued chatter, the door banging - and they were gone; although as a parting shot, just before leaving, my original inquisitor did stridently demand: "Just 'oo the 'ell *is* that in there, then?" before she, too, left, flummoxed.

They never knew for certain if I was the groundsman, a caretaker, a mislaid parent, or me.

Nor did I enlighten them.

My lecture went off 'reasonably' well, but I do not like being associated with something I cannot do properly, or feel myself to be unequipped to contribute to wholly. MGM's Louis B. Meyer had a framed credo on his desk, which I love: *Do It Right; Do It Big; Give It Class.*

"How did it go?" Pat Honan asked in the office next morning.

"All right, I suppose," I said, shuffling a bit, twiddling a paperclip.

"I see. What went wrong?"

"I got by alright, but I wasn't on top of it. I don't really know the first thing about lecturing. I'm a baby-faced twenty-one-year old. It's difficult for me to put stuff across with conviction, without having any tricks of the trade to help me. If I am going to be expected to represent the Company to the public I need to be equipped to do it properly, to save embarrassment, to myself *and* to the Company.

"I agree absolutely," said Pat. "What do you suggest is the remedy?"

"Surely there must be a course or something, that I could go on?"

"Is there? Probably there is. I don't know. I'm sure you're right though. It's a good idea. Why don't you find one, and I'll see if we can arrange to send you on it."

Find one, I did.

Born in poverty on a farm in Missouri, in 1888, and suffering all manner of early privations and setbacks, in his teens, though still having to get up at 4 a.m. every day to milk his parents' cows, he managed to get educated at the State Teacher's College in Warrensburg. His first job after college was selling correspondence courses to ranchers; then he moved on to selling bacon, soap and lard for Armour & Company. He was successful to the point of making his sales territory of South Omaha, Nebraska the national leader for the firm.

Dale Carnegie later became an American writer and lecturer, and the developer of famous courses in self-

40

improvement, salesmanship, corporate training, public speaking, and interpersonal skills.

He was the well known author of the book *How to Win Friends and Influence People.*

First published in 1936, it enjoyed its 17th reprint within a few months and became a massive bestseller that still remains popular today. By the time of Carnegie's death, from Hodgkin's Disease, in 1955, aged 66, the book had sold five-million copies in 31 languages, and there had been 450,000 graduates of his Dale Carnegie Institute.

His first collection of writings was *Public Speaking: a Practical Course for Business Men* (1926), later entitled *Public Speaking and Influencing Men in Business* (1932).

A combination of all these personal development skills and 'lore' was just exactly what I was looking for, and it so happened that Fate was fortuitously going to put my way the wherewithal to do so.

It has long been fashionable in some circles to deride Dale Carnegie's philosophy. For some reason both my mother and brother considered my involvement with the organisation to have been the worst thing I ever did, turning me from the sweet, innocent lad that I was, into an OTT braggart, but it certainly gave me the confidence to be able to say "boo" to geese, and much, much more besides.

One of the hardest tests and worst experiences an untrained or unprepared person can have in life, is to find himself being called upon to speak extemporaneously, and effectively, in public.

It is a well documented and oft quoted fact that some fear the prospect even more than death itself.

I'd managed to survive my first ordeal by fire, by addressing that Horsham women's club, but I knew I had been ill equipped to do so, and now I was eager to add the ability to my small but burgeoning armoury of newly acquired life skills.

The very day following my talk with Pat Honan, I chanced to see in Brighton's *Evening Argus* an advertisement stating that the Dale Carnegie Organisation would shortly be holding a fourteen-week course in Public Speaking and Human Relations at Hove's New Imperial Hotel, where there was to be an introductory demonstration *that very evening.*

I couldn't wait to get along to it.

At the end of their presentation I was so wildly enthusiastic about what was being offered that I could hardly wait to tell Pat Honan about it next morning.

The following week both he, and Mr JR Morris, Ronuk's Managing Director, came along to the second introductory meeting with me. They, too, were impressed, and so the Company agreed to pay the £40 fee (£700) and sponsor my attendance on the course, every Monday evening for the next fourteen weeks.

I was cock-a-hoop with excitement.

There were twenty-six of us.

It was all terrific fun, and I made lots of new friends, as week on week I could feel myself shedding inhibitions, gaining self confidence, and acquiring basic public speaking skills.

The Dale Carnegie course had been running in America since 1912, but the first UK franchise had only come to Britain in 1955 (the year Carnegie died) - operated out of his Oxford Street office by a big, bluff, warm hearted, extremely vibrant and extraordinarily personable fellow, who exuded extreme confidence, called Michael Adam.

At that time the course was being run in 750 cities around the world, and Michael Adam had got it set up in over 20 centres in UK.

By then the courses overall had been attended by more than 700,000 men and women globally.

They had to be getting something right.

Today, more than 2,700 instructors present Dale Carnegie Training Programmes in more than 25 languages, and now more than seven million people have completed their courses worldwide.

In the UK, post-course Carnegie clubs were being formed up and down the country.

There had already been two previous courses held in Hove.

Those who attended them had formed their own club afterwards, which went on to become the official Sussex branch. When our own course finished we were invited to join this club as well, which several of us did. A couple of dozen of us and our wives/husbands used to meet once a week to consolidate what we had learned, and help keep ourselves up to speed by giving short, prepared, or spontaneous speeches, which the floor then criticised constructively before we all repaired to the bar.

Unfortunately, it seemed those three courses had been sufficient to satisfy the requirement of all those Brightonians and Hoverians who had ever sought to become self assured public speakers.

Successful and popular as the initial three courses had been, the paucity of later advertising response suggested to Michael Adam that he could not justify launching a fourth course in the area.

That well known British ennui had won through once more, and as a result, our post-course club membership began to dwindle. I was now the club secretary/treasurer and Peter Hogg, a genial, humorous Australian RAF pilot/businessman who had married Joan and settled here after the war, was president.

Together Peter and I decided we should try to acquire some new lifeblood.

How to do it?

We set about finding out if there were any other locally run public speaking courses taking place anywhere, and to our delight discovered that one had already started just the previous week, at a nearby school.

The following Monday evening Peter and I went along there, for a recce.

We found around three dozen disparate and unenthused people sitting spread round the school's vast assembly hall, listening disinterestedly while one of their number on stage struggled to give an amusing talk about his summer holiday. One or two more sympathetically aware attendees tittered gamely for him, whenever or where it was not too impolite to do so, but other than that it was a pretty sterile gathering. Peter and I, by now both heavy duty professionals of course, sitting back with our arms folded, felt incredibly smug.

In fairness it *was* only the second week of their course, and they *had* enrolled with the express intention of learning - but even so it was possible to sense that their week 14, if ever there was one, would not be an evening of riotous celebration or achievement.

Peter and I glanced at each other, trying to conceal our superior, self satisfied smirks.

Having arrived late and crept in at the back we had not yet had an opportunity to present our credentials to the course instructor, a harassed and aging little *ingénue manqué* who looked is if her day job was either running a cats' home (no, not that sort) (in Hove?) (oh, very well - *these* days, perhaps; but certainly not back then) or else some kindergarten art class. Watching her work, however, we realised that to reveal who we were might be rather patronising and naughty, and fluster her even further, so by mute agreement and a tacit nod, we let sleeping dogs lie.

All the others but one, and us, now having spoken, we were invited to take our turn on stage, to perform. We felt a bit like John Gielgud and Richard Burton might have done, if they'd gone along incognito to suss out some local drama group.

Peter took the stage first.

He was a study to watch, as he struggled to play himself down and act the novice.

To no avail.

The harder he worked at making his talk seem dull and uninteresting, the more it sparkled. The class steadily stirred in their seats; began to sit upright; became fully awake; leaned forward intently; paid rapt attention, and suddenly roared with appreciative laughter as Peter's stentorian voice with its antipodean twang bounced mellifluously round the auditorium. Despite the conscious suppression of his real ability, the high note of his finale still left them gasping for more.

Then it was my turn.

I was the 'more'.

Between us we wowed 'em.

One woman in the audience kept emitting the most extraordinary and distinctive 'braying' laugh.

Barely able to stop herself collapsing in the aisle from cracking up, she was giving us her all, appreciation-wise.

We loved her.

She was too much.

When I had wound up telling everyone about *my* summer holiday, and had almost received a spontaneous standing ovation (no, not really) this self-same laughing lady was the only person left who had still not spoken. Then aged 54, she clambered gamely up on stage with a happy grin, and then with a natural and infectious ebullience like you've never seen, set about up-staging the lot of us.

She was a natural born riot, and brought the house down.

Peter and I collared her eagerly afterwards, told her who we were and why we were there, and that there were much better pickings for her to be had down the road at *our* club. She was delighted with this intelligence, clapped her hands with joy, accepted our invitation with alacrity, and came along promptly to our very next meeting the following week.

Her name was Margaret.

All her life she had been a domestic servant.

With her children finally off her hands, she had now decided to embark upon a programme of self improvement. Concurrently she was already studying GCE O-Level English, as a prelude to greater things.

Margaret took to all of us and to the Dale Carnegie concept like a duckling with happy pills would to a weir. Some of our club's more staid lady members found her personality a trifle overpowering, and cringed a bit, but the sheer warmth and unbridled enthusiasm and vitality of the woman completely knocked us out.

Eight years later, when I was living and working in Hanover, in Germany, and time and distance had severed most of my Dale Carnegie connections, I was scanning the *Sunday Express* one day when my eye caught an article by the late Robert Pitman, on his Book Review page, in which he raved about a new autobiography that had just been published, called *Below Stairs*. Without reading beyond his third paragraph, I knew exactly who he was talking about.

Margaret Powell.

Our Margaret - who then went on to write several more best selling autobiographical 'below stairs' romps, as well as becoming a well known TV personality.

Married to Albert, her milkman husband, she died in 1984, aged 77.

Dammit, now she's dead Brighton City has even named one of their buses after her! *And* put a blue plaque on her old house.

Margaret's unsuppressed late flowering talent was always going to erupt into the public domain. Not even 'launched' myself yet though, it was still satisfying to know that at least I had acted as part of the handrail for her ascent.

Peter and Joan Bain-Hogg lived in a gloriously converted 19th century seafront apartment on the corner of Westbourne Villas and Kingsway, just opposite Hove Lawns. They operated a successful business in London, buying, refurbishing, and selling second-hand printing and publishing machinery. They both smoked and drank - we all did - and one day Peter, who was quite a 'large' chap, aged about 42, said: "Mike, do you think it would do me any good if I was to come along with you to your weight training club, to try to shed a few pounds?"

"Course it would," I said.

The Manorbe Gym was downstairs, beneath the ice rink, which adjoined the old Odeon cinema, south of the clock tower, at the bottom of West Street. A couple of weight-lifters - Derek Manthorpe and Dick Orbell (clever, eh: ManOrbe: gerrit?) - were running it as a pretty good place for blokes to meet up and pump iron.

Brighton's Manorbe Gym in 1962 was probably the *real* origin of the term sweat shop, and no place for a lady, *although . . .?*

Anyway, a big, bullet-headed blonde guy called Adrian was *our* great white hope for a Mr Universe title. He was Brighton's answer to Arnold Schwarzenegger, before the latter was ever heard of. Adrian, who I believe was a gas fitter by trade, was our role model.

Charlie had abs to die for.

Bill curled unbelievable weights and could crush nuts with his biceps.

Johnny had pecs like dustbin lids and could make them twitch to the music of time, just by squeezing his palms together . . .

. . . and having lugged ammunition boxes up frozen Korean passes, I had a reasonable pair of calves, but there was a lot of work (still uncompleted) to do on the rest of me.

And there were a hundred other members who would drift in and out at various times, religiously performing their own particular workout schedules, in order to achieve what they aspired to; but it was Adrian who was the only fully formed, honed, defined, ripped and oiled all round finished article.

Nigel Green used to work out regularly with us too, the then 38-year old South African born British character actor.

He was such a nice chap.

Because of his strapping build and commanding demeanour, he would often be found playing military types, and men of action, in such classic sixties films as *Jason and the Argonauts* in which he played Hercules, Colour Sergeant Frank Bourne in *Zulu* - and Major Dalby, Michael Caine's boss in *The Ipcress File*. He played Little John in *The Sword of Sherwood Forest,* General Wolseley in *Khartoum* and Colonel Harker in *Tobruk,* as well as many other roles. My contribution to helping this well known and popular Brightonian achieve these roles and be fit enough to play them, was to stand in and 'catch' for him when he was bench pressing awesome amounts.

Sadly, Nigel was to die, from an accidental overdose of sleeping pills, aged only 47, in 1972.

Peter and I used to go to Manorbe to train from 6 p.m. to 8 p.m. on Mondays, Wednesdays and Fridays. He thoroughly enjoyed his workouts, which he was convinced were doing him good. They should have done; he went at it like a bull in a china shop.

He and Joan were unable to have children, and so recently had adopted a lovely little baby boy, whom they'd christened Jocelyn.

Only three weeks later Peter had a massive heart attack in his sleep, and when Joan awoke that Sunday morning it was to find her beloved husband lying dead beside her in their bed.

Convinced (hopefully incorrectly) that it was the sudden burst of weight training that had killed Peter, Joan stoically continued to run their business and rear young Jocelyn. She never remarried.

Jocelyn (now 47) eventually grew up to leave home and become a good and successful professional photographer. In the meantime Joan had disposed of the business, and slipped into graceful retirement.

I had never met Jocelyn.

One day Joan (now aged 90) and I touched base again after almost half a century of exchanging Christmas cards, and I went for Sunday lunch. That's when I met Jocelyn for the first time. Because I didn't want to put my foot in it, I had earlier asked Joan if he knew he had been adopted. He did - and sometime in his 20s had successfully set about meeting his natural father, whom it turned out was a bit of a vagabond '60s playboy, called Tom Cyffin, then living in Devon.

"Not the Old Etonian, ex RN, ex racing driver tobacco heir who dissipated his inherited family fortune?" I asked.

"Good God; *yes*," replied Jocelyn and his mother, flabbergasted. "But how on *earth* . . .?"

"In 1994 I was a sales manager covering the west of England," I related, even more incredulous than they were. "Tom was one of my team. We became quite good friends. Small world, eh?"

One day I broke my usual routine and went to Manorbe, on my own, to have an earlier than usual workout, at 4.0-o'clock in the afternoon.

48

The place was completely empty, giving me unimpeded access to all the equipment, as and when I wanted to use it, without having to queue. Instead of inhaling the usual steam-heat, and bayou type air awash with pheremonal male perspiration, the atomosphere was reasonably fresh for once.

Just as I was starting my second set of dumbell presses, however, the door opened, and Harvey Holford walked in.

The handsome, dark and bearded Harvey was the 34-year old *demi-monde* owner of Brighton's *Blue Gardenia Club* in Queen's Square.

He was married to an attractive, 21-year old blonde, called Christine.

They were well known Hollywood-style figures around the town, usually to be seen cruising about imposingly in their scarlet open-top Pontiac Parisienne, with their motor boat and trailer in tow.

Harvey didn't come to the gym all that often, and because we were both there to work-out, not to socialise, I only exchanged some desultory small talk with him; but it was to transpire that I would be the last person from the gym to talk to him for quite a while after that. No, he didn't have a stroke or a heart attack, but went on home and later that night murdered his wife, Christine.

It turned out that she was a serial adulteress, who had been two-timing him big time.

They had been married two years previously, in November 1960, and Christine had given birth to their daughter, Karen, in May 1961. Soon after that she started drinking heavily and putting-herself-about-a-bit, and then in the summer of 1962 she had left little Karen in the care of her mother-in-law, and gone off to the south of France on holiday with a girlfriend. There she enjoyed some more 'flings' with different fellows, but also met and embarked upon a relationship with the washing machine magnate, John Bloom. Back home in England she taunted poor Harvey with all of this, and told him she was leaving him. Shortly afterwards is when he came into the gym and engaged in distracted small talk with me, slowly pumping iron while those burning thoughts were racing through his distraught mind.

Upstairs in their penthouse later that night, the couple had their last, disastrous confrontation. Harvey apparently said to Christine: "What about Karen? Even a slut would not leave Karen. What do I tell her when she is older, that her mother is a whore?"

Christine reportedly shouted back: "I am a whore, am I? I will tell you something." Then she uttered her last words. "You can stop crying about Karen, because she is not yours."

Later Harvey said: "I felt something go. I snatched a gun out of the cupboard, and shot her. I just fired at her."

He picked Christine's body from where she fell, and laid her on the bed. Then he went to the kitchen and swallowed all the tablets he could find. "Then I went back to bed and cuddled her."

When the police arrived they shone their torches through the glass doors into the bedroom, and saw Harvey wearing only a white singlet, sitting up in bed with his arm around Christine, who was dressed in a white pullover, black matador tights, and a green blouse. Their heads were together, and they appeared to be asleep. But by the light of his torch, Detective Constable Sullivan could see that Christine's face was bloodstained. Her right eye was wide open, fixed and staring towards the ceiling. As the bedclothes were pulled back, she was found to be lying in a pool of blood. She had been shot three times in the head - through the front of the lower jaw, through the right temple and through the left ear - and three times in the body, including once through the genitals. Harvey, who was cradling her in his arms, was deeply unconscious from an overdose of the barbiturate, Seconal. Under the bed on his side was discovered a .38 revolver.

Harvey was rushed to hospital, and did not recover consciousness for 82 hours. Remanded in custody in Lewes Prison, he was committed for trial at Sussex Assizes on a charge of murder, but on the day before the trial, he hurled himself 15-feet from a first-floor landing, and fractured his skull.

50

He was moved to an outside hospital, and eventually recovered. His delayed trial opened in March 1963, before an all-male jury. In his remarkably sympathetic summing-up (untypical of the times), the judge, Mr Justice Streatfield, said of Christine's final taunt that Karen was not Harvey's child: "Can you imagine any words more calculated not only to sear and cut deeply into the soul of any man, but to rub salt into the wound at the same time?"

And, referring to the fact that Christine had once called Harvey a 'little boy', the judge added: "Think of the contempt in those last two words."

The jury cleared Harvey of capital murder, and returned a verdict of manslaughter, on the grounds of provocation and diminished responsibility. After applause from the public gallery, the judge sentenced him to three years in prison, telling him: "There must be few men indeed who have been subjected to greater provocation than you were."

He was paroled on 2 October 1964.

He changed his name to Robert Keith Beaumont, and went to work as an estate agent.

Astonishingly, ten years later, he stood at both General Elections, in 1974, polling 428 votes in the first, as an independent candidate for the Brighton Pavilion constituency - and 155 votes, in the second, as the English National Party candidate for Brighton Kemptown.

After the mild form of leukaemia he had, suddenly became malignant, he died in June 2006, at the age of 77, at Brighton's Royal Sussex County Hospital, the place where, 44 years before, he had recovered consciousness after killing his wife.

All sorts of 'arty-farty' things used to go on in Brighton in those days, too.

There was a flamboyant businessman called Barry Langford, who had one foot in the music business. He also had a magnificent antique jewellery and silver emporium, in a splendid corner shop at the junction of Middle Street and Duke's Lane, at The Lanes' westermost entrance. One Saturday morning, when Rachel and I were out strolling, we found ourselves merging with a packed throng of people massed around Barry's shop, 'waiting for something to happen'. When it did, it was worth waiting for, because five minutes later a great big open top white Cadillac came cruising slowly round the corner, with one of the most glamorous blondes you could ever imagine puncturing the red leathered front seat with her stiletto heels, standing up clutching an enormous bouquet of flowers, waving and flashing everyone the most radiant of smiles. It was Britain's answer to Marilyn Monroe - Diana Dors. Then at the peak of her notoriety and fame, she alighted from the car and, subjected to photographers galore, teetered elegantly into Langford's emporium to queen-it at his latest cocktails and canapés promotion, while the rest of us dispersed and went about our own more mundane business.

That evening - wrong, that *night* Rachel and I went to the cinema, but it had nothing to do with Diana Dors this time. The French director Marcel Camus had just made a film in Brazil called *Black Orpheus*, an adaptation of the Greek legend Orpheus and Eurydice, set in the modern context of Rio de Janeiro, during the Carnival, with a soundtrack by the bossa nova legend, Antonio Carlos Jobim. For some reason best known to someone whom I can now no longer recall, it was arranged that there should be a midnight UK premier of the film, to be shown at the then delightful Victorian art house Paris Cinema (now demolished, of course) just along from the Theatre Royal in New Road. All the good, the beautiful, the interesting and the press corps of Brighton had been invited to attend. It was a fun, and quite exciting night. Rachel and I were sitting in the front row of the circle, and although the place was completely packed, the two aisle seats beside me still remained vacant.

Until the lights dimmed.

Just as they began to do so I turned round to see if I would be lucky, or whether there were going to be two last minute arrivals turning up to cramp my leg space.

Inevitably; the latter.

In those final few seconds, just before the auditorium was plunged into darkness, the 53-year old Sir Laurence Olivier and his deliciously perfumed 33-year old wife, Joan Plowright, came quickly down the stairs and slipped quietly into the two seats beside me.

At least they didn't ruin the film munching popcorn.

FOUR

ON 3 NOVEMBER, 1960, I got ill.

I still had the MG at the time, but it was round in its backstreet garage again, having more minor repairs done, which meant I had to take a bus to work.

The walk to the bus stop and the three-mile journey made me feel queasy.

It was a cold, wet, windy, wintry day.

The office windows rattled in their frames, we were desperately busy - and I felt like death the whole day. My previous military training and self discipline, foolhardiness, embarrassment and the possibility of being considered a shirker when under pressure - all of this combined to drive me sluggishly on, but I was acutely aware that I was noticeably being the least effective member of the team, and my colleagues were beginning to cast sideways glances at me, raise their eyebrows and tut.

I couldn't wait to get home.

"We're desperately behind schedule with this one," Pat Honan snapped during a hastily grabbed tea break. (Yes, I know; but tea does revive the flagging spirit) "and we've simply got to get this shipment out to Honduras today. I need to ask if you would all mind working on a little later this evening, please."

"Sure," came the false response from everyone, all eager to impress, score points, and get promoted.

"Actually," I said, "if you don't mind, I think *I'd* like to knock off early for once. Now, in fact."

Ever farted in church?

Pat Honan's mouth dropped open with incredulity.

Every head in the room turned to face me, with disbelief.

"I'm sorry; but I've been feeling pretty rotten all day. So much so, in fact, that as my own car's in the garage I am going to have to ask if one of the company's cars could possibly run me home, please?"

"Of course," Pat Honan said. "And please don't come in tomorrow if you're still feeling bad, will you. Most of the work will have been done by then anyway."

Point made.

One of the company's cars dropped me at our front door, before roaring off with a trail of disgusted exhaust smoke writhing derisively in the air behind it, making me wonder whether when I did return to work it would be to find a white feather on my blotter.

It was 4.30 p.m.

Rachel wouldn't be home for another hour yet.

I crawled upstairs to bed, and when I say crawled, I mean crawled. I wasn't awash with pain, or screaming with agony, but something still told me it would be better if I crawled.

I clawed my way gingerly onto the edge of our bed, wriggled carefully out of my clothes, like Houdini in slow motion, and slithered uncomfortably between the sheets to assume the foetal position.

It was wonderful when I heard Rachel's key in the door.

"I must say, you're a lovely shade of green," she told me. "I'll fetch a hot water bottle."

That's when I threw up.

"I'm ever so sorry, darling," I said, "but – well - do you think you could possibly telephone the doctor for me, please?"

My mother had gone to great pains to instil in me that consideration for others was always of paramount importance, with the result that in its constant practice I had developed something of an inferiority complex. I was hesitant ever to ask anyone for anything, in case I interrupted a sneeze, or I might have disturbed some thought process that was just entering their mind. And no one, but *no* one, of any breeding, *ever* disturbed a *doctor*. They were not plumbers, after all. They were *doctors* - put on earth to sign the back of passport photographs - and would have to come all the way down from their home on Olympus to attend one's actual *bed*side. According to Mother.

Therefore, Rachel knew I was serious.

She telephoned the doctor.

No sooner had she done so, than I felt better.

The gnawing pain eased.

Colly-wobbles all gone.

God what a ham!

"Darling, why not cancel the doctor?" I suggested.

"You sound like some Mafia killer proposing a contract on the poor man's life. He's coming, and that's that. Besides, you look dreadful."

Doctor Buckmaster arrived an hour later.

"So what seems to be the trouble, then?"

He put his black bag down on the floor and slung his coat across a chair.

"Tummy ache, Doc. All gone now, though."

"I see. Well, let's just have a quick look then, shall we?"

"Aghhhh . . .," I writhed.

"Hurt?"

"No; stethoscope's cold."

"How about this?" He prodded my ribcage.

"Yes. It's painful. A little. There's not a lot of flesh there, so when you bash it, it hurts a bit." I was trying to be helpful.

"How about this, then?"

"Ayeeeeeeee . . . Keeri*st* yes, *that* hurts. Does it ever. *Phew.*" I jack-knifed, grunted, and swiped an outbreak of sweat from my brow as he withdrew his finger from poking my abdomen.

He smiled knowingly.

Putting his stethoscope back in his bag, he closed it, and asked if he could use the telephone.

He dialled a number, pretending to admire one of the pictures on the wall while he waited. Then he spoke.

My God!

He was calling an ambulance.

Rachel subsided weakly onto the bed beside me, taking my hand.

They were going to take away her sex machine.

How *dare* they.

Doctor Buckmaster replaced the handset, turned round, grinned and patted my knee. "Ambulance on its way," he said. "They'll take you out on a stretcher and cart you off to the Royal Sussex County Hospital in Brighton. You'll be fine again in a few days, and . . ."

"Yes, but Doctor . . . what *is* it?" Rachel and I both blurted together.

"Oh, I'm sorry; didn't I tell you?" He laughed. "You've got an acute appendicitis. Quite a ripe one, I'd say. Ready to pop at any second. I should think that with a bit of luck we've just about got it in time though. Good job you called me when you did, wasn't it!"

That was it, then.

I was going to die.

No one had ever operated on me before.

They were going to stick needles in me, put a gas mask over my face and cut into me like they did with hundreds of others each week. But in my case it would go wrong. That would mean ripping up my carcass afterwards to discover why. And I felt fine now. Really I did. Once I'd spewed, the gnawing ache had subsided. Just the same . . .

. . . if I was going to go out, I decided I would go out in style.

While Rachel showed the doctor out, I climbed carefully off the bed and started to assemble the things I thought I would need for a stay in hospital.

Gosh - this was exciting.

I would love to have been able to see Pat Honan's face in the morning, when he'd find out. It was a good job I had heeded nature's nudge to come home when I did, otherwise the damn' thing might have burst in the office.

Donning trousers, slippers, my paisley robe and a foulard choker, I laid out the things I would need, on the bed. Books to read. Papers and a pen to write with. My guitar, to strum. My chess set, to play with. My portable typewriter; cigarette holder; monocle . . .”

“Just what the *hell* do you think you’re doing?” Rachel demanded, when she came back into the room. “Get back into bed this instant. If that thing goes off, you’ll ruin the carpet. And where the hell do you think you’re going? A river cruise with Noël Coward? You’re ridiculous, you know that . . .?”

She continued to rant along these lines, until the ambulance arrived ten minutes later.

“Right Guv, no stretcher then,” one of the medics agreed, “but it’ll be more than our jobs’re worth not to put you in a wheelchair. If that thing of yours explodes on our watch, Fred and me’ll be losing ourselves a whole load of brownie points on your account. *Capisce*?”

They couldn’t convince me.

I was only twenty-two-years old.

I didn’t need a wheelchair.

I glanced through the curtain down onto the pavement below.

London’s commuter train had just pulled in to Hove Station.

Hordes of people were streaming down the road.

The blue light on *my* ambulance flashed its eerie glow across the ceiling. Its back doors were open wide, expectantly. A curious little throng had already gathered. It was almost time for my appearance.

I turned from the window.

“Right, gentlemen,” I said, offering my arm to my wife. “Shall we descend?”

“For God’s sake, stop pissing about,” Rachel hissed. “You’re not impressing *any*one.”

“Maybe not,” I retorted, “but *I’m* having a wonderful time.”

When we reached the already open front door downstairs, I paused. The two blue-suited ambulance men had gone on ahead of me across the pavement, unaware that I had deliberately dropped behind. By now quite a nice little patiently fidgeting crowd had formed, all of them eagerly awaiting my appearance, although one or two seemed disappointed not to see an advance trail of blood seeping into view. Pausing for just a moment longer - timing is all - I stepped from the porch, out onto the pavement, and the glare of my public at large. My monocle and cigarette holder proved effective, but by the cringe it was cold out there. I wished I had worn my woolly dressing gown instead of that lightweight paisley job. I also wished I'd had a carnation in my buttonhole, and an underarm poodle to carry. Taking three paces towards the ambulance, I lurched. The crowd gave a collective gasp. One or two clasped their hands to their mouths, but one woman stepped boldly forward and waved her shopping list under my nose for me to sign. Then a gruff voice at the back brought me back to earth with a bump.

"Ooh the 'ell *is* this burk, then?"

He'd made his point.

Did me a favour.

Huffily I quit play acting, pulled back my shoulders, and stepped determinedly towards the ambulance. Suddenly a piercing stab of real pain went ripping through me. I gasped, clutched at my side and trod into a freshly laid dog turd on the pavement, before falling into the arms of the rightly annoyed ambulance men who pulled me quickly inside, stretched me out, clunked the doors shut, and the ambulance pulled deftly out into the traffic.

Fifteen minutes later I was being wheeled into Jowers Ward, at Brighton's Royal Sussex County Hospital.

When the Army had posted me to the Far East four years earlier, they had issued me with a lovely pair of powder blue tropical pyjamas. Apart from wearing their bottoms once or twice, with a red PT vest, to gain access to the teeming thoroughfares of Hong Kong, whilst transiting through there for a few weeks on our way up to Korea, those pyjamas had never been worn for slumber, but spent their entire military career pressed and neatly folded ready for kit inspections. When I handed them back, along with the rest of my kit, at the end of my service, and the QM storeman shook them out, they fell neatly apart at the seams, as if they'd been sliced with a samurai sword. Since then, I had never owned or worn another pair of pyjamas, but always slept in the raw.

Still do.

Always shall.

Rachel, however, on this occasion, in Brighton, in 1960, thought that for me to do so then would indicate a dereliction of her wifely duties, so she had shoved into my valise a pair of her own fluffy pink winceyette teenage jim-jams, with her initial $\mathscr{R}$ embroidered in chocolate brown above the left breast. Dressed like this I looked very twee indeed, sitting up in my hospital bed waiting for a doctor to come and see me and, if I had but known it, to shove a greased, rubber-gloved middle finger up my backside for an exploratory wiggle. What the connection was between my prostate and my appendix I could only guess, but as she was an extremely attractive young doctor, writhing about in mid air impaled on her digit like that, I had my time cut out trying not to enjoy it too much, break wind, or worse.

At 1.00 a.m. they operated.

Next morning I woke up early to the ghastly realisation that something was missing.

Part of me had gone.

With cold sweat bouncing from my brow I felt gingerly beneath the bedclothes.

It was no longer there.

They had taken away my pink pyjama top.

It had been replaced by a hospital gown. And . . .

. . . what the hell was that great lump of plaster stuck across my midriff? I toyed with it a bit, and then tried a prod. An excruciating wave of pain coursed through my body. I howled. A night nurse, waiting to go off duty, came scurrying across the floor from her cubicle, brandishing a hypodermic at the high port. Whopping its 24-inches of cold steel straight into my right buttock, she plunged the pain killer into my system, swabbed the wound with a piece of petrol soaked mutton cloth, and disappeared back from whence she had come.

After breakfast, Sister brought Matron round. At the foot of my bed they both stopped and appraised me benignly, lying there with the sheet pulled tightly up to my chin.

"This little boy came in last night, Matron."

Que? Moi?

My big blue eyes started in their sockets. Sister must either have misread my notes, or had had something of a night of it; lucky girl. The average age of Jowers' Ward's inmates might have been 70-plus, but that still didn't make a married chap of 22 'a little boy'.

"Well, young man - and how are your legs today?"

"Fine thanks, Matron. How are yours?"

The smiles froze on their well scrubbed, well made up faces. Unclasping her hands Sister grabbed the sales bulletin thing that hung from my bottom bedrail, and was just going to read it anew when a male doctor hove into view.

"Morning ladies. Hallo, old chap. How are you feeling this morning? Bit sore I expect. It was a real beaut you had there, you know. Ripe as a cherry. Just ready to go off. I got it out without a minute to spare."

"Gee, thanks Doc," I said, fully meaning it.

Later that morning I awoke from a light doze to find that half a fruit garden had been placed on my locker, in a precariously balanced, beribboned basket.

Ronuk wanted to give me diarrhoea perhaps?

Or contrite forgiveness?

At three-o' clock a genially smiling, but slightly penitent, Pat Honan popped in to see me, assuring me that my reneging from the previous afternoon's workload had now been expunged from the record. Apparently I was now quite a *cause célèbre* at Ronuk, being the most exciting *divertissement* the firm had known for *ages,* ever since young Etherington, in packaging, had dropped everything to go off and join the Boer War, in fact.

My dressing became unstuck, dislodged itself, and fell off in the night, and I discovered that instead of stitches I was being held together with five little steel clips. Next morning one of the nurses brought over a pair of economy-sized wire cutters to my bedside, closed my curtain, and proceeded to prise the clips out, dropping each one with a clatter into a surgical bowl, reminiscent of bullet-plucking in the Old West. This impression was enhanced by my two-day growth of chin stubble, but back wearing Rachel's pink winceyette pyjama top once more, I felt more like the Lavender Cowboy than John Wayne.

Half an hour later I was allowed out.

Appendectomy had now been added to my ignominious list of dysentery, chilblains, and common cold (recurring).

My five buckled steel clips, with their milligrams of dried flesh still adhered to them, like biltong, or carrion to teeth, macabrely adorned Rachel's charm bracelet for years.

They weren't particularly attractive, but did make for interesting conversation at cocktail parties.

FIVE

MEANWHILE, BACK AT THE RANCH Ronuk was in the throes of being taken over by the Sheffield firm of Izal, which produced slip-n-slide loo rolls, disinfectant and a host of ancilliary items.

Last in?

First out.

I was stood down, paid off, and sent home.

The late, great comedian, Kenneth Horne, was a Ronuk director. I would bump into him in the loo just inside our head office front door there occasionally, when he used to come down for board meetings. Not by prior arrangement, you understand. It is just that we seemed to share a similar metabolic requirement at around 3.37 p.m. each day - but now all that hobnobbing with the famous would cease.

Sitting at home in 74, Goldstone Villas, still wincing from my recently incised stomach muscles, while re-counting my meagre severance pay, I tried to plan the next step up in my downwardly spiralling future. My father had been right. I should have worked harder at school; got myself a proper job; become a doctor; whatever.

The doorbell rang.

It was Pat Honan.

"Got another job yet?" he asked.

"Do us a favour," I said. "I was only fired yesterday."

"How would you like to go out on the road, for Izal?"

There was an option?

"Okay," I said.

That's how I got a cauliflower-coloured Austin Farina rep's car full of samples, and Kent.

First of all I had to go up to Sheffield, for a month's induction course, to learn all about the Izal range of products. I was put up in a boarding house, and didn't enjoy a single moment of the entire experience. Nor was I much enamoured with the ensuing few months, either, spent flogging disinfectant round the Garden of England.

Early each Monday morning I would wave goodbye to Rachel, and slog off eastward towards Maidstone, Ramsgate and Folkestone, where I would stay at a succession of third rate hotels with the rest of the commercial fraternity, who were plying that beat with their various wares. If I'd been selling arms to warlords, Aston Martins to film stars, or high heels in Bond Street, each of those callings might have had more *oomph* to it, but I felt that purveying loo rolls, disinfectant and floor polish did little for my image, or self esteem, and even less to satisfy my artistic craving, or general lust for life. Often I wondered how I'd managed to find myself in such a position, an unargumentative piece of flotsam, ferried about at the convenience of others.

What was I meant to *do* to redirect my future?

I couldn't sing or dance.

I wasn't a mind boggling body builder, magician, or juggler.

I had no skills, and I had no calling.

I knew the sort of thing I didn't want to do. I was doing it. But I couldn't think what I did want to do - except to be a successful writer one day soon.

That is when my Dale Carnegie connection stepped in with a dividend.

Douglas Tyler was a dear old boy, who owned a Hong Kong import/export business.

He and his delightful wife, Josie, had been on the same Carnegie course as me. He cornered me at a club meeting, one evening.

"Michael, I can see you're not happy," he said. "Gone is the ebullient young chap who used to enthuse us all so much with his merry quips and scintillating talks. Job getting you down, is it?"

Sagacious old sod; hit the nail in one.

"As a matter of fact it is rather, Douglas, yes. How did you know?"

"Doesn't matter. I've been around. I know about these things. Would you be interested in a change of scene?"

"You mean Hong Kong? *Any* time," I said, grinning broadly at him, scarcely believing my luck.

"No; no - I can't do anything for you there, I'm afraid," he replied quickly, "but a friend of mine, Patrick Durrant-Oxley, is looking for someone to join his company in London. Funnily enough, he did the Carnegie course himself a couple of years ago, but is too busy these days to be able to get along to the meetings. He is a charming chap. He lives here in Hove, and is on the look out for a bright young man like yourself. I've told him all about you, and if you are at all interested, I know he would very much like to meet you."

Patrick Durrant-Oxley Esquire owned two companies; Francis Hollings (Advertising) and H. Costa (Cigar Importers.)

The two companies were co-located at the junction of Clifton Street, with Holywell Row, in the City of London's Hackney district.

Each of them was a small family concern, which he was looking to expand.

I was to become part of that expansion programme.

I started on 5 June 1961, and continued there happily for the next eighteen months.

In my specially-purchased-by-the-company battleship grey Triumph Herald, I covered the whole of southern England.

There is a lot of southern England to cover, when you're one man, and you've got to cover it.

It stretches from Kent, to Cornwall, with lots in between.

It was my intention to do well for Patrick Durrant-Oxley, because he was a charming and personable gentleman who didn't know how to be anything but nice to people. Besides which, he was selling good products.

Although I also represented Francis Hollings Advertising, which was in the business of providing corporate gifts, I majored more on the cigar side of life.

My new employer was the purveyor, to upmarket punters, of a veritable cornucopia of cigar products from the Caribbean and Holland, but in addition to all of this, at the time he was the sole importer to the UK of the only hand made Havana whiff in the world.

It was called Royal Dutch.

Whiffs were popularly made from tobacco off-cuts, droppings and sweepings, stuck together with sweetly flavoured paste.

Not so Royal Dutch.

Whether these exquisite little fellows were ever rolled up and down a curvaceous Cuban thigh, I don't know - perhaps being only a whiff, the teenagers worked them - but they were a damned fine smoke, as well they should be, being hand rolled from Havana tobacco.

Such was my belief in the product, my dedication to the task, and the enthusiasm of my sales pitch, that within a month every pub and tobacconist in Kent and Sussex that was going to, had already taken delivery of their first consignment of stock.

Mr Durrant-Oxley was delighted.

He even gave me a cigar for my trouble.

A big one.

Royal Dutch whiffs were not my only merchandise.

My leather sample case groaned with coronas, corona-coronas, panatelas, Macanudos, Romeo y Juliets, Punch, Monte Cristo and matches. I was hooked on the things. I would light up a Jamaican after breakfast, a Havana after lunch, puff whiffs all day, and collapse in a soggy green stupor each evening, smoking a luscious H. Upmann. I only ever saw one fellow in a worse state than me. He was a 22-stone Danish doctor with whom I shared an early breakfast at a hotel once. His 6.00 a.m. repaste? Corn flakes, a pint of lager and a cigar!

One tobacconist I visited at The Arcade in Worthing, was not struck on cigars at all. *He* was a dyed-in-the-wool pipe man. His shelves were laden with lovely multi-coloured jars of tobacco blends, which he mixed himself for a specially discerning coterie of pernickety olde-worlde customers.

"I'm also a keen fisherman," he told me, "and on summer evenings along the river bank I used to get so fed up with the clouds of flies, bugs and midges plaguing me the whole time, that I took up pipe smoking, just to keep the buggers at bay."

"Did it work?"

"I'll say," he roared, slapping his thigh with merriment. "Why - the stuff I mix . . .? even the crows were flying at forty-feet!"

I am an avid sun worshipper.

One hot summer's day I had finished my 11.00 a.m. appointment in East Grinstead and decided that as it was Thursday and I'd had a good week, I would take the rest of the day off, hurry home, and go down to the beach for a swim.

Putting my foot down, in my eagerness to get stripped off in the sun I got the Triumph bucketing flat out down the A22 at its top speed of 70mph. In front of me a little beige-colured Renault something-or-other was tootling along at 30mph without a care in the world, impeding my hell-for-leather advance south, so like a *whooshing* meteorite I pulled out to overtake.

At that moment the Renault decided to turn right, into Hobbs Barracks, just to the west of the road.

Too late, I saw its flashing amber indicator light winking at the top of the central door column, obscured by mud and the bright sunlight.

To avoid a 70mph broadside I yanked the wheel to the left and cleared the Renault's unsuspecting boot, but before I could straighten up again I'd lost control completely and the

Triumph went hurtling head over heels in a triple somersault into the wood beside the road.

It was like being in a crashing plane.

Foliage whipped past the disintegrating windscreen and my whole topsy-turvy world was revolving at a slow motion rate of knots.

With a juddering crash and a shudder the car finally came to rest the right way up.

Seconds later I found myself standing beside it surveying the damage and rubbing my bruised buttock, acquired bouncing up and down on the gear lever.

How I got out of the car alive and was able to stand there looking at it, was beyond me: a miracle.

It was my first experience of the paranormal.

The driver's door was lodged against a tree, and the passenger door a completely buckled piece of wreckage.

There was no way I could have got out of that vehicle; but I had.

Feeling weak at the knees I crossed the road and strolled up the side road to Hobbs Barracks guard room, by their main gate. There they let me use the telephone to call and report my mishap to Mr Durrant-Oxley, in London. Forever the gentleman, his first concern was for my welfare. He made me promise to get a taxi to take me home to Hove, and then I gave him the necessary information to have the car collected.

Twenty minutes (and a cup of tea) later, a taxi pulled up outside the guard room, and an hour after that drew up outside our flat in Goldstone Villas, by Hove Station. Thanking the driver and paying his exorbitant fare, I noticed there was a chap with a briefcase standing on the step of our apartment, having just rung the doorbell. Curiosity aroused, I asked: "Can I help you?"

"Er . . . how do you do, sir," he said pleasantly, offering me his hand. "It's just by way of being a cold courtesy call, really. I'm from the Prudential Insurance Company, and sell life insurance policies. . ."

"Come on in," I said. "You've just sold one."

When Christmas arrived, I got to know London well. All the 'selling' had been done and 'delivery' was now the cry. Big name customers who had ordered cigars from us for Christmas, expected to get their cigars for Christmas. Even back then the GPO (General Post Office; the precursor to Royal Mail) could not be relied upon to complete deliveries satisfactorily, so my trusty little – amazingly, not written-off, but refurbished Triumph Herald and I were commandeered from our provincial outpost and deputed to run deliveries, in order to help the company retain its good name. I slept on a camp bed on the office floor, and for two weeks the Triumph would be loaded up each morning with boxes and boxes of gift-wrapped cigars from H. Costa's lavish humidor, which my idiot wife, bless her cotton socks, insisted on calling our thermidor. With the London A-Z open on the seat beside me, I would drive from Sir Charles Clore's place, via most of the embassies, to Sir Lew Grade's, dropping off all their goodies along the way. No parking meters or traffic wardens. No congestion charge. No fines. No time limits. Everything flowed beautifully. I felt like a small boat skipper evacuating Dunkirk single handed, and by the end of the fortnight I reckon I could have given any novice London cabbie a run for his money.

And my grateful lungs enjoyed a better class of smoke.

SIX

RACHEL AND I HAD BEEN MARRIED two years now, and the sort of thing that almost invariably happened to hot blooded Gibraltarian girls nine months and seven minutes after their wedding night, hadn't.

Back home on The Rock this first caused amused speculation about her husband's virility, leading pretty soon to probing enquiries from batteries of inquisitive and opinionated aunts, which then became pointed and persistent questioning that eventually culminated in their angry embarrassment and despair - and thereafter (thankfully) perplexed silence for a while. The fact simply seemed to have eluded all of them that it was by personal choice that Rachel and I had decided to enjoy a few years' 'getting to know you' adjustment and happiness time together first, before hitting the nappy scene with a new arrival.

Then a couple of years later the harassment started all over again.

The whole object of marriage, surely, was to produce children? Hadn't we got it together yet? Couldn't we find the recipe? Did we neither realise nor care that we had become the talking point of Gibraltar, and people were now even discussing and thinking of submitting anonymous suggestions for the treatment of impotence, sterility and worse - ? - all of which sounded very important indeed when shouted volubly in Spanish across a kitchen table.

"*Okay*," I said at last, one evening in spring, "to silence the chattering classes I suppose we'd better concentrate our minds and get down to it, eh! What shall we go for? Boy - or a girl?"

"Anything," Rachel cooed, all starry eyed.

"Goldfish?"

"No - one or other of what you said first."

"Boy, or girl?"

"Yup; them."

"Which one?" I persisted.

"Either would be lovely." She cooed again. "Or one of each, perhaps. Whichever you like. Whichever comes first. In any case, there's not very much you can do about it . . ."

"What do you mean, there's not very much I can do about it?" I bridled. "You come here this instant woman, and I'll soon show you whether there's very much I can do about it or not."

"Idiot. I mean there's not very much you can do to determine its sex."

"Maybe not, but *you* can," I countered. "Rather than think of England, just think pink please. I'd like a daughter."

We dispensed with contraception.

The savings were considerable!

They boosted our holiday fund, and enabled us both to fly to Gibraltar for a break that summer.

That's where our daughter Natalia was conceived one night.

Don't ask me how I know, but in the same way that a woman usually knows who the father is, unless he's out of his box on lager a man also knows when his seed has made an impact. There is a portentous and spiritually induced shifting of bone marrow, which tells him he's done his stuff, that he's hit the spot, and now both parties only have to wait for the gestation period to run its natural course.

Best done with the right woman.

Suntanned and gorgeous, me beaming, and Rachel on Day Fourteen of Operation Bloat, we flew back to England, and moved from 74, Goldstone Villas, into a super new flat in Hillcrest Court, which my increased salary now enabled us to afford.

71

Rachel continued to soldier-on in her secretarial role at Plummer Roddis, until early April, by which time her knicker elastic had become far too overstretched, and getting in and out from behind her desk all too difficult to do.

She was admitted to Southlands Hospital, in Shoreham, where, fortuitously, my paternal aunt had been Sister Tutor for many years, and it was there, at six-o'clock on the evening of Thursday 19 April 1962, that a new princess arrived in England. She was small, dark haired and lay angelically curled in her crib at the foot of Rachel's bed. One of my greatest regrets was that my brother Anthony and I had never had a sister, so ever since I was a lad I had dreamed of having a daughter. I picked her up and held her to me preciously, gazed down at her chubby little face, flicked her perfect little nose, and felt I had paid my dues to mankind and been justly rewarded.

"Well done, Lump," I said, patting Rachel's lately vacated tum, now depleted like a barrage balloon that's hit a spike. "Suppose I'd better go and spread the glad tidings."

"You do that," she agreed, smiling lovingly at me. "Just don't get yourself too smashed in the process. Come back and see *me* again sometime, too. Remember, now there are two women in your life, and we both need you. Big man."

Actually, she didn't say that last bit. I just put it in.

Why we named our delightful daughter Natalia, born in April, I have no idea, except that her mother liked and chose the name, so that was reason enough. She quickly became known as Tali, and was an adorable little girl. She had beautiful green eyes, and in no time at all her brown hair had turned blonde. She went to a nice school, had nice friends, married a nice guy, produced two nice children, divorced the nice guy (who by then had become a bad guy) and then, aged forty-five, partnered another nice guy, one who worships the ground she walks on and brought the sparkle back to those lovely green eyes of hers - but more of all this in due course.

Meanwhile - what had been happening to the rest of my family?

SEVEN

IN 1954 MY PARENTS SEPARATED as a prelude to their pending divorce.

Then aged 44, my father departed - it has to be said with varying degrees of reluctance and relief - to recommence a bachelor lifestyle, subsisting on beans in a bungalow, and as soon as their decree nisi came through and I had gone to Korea with the army, mother upped sticks and sailed off to South Africa, taking my sixteen-year old brother, Anthony, along with her.

It was now 1958.

Ever since she was a little girl, the Dark Continent had always held an enormous fascination for mother. Now aged 45, footloose and fancy free at last, she was able to embrace her new opportunity with a considerable degree of enthusiasm.

Within minutes of her arrival there, it seemed, she had found herself a job working as a fashion buyer for Garlick's, the Cape Town Department Store.

Anthony got himself sorted out in a library, but after a year decided he had been hanging on to mother's apron strings a tad too long, and felt it was time to bug out and start a man's life of his own.

We had none of us seen each other since I'd set sail for Korea, and now that I was back in England once more, Anthony felt he would like to try mixing it with his big brother again. Although knowing that she would miss him dreadfully, mother knew the time had come, and that it was right and proper for him to leave, so she financed his return trip and bade him a nicely restrained tearful farewell at the South African dockside.

Back home in Sussex, he moved onto my recently vacated floor space in dad's bungalow, and took a job - also as an advertisement representative - with the Brighton *Evening Argus*. After just a few months of this he realised that perhaps his big brother didn't hold quite the attraction he'd thought he would, and that in order to get some hair onto his own chest he was going to have to strike out even further afield. For some reason best known to himself, and to this day he's never been too sure what that was, he chose Canada to go and do it in.

He was there for about three weeks.

Somewhere half way across Canada, he got a job on a farm the size of a small country, but by tea-time on Day One decided he wasn't happy with it. Confronted by the harsh reality of Canada's ruggedness, he discovered that his John Wayne gene wasn't as pronounced as he'd thought it was. At 5-o'clock that morning the farmer had asked him to go mend a fence. This was not just a common or garden fence, a difficult enough task at the best of times for any of the non-DIY inclined George boys, but a real fence - a several miles long cowboy fence, that skirted a glacier, or a canyon, or something. Each time Anthony hit a fresh bit of it with his tack hammer, previous sections of it he'd just repaired (sort of) would fall down again. By 11-o'clock he felt a whimper coming on, and wondered why he'd left the *Evening Argus*. His hay fever had kicked in and was playing up a bit too, so what with one thing and another, he was dispirited.

He decided there and then that he'd 'had' Canada, and would prefer Southampton.

Unfortunately, he got on the wrong bus.

The American police found him wandering about a Chicago stock yard at 5-o'clock one morning, so pointed him back towards Canada again. This time he made it to Montreal, where he took a job dispensing coca-cola, from a tray, to punters beneath a circus big top, while awaiting his sea passage home.

74

But what of mother, left standing there with a brave face, waving farewell to him on the jetty back at Cape Town, in 1959?

By now she was fully *au fait* with the life style, had loads of friends, was professionally secure, and felt that she knew a bit about the Cape Province and its undercurrent of political unrest, which she found had been getting to her lately.

And then, to aid her decision making, as she was walking home from a drinks party one evening, she was accosted by a black man.

Although he became the recipient of a stream of unladylike abuse, and a quite unexpected knee to his groin (something mother had been waiting all her life to administer, and even down a dark alley, without any cameras to record the deed for posterity, she wasn't going to miss a chance like that when it was handed to her) the incident brought a flush to her cheeks, and the realisation that she was beginning to feel homesick for Britain. After two years there, she'd now 'done' Africa. Perhaps it was time to move on. Not for her, though, a long sea voyage, or even a swift air flight. There was still a lot more of the place she'd like to see before quitting it completely, so as soon as she'd packed up in Cape Town, she decided to come home overland.

She was nearly fifty.

She joined a photographic safari.

Travelling 1,400 miles over the Hex River and across the burning Karoo, mother joined her new companions in Johannesburg, their expedition departing from there on 14 March 1960.

The journey home took three months.

Leaving Rhodesia, they crossed the newly constructed Kariba Dam, that had then recently been completed on Zambia's Zambezi River, and then moved on up into Tanganyika. She laughingly recalled having a bath here, in a primitive shed while a huge bat looped the loop above her.

From Mombasa, on the Kenyan coast, she and her party then moved inland to Nairobi, passing Kilimanjaro, thrillingly encountering wandering lions and lionesses, and on up to

Kampala in Uganda (this pre Idi Amin's era, thank God – otherwise mother might have had to have words with him.)

From Gulu, in northern Uganda, they crossed into southern Sudan's regional capital, Juba, where at a nearby river crossing they encountered a naked party of seven-foot Dinka tribesmen, smothered in blood and flies, carrying home their kill of buck and leopard.

Mother had protruding front teeth.

Protruding front teeth was quite a pronounced feature of the Dinka physiognomy as well.

Their local chief caught sight of mother, and meeting a European woman who shared his tribe's dental peculiarity, he took rather a shine to her.

White goddess?

"I think he quite fancies me," she wrote on one of her postcards, "so if you receive an animal skin shield (or similar) in the post, it'll probably be part of my purchase price, meaning I've decided to stay: you'll have a Sudanese step-dad, and I'll be wife number twenty-three."

We didn't take her seriously of course, and the shield never arrived, so we assumed she had continued safely on her way.

She had . . .

. . . to Khartoum - where the 118 degrees of heat was so intense that she was unable to eat, and for three days subsisted on brandy; which wouldn't have been too much of a hardship for mother.

Crossing the Nubian desert, the party eventually arrived at Wadi Halfa, where they rested for a couple of days, before taking a steamer up the Nile. They passed the 13th century BC Abu Simbel Temple, Pharaoh Ramesses II's lasting monument to himself, and his Queen Nefertari, built to commemorate his alleged victory at the Battle of Kadesh, and to intimidate his Nubian neighbours. This entire complex was uprooted shortly afterwards (in the early 1960s) to be relocated on an artificial hill, to avoid its submersion during the creation of Lake Nasser, the massive artificial water reservoir formed after the building of the Aswan Dam.

Docking at Shellal, mother and her party took the train to Luxor, for a visit to the Valley of the Kings, and then at 3.30 next morning trained themselves the 400 miles up to Cairo.

From Alexandria they shipped across to Piraeus, and went on up to Athens, on up through Albania, Salonika, Skopje and Belgrade, and then to Zagreb; here they slept out in the woods, receiving a visit during the night by a curious army patrol, wanting to know who they were.

They crossed into Austria, and passed through many of its delightful towns en route to Vienna, Munich, Frankfurt, and Brussels - finally disembarking from the cross channel ferry, in Dover, in the pouring rain, and so realised they were home at last.

Having shaken the sand from her hair and had a good long soak (in a bat-less bath this time, not brandy) at a room in the Albion Hotel, in Brighton, mother telephoned to let us know she'd arrived.

Rachel, my brother Anthony and I duly fetched up to greet her - Rachel to meet her zany mother-in-law for the first time, Anthony and me for a grand reunion.

The 'theatre' lies only skin deep in our family.

Mother was a ham of the first water.

She wasn't downstairs to meet us in the foyer or bar, but had suggested we might like to go up to her room.

She must have been tearing her hanky to shreds, before the lift doors opened and she heard us chattering and laughing our way along the carpeted corridor outside.

Her door was ajar.

I pushed it fully open - and there she stood, looking resplendent in purple and pearls, positioned to wonderful effect by the window, hand to mouth, gazing out at the sunset over the English Channel like some Noël Coward leading lady on a 1920's theatre programme.

She'd even got the inadequate lighting right too.

Turning as we entered, as though we'd caught her by surprise (hah), she clutched at her throat with a sweet little choke of emotion, placed one small sun bronzed fist to her lips, and breathlessly gasped something like "My sons, my sons," although having just been living on hard tack and brandy for three months, it might have been "My gums, my gums."

Switching her gaze to appraise her new daughter-in-law she gave a gasp of relief and obvious approval in that direction, but was then unable to sustain her act a moment longer.

Slapping both thighs, she threw back her head, roared "Holy shit, you guys . . ." and then emitted a raucous burst of nervously released laughter.

She was our old mum again, whom I had not seen since I'd set sail for Korea four years before.

She gave us all a heartfelt hug, Anthony a coat hanger and me a poison spear, and we all went off to dinner.

Shortly afterwards, our now reacclimatised mother took up the appointment of overseas sportswear buyer for the House of Fraser's Birmingham outlet, Rackhams. This entailed her flying off to various fashion shows around Europe, but between sedately whooping it up in either Paris or Milan, back in Birmingham one day, she met up again, out of the blue, with a couple called Nicholas and Biddy Eggleton, who had been friends in the next road to us, when we had been living as a family in Sussex during the war. Their young son Graham and I used to smash up our Dinky toys together on one or other's drawing room carpet, when Hitler had been bombing seven kinds of shit out of us upstairs.

Sadly, by the time they rekindled their friendship 20-years later, Nicholas - or 'Egg' as he was always known - was a sick man, and Biddy had been an invalid for seven years.

Soon afterwards she became terminally hospitalised.

When 'Egg' and mother went to visit Biddy together one afternoon, they were appalled to find that she had lost her power of speech.

During a subsequent visit, knowing she didn't have long to live, Biddy feebly indicated to them the gold band on her wedding finger, pointed at mother, offered her a lopsided but heartfelt little smile, then pointed to her husband - and nodded.

It was a deeply touching, romantic, and unforgettable gesture, and its thought and implication did not leave them unmoved.

As a consequence, a reasonable time after Biddy had died, mother accepted Egg's hesitant proposal, and they were married.

Not long afterwards, they were driving home in foul weather, late one night past, an ill lit building site. The car skidded on some mud, went out of control and hit a projecting steel girder. The shock of the impact whip-lashed mother's neck, while the corner of the girder smashed through the windscreen and tore out the left side of her skull.

This experience did neither of them much good, and soon afterwards mother realised that the bang on her head had been sufficient to impair her business acumen. By now Egg had retired, so mother gave up fashion and sportswear buying, and they went out to live in Majorca. After a season there, they returned to Birmingham, where, sadly, Egg went into a sudden and rapid cancerous decline, and died.

It was shortly after this that mother decided to go to New Zealand.

By sea.

On board, she had a fling with one of the ship's officers, to whom she bade a fond farewell at Auckland.

Ashore, she appeared on *Woman's Hour* and gave a couple of press interviews, but then found that she was bored with New Zealand already, so she re-embarked to complete the trip to Australia, doubtless attracted by the possibility of some long term development evolving with her particular ship's officer, but then these hopes were somewhat dashed for her when they finally docked at Sydney to be met by his wife and family, whom he'd conveniently forgotten to mention; so - having dusted herself down, and always wanting to be at the centre of things, mother then made tracks for Alice Springs, where she took a job as a cook on a cattle station.

Having 'done' that, next she went across to Brisbane, where she became social secretary for a high court judge, but when he decided to become amorous she decided she'd had enough antipodean adventures for a while, and once more returned to base; to England.

Funnily enough, I can't remember what she did after that, but it wasn't long before she'd upped sticks again, and this time headed for America.

It was here, finally, that she 'found' herself.

Our good neighbours at Ferrers Road, in Lewes, where we lived during the war, used to smile indulgently at mother's outlandish antics whenever the *Luftwaffe* appeared overhead, and she would stand in the garden defiantly shaking her fist at them, blowing them raspberries on a purloined police whistle.

Seemed to work.

We won.

But many of those neighbours were still living there, in the same homes, forty years later. Their bomb damage had been repaired, and they all had lovely gardens surrounding their well appointed homes, with pictures of their grandchildren proudly on display, and pretty little doilies under their cake trays should you ever visit - but what ain't they got?

They ain't got balls!

My mother could play a mouth organ.

Ukelele, too.

From being a mundane, passed over little housewife, she built herself up to become a top flight international fashion buyer. She travelled the length and breadth of Europe, Africa and Australia. She married a dying man to nurse him, and conducted her whole life on a shoe string. Every penny she ever spent she had earned for herself first. She set out on her adventures with no illusions, but a great faith in humanity, and her own wit, charm and personality. If she met a sophisticated society hostess with a problem, mother's solution to it would be the same as that offered to a friend over a cup of tea at the kitchen table at home, but in an international setting was taken as being the pearly words of wisdom of a gifted latter day saint. She once met a little boy in America who had constipation. Behind his worried parents' back she forced stewed apple down his throat for a week, and gave him a good old clean out that way.

Everyone thought she was wonderful.

Thereafter the kid's parents used to consult mother about their psychological problems, and somehow her 'Forrest Gump' style philosophising used to help them, too.

In the midst of the Detroit race riots, in 1967, mother happened to find herself sitting in a bus station there. Three aggressive coloured gentlemen carrying iron bars came and sat down beside her.

"Do you mind if we sit here, lady?" they asked, swinging their iron bars with intent.

"Not in the least," mother retorted, smiling sweetly. "After all, you're no better than me."

They were still puzzling that one out when the enigmatic little English lady climbed aboard her bus to set off for her next adventure.

That was to be in California.

This is where she met and fell in love with a fringed buckskin-clad six-foot-five John Wayne / Gary Cooper look-alike, called Dave Bush.

They were married on 12 July 1969 (mother's fifty-seventh birthday.)

It was a love match made in heaven.

Mother had never learned to drive.

After she'd married Dave, she took her test and passed.

Soon afterwards she wrote to tell us that she had acquired a set of wheels.

"What sort of car have you got, Mum?" we asked her excitedly.

"I don't know, dear," she wrote in her next letter, now in her sixties and owning her first ever car. "I think it's called a Mustang Ford, or something."

At one stage in my life I was keen to relocate to an English speaking community in the sun.

Obviously, it had to be California.

The US Immigration Department has a preference list for those seeking a green card to work there.

My priority lay somewhere around Z-minus, slightly beneath that of the Vietnamese Boat People.

Although mother was now married to an American, she still proudly possessed her British nationality. If she was to take out American citizenship however, she would then become eligible to 'claim' me, thereby elevating my position on the immigration preference list to A1.

For months everything had been orchestrated between us to this end.

I was already out there in California, with a job lined up and waiting for me, but the whole ploy was dependent upon mother passing her test.

Came the day.

"Don't *worry*, darling," she assured me, climbing into her racing green 'Mustang Ford' that fateful morning to drive to the court to be examined and, if successful, to swear her allegiance etc. "I've studied so hard they won't only grant me citizenship, come tea-time they'll probably ask me to run for President."

Half way there she was involved in a car smash, never made the court, and wasn't able to have another go for months, by which time my plans all bit the dust and I returned to UK to do something else. (More than once the thought crossed my mind that perhaps she'd pranged the car deliberately, believing America wasn't big enough for both of us.)

Dave was a consummate gardener. He had only to tickle the tip of a plastic shrub for it to burst into life, bloom and procreate.

He was head honcho at Rogers Gardens, one of the most beautiful and well known gardens in California, at Corona del Mar, near the Pacific Ocean. Through this he was invited to maintain the gardens of President Nixon's Summer White House, at San Clemente, which he and mother came to know well.

Later down the line, mother wrote to say that they had decided to branch out on their own.

They bought a cement mixing business.

When my brother Anthony went out to visit them, he said he could scarcely believe his eyes. There was mother, all 8st 6lbs of her, with wrists like matchsticks, humping cement bags about the place, mixing the stuff with a shovel, and pouring it herself. This was all a prelude to the statuary business they were to set up, selling replica stone fauna for gardens and rockeries.

Once a year they would take their truck up north to collect driftwood from the beaches of Oregon, which they would load up, drive back, and turn into the most beautiful of garden ornaments and planters.

Then they bought themselves a Winnebago motor-home, in which they spent weeks at a time away on trips, camping and exploring the farthest reaches of the West. "Growing old disgracefully," is how she used to describe themselves and their shenanigans, to which remark Dave would gaze at her with dumb adoration, going along with everything she said, and chuckling with delight.

Although her doctor had strongly advised her to desist, at the age of eighty-seven she was still doing handstands against the garage wall. It wasn't a particularly edifying spectacle, but the squeal of enjoyment she emitted each time she managed it, was worth all the tea in China, and the feat made her a firm favourite with kids from the Indian reservation out near her desert home.

"Whoops; there goes another one," she would remark with a shriek, each time she committed a *faux pas* or uttered another malapropism, implying that she realised another of her diminishing set of marbles had just popped its casing and ceased operating effectively; a bit like a small light bulb packing up and calling it quits, or an icon disappearing from a computer screen.

"What would you like to drink, mother?" I asked her at a restaurant once. Mother had always enjoyed quaffing tipples of one sort or another, so how was I to know she'd recently quit?

"Drink?" she expostulated. *"I* don't drink. Darling, these days you've only got to show me a grape, and I'll try to open a door by its hinges."

Twenty-six years later - in 1995 - mother was to lose her life's companion, to bladder cancer, which shook her badly. But this gutsy little old lady, still with all her own teeth and only one filling, was to soldier gamely on for another decade, during which time she reckoned that half of what should have been inside her body was beginning to fetch up on the outside, which she seemed to find amusing rather than disquieting, as she kept trying to tuck it all back in again.

"I'm packed and ready to go," she kept telling us, "but the bus won't come."

Then finally it did.

At the age of ninety-one, she fell and broke her hip.

Lying there wired up to hospital drips, she was fearful of turning in her sleep lest she should dislodge one of the tubes, so she spent the whole night with a firm grip on the most important looking one of all.

Her nurse told her over breakfast it was the radio cable.

Mother left us on 26 December 2004, about the same time the Boxing Day tsunami hit Asia.

We have often wondered about the connection . . .

She had an obsession about 'stocking up' with things, such as bottled water, loo rolls, cans of food etc., in preparation for 'the next war'; an earthquake (she lived slap-bang astride the San Andreas Fault); an armed rebellion in the village; an outbreak of typhus; a nuclear explosion, or whatever.

After she died we found shelf after shelf of *dented* tins of foodstuff in her kitchen cupboard.

"From all the banging and swearing that went on in there around lunchtime each day," one of her neighbours told us, "we thought she must have been prospecting, or something."

We then realised that because she was no longer able to handle a tin opener, she had vainly been trying to use a hammer and one of Dave's screwdrivers to get at her lunch each day.

Mother kept a wall chart diary on her kitchen wall, upon which she would crayon her appointments: Dentist: Take Pills: Do This; Do That and then Do The Other sort of thing. The week before she died, her identical little plaintive four-day consecutive entry read: *I seem to have lost my way.*

We reckoned she'd suffered a mental white out.

She was cremated, and her ashes were spread at sea, the same as her beloved Dave's.

Three months after her demise, Anthony and I received a communiqué from the undertakers, which read

In loving memory of Vera Bush
Entered Into Life July 12th 1913
Entered Into Eternal Rest December 26th 2004
Scattered at Sea Off Coast of Orange County
North 33 Degrees 32.273
West 117 Degrees 59.171
On March 18th, 2005
As requested by Miller-Jones Mortuary and
Crematory, Hemet, California.

EIGHT

BACK HOME IN BRIGHTON Patrick Durrant-Oxley, the managing director of Francis Hollings Advertising (and H. Costa Cigars) - my boss - had just bought himself a brand new Jaguar Mark X, the largest, widest saloon car Jaguar had ever built.

Occasionally he would pick me up from our flat at Hillcrest Court, and we would drive up to the London office in it together.

P.D-O was the epitome of sartorial elegance, always attired in hand-made black Lobb shoes, the finest quality navy blue chalk-stripe suit with a crisp collared (detached cutaway) shirt, and pure silk tie. He made *The Avengers'* Patrick McNee look almost chav-like, and was unquestionably my newest role model.

The Jag's magnificent wood-trimmed interior was immaculate. P.D-O always wore a pair of white kid gloves with which to drive in it, with a trademark box of Havana cigars lying open beside him. Cruising imperiously up the A23, exhaling richly aromad blue smoke through his half open quarter-light, he would sniff with mock disdain at everyone we overtook, murmuring: "I wonder why he doesn't work harder; buy a *prop*er car?"

Everything about Durrant-Oxley reeked of class. I tried desperately to emulate him, but there was no way my fourteen-guinea Burton's suit was ever going to match his £200 Huntsman. I did get to smoke expensive cigars, but only because he provided them for me. I owed this gentleman

86

much, but was nevertheless still beginning to feel that in the long term I owed myself and family more.

I had been out of the Army four years now, and really did not seem to be making much headway at all in civvy street. Many of my peers were in the same plight. We were all beating ourselves to death trying to acquire position and wealth, by building up various embryo businesses, commission agencies and what have you, but finding our ambitions thwarted every inch of the way by bureaucracy, bullies and/or established monopolies. With hindsight I realise that I was too well mannered, considerate and caring, and possessed only ten per cent of the ruthlessness needed to become a successful businessman, but I didn't know that at the time and so daily life was a struggle for existence, and to pay the bills.

There seemed very little enjoyment to be had.

I know I was only twenty-four, but still I wanted to be able to afford Havana cigars of my own, silk shirts and a shiny Mark X Jag.

I was bored, directionless and miserable.

England, and our lifestyle, were depressing.

I couldn't afford to entertain.

It seemed I could hardly afford to live.

I was a little man who wanted to be big, and couldn't, because I didn't know how to go about it. So in desperation and with a giant leap of faith, what did I decide to do . . .?

My father had now sold his bungalow in Southwick, so my brother's and my fall-back bed space had been irretrievably removed. Dad, aged 53, now lived in Hastings. Always a keen amateur thespian and operatic songster, in no time at all he had joined The Stables Theatre Club. There he met a talented twenty-five-year old local singer, Susan Barker. They hit it off, and, again in no time at all she had become the next Mrs George.

Dad was a joy to watch.

Since his and mother's divorce he had spent ten years in the wilderness.

Dad (aged 53) marries again – Sue Barker, who was slightly
younger-1963

Now he was like a boy with a new bat, his life full of sunshine and purpose again. To accommodate his new bride he bought a new house - and a Jag! How pleased we were that he did, because as things turned out Fate was only going to allow him eight more years to enjoy them all.

Mother was still either plying some sea somewhere, or attending a Milan fashion show, while my brother Anthony was away in Pantomime, down in Bournemouth.

Perhaps I was a late developer: either that or an incurable romantic. I still wanted to be a cowboy: make love to a film star: win the Mr Universe contest so that I could walk forever unmolested around the water front bars of the world: be an internationally acclaimed concert pianist/guitarist/tap-dancer - or an operatic tenor: enjoy the fame of a racing driver . . . and make a few thou along the way. Above all else though, I had come to realise that what I had always really wanted to be was an army officer, and writer - both of which were more realistically within my reach.

So I offered Mr Durrant-Oxley my resignation, which he accepted with regret - and rejoined the army.

Apart from marriage and my daughter, although I had been disillusioned at times, my three years spent with The Royal Sussex Regiment had been the high spot of my life thus far. As a soldier I had merely been another piece of expendable cannon fodder, humping coal, ammunition boxes, pick helves and a rifle about the place, but I had definitely valued all the close camaraderie and the opportunities we had - even in steerage - for travel. I had kept a diary, and most days there had been something interesting to put in it: *Saw sharks today; dolphins; an explosion; was on firing party for burial at sea;* stuff like that. Now my diary was kept in a drawer, because lately there had been fewer and fewer occasions for me to post any entries.

Suntanned and handsome, a hint of blonde hair curling under his bleached service dress cap and the certainty that if his feet had been visible they would have been shod in faded suede chukker boots, he stood hawk-eyed and intent in a scout

89

car turret in the Libyan desert advertising the fact that a three-year short service commission in the Army was a pretty cool thing to go for . . . this was the artist's line drawn impression of an end product of Mons Officer Cadet School, used regularly in a *Daily Telegraph* advertisement in the 1960s. National Service had finished and Britain's new, all regular army - the *Professionals* - was in the process of being formed.

The more I thought about it, and I thought about it a lot, the more appealing the proposition of a full blown army career seemed to be. With their own experience still recently in mind, fathers could be proud of their sons donning khaki for a living. There was still an ongoing Father/Son, Queen and Country feel about service life. The Army was a respectable calling. Korea, Malaya, Kenya; Cyprus, Borneo, Suez, Aden - everyone had recently had someone doing something, somewhere, in uniform, even if it was only two years spud bashing at Catterick.

Six years on, the military was to become engaged in its protracted Northern Ireland confrontation; twenty years on - the Falklands War; thirty years on - the two Gulf Wars, and the prolonged misery and arguable inadvisability of Bosnia, Iraq and Afghanistan. By the time he was thirty my nephew (not yet born) was going to sport more medals on his chest than those acquired by twelve of my peers, two brigadiers, and me combined, but between Britain's withdrawal from Aden in 1967 and the Falklands War in 1982, the world stage enjoyed a reasonably quiescent time of it, punch-up-wise - which is when I rejoined: so I got that bit right for once, didn't I.

My peer group did not fight in India, South Africa or the trenches, North Africa, storm Cassino, or get shot at terribly much, but if we had been there at the time and been given the task I am sure we would have done just as well as our forebears. In the meantime, the Army still had to be manned, the Colours kept flying, the drums beating and the regimental mortgage payments flowing during the build-up to the wind-down of repossession, rifting, and the sanitised new streamline product which serves us today. So apart from me becoming one of the Cold War team helping to keep the Russian Bear at bay across the River Weser, as a BAOR officer during the that period, there will be no swashbuckling, blood and guts deeds of history-making derring-do here.

But what *of* the army I had left behind four years ago? How had it been faring without me?

With the end of National Service and no longer any Empire left to administer, in a 're-shaping' process our Whitehall masters were offering redundancy terms to certain categories of the 'new professionals', inviting them to quit khaki and don mufti once more: very much as generations of their forebears had been asked to do when their services were expediently no longer required, and they'd all gone off to run chicken farms or sell water purifiers for a living.

To aid this reduction in military strength great regiments were compressed and amalgamated and hard won and proudly worn cap badges were relegated to lapel-wear as collar dogs, the resultant hybrid expected to rise again like a military phoenix of renewed efficiency on a cloud of instant tradition. All this while the Russian war machine was trebling itself, socialism boiled and bubbled throughout the land, and communism was crawling ever closer across the drawing room carpet to envelop us. No - really: this was the '60s, and this is how we all felt about our daily lives. Sure, they were the 'swinging sixties' and Carnaby Street was all the rage, but those of us 'in the know' still genuinely expected to wake up one morning to find Russian tanks rumbling up The Mall and a hammer and sickle flag flying above Buckingham Palace.

Despite its weeding and overall reduction programme the military still had to attract new blood though, and although for many young men industry, commerce, the pop scene, emigration or the dole would have been infinitely more preferable than becoming a soldier, Dartmouth, Sandhurst and Cranwell were still successfully able to attract more than just the average 'few'. This time round, however, your Officer Cadet Nigel Playfaire-Smythe of independent means was not quite so apparent. Such 'Ruperts' were still very much in evidence of course, leaving Eton and Harrow, Marlborough, Wellington and Radley to come on to be trained up for a stint in their father's old regiment; still acknowledged by most as being the finest finishing school for blokes ever devised. However, there was also now a distinct upsurge of unhyphenated grammar school boys and others applying to attend the Services' stringent selection boards, with a nonchalantly suppressed eagerness to become members of the officer corps. These potential officers would be dependent on their military salary alone, so they certainly weren't queuing up for the money! Whether these Gentlemen-Come-Latelys believed their decision to be a calling, a career or just 'a job', they nevertheless soon became drilled in and imbued by the elitist ethos of past military glories and achievements that permeates all officer training establishments. Setting-to with a will they underwent the rigours, learned the cries and feverishly polished their fathers' hand-me-down National Service Sam Browne belts in readiness for that days of days when with their single pips gleaming heroically on their epaulettes, a ceremonial war sword by Wilkinson gird about their loins and Williams & Glyn's wresting with the meagre contents of their bank accounts, they would sally forth as freshly gazetted Officers of The Queen.

I had already spent three years as a soldier. I knew what soldiers thought; what pleased and annoyed soldiers; what qualities soldiers admired, and, more important what qualities they disliked. I had learned my lessons well. I had been a soldier and suffered and enjoyed the consequences of that lowly station.

Now I intended to apply for a commission.

What sort of an officer would I be?

On reflection, there seemed to have been very few officers whom my bunkmates and I had found ourselves genuinely able to respect without reservation. Maybe we had expected too much of them. They were officers, therefore they were imbued with the myth of divine right and impregnability which their uniform and rank bestowed upon them, but most of those we encountered had either been fresh faced youngsters like ourselves, eighteen and twenty-year old virgin platoon commanders who made silly mistakes and then stood on their dignity to cover them while usually being too callow to do so effectively - or grizzly old majors. Old? We were eighteen. To us, thirty-five was old. But our grizzly thirty-five-year old majors had fought against Rommel in the North African desert and up through Italy to take part in D-Day.

Then there were career paths to be thought about.

The reality of peacetime soldiering is that successful advancement up the promotion ladder has to be worked for and sometimes worked for most deviously. These men had families and responsibilities. The higher their rank when the time came for them to hang up their swords, the greater their pension. The greater their pension, the more spending power they would have and the happier they would be, so they were all on the "Yes, Colonel," "No, Colonel," "Whatever you say, Colonel" path, in order to attract 'Excellent' annual confidential reports, which were essential for anyone hoping to be elevated to the next rank.

War time officers are the real stuff.

War produces twenty-four-year old brigadiers.

Peace time officers would like to be the real stuff, and fancy themselves as such, and no doubt could be when push came to shove, but whilst awaiting the arrival of their war, the system usually manages to mould them into brown nosed poodle-fakers who can all too often become possessed by self-interested wrong values in their ruthless quest for self advancement. Officers' careers have been affected by how well they can organise cocktail parties and dinner nights, or how successfully their wives can arrange flowers in the garrison church. At an officer's garden party once I heard one junior major splutter through his strawberries to admonish his errant ten-year old son, idly straddling the pretty little white picket fence erected around the marquee. "Don't do that Timothy," he called out, then, when he saw the brigadier hoving into view, hastily added: "Your father wouldn't like it."

"That officer there," I once heard a soldier inform his mate, "is so far up the CO's arse he'll soon come across the Adjutant."

If the Army had been a private company, back then in the early '60s we believed it would soon be in the history books of liquidation. Its teeth had been pulled. It was weak, mangy and politically unloved. Its tail twitched occasionally and it still pricked up its ears from time to time and could put ribbons round its neck on Open Days, but the heartbeat was faltering and it was old enough to have its first serious coronary. It could scarce afford any form of global roar any more. Its main occupation was survival and swiping ticks from its back. And this was then. Just think where it has been sent and what has happened to it since - and still it survives.

- *Plus c'est la même chose.*

So - not a bad mob to belong to really.

Despite the foregoing misgivings, when I decided that I would like to rejoin the Professionals there was still little about their imagery which did not appeal to me. Recollections of my previous three years in the infantry sprang readily to mind: the bands, the bombs and the bayonets; the bandoliers of machine-gun ammunition slung across brawny, khaki-clad shoulders criss-crossed with tough green webbing equipment; the tattooed forearms; the badges, the bravery and the whole romantic gamut of the game grabbed my soul like the sight of a tattered Union Jack – Union Flag – whichever you like, fluttering in a sun baked jungle clearing while the silver notes from a dying bugle faded from some nearby mountain fortress. Yup: I felt I was ready to spill blood for a bit of that.

"If you don't like the sound of marching feet and can't take a joke, you shouldn't have joined," I remembered them laughing out to us in my original basic training.

I liked both, yet by Week Three of generating Royal Sussex sweat over hill, dale and tarmac, the glamour *had* begun to pall. My head had been shorn; *"We don't want you spreading lice about the place, nor do we want your lovely locks to get caught up in your breech-block:"* my boils were ripe; blood squelched from the lace holes of my boots; my blisters became blistered; my suppurating knuckles were permanently chipped, knocked, scarred, scabbed and grime-encrusted. I knew what shaver's rash was alright too, having acquired it more than once shaving in cold water with a blunt blade on a sub-zero early morning hill in Korea. My calves and kneecaps had been rubbed bald and shiny, and rain water always seemed to be trickling uncomfortably down the back of my neck. However browned off we became the thought never entered our heads to lay down our arms *en masse* and refuse to soldier though. That would have been mutiny and would have incurred a considerable amount of wrath descending on us via the Manual of Military Law. Even a small locally administered parochial tweak on the ear by the MML stung you quite hard. As a result, we were taken for granted and abused. We were made to run up mountains in full kit and then run back down them again; to bleed, to hurt, to get out of breath . . . even to die, sometimes, some of us did, yet still we were remorselessly driven on and still we would grin foolishly and think of England and our girlfriends. It was called Discipline. But it was great and it worked. We, its recipients, knew what it was and what it was for and that we had to have it. Those were the rules of the game. By those rules the British used to win wars, brush fires and skirmishes and looked incredibly good on the parade square. I had first been licensed to kill about the time James Bond hit us. He used a Walther PPK and did so whenever he felt it expedient. I often felt it expedient but my .303 Lee Enfield was locked away in the armoury. I could only get it out if it said so on Part One Orders, and then only to shoot at targets and not tin cans, cats or stray dogs, let alone people I didn't like.

Mainly it was the rain water trickling down the back of my neck that decided me this next time round that a commission was called for. Officers got to wear nice clean, stiff white Moss Bros riding macs with their collars turned up. They managed to keep them clean, stiff and white because they didn't have to flog round with a pick helve guarding the coal store in the wee small hours, stoking the boiler and standing guard duty beneath cracked and overflowing drainpipes. They were required merely to don their best blue Number One Dress uniforms, mount the Guard (not literally you understand) and then come back and check on it for a few minutes at 01.00 before turning in for the night.

That was the theory anyway.

"Why do you want to be an officer?" was one of the telling questions they asked us at RCB.

"As a personal insurance in the event of war, sir. I believe officers get cushier billets. Plus I simply adore that *gorgeous* beige overcoat they wear; also I rather like the idea of standing out in front with a sword."

I knew I still had a lot to learn.

Back then I used to trust and respect my superiors. We all did. They knew the bigger picture, and how we fitted in. "There's no need for you to befuddle your young brains and run the risk of them catching fire," we were assured by our CSM. The more we matured, however, the more we posed questions. For self satisfaction, those questions needed to be answered, and more often than not I found the answers wanting. Eventually I came to the conclusion that in many cases our masters were as much in the dark about things as us: nor, it seemed, did they have too much sway in affecting certain pre-determined courses of action, which invariably resulted in the soldiery bearing the brunt.

Overall, though, the military panoply still appealed to me, especially the ceremonial. Yet I had always felt strangely detached from any proceedings of which I was a part. As the immaculate khaki clad figures marched, wheeled and counter marched, tick-tocked in general and carried out the entire choreographic content of the Army's Drill Manual with sufficient precision to render a Swiss watchmaker impotent, even though I was usually in the front rank I had always felt superfluous. The officers were all part of it, of course; those magnificent creatures upon whose shoulders the mantle of God had descended, those wonderful chaps who stood between us and the outside world, with their swords drawn gleaming and rock steady before them, the peaks of their caps touching the tips of their patrician noses, casting shadows over gunsight eyes . . . they were a part of it alright. It was their regiment. They were infused and committed. We all knew their names, the names of their dogs, their idiosyncrasies and which sports they excelled at. We, on the other hand, were just the hired hands. We were not personalities, allowed to guffaw out loud in company. We were rent-a-crowd. There were plenty more of us where we came from.

It was this, also, then, that decided me this time round to take a commission - to stop the rain water getting down my neck and to start shaping some destiny for myself.

For the past four years I had been a civilian. This enabled me to compare both lifestyles. On reflection, the prospect of visiting foreign climes with my diary once more, held more appeal than continuing to flog round south-east England as a sales rep in a low status company car. My daughter, Natalia, was nearly nine months old. I was behind with the rent. A khaki career path (bolt hole?) and the incentive and opportunity to write, seemed an appealing prospect. I discussed the idea with Rachel and she agreed that a period at home in the Gibraltar sunshine with her family while I underwent the rigours of Mons OCS for four months, seemed like a good idea.

Now for the second time in my life I was at the threshold of a new careeer. I had packed the family's belongings. Rachel and Natalia had flown home to Gibraltar for the duration, and I handed our Hillcrest Court flat back to its owner. It was February 1963, when the snow lay not deep and crisp or even on the ground, but in great big heaps of filthy frozen chunks.

Army wives in peacetime affectionately refer to their husbands' operational training exercises and manoeuvres as: "Oh, Jeremy's off playing at soldiers again this weekend."

I was now off, once more, to play at soldiers again.

NINE

AT WESTBURY in Wiltshire there is a large converted country manor called Leighton House. It is the home of the Army's Regular Commission Board (RCB).

Leighton House was built by Thomas Henry Phipps Esquire, on land originally owned by the Thynne family (Marquess of Bath), in about 1800. In 1888 it was purchased by W.H.Laverton Esquire, then Managing Director of the Laverton Mill in Westbury. He enlarged the house and built its stable block (now the Board Office), road bridge and a large private theatre.

By the end of the 19th Century, Leighton Park had become one of the showplaces of Wiltshire. The 'Test Matches' between Mr Laverton's XI and the Australians drew crowds from far and wide, if only to see the great W.G. Grace in action. Famous stage stars of the day such as Melba, Caruso, and Dan Leno used to entertain the house parties and the cricket teams in the Theatre.

By 1921, Leighton Park had become a school - the Victoria College - and it is still referred to locally as The College, or Victoria House. When the school was forced to close down in 1936, the estate lay derelict for two years. Destined to become a Roman Catholic training college, it was instead requisitioned and later bought freehold by the War Department.

During the Second World War, Leighton Park housed part of the Royal Victoria Hospital from Netley, Southampton, together with No. 111 Convalescent Depot. By 1945 the military population had risen to over 1,000 and the old theatre, demolished in 1964, did sterling service both as a concert hall and as a cinema.

When the war ended, Victoria House became one of the several War Office Selection Boards (WOSB) for National Service Officers, and in 1949 it was chosen as the permanent home of the Regular Commissions Board, which had formerly been at Knepp Castle, Horsham. The present candidates' living quarters were then built along the drive, and in 1951 the main building became the Officers' Mess and reverted to its old name - Leighton House.

In September 2006 the RCB was to become renamed the AOSB (Army Officer Selection Board) - but when I took a few days leave from work in order to sneak off to Leighton House to undergo my assessment tests there in 1962, it was still known as the RCB.

For three days I underwent all manner of physical and psychological appraisals to have my officer-like qualities and potential professionally assessed by the RCB's resident team of regular serving officers, presided over by a major-general, all of whom knew what they were about. Well - to a degree they did: I passed.

I was over the first hurdle.

When National Service was at its zenith there used to be an 80% pass rate at RCB (or WOSB as it then was). During the time that I attended (just after National Service had finished), with the same tests and standards, there was an 80% failure rate. This is why despite redundancy and the formation of a smaller army, advertisements were still appearing in the press for more army officers. It was reassuring that the Army so steadfastly maintained its standards, but it was a salutary reflection on the declining state of the nation's youth that so few applicants now seemed able to meet those standards. Although scions of the Old School were still fetching up by rote to join their fathers' regiments as a familial rite of passage for a while, before going on into the City, the Army generally seemed not to be quite such a popular career as it used to be. Assuming a candidate's given and understood inherent ability, country seats and private means were no longer the other prime requisites for a commission, although the correct social connections and background were (and still are) required for the Household Brigade and some cavalry regiments. There is that well known apocryphal tale of the Sandhurst cadet being interviewed for acceptance by the Colonel of The Blues and Royals.

"Can you tell me why the Blues wear blue jackets, young man?"

"Of course I can, sir," the well briefed and savvy cadet promptly replied. "So that their blood doesn't show when they're wounded."

Many of the young men who were starting to arrive at Westbury in my day, and subsequently, were doing so straight from school or the shop floor. Many of them were turning up not with hacking jackets and cords, but with flowing locks, wearing flared jeans and Frankenstein boots. Unaware of the proper form, they had applied on a wing and a prayer just to give it a shot. The appearance of such candidates could and did stick in the craw of many a professional army man, who despite his full awareness that it was now the twentieth century, was still pretty imbued with traditional conservative standards.

RCB was the processing cell for potential officers of all branches, from the Army Catering Corps to the Brigade of Guards. However well qualified he might turn out to be as a leader of cooks, certain young men could still find it daunting to be competing at Westbury with a sea of Old Etonians and Harrovians poncing effortlessly about as to the manner born, all seeming to know each other and each others' sisters and with any thought or likelihood of failure furthest from their minds. The RCB team, of course, was nicely aware of the different social expectations of a top line cavalry regiment *vis-à-vis* the arguably more pedestrian requirements of a technically oriented arm or corps, and with appropriate recommendations they would channel their selections accordingly towards the most suitable end cap badge.

At completion of their three-days' Westbury ordeal, candidates heaved an enormous sigh of relief and departed to their respective home bases to await the verdict. They were notified of this a few days later by the arrival in the post of a buff coloured envelope conveying the message. Those who had been successful, be he Guardee, Gurkha, Engineer or Cook, then proceeded to officer training at one of two establishments. At that time these were The Royal Military Academy, Sandhurst (RMAS) - or Mons Officer Cadet School (OCS), Aldershot.

After the Second World War, all fit men were conscripted, after reaching their eighteenth birthday, for National Service of up to two years with the colours followed by three in the Territorial Army or other part-time Reserves. National Service and Short Service commissions were granted to provide the large numbers of junior officers required by a large army, but as both categories were only engaged for a limited period, the time available for Officer Cadet training was restricted to a few months. The war-time OCTU system was adopted for this purpose, and two Officer Cadet Schools were set up. One was at Mons Barracks, Aldershot, previously used by 161 Inf OCTU (RMC) - and the other was at Eaton Hall, in Cheshire. Officer cadets of the Royal Armoured Corps or Royal Artillery went to Mons, while those of the other arms and services went to Eaton Hall. When National service was abolished in 1960 it was decided to retain the Short Service system, as this improved the long-term prospects available to career officers. Eaton Hall OCS was closed and Mons OCS became responsible for training all Short Service Officer Cadets, as well as all those joining the Regular Army as graduates. As the supply of ex-NS officers dwindled, Mons also undertook the final training of candidates for Territorial Army commissions.

This proved very successful. The intensive OCS system trained cadets solely to perform the duties of subalterns, and was thus cheaper and quicker than the Military Academy system (Sandhurst), which was intended to produce future field officers and generals. Some commanding officers found the former more useful than the latter. Increasingly, potential officers preferred to train at Mons, where they could gain all the benefits of a commission in six months, while their Sandhurst contemporaries were still serving as cadets for a further eighteen.

In 1972 Mons OCS moved the few miles from its ageing barracks at Aldershot to the empty New College at RMAS. The original plan that the two establishments should simply be co-located did not prove feasible, so the decision was then taken to restructure the entire system of Officer Cadet training, with Mons College as the major element of the RMAS.

All this was to be in the long term.

In the meantime, I was off to attend the earlier version of Mons OCS.

Not for us the leisurely academic terms of Sandhurst.

Mons boys were originally in for 'the duration' (of the war): Train fast; train hard. Forget the cocktail party circuit, there wasn't time. Sort out the Hun and back to Blighty. This was the lusty, thrusting Mons tradition that grew up over the years and was apparent still when my intake and I arrived there in February 1963. Sandhurst was for future generals; Mons for the instant warrior. *Serve To Lead* was Sandhurst's motto. *Leadership* was Mons'. In an action packed five months the Mons product had to be ready to command the lives of 30 men in a desert, jungle, snow or mountainous environment. The course worked well. It had to.

Architecturally Mons Barracks was evocative of an Alaskan lumber camp. We resided in a complex network of elevated wooden huts known as 'spiders'. The rest of the school consisted of the usual guard room, garages, drill square, playing fields, obstacle courses, gymnasium, cookhouse, MI Room, armoury, lecture halls, class rooms, the commandant's and adjutant's offices - and the administrative wing, the latter being referred to as 'The Tramlines' because they consisted of two parallel lines of offices. The whole place was so gloriously disorientated as to bear only the slightest resemblance to most known military establishments and created the utmost confusion in the minds of newcomers to its portals. Portals? There were none. One simply turned off Queen's Avenue, Aldershot, and there at the end of a long road was Mons OCS sprawled about all over the place.

Queen's Avenue is Aldershot's answer to London's The Mall. When I was 15 I was first driven along it at 10.00-o'clock one Saturday night in 1953 with my father. National Service and the Korean War were in full spate at the time, and a khaki-clad flood of humanity was swelling, milling and flowing along Queen's Avenue as if it was Oxford Street in the rush hour. The place pulsed with this seething military throng. Seen in retrospect it was like finding myself dropped into the midst of a teeming ancient civilisation in some sort of real time, when in 1963, a decade later, National Service over and done with, it seemed almost deserted by comparison.

The Commandant at Mons was a brigadier, Brigadier P.W.G. Pope, DSO, MC. His pug was a bitch. His second-in-command was the moustached and monocled, extremely dapper Lieutenant-Colonel T.J. 'Bill' Bowen, MC, of The Worcestershire Regiment. His adjutant was a captain in the Coldstream Guards, P.E.W. Gibbs, who had an Afghan hound. (Dogs are an essential part of an army officer's kit; especially those with spotted handkerchiefs tucked up their sleeves.) His two company commanders were majors (golden retrievers), whose 2i/cs were captains, for whom – unless they were cavalry – an Afghan would be rather pretentious, so it is usually a black Lab or Jack Russell –sometimes even both; one of each.

Mons consisted of Salerno and Kohima Companies, each company being commanded by one or other of the two majors mentioned above.

(Never, under any circumstance, a Chihuahua though.)

Each company carried out identical training, but alternately did so ahead of the other company. For example, I was in Salerno Company, the senior company, the members of which were due to be commissioned in July. Kohima Company was the junior company, to be commissioned a few weeks after us. In between our (Salerno's) commissioning parade and

Kohima's, a fresh Salerno company would be formed from new arrivals, and commence its training as the new junior company, and so on.

The senior and junior companies were each made up of three platoons, overseen by our three captains above who would strut, stroll, mince and otherwise motivate themselves about the place in accordance with their respective regimental customs, tempered with locally adopted idiosyncrasies and as much personal affectation as they thought they might subtly get away with. We really were twitching out the last days of the Raj there in our grey and dismal Hampshire cantonement - but the ritual was still meaningful, stressful, character building, and fun.

Further on down the chain - just beneath the watermark, so to speak - one encountered a national characteristic which, with the military being one of the Establishment's last strongholds, was as fervently nurtured at Mons as ever it had been anywhere throughout the length and breadth of Great Britain's once vehemently vermilion empire. Although it was an invisible wall, its effect was as powerful as a high voltage fence erected around such places as the car park, the lavatories, the seating arrangements, the petty priorities and all the other niceties of life. In short, it was The Social Barrier.

Beneath our three platoon commander captains there stood one lonely Black Watch subaltern. He commanded the school's Demonstration Infantry Platoon of Black Watch jocks, used as toy soldiers to show us how things really *should* be done if we were going to do them properly. Like a kilted Horatio he bridged the gap, standing lonely sentinel on the right side of the seldom scaled invisible wall. On the *other* side . . .

. . . groping at its hitherto rarely assailed brickwork, clamoured those lesser of God's mortals, sometime serfs and peasants, one time Bowmen of England - the Other Ranks (ORs.) To a man as worthy a band of cohorts as one could wish to meet, at the top of this heap was the RSM (Regimental Sergeant Major), otherwise known as **God**. At Sandhurst and Mons the RSM was always traditionally a Guardsman, a niche market which historically the Brigade had always successfully managed to corner for itself, and such was their power that possession being nine-tenths of the law no one was ever going to dream of gainsaying them this time-honoured right of theirs.

Our **God** at Mons OCS at this time was the fearsome Sergeant Major S.A.J. Blake, of The Coldstream Guards.

Salerno Company was commanded by Major John 'Bungey' Tavistock, MC 11th Hussars (nick-named after his Golden Retriever). He was; not his regiment.

The three platoon commanders were Captain Tony Dove-Medows, a Sherwood Forrester, Captain 'Dickie' Dutton, King's Own Yorkshire Light Infantry, and Captain David Swinburn, a Sapper.

The Company Sergeant Major was CSM 'Daisy' (don't ask) *'I couldn't give fifty-thousand monkeys' fucks, sir'* Bracknell, Coldstream Guards, and our three platoon sergeants were Sanderson, Scots Guards; Scott, the Middlesex Regiment, and Jackson, Coldstream Guards. And there you have it.

By nature of his calling CSM Bracknell was a strict disciplinarian and tyrant but beneath these assumed characteristics of his there beat a kindly heart and a warm and humorous personality. He was a veritable music hall turn. After I was commissioned I once had to go back to Mons for something, and happened to bump into 'Daisy' just coming out of the RSM's office. It being the appropriate time of day he kindly invited me across to the Sergeants' Mess for lunch. After the waiter had served me a dollop of green processed mush the CSM leaned over and apologised, saying: "Sorry about the OR pattern peas, sir. The Mess caterer hasn't been able to get hold of the officers' sort for some time."

This then was the team expectantly poised to greet the arrival from Aldershot station of that season's first batch of young hopefuls to Salerno Company.

TEN

SALERNO COMPANY, MONS OCS, Aldershot, Hampshire had drawn its kit, had its hair cut and eggs for tea and with its past experience parcelled up individually in brown paper and string and posted home to country seat, town house or urban semi, lay itself down to sleep in neat little rows beneath course War Department blankets and the darkened eaves of barrack rooms whose wooden beams and walls creaked at the joists and could tell a tale or two.

The Ministry of Public Buildings and works (MPBW - later to become the Department of the Environment {DOE} and then the Property Services Agency {PSA}- and even then still not quite sure exactly what they were meant to be doing) had submitted their report on the creaking. Whatever the structural reason might have been, the more romantic of us who slept there each night and heard it straining its bowels, attributed it to a supreme effort on the walls' behalf to impart to the latest Salerno intake the horrors of what was to come.

Oh, if only they had succeeded . . .

. . . they could have been published as a Baedeker of military tips; how best to burnish brasses, bull boots and blanco belts; how to bumper the floor and elude authority, in short . . . how to get through the coming months of toil by expending the minimum of heartbreak, sweat and frustration. Yet they were only walls that could only creak and let the latest intake sleep on.

Or were they sleeping?

The sandman, if he had passed, would have clearly perceived the spirals of smoke illuminated by the glowing tips of several cigarettes burning in the night: or the white blur of

106

arms folded behind a pensive young head still awake with confused thoughts of the morrow. Perhaps the sandman's attuned ear might even have detected the almost inaudible sniff of a young man fresh from home or wife or girlfriend, his mind a turmoil of nervous anticipation about how he would acquit himself. Would he do well, by not letting down family and friends?

The next few weeks would tell.

Officer Cadet Joshua Nguli (soon to become known as One Ball) of the King's African Rifles lay in his bed in the far corner of 'D' Spider's Room 3.

He had only been in England four days, and so far - his illusions shattered - he didn't like it. At home in Kenya he had visualised England as being a kind of Utopia where no hate, unfriendliness or rudeness ever existed; where there was no poverty, and visitors would be welcome in every household. He had now found that English people really did spend the whole time referring to and discussing their truly ghastly weather. The grey skies, the rain and the cold seemed to affect everyone he met, making them tight, pinched and mean of countenance and spirit. Everyone seemed to be so defensively aggressive the whole time and didn't seem to be in the least bit friendly or cooperative. Everywhere he went it seemed as if he was an unwelcome intruder. At home in Kenya you could strike up a friendly conversation with almost anyone, but apparently that was not the case over here. He had expected to find the British way of life over here even better than that led by the white administrators at home, but this was not so. One almost gained the impression that the officials at home were atypical of their race, and being aware of this had emigrated to Kenya to lead their own lives rather than remain and be ground down in this drab mother country of theirs. At home the wives of some of the British soldiers had not been the best advertisement for Anglo-Saxon womanhood, but the majority of other white women had been real ladies. Now he was finding that those soldiers' wives had been beauty queens compared to some of the slatterns he was seeing around him;

cheap, gross, ignorant - could they possibly be British? It was the first time he had seen white women work - and so *menially.* And the so called Christian faith which was so strongly espoused at home, seemed to be totally absent here in England. It was shocking.

Joshua, and his cousin Martin Matu, had flown in from Nairobi bursting with pride that their government had chosen to send them on this course, while outwardly giving the impression that they felt it was no more than their due. In five months time they would at last be able to don the coveted service dress cap and Sam Browne belt and return home to command a platoon of *Askaris.* Out of personal pride they would have to display a certain amount of effort over the coming months, but not so much as the British cadets. It had become obvious over the years that overseas cadets were seldom relegated or RTU'd: if they had been, their governments would have stopped paying Britain's treasury as handsomely as they did for training them.

Joshua was in 1 Platoon, and his cousin Martin in 3 Platoon which was a shame. This meant they were unable to sleep in adjoining beds, when they could have conversed together. What was it he had heard that big red-haired fellow say? Joshua had just been coming back into the spider after tea. Pausing in the doorway to light a cigarette he had not been noticed by the group gathered inside the room with their backs to him. It was funny the way British men stood when talking amongst themselves. Almost invariably they sunk their hands in their pockets and shuffled from one foot to the other, intermittently banging the welts of their shoes together as if they were cold.

"Christ though, these bloody wogs crawling all over the place get right up my nose, don't they you? My brother told me that twenty percent of each intake is coloured, but I thought he was exaggerating. Now I see what he meant. There's an incredible number of them, don't you think? Thank God we've only got one of 'em in here: it'll be bad enough as it is in summer. At least he's over there in the corner. At least the powers that be seem to have got the dispersal plan correct. Imagine if we had a whole gaggle of them sleeping together."

"Is that right, Charles? Surely 'gaggle' isn't the collective noun for wogs, is it?"

"No, I suppose 'tribe' might be more appropriate, really," said one.

"Sorry, old boy; Charles is right," put in another. "A tribe is when you've got all of them. A gaggle is just bits and pieces. Well - it is in my book, anyway."

This remark had been greeted with appreciative guffaws of inane laughter, but then one of them had caught sight of Joshua standing there shocked and surprised in the doorway. Smiling to conceal his burning hurt he walked quickly over to his bedspace and reached up to take his photograph album down from his locker. The group of malicious Brits had dissolved with embarrassed grins at each other and silly little coughs at nothing in particular, dispersing to their respective bedspaces to busy themselves sorting kit.

The happy, smiling face of his fiancée Elizabeth seemed many miles away that night. Joshua had no particular reason to like the Brits. All they had so far offered him was disinterested surliness and insults behind his back, and cold indifference to his face. It was difficult for any young man to evolve a workable philosophy in his teens to aid him against the knocks he would encounter, but a black man in a white man's country really did have problems. Still, at least he was in a white man's country, eating white man's food (filthy stuff that it was) and living with them. Perhaps in the future a wind of change would blow its course and his descendants could show compassion on the British. Besides, he had known white men who smelled none to pleasant in summer. He always had suffered from sweaty feet.

He slept.

Charles Mackay was a Scot; ex Gordonstoun - and tough.

His shock of wiry red hair was the bane of his life. If it had not been such a drastic step he would have had it dyed, or shaved. The camp barber's efforts that afternoon had not been

109

far short of the latter, but as he lay on his bed trying to sleep he still felt like a E-Type carrot in its garage for the night. Yet his fiery hair belied his nature. Despite his rugged appearance his grandmother in Dundee still referred to him as a sweet natured boy, and this funnily enough was a fair appraisal. He was desperately sorry he had upset that bloody black man earlier. He had honestly not seen him standing in the doorway, but he had to try to get in with the other chaps. His broad burr was not always acceptable in every circle so he had to try to make his mark on the rugger field, and making facetious remarks. Oh, well: no good crying over spilt milk. Perhaps in due course he'd get a chance to make amends. Silently saying his prayers he mentally hummed a few bars of the *Skye Boat Song*, turned over and went to sleep.

Fraser Alan-Hunter had been to Mons before.

After three days there he had become so incensed in an argument that despite the warnings of the Brigadier and his staff to the effect that overseas cadets should be treated with an especial courtesy, he had smashed an infuriating little Thai police trainee so hard in the face that if it was at all possible the oriental nose had looked even flatter than before. Neither the Thai nor the Commandant had looked favourably on this occurrence. William Hickey had considered it a newsworthy enough titbit to put in his gossip column though, so the incident had appeared in humorously couched journalese in the *Daily Express* just a couple of days later. A disgraced but seemingly indifferent Alan-Hunter had duly been returned to his regiment, the 15th/19th King's Royal Hussars in Germany, where with immaculately tapered trousers he had sallied forth once again as a mere trooper to support the surrounding fleshpots and bars. After a decent lapse of time during which he smashed up two cars, a home and an engagement, his not entirely un-influential father made representation through the appropriate channels to have his son reinstated, and so his father being a cabinet minister Alan-Hunter was once again admitted through the non existent portals of Mons OCS for a second chance.

110

Despite the lateness of the hour and the import of the morrow, Alan-Hunter was not curled up asleep beside his fellows in Hampshire, but had just arisen from a very warm and scented double bed off Cadogan Square, donned his sheepskin jacket and leaving the sated deb to worry alone for the next few weeks removed the parking ticket from his green Austin-Healey 3000 and gunned the big car westward back to Mons.

At 03.15 they started to remove what remained of Fraser's car, his body, and the motorcyclist with whom he was splashed in a fatal embrace, from around a badly bent stanchion of the Hammersmith Flyover. He hadn't yet even bothered to get his hair cut.

It is a character trait in some people - we've all met them - that they go roaring off on life's path hell bent on a frenetic quest for a premature, seemingly pre-ordained and dramatic demise.

ELEVEN

08.00 FRIDAY 29 FEBRUARY.

One hundred of us officer cadets milled round the entrance to our billets, split into desultorily conversing groups. Names, cigarettes, point of view and inane banalities were the currency of our nervous exchanges. The majority of my peers there had just spent their first night in the army and endured their first army breakfast. Gourmets amongst us were not the happiest of men.

The sun was making a brave effort to shine on our initial endeavours and the frost was still begrudgingly departing its night's resting place. A sociologist would have been enthralled. One hundred young men brought together under the complete and absolute command of a mere handful of officers, NCOs and a system, each of whom we were yet to meet and who in turn were waiting in the wings to shout, coax, push, insinuate and force as many of us as possible through the forthcoming five rigorous months of training. Most of us would make it. A few would not. Any one of us might be RTUd for disciplinary reasons or unsuitability: or we might be relegated to the next intake for having broken our leg or being slow in the classroom or physically incapable of such sustained gymnastic feats as raising our shins to the beam. Then there might be the occasional unfortunate soul who would come unstuck for no apparent reason at all; in all respects a first class chap, but for some reason which no one would disclose to him and of which he was unaware, his face may not fit and he would be destined for pastures other than khaki.

There we stood . . .

Etonians; Harrovians; Grammarians; Glaswegians; Kenyans; Nigerians; Colonials; Honourables - all of one accord, hopefuls. A mixed bag, all of whom had managed to impress our respective selection boards that we possessed that one indefinable quality - leadership, in many cases still dormant, which categorised us as potential officer material. We were there to have this quality drawn out, developed, recognised and exploited in our own and the nation's interest. For the next five months we would learn to shoot, march, run, salute and throw things; to lead, command, instruct, lecture, sweat and suffer; to undergo privation, physical discomfort of no mean order, spit, polish and eventually to emerge on that day of days, seemingly so far distant now, as newly commissioned officers.

Major John Tavistock, MC, was a 'cherry picking' 11th Hussar, the nickname coming from an incident during the Peninsular War in which the 11th Light Dragoons (as the regiment was then named) were attacked while raiding an orchard at *San Martin de Trebejo* in Spain. When the regiment became the 11th (Prince Albert's Own) Hussars in 1840, their new uniform by coincidence included crimson (i.e. cherry) coloured trousers, unique among British regiments and worn since in all orders of uniform except battledress - not in memory of the orchard incident, but to reflect the crimson livery of Prince Albert's House: Saxe-Coburg and Gotha.

The 11th Hussars famously charged with the Light Brigade, commanded by their previous Colonel, Lord Cardigan, at Balaklava during the Crimean War.

In 1928, it became the first British regiment to be mechanized. There was an apocryphal tale doing the rounds at the time of another cavalry regiment, whose motto was *Love And Ride On*. When they switched from horses to tanks they changed their motto to *Screw And Bolt*.

John Tavistock's association started in 1939 when as a polo playing subaltern he had joined his regiment from Sandhurst. In 1940, the 11th was located in Egypt when Italy declared war on Britain and France. It was part of the 'Divisional Troops of the 7th Armoured Division (known as the 'Desert Rats'.) When they began to conduct various raids against Italian positions during the Western Desert Campaign, Captain Tavistock had found himself in the turret of one of his regiment's obsolete Rolls Royce armoured cars pounding along a dust choked route in the lead formation. To the quickly battle-hardened twenty-four-year old captain it had seemed only a few months before that he had been on manoeuvres in the mud of Long Valley, back home in Aldershot, when controversial discussion were still raging about the relative merits of tanks and armoured cars *vis-à-vis* horses. When the cavalry had first become mechanised its officers had been dismayed to find there were no means of communication from the turrets of their new vehicles to the virtually blind drivers, cut off in the bowels of the beasts by the roar of their mighty engines as they screamed to scale one hump, only to topple over and plummet down the side of the next. The ghostly echoes of a million fading hooves and creaking saddlery answered the call. The erring armoured drivers then found themselves with reins strapped to their shoulders. The commander in the turret could yank his driver's reigns to left or right to indicate direction as he pleased. Unfortunately some of these signals were conveyed with such ferocity that sometimes even the toughest shoulders were jerked into dislocation. As if that was not enough, when the turret revolved the harness became so viciously snarled that the driver would be ejected backwards from his seat to dent his head like a saucepan against the steel roof. It only took a few drivers slumped over their controls with fractured skulls before the communications system was improved, but the early days of John Tavistock's war had been mostly ones of trial and error.

In 1944 he had been promoted to major, but in 1945 lost his crown along with the lower half of his left leg and reverted to his substantive rank of captain with a strapped on limb which gave him gyp in winter and wore his shoe down in an irregular pattern. In 1946 he was adjutant at the depot for a while, and thought this was a good enough time to marry Sheila Melanie Athlone beneath an archway of flashbulbs and sabres. In 1947 the new Mrs Tavistock presented him with a son, Derek, and in 1948 a daughter, Janine.

So the ensuing years rolled on between Germany, the Far East and the War Office, and now, just as Derek was about to start his first term at Sandhurst and Janine was becoming increasingly aware of herself as a young woman, Major and Mrs John Tavistock found themselves quartered in Camberley, with him commuting over to Aldershot every day in his grey Mercedes 220SE, to where he was fulfilling his latest appointment as Company Commander of Salerno Company, Mons OCS.

John Tavistock was no fool, but major he was and unless he became very lucky indeed at the eleventh hour, major he knew he would remain. At forty-seven he had had a good life, but really and truly he had left it eight years too long to get out and start something afresh. Eight years ago he had been having a ball in Singapore at GHQ FARELF. Despite the writing on the wall regarding lack of promotion, who in their right mind would have left the glorious Far East that summer to go and sit in some dingy office off Moorgate? But they had left eventually, and returned for the second time to Bielefeld where perhaps with some premonition of a pending change, he had lashed out and invested in his brand new Merc.

Now they were back living in Camberley again.

Each day he passed the impressive white Academy gates of Sandhurst on his way to Mons. This would definitely have to be his last tour. Fitting, perhaps, that he should go out as father figure to a lot of officer cadets still wet behind the ears, as he himself had once been. Not quite the same as the Academy, this, but they had started churning out officers here during the war in a compressed and vital course and if results weren't the true test of success or failure then he didn't know what was. *Serve to Lead* was Sandhurst's motto. Mons was simply *Leadership*. Must be a message there somewhere. Everything had to have a message these days. These Mons chaps probably came from a wider age bracket and background than the

Sandhurst entrants and in only five months they were doing the job which the Sandhurst chap would have to wait two years for. Yet they were eventually doing it together; side by side in some far flung corners of foreign fields, and unless anyone asked there was no particular hallmark to differentiate between them. He sucked momentarily on his pipe and still musing gazed at the flaking ceiling of his austere little office in the 'Tramlines'. There were two Bateman prints on one wall, a very discreet pin-up calendar on the other, various framed photographs of himself seated with groups of fellow officers, or crews; a photo of his first armoured car; a watercolour caricature of himself in Mess kit, and curled up at his feet under the table, his golden retriever bitch *Bungey*. Raising her head and cocking an ear she sensed his decision to move and slowly uncurling herself waddled across to retrieve his riding crop for him from the chair. He in turn arose to his feet, knocked the dottle from his pipe, rifted cursorily through his 'in' tray and donning his stained SD cap opened the door to step outside. Only he realised at that moment and then only subconsciously perhaps that this would probably be the last intake of cadets he would be welcoming to Mons.

Patting *Bungey's* head he casually acknowledged the early morning salutes from the permanent staff he passed, and limped across to the main lecture hall with *Bungey* lolloping faithfully at his heels.

CSM Edward Bracknell, BEM, Coldstream Guards, thirty-eight-years of age, was a bastard. On parade. Off parade, unless it suited him to be otherwise, he was really quite a decent sort.

Everyone knew the outrageous language and behaviour of army WOs and NCOs were merely a stylized charade, but a CSM has to possess these qualities in abundance. He has to have a tremendous personality, larger than his boots, and the strength to carry it *and* he has to have the ability to act Olivier off the stage.

Bracknell possessed both.

He had seen action in most theatres since 1945. He had his

Army Certificate of Education 1st Class and was studying three subjects for GCE. He spoke extremely good German and had what was reputed to be one of the finest set of whiskers in the British Army. He stood six-foot-three in his ammunition boots, weighed 200-pounds and could manipulate his pace stick with an expertise that would put a Royal Marines drum major to shame. He was affectionately by some and otherwise by others known as 'Daisy'.

It was now 08.10 on Friday 29 January. 'Daisy' Bracknell with his three accompanying platoon sergeants hot in his wake came swiftly steaming and bristling up the gravel road between his office and our accommodation. Of one accord the one-hundred of us seemed to sense 'Daisy''s impending arrival with his outrider entourage, and men who only hours before had been long haired civilians instinctively stubbed out half-finished cigarettes, swallowed hard and began shuffling ourselves into some semblance of order.

The herd sensed collective fear.

'Daisy' hove to starboard while his three sergeants deployed themselves strategically at our assembly's flanks, as if to close exits and cut off all escape routes.

Silence fell.

Seconds ticked by without a sound but the almost inaudible crackle of the still withdrawing early morning frost. One cadet coughed nervously and the ninety-nine others of us stole a shifty glance in his direction thinking he might be spirited away, thankful it had not been any of *us* whose throat had tickled.

'Daisy' continued to gaze steadfastly at the sky; possibly offering guidance thereto, certainly not receiving it. Then turning a transformed and beaming countenance upon us he opened wide his mouth like the MGM lion and emitted a gently rolling bass that left no doubt as to the resounding volume that was held in reserve.

"It is now quarter-past-eight. If you young gentlemen would care to shamble over here towards me and arrange yourselves as a more presentable looking entity we will call the roll prior to gripping you. *You*, sir . . . that knock-kneed, brothel-bred bastard over there who looks as if the best part of him ran down his mother's leg . . . yes, sir - *you*, sir . . . the pale faced gentleman clenching his fists . . ." - he jabbed the brass ferule of his pace stick to indicate a callow, cowering, quivering, blond-haired youth of nineteen tremulous summers who obviously hadn't *ever* been spoken to like that in his life before. "Would you be so kind as to step over here and act as Right Marker, please? If you were ever a member of your school's cadet force you will no doubt recall what exalted position that is. If not, then you will very soon learn. That's right, sir. You've got the idea. Very good indeed, sir. And what is your name, if I may be so bold as to ask, sir?"

"Martin . . . Sergeant."

"I see. Well, I'm not actually a sergeant, you see, Mister Martin, sir. Those three gentlemen waiting over there at your flanks are sergeants. They're important; but I'm even more important than they are. Just this once, seeing as how you're a new boy, sir, we'll overlook your silly little slip, shall we? But let it be known that from this moment on, should you ever happen to call me sergeant again, I shall kill you. You will call me Sir, sir. DO YOU UNDERSTAND?"

"Yes, sir. But I think I'd better clear up a slight misunderstanding first, if I may. You see, I'm actually Officer Cadet *Johnson*. Martin is my Christian name."

"*Is* it indeed? Well now, fancy that. What a lovely name. And there you are being all friendly and wanting us to be on first name terms on initial acquaintance like that. I had a goldfish once. We called *him* Martin. He died. RIGHT, gentlemen . . . if you would now care to fall-in on this little twerp, Officer Cadet *Martin* Johnson - and if some of you should accidentally manage to trample him painfully underfoot as you do so please be assured that on this occasion I shall deliberately fail to notice - we will continue with the proceedings."

The bolder among us allowed ourselves a swift chuckle to release our tension as we shuffled into three horribly ragged lines.

The CSM still stood apart and some would have sworn

that an ethereal plinth had elevated him even farther from the ground. He surveyed us with a smile (or perhaps it was a leer) of studied patience while his three subordinates paced swiftly up and down like collies nipping our assembled lines into shape. Job done, as though by some prearranged signal they all peeled off, came together before the CSM, smashed their boots into the gravel roadway, swivelled about and flattened the road surface once more, once again stamped a foot away from their original indentations and in that way arrived in the 'at ease' position.

The heavens waited.

"Gentlemen, I am the first person to welcome you officially to Mons Officer Cadet School. Welcome. Let us have no mistakes. I *am* a person. From time to time, almost hourly in fact, there will be those among you who will have occasion to doubt this. Nevertheless, it is true. I am Warrant Officer Second Class Bracknell E. of the Second Battalion the Coldstream Guards. Sergeant Scott - the young gentleman third from the right in the centre rank whispered something to the effect that First Class must have been full would you please arrange to have him removed this instant thank you . . ."

"SAH . . ." *Crash - CRASH - crump - swivel - crunch – crunch - CRUNCH.* "_YOU_, sir. Out. Now. Left turn. Quick March. Right Wheel. Leftrightleftrightleftrightleftright . . ."

Two little clouds of rapidly spiralling dust disappeared towards the Guard Room at such a rate of knots it was mind boggling. We wondered if we would ever see that man again. Completely unfazed, the CSM continued.

"You will perceive gentlemen, that things here at Mons are executed with expeditious efficiency. We haven't got time to mess about. I sincerely hope that you will enjoy your stay with us, but I am confident that you won't enjoy all of it. We were not designed to be a holiday camp. Officially I should say that it is up to you. We all know better than that though, don't we. If you try to butter up to me, I dislike it. On the other hand, if you should refrain from showing me the requisite amount of deference should I approach and deign to speak to you, I also dislike it. So you will, I think, agree that the school's motto

119

Leadership is not quite so apt as *You Can't Win*. Nevertheless, I wish you all the best of luck. Work very hard and we'll see if we can't get some of you through. You may now relax, and smile . . . all *right*, that's *enough;* No need to tear the arse out of it."

The wind rustled. Leaves stirred on the trees and the CSM departed, having created in the mass mind of his stunned audience exactly the impression he had intended. It was all an act, of course. A great, big, wonderful, much rehearsed, refined, honed and polished act, and one that worked every time.

One of the sergeants assumed the lately vacated hallowed spot and commenced to sort us slowly reviving cadets into three separate platoons.

"You will now fall-in to your respective platoons, gentlemen, and we shall march across to Number One Lecture Hall where you will hear the Commandant's opening address."

A good drill turnout requires the knowledge of the instructor and the backing and precision of a well trained platoon. Suffice to say that on this occasion the instructor's knowledge, and patience, were second to none, and we got there.

Our three platoons (hereinafter known collectively as The Company) arrived at the Lecture Hall and filed into the chairs mounted on tiers surrounding a battlefield diorama built on a dais. 'Daisy' was there to welcome us with a moment's brief instruction on how to simulate the position of attention while seated. This briefing was curtailed by a flurry at the door. It was 'Daisy''s cue to give the Company its first command.

"COMPANEE*eeeeee . . . TSHA.*"

Ninety-nine cadets (one had gone sick already) (but the processed miscreant who had been hurried off to the guard room had been released and sheepishly returned to us) galvanised our spinal cords into instant rigidity and flashed our arms to the sides of our tightly packed chairs. Ninety-nine subdued *"Ahhhhs"* then rent the air as 990 knuckles rasped the chair frames to each side of them.

Major John Tavistock was the first to limp into the

limelight, flanked by his adoring *Bungey* and accompanied by Captains Tony Dove-Medows, Dickie Dutton and David Swinburn. Casually seating themselves and crossing their elegantly tapered legs they commenced conversing with one another in subdued tones via the major, gently tickling *Bungey's* head. This magnificent four (plus dog) put up a wonderful performance of being totally unaware of the presence of 99 pairs of eyes boring inquisitively into them, wondering 'which is ours' and 'what's he like?' Yet who could know other than themselves that every breath, every inflection and every insouciant twitch was each calculated for maximum theatrical effect.

Their desultory chat continued, punctuated by the occasional subdued ripple of mirth, like VIth Form prefects having a mature giggle at the front of school assembly, but then there came an even bigger flurry at the door and again 'Daisy' effected his ear shattering command:

"COMPANEeeeee . . . TSHA.".

In one-thousandth of a millisecond our spines grew one-eighth of an inch and with as much temerity allowed in a drill movement sore knuckles plunged to our sides again. This time all that was lacking was a fanfare of golden trumpets as the Commandant strolled casually into the hall, saluted airily at something in the far ceiling, dropped his cane on the floor, and said:

"Sit easy please, gentlemen. I'm afraid we can't let you smoke in here; it causes a fire risk, you know. Well now, I suppose I'd best start by welcoming you to the school . . ."

His address was brief, clipped, and not very much to the point. No doubt with the recent late Fraser Alan-Hunter's tragic debacle in mind the only point he really seemed interested in making was not to drive fast at weekends. The administrative dovecotes would be all of a flutter that day arranging the disposal of Alan-Hunter's rather badly dented body, not his car's so much as his. We should always leave in sufficient time to complete our journeys safely and on time. The Commandant was of the opinion that it was not possible to make up lost time by driving fast. He was probably quite right of course: the old kill joy.

He then introduced Major Tavistock to us, said: "Carry on John, would you please," and with another airy salute at the roof and a further brain numbing bellow from 'Daisy' Bracknell, departed, accompanied by his willowy Coldstream Guards adjutant who had been standing there holding two more dogs in the wings, Captain P.E.W. Gibbs.

The doors having closed behind them, all eyes now turned to Major Tavistock who was mounting the dais with difficulty because it was winter and his stump was playing up.

"Well, chaps," he said, smiling an endearing crooked toothed smile, making him instantly liked. "Our next five months together are going to be spent something like this . . ."

He then outlined at length what was in store for us all.

When he'd finished we were given ten minutes tea break before starting Map Reading.

One of the hardest aspects of our life at Mons was deciding which way to turn when we were genuinely up against it, with some *real* problem, one that had not been inserted as one of the syllabus's built-in 'buggeration' factors. Because part of our training was learning to be prepared to meet the unexpected, a buggeration factor was a deliberately contrived gremlin they would produce at an appropriate stage during an exercise to help things become even more difficult should they ever appear to be going well.

The syllabus was tough.

It had to be.

In five months they had to train us to be competent platoon commanders, equipped to take on responsibility for the lives and destinies of thirty men in day, night, desert, steppe or jungle. Training for such a vocation had to be thorough. Unwavering discipline constantly needed to be applied and practised. Wasters swiftly needed to be wasted. The pressure was on. When the pressure's on, things can burst. Things such as brain cells. We were all constantly on the QV 24-hours a day in case we should feel ourselves slipping from the razor's edge. The bogey of failure, of being RTUd for any misdemeanour, however slight, assumed terrifying proportions. Although people did mysteriously disappear back from whence they had come, they were isolated cases. Nevertheless, Officer Cadet George, who was determined not to get the sack having come this far in life, was still reticent about forming up, as I did one day - to complain about the food.

I was aware that Mons was not *The Ritz*, but with all our dashing about we were burning up zillions of calories the whole time and needed adequate refuelling, otherwise blokes would be shooting each other by mistake, or keeling over clifftops on night exercises.

Initially the standard of food was just another aspect of the bitter pill of 'ruggedness' we had to swallow. "After three weeks in the jungle, a meal like this would be viewed as a gourmet's gargantuan delight" we were once told. After a while, though, it became apparent that the stuff we were being given was simply too foul to be a proper part of the official scheme of things. We felt that some of us might even die from eating such muck. Those of us who could afford to eat out (should we ever have a minute to spare) or purchase cans of ravioli to keep in our lockers to prepare at will, did so. The rest of us got grudgingly on with it, and suffered.

Was the predicament a genuine cause for complaint - or was it a deliberate buggeration factor, part of the course, to see how we would cope?

Tough call.

But we decided among us that the problem was real; described by the army as being a 'no duff' situation: e.g. kosher, such as having to call an ambulance for real to ferry out a genuine broken leg victim from some exercise manoeuvre.

We felt that the root cause of the trouble probably lay in the cookhouse itself, and had to do with the low morale of the ACC cooks who manned it.

The dining hall/cookhouse building was a vast, white hangar of a place that had been expediently slung together in the war. A new one was in the process of being built, but the disillusioned guys who operated the existing antediluvian monstrosity could obviously see little or no reason for putting their all into making meal times the most pleasant hour of the day for a lot of snotty-nosed officer cadets - hence what probably started out as reasonable fayre when it was offloaded at the kitchen entrance, ended up on our plates as hash. Nobody *did* die, but if the offending muck hadn't been sweated off through the soles of our boots each day there could well have been the ghastliest outbreak of boils and associated eruptions.

The time had come to complain.

This would be a hazardous test of someone's mettle.

Mine.

I formed up on Interview Parade, to be seen by Major Tavistock. Prefacing my report to him with the heartfelt assurance that I was not a natural born whinger and was speaking on behalf of Salerno Company as a whole, I lodged our collective complaint with him.

"Okay, George," he said. "Point noted, accepted and taken. I'll arrange to have it checked out."

"Thank you very much, sir. We'd all be most grateful." I saluted (smartly, of course) and marched out.

Next day I sat in the dining hall partaking of the most sumptuous lunch ever known to man.

Of course, word had leaked that at my instigation the Company Commander was coming round to inspect the cookhouse that day. With an understandable spirit of self preservation the cooks had all pulled their fingers out at last.

The doors opened.

Surprise; surprise.

In limped Major Tavistock, accompanied by Captain Dove-Medows and a scowling CSM Bracknell. They strolled between the tables gazing nonchalantly about, as though they had simply dropped by in passing, to look at the plastic flowers on the window sill or something. And what did they see? Ninety-nine (ninety-eight, actually) happily smiling officer cadets all contentedly wolfing down great platefuls of glorious food.

Within minutes every platter was spotless.

Except mine.

I sat huddled in a far corner, my face buried with defeat in a soup plate. It could only be half-an-hour at most before I would be invited to pack my bag and leave, to seek my future sustenance in civvy street.

In the event my 'snitch' on the cooks was not deemed to be quite such a heinous crime as I thought it might, plus after that the food did actually improve for a while, and I was allowed to soldier-on to suffer even further mishap and privation.

THIRTEEN

THE INFRASTRUCTURE, ORGANISATION, battle tactics, ceremonial and uniforms of the British Army have for generations been admired, striven after, adopted and emulated by emergent ex colonial and Arab countries. King Hussein of Jordan and his sons, as well as Sultan Qaboos of Oman and King Hamad of Bahrain were only five of a string of notable overseas personages who have attended either Sandhurst or Mons over the years, both as their finishing and starting school. Arab princes and princelings and the sons, cousins and nephews of African tribal chiefs have in their time - prior to their succession and/or assassination - had their respective treasuries transfer substantial course fees to Britain's kitty, so that on their country's behalf they could acquire the basics of soldiering and the British officer style and technique. After their assumption of power at home, they have then sent a stream of their subordinates here to England for refresher courses on this, or familiarisation courses on that. Twenty-three percent of our Mons cadets came from south of Dover, few of whom seemed to share quite the same sense of personal pride, incentive or urgency to pass the course with honour, that we did. As long as they had 'attended' a course in England, no sooner had they returned home again than they were viewed by their fellow countrymen and the hierarchy as being absolute 'mustard'. Payment for their various courses having been gratefully received, the British Government was loathe to have any of its overseas clientele subsequently fail or be RTUd, in case their country became piqued and withdrew from the scheme, thereby channelling no more funds into our own ever needful coffers. The result of this on the British cadets was two-pronged. On the one hand it reinforced our sense of pride and superiority, but it was also the cause of a considerable degree of resentment. So it was rare, if ever, that an overseas cadet failed the course, yet they used to get up to and have a blind eye turned to the most lamentable behaviour that would have guaranteed instant and ignominious dismissal if perpetrated by a British cadet.

Apart from their general behaviour, most of their thoughtless misdeeds had to do with weapons handling. Even if they weren't farmers or were never to bear arms professionally, it has still always been the given and mandatory lot of a British father to instil gun lore into his son as soon as he is given his first plastic pistol. "Even if you are absolutely certain that it is empty, Giles, you never, ever point a weapon at anyone - not even in jest." (Thus indoctrinated it is hard to understand how we won so many wars).

African fathers, on the other hand, may have taught their sons a trick or two with an *assegai,* but real, live guns, it seemed, must have been treated with the same disregard as Lego.

"This is a very nice t'ing," one African student told me, chuckling with delight as he lovingly weighed a nicely blued, slickly oiled 9mm Browning in the sweaty, off-pink palm of his hand, grinning lasciviously and letting both eyes roll upwards. "When I get back to my country, I shall buy one of these guns," he said.

"What for?" I asked. "What on earth will you do with it?"

"Shoot my uncle," came the matter of fact reply.

On another occasion twenty cadets had just thundered down the range with hoarfrost, grime and sweat steaming in visibly gaseous vapour from their combat kit and webbing, hurled themselves panting in a dead-bounce position onto the firing point, loaded and cocked their bren-guns and were simultaneously about to depress the trigger of each weapon to send 300 rounds zipping into the Figure-11 targets 200-yards away in the butts, when there was a slow stirring from the line of gorse in front of them. The movement went unobserved for a moment by all but the ever vigilant platoon sergeant. Was it some luckless stray dog perhaps? A soon-to-be-blasted fox?

No.

It was a stray black man.

"STOOOOOOOOOOPPPPPPPPPPPP," screamed the platoon sergeant at the top of his lungs, leaping along the line of guns and waving his arms in a paroxysm of concern.

"Mister *M'Bouta*, sir. You *IDIOT*," he screamed, whirling down range, fists clenching and unclenching, snarling through quivering, foam-flecked, gnashing, white-lipped teeth at the African prince who was picking his way nonchalantly back through the bracken, tugging at fern stalks as he proceeded unconcernedly towards us as if chewing grass. "What-the-bloody-fucking-hell-do-you-fucking-think you're fucking-*DOING?* Sir? Another fucking second . . . just one more fucking second and you would have been cut to fucking paste. Cor, s'truth. Cor, blimey. *Christ,* Mister M'Bouta, I despair. These guns are *British* guns, Mister M'Bouta. These guns can cut down *trees,* Mister M'Bouta. As the good Lord God is my witness I ought to kill you, revive you and then kill you *again. Bloody* hell."

Incan*descen*t with rage he tore off his beret, hurled it to the ground, stamped on it, stopped, glared, felt better, stamped on it again for luck and then bent to retrieve and dust it down against his denimed leg.

"I was feeling tired, sah," our surprised black prince retorted, after the essence of this verbal onslaught like no other had impressed itself fully upon him, "and did lie down to sleep for a while."

"Do anything like that again Mister M'Bouta, sir, and you'll be lying down to sleep for a very long while indeed: in two bits," wailed the sergeant with continuing frustrated resignation at his lot. If through M'Bouta's own stupidity he had been torn to shreds by a hail of 7.62 lead, the sergeant would have been court martialled.

We carried these students through the course on sufferance, and received little but condescension from them in return. They would lay down their arms and refuse to carry them, because they were 'too heavy'. They would get half way up a cliff face, freeze, stick, refuse to budge, whimper and have to be winched to the top, grinning. Or, better yet, lowered swiftly back down again, yelling, flailing their arms and legs about, complaining at our gleefully inspired rate of their descent, which they hadn't quite bargained for. At weekends they would bring badly peroxided East End tarts into camp in their Jaguars, and at mealtimes would smother their meat and two veg with custard and their prunes with gravy. It has to be said that with our own future livelihoods at stake, being obliged to ride shotgun on this gaggle of kindergarten coloureds with banana juice down their spines instead of marrow, and with no compensation or consideration for doing so, many were the times under pressure when a trigger was very nearly accidentally squeezed on purpose by a sorely stretched white finger.

After commissioning, the majority of us went on to enjoy a normal military career with promotion through the rank structure dependent upon age, experience, ability, examination and recommendation. Yet half these incompetent coons with whom we trained returned to their tribally oriented systems to take part in uprisings and coups and gain overnight promotion to brigadier on the strength of the skills they'd remembered from those that our people had endeavoured to impart to them under duress. On subsequent visits back to Britain they would then enjoy the respect and privileges accorded to their rank while we, still junior to them, would have to salute and call them 'sir'.

It was the routine of one of our administrative colour sergeants to load crates of pop and Mars Bars into the back of a Land Rover to take out to our exercise areas for resale to us appreciative cadets. With bracken and uprooted shrubs adorning our steel helmets and camouflaged persons, groups of us would emerge from the trees of Blueland to form orderly queues and purchase these goodies. The C/Sgt's Land Rover canteen used to remain open for half-an-hour. He would then repack everything, drop the flap, have a fag and drive off back to camp, or to another location. Just after he'd thrown away his fag and was clambering back into his cab one day, having called last orders fifteen minutes before, a lone Arab detached himself from a thicket and wandered aimlessly across to the C/Sgt's vehicle.

"Me want Mars Bar, he said.

"I'm very sorry, sir," the C/Sgt said, reasonably. "I'm just off to another location now. I did call last orders fifteen minutes ago, sir. I'm afraid everything's packed away now."

"Me want Mars Bar."

"Well now, look old cocker, it's like I said, see. The shop's closed: savvy? I've got to go now."

"Me Arab prince. Me want Mars Bar."

"I'm very sorry, sir, but like I said, I can't oblige you, I'm afraid," said the C/Sgt, fighting to retain his cool. "Now if you'll excuse me I'm in a hurry and must . . ."

"Me Arab prince. Me got plenty of money . . . and me want Mars Bar."

"Now, look here sir," said the C/Sgt . . . and then screamed: *"You may be a fucking Arab prince, for all I care. Your father may be the Sheik of fucking Araby himself for all I care, and own every oil well, tent, oasis and camel turd in the whole fucking desert. For all I care you and your kinfolk and the donkeys may own all the fucking money in the whole fucking world . . . sir — but I've still got the Mars Bars. Now fuck off,* please. Sir." Slamming his vehicle into gear he then shot off down the rutted track, showering the Arab with even more fir cones, pine needles and twigs.

Exercise Marathon was a defensive exercise.

We had lumbered about from location to location for two days and then been ordered to dig-in on Hankley Common.

It was a cold, bleak and windy, rainy night.

My digging partner and trench mate on this occasion was a slender little coal black Somali called Jama Hassan Mohamoud. This meant I had to do most of the digging. Not because of his name so much, but because of his size, origin and inclination.

Coincidentally, during the day media reports had been

coming in ('no duff'; for real) about some political upheaval that was unfolding in Somalia, so Mohammed (as we called him) had been the butt of affectionate raillery from the rest of us, because as overseas gentlemen went he wasn't a bad little lad really.

Somalia had severed diplomatic relations with the United Kingdom following a dispute over Kenya's northeastern region, an area inhabited mainly by Somalis. Somalia urged self-determination for the people of the area, while Kenya had refused to consider any steps that might threaten its territorial integrity.

At 04.00 the platoon commander loomed out of the darkness and started to hover uncomfortably about the edge of our 4' x 3' x 5' trench, dislodging pebbles and loose scree down my trouser leg as he shuffled about from foot to foot, considering us from the loosely packed spoil of our mini earth revetment above. He was either busting for a pee, or else was desperate for a new friend. He had obviously been tasked to say something unpleasant and didn't quite know how to broach the matter. Mohammed and I gazed up at him like expectant goldfish at feeding time. We regarded each other blankly, then looked up at him again, wondering if he'd worked out what it was he wanted yet. After a moment of this scrutiny he stopped squiffing about, remembered he'd been sent on a mission, braced himself and squatted down beside me as close as he could get without falling in.

"George," he said, beckoning me with his finger in the darkness. "A word in your ear."

"Of course, sir," I said, doing a double take at the equally puzzled Mohammed standing by my left shoulder, who then shrugged and politely turned the other way to pretend fiddling with some dirt. I scuffed nine-inches to the right, which without starting to climb out of it was all the trench would allow. The platoon commander leaned forward, bracing himself with one hand on my shoulder to prevent toppling over. *Oh, oh,* I thought: a friend of mine had told me this might happen one day. *He likes me.*

"This is a bit of an absurd situation," he whispered. "I

don't quite know how to advise you to handle it.

It seems he likes me a lot.

"It's just come over the radio that Great Britain has severed diplomatic relations with Somalia. This chap you're sharing your ditch with may be recalled and find himself on a plane back tomorrow. We're awaiting advice on it. Meanwhile, I'm afraid it befalls you to entertain him diplomatically for the rest of the night."

"Champagne, sir? Caviare? Couple of sheeps' eyes?"

"Very droll; no, but it'll be a jolly good piece of additional officer training for you."

"Well, if you hadn't told me about it we'd have been all right carrying on as we were really, wouldn't we, sir."

"I suppose you're right George, yes, I must say hadn't looked at it that way. Anyway, I thought it only fair to let you know the form. Technically, you see, I don't think you're supposed to talk to him."

"Would it be all right if *I* talked to *him* then, sir?" interjected Mohammed from the far end of the trench, nine-inches away, unable to help overhearing the whole asinine exchange and wanting to help out of he could.

Just then a thunderflash went off.

We were under attack from the 'enemy'.

Next morning we went back to Mons.

Mohammed was not repatriated.

In July he passed out as a 2/Lt with the rest of us, and then went home to command a battalion.

A week later Captain Dove-Medows pounced on me again

"Oh, sir," I squealed. *(Now he likes me even more.)*

"George - I'm told you're something of a dab hand with a pen. We're trying to drum up contributions for the school magazine. Do you think you could do me an account of *Exercise Marathon* and let me have it by tomorrow, please?"

He didn't mention a fee.

I deemed it politic not to do so either.

The required article was duly delivered.

I was slightly dischuffed to see him place it irreverently

atop a pile of similar pieces from other press-ganged contributors who he obviously thought must also have possessed a degree of literacy, but then after scanning them all in his room in the Mess that evening, it was mine he selected to put into print.

No copyright is being infringed . . .

EXERCISE MARATHON

Contrary to the popular belief that only stiffs and worms live in holes in the ground, there are in fact several other species who do so. Frogs, moles, the contents of refuse tips, roots of plants, and by no means least of all - Mons officer cadets.

On second days of the second quarter, when the wind howls across the moor, the sky is overcast and human beings are all a'bed, the unsuspecting traveller on Hankley Common may well happen upon some of these grubby mons-trosities standing neck high in their subterranean lairs. Should you be interested in tracking them down and their exact locale eludes you (as it does their own incoming patrols from time to time) there are several effortless ruses that can be employed to draw them out. One of these is to wander aimlessly about the countryside, muttering any of the following:

    1.   Christine Keeler is in the admin area. One volunteer needed to help her unpack. (This was in 1963, remember. God knows who today's equivalent would be.)

or

    2.   Hot water; clean sheets; feather pillows . . .

or

    3.   Breakfast from 8.15 a.m. to 9.30 a.m. . . .

or

    4.   Feelthy peectures

Should you have a party of friends with you and think it would be rather fun to see a demonstration of the fire power of 1 Mons Rifles, try screaming through a loud hailer something like this:

1.   The whole of One Platoon will be simulating the role of Company Commander, not for twenty-four hours, but for an entire week . . .

or

2.   There will be not one, but ten patrols going out tonight or

3.   No smoking in the trenches . . .

or

4.   Christine Keeler is in the . . .

Any of the foregoing is guaranteed to bring about your ears (especially if you are standing beneath a bushy topped tree) a fusillade of blank shot from each hitherto heather-bedecked hole.

This, then, is the new sport indulged in by the smart set: MOC baiting. It is a lot of fun and guaranteed for laughs. But from the other side of the bush - what are the attractions of a hole?

What draws Mons officer cadets to them?

How would *you* become a MOC, apart from suffering temporary mental derangement or too much the previous night? To discover the answer to this, and other pertinent questions about the future defenders of the realm, we sent our roving reporter along to Aldershot recently to observe the latest batch of officer cadets enduring the rigours of *Exercise Marathon*, the Army's current scheme for initiating its potential officers to the beauties of an underground life. This is his report:

THEY WERE GOING TO HAVE it on a Monday, but as there was only a slight drizzle that day they waited until Tuesday's torrential downpour when it was bucketing down and then we set off, me - and the Human Pack Transport Company of 1 Mons Rifles.

The first leg of the march to a place called Jubilee Firs was uneventful, with the possible exception of one overseas cadet whose repetitious: "I sho wish mah pappy had never had that last blow through," left us in no doubt

134

that he was feeling uncomfortable from the ongoing loss of skin on his feet.

Arriving at their destination the Company peeled off to its respectively designated platoon positions and commenced digging in. This was the purpose of my visit. You may recall that last month I wrote a series of articles about the versatility of the MOC, his remarkable ability to embrace with equal aptitude and fervour a magnitude of tasks vital to his well being and future career requirements; tasks such as bog washing; window cleaning; company areas (cleaning-up-of); floor polishing (great emphasis being laid on the importance of this skill) and now this more recent innovation of the nuclear age, ditch digging.

With pencil poised stubbily above my soggy notebook I advanced upon two aloof looking MOCs who with noses upturned in disgust were slowly and deliberately removing pieces of our national heritage with the air of a distinguished brace of surgeons called upon to remove a particularly grubby appendix.

"Pick?"

"Pick."

"Shovel?"

"Shovel."

"I say, Jeremy; do take care, there's a good fellow. That last lot went down my boot. Try not to be quite so spastic."

"Sorry, John. I say, what time's dins? I'm positively ravishing."

"Yes, I know you are, m'dear, and isn't it such fun being in the same ditch together?"

"Don't be such an ass, Jeremy. Someone might hear us. Anyway, I tried laying on that private catering firm, but since my cheque bounced after *Footslog* they don't seem to care if I starve."

"Not to worry, old boy. I've brought my primus and several tins of salmon and ravioli in my pack, so we should be able to get through till brekkers okay. Sorry, no lemon though. I had to bring along a spare pair of socks instead.

At this juncture I felt I should introduce myself.

"Excuse me," I said. "What do you intend to do with this rather splendid hole of yours when it's dug?"

"Oh, do you like it? Really? We're ever so pleased. It *is* rather a good one, isn't it! Well, actually, we shall probably just sit in it until last light, and then bung the dirt back in again before leaving."

"Why last light?" I asked. "You make it sound like some mystic ceremony."

"Oh, but it is: well, no, it isn't: not really. You see, in the Army there are only six times for doing anything. Night; day; last light; first light; 23.59 hours and CO's Orders at ten, but we don't count that because it coincides with NAAFI break."

Undaunted, I persisted.

"But doesn't it seem a little pointless, digging a trench just to fill it in again?"

"Most certainly."

"Then why do it? What's the point?"

"To make us tired."

"But that's ridiculous, wearing out a perfectly good shovel and tearing up the countryside just to make you tired. You've got a perfectly good barrack square at home. Why not burn round that a few more times instead?"

"We did. Earlier today."

"Oh."

"Yes."

"Oh."

"Look . . .," like a meerkat peering above his rampart, he looked quickly around. Satisfied that there was no real officer eavesdropping on the enormous scoop I felt he was about to divulge, he flung his shovel to the ground and pointed a dirty but otherwise well manicured digit at me.

"You don't seem to understand the importance of ditch digging, my friend, do you? Firstly - it teaches you discipline. Unless he's a keen gardener it is against an officer's natural instinct to want to dig a ditch, therefore to do so must be good for him. It's character building.

136

Secondly - it shelters you from a nuclear strike . . . I think; oh yes, and shelling. I know we're not at war, well, this week we're not, at least I don't think we are, but one never knows when one might actually be about to be shelled. Yes, from Larkhill. *(The Royal Artillery Training Establishment, in Wiltshire.)* Thirdly - think of the advantages of living in a hole? Yes, of course it's damp and cramped and dirty and miserable . . . oh *do* stop snivelling, Jeremy . . . but there's no rent to pay; no wear and tear; no fuel bills; you're at one with nature, and - yes – on that point I'm afraid we have to do it in a paper bag. But we do bury it afterwards. We have the technology. Die of pneumonia? Yes, I suppose that's possible. Constipation? Sometimes. Boredom? Never. One can spend simply hours cross breeding earwigs and bits of twig and sand and stuff out of one's hair. Refuse? Oh, we chuck that at the enemy. *Course* there's enemy. What on earth do you think we're here for? They're just over the crest of that hill. *Fantasians* from *Redland*; yes, absolutely hordes of them. Mechanised battalions by the truckload. We've been killing 'em off for years. Ever since school CCF, in fact. This last lot dropped by parachute during the night . . ."

Gentle reader - after filling in all their lovely ditches, withdrawing from Jubilee Firs and enduring a night march of many a long league, 1 Mons Rifles arrived at their destination, the middle of Hankley Common, just after first light next morning. Having dispersed into warrens, burrows, hides, scrapes and holes, they sat back and waited. *Marathon* was a defensive exercise. Patrols were sent out at intervals to ensure that the *Fantasian* forces *were* in fact just over the neighbouring hilltop, and not the figment of some deranged person's fertile imagination. Intelligence couldn't be wrong. Could it? Satisfied, the patrols returned. No, they hadn't actually *seen* them but they were definitely very probably there all right . . . they had to be; they always were, weren't they . . . after all, the Directing Staff said they were; so they must be.

Bored by the inactivity *Holdfast* (Royal Engineers) and *Shelldrake* (Royal Artillery) decided to vye with one another to see who could produce the biggest bang. Having loosened the roofs of all the trenches, the CO, or the enemy, or some other like-minded sod behind the scenes called down reciprocal raindrops in no mean quantity. Morale was withdrawn and returned to the company stores to be painted for commissioning parade. The cardboard replicas came to life, attacked and were duly repulsed (wouldn't you be) and that afternoon the second lot of holes were all filled in again - with perhaps a pang or two of regret? *Exercise Marathon* had been and gone and our weary Soldiers of the Sixties could look forward to riding back to Mons in trucks for their tea and to wallow and luxuriate in glorious hot baths and showers . . . okay so the water was off. It helps toughen you up, and what's a few smells between friends, anyway?

Soldiering.

Such a noble profession.

FOURTEEN

ONE EVENING AFTER TEA I was sitting on my bed polishing my bayonet.

Swords, knives and any sleek sliver of steel have always fascinated me.

On an impulse I tossed my gleaming bayonet into the air, caught it by its blade, drew back my arm and sent it flashing across the room to imbed itself with a satisfyingly solid *thwunk* into one of the timber beams above.

"Christ, Mike; how'd you do that?" yelled out The Honourable Nicholas Brooksbank, looking up from bulling his belt-brasses on his bed beneath the beam at the far end of the room.

"With a considerable degree of style," I retorted, smugly relieved that the bayonet hadn't arrived at its destination in reverse and came bouncing back by the boss of its haft, like it usually did when I tried it on trees.

"Do it again," Nick insisted.

"Yeah," piped up several other voices from around the room, where the rest of the guys were engaged busily buffing up various bits and pieces of their kit.

Getting up from my bed I strolled casually down to the far end of the room, reached up and tugged the bayonet loose, spun round and hurled it straight back up the room into one of the pillars at the opposite end. God, I was on a roll; pushing my luck though. Enough. No more. I knew when to stop.

"Hey, that's *terrific,*" they all yelled.

"Boy Scout once, wasn't I," I replied, grinning.

"Do you know how to evade a knife attack"? asked the cadet with the distinctive Donald Sinden voice, who slept in the bed opposite me.

"Run?"

"No, seriously Mike - do you?"

"Yes, I do as a matter of fact."

This Old Etonian, whose father had famously died of his wounds after commanding the Royal Scots Greys in North Africa, unwound his legs from beneath his six-foot frame and rose gracefully to the perpendicular. He was aged nineteen then, and tough. Even in Korea I had not met anyone with quite the same incredible stamina or powers of endurance. Belying his inner strength he didn't look particularly tensile, having a streaky rather than a muscular appearance, but I am sure those streaks were striated with steel sinew and piano wire. In our few short weeks there at Mons he had already built a legend about himself for physical prowess and determined rebelliousness.

Tossing him the bayonet I told him to come at me – slowly, mind - in (simulated, I hastened to add) aggressive mode.

It only took three attempts for him to perfect the block and parry technique, which I could see him itching to go out and try on some poor luckless sod for real somewhere, as soon as he possibly could.

He was commissioned into his father's old regiment.

After serving with them for a short while he then joined the SAS and subsequently went out to fight in the Dhofar War, in Oman.

I remember saying to him once at Mons, "There's only one thing for you to do when you're older, and that's to become an explorer."

It was one of the most prescient remarks I have ever made, because the whole world knows that that's exactly what Sir Ranulph Twistleton Wykham-Fiennes, Bart., known to us all as 'Ran', did go on to do.

I often wondered whether in his travels he ever had occasion to use that piece of knife drill I showed him.

1 PLATOON - SALERNO COMPANY

Mons OCS, Feb-Jul 1963

Rear L-R: **Bob Williams;** Ali; **Chris Seel;** N/K; **Geoff Van Cutsem;** Jama Hassan Mohamoud; **Author;** Mayalarp:
Middle: **Bob Millum;** Abbas; **Simon (Lord) (Glen) Arthur;** Jeremy Hope; **Paddy O'Neill;** Andrew Black;
George Lambert; Richard Heywood; **Carl Renwick:**
Front: N/K; **Gavin Thompson;** Paul Sugden; **Tony Brassey;** Sgt Jackson; **Sir Ranulph Twistleton-Wykeham Fiennes;**
Bob Campbell; **Nick Brooksbank:**

141

Another new boy joins the fold:
2/Lt M.A. George - July 1963

These are what are known as
'bull-shit' shots: as can be seen,
the author has several of them …
and as if you hadn't guessed, this
is his *I Love Me* page …

Diyarbakir, Turkey – Nato ACE
Mobile Force Exercise *Eastern
Express* – 1965:
Author, in front of his abode

We made mistakes, we made headway and we made friends. Then, one day in July, after three marathon exercises and five marathon months, we made the *London Gazette*. Our passing out parade was deemed a great success. No one fainted. No one boobed or in any way detracted from the general spleandour of the occasion. Our parents, guests and dignitaries arrived on time (in order of precedence, of course) into the stands beside the gaily flag-bedecked parade ground.

At 14.15 the Band of The Welsh Guards struck up a rousing march and Kohima's 100-strong Junior Company swung proudly down the ramp and right wheeled onto their pre-positioned markers on the square. They halted, left turned, right dressed, were stood at ease - and waited. From the stands anxious parents strained to see proud sons, but to no avail. This was the Junior Company, still undergoing the throes of its own gruelling training. Their parents hadn't been invited. There wasn't room. It wouldn't be their day for another three months yet. Their role today was as our supporting cast.

Other than steady breathing and the murmur of conversation from the stands, all activity on the square had stilled.

The Director of Music, Captain H.A. Kenny, raised his baton a second time and the gold and silver instruments at his command trumpeted a tune of glory that rent the air in unison with Salerno Company Senior Under Officer John Black's authoritative word of command. Straighter, smarter, better and justly more proud - after all, we had successfully survived the course's culminating *Battle Camp* in Wales, dammit - we swung down the ramp and right wheeled with a fraction more precision onto our own markers, left turned, right dressed, were stood at ease - and waited.

From the blur of faces staring at us intently from the stands we were able to pick out hats, coats, faces, friends, parents and relatives (only two each, though) who in turn were now able to identify Simon, Rodney, Tim and in microcosm noticed that perhaps David's left foot was slightly out of line, Peter's cap had slipped slightly over his right eye, and that Paul had a minute spot of white blanco on his left sleeve.

143

Like a sniper some hidden being then gave a secret signal from a nearby rooftop. The Director of Music raised his baton for the third time. All over the world millions of different things were happening. During that moment people were dying, being born, making love, being shot, pleasured, having an operation, making and losing vast sums of money and driving too fast round corners, but on our particular dot of the universe at that particular moment in time all else was of no accord as the Royal car glode gracefully and silently to a gentle standstill beside the dais, and its inmates alighted.

The guests arose.

Gentlemen either removed their hats or retained them and saluted. The band struck up The National Anthem and John Black, our Senior Under Officer, gave the command *"Royal* Salute - *Preeee*sent . . . *ARMS,"* which galvanised both companies into the time honoured stance for The Royal Salute.

Flanked on the dais by her requisite aides and courtiers, our then 37-year old monarch, Her Majesty Queen Elizabeth II, smiled out serenely at us.

Ma'am inspected us.

Ma'am made a very nice speech to us.

We marched Slowly past Ma'am, giving her a misty Eyes Right.

We marched Quickly past Ma'am, and gave her a proud Eyes Right.

While the Junior Company gave us our own Present Arms, with our breasts straining with pride we newly commissioned gentlemen then marched slowly off parade, dividing to march each side of the dais upon which stood our Queen, our eyes gazing individually and steadfastly up into those of our Sovereign Monarch and Most Gracious Majesty whose Land Forces Commission she had just bestowed upon us.

The lamenting strains of Auld Lang Syne played us off parade.

We broke ranks in the green field beyond the square and with quavering but jubilant voices spontaneously proffered clammy and blanco stained congratulatory palms to each other. Caps were hurled into the air. There were whoops and high-fives all round. We'd done it. We'd been judged, and not found wanting. We were there. We hadn't fallen by the wayside. She'd commissioned us. It was our day. Our precious, once in a lifetime moment. Thousands before us had experienced the same euphoric occasion: millions hadn't, nor ever would.

We were British Army officers.

Parents now burst forth to besiege us with more congratulations of their own. There were more handshakes, kisses and restrained little hugs and then we all filtered across to the large, white marquee where tea, strawberries and cream, conversations and introductions were taking place, while all eyes kept flickering glances across to the smaller, whiter marquee where the Commandant and entourage were entertaining our Commander in Chief to *her* strawberries and cream.

All the five star hotels down to the lowliest B&B within a 20-mile radius of Aldershot were fully booked for the night. We formally attired young subalterns, wearing our Mess wellingtons for the first time with our DJs, were entertaining our evening-dressed families and girlfriends to dinner in various surrounding hostelries, before returning in our cars to the marquees again, back at Mons, where their interiors had now been transformed to cater for 300 dancers and champagne sipping, prawn cocktail consuming, merry making people. It was The Ball of the year. *Tatler* gave it full page coverage. Tommy Kinsman's high society 'Debs' Delight' band gave it what it needed, and the debs and girlfriends and ladies let their hair down to give the newly christened leaders what they said *they* wanted, or, at least, what they thought they'd rather like, if that was at all possible; please.

Cyprus; Aden; Borneo and the reality of the morrow seemed as far away as the first room inspection and route march.

The room inspections were over now.

The new tomorrow had yet to be met.

FIFTEEN

BULLER BARRACKS, Aldershot.

Alan Wade, Mike Rutherford, Richard Powell and I had been commissioned from Mons into the RASC (Royal Army Service Corps) whose home was at Buller Barracks, named after General Sir Redvers Buller, VC, of Zulu and Boer War fame.

We were commissioned on Friday 26 July. On Saturday 27 July I was on a plane down to Gibraltar for three weeks well deserved leave, eager to flash my two shiny new staybrite pips at my wife and baby daughter, Rachel and Natalia.

Suntanned and juicy I then returned to Aldershot to attend a three months RASC Junior Officers' Course (JOC) at Buller.

Mons had trained us in basic infantry officer tactics. Now we had to learn the tricks of the specialist arm of the service to which we had been designated.

After commissioning, the cavalry went on to Bovington in Dorset to learn how to handle their tanks and armoured cars. The Gunners went to Larkhill in Wiltshire to learn how to fire their big guns, and along with 24 newly commissioned Sandhurst cadets (two of whom were from Africa), Alan, Mike, Richard and I (from Mons) now formed part of the combined Number 82 JOC (them) and 9 Short Service Officers' (us) Course, scheduled to run from 28 August until 11 December, designed to instil into us the entire ethos of our new Corps' lore and protocols, as well as teaching us everything we would need to know about its *raison d'être:* motor transport and supply.

Richard Powell and I were paired off to share the same room in the Mess there together for the duration, and thereby formed a lifelong friendship.

Before commissioning Richard had been a piper in the Scots Guards, and by all accounts, mostly his, a very good one too.

After lunch in the Mess at Buller each day, we would go up to our room for a wash and brush up, when to keep his hand in Richard would always take the opportunity to practise fingerwork on his chanter, and I am not speaking at all euphemistically here.

With this reedy wailing going on there was little else I could do but join in, thwacking out an accompanying rhythm with a pair of drumsticks on the back of our room's padded club chair.

Later in life Richard went on to help organise the Edinburgh Tattoo, and to become a recognised world authority on military music.

Richard always displayed a great regard and fondness for matters ceremonial. He had a flame red lining in his service dress jacket, and was the only officer I ever knew who also wore with it a waistcoat. He didn't sport a monocle or take snuff, but both would have suited him rather well.

Although they had done it at Sandhurst, at Mons OCS they'd never got around to teaching us sword drill. Through determination and practice those of us with any flair to our personality had become quite nifty at twirling our little bamboo swagger canes about, but no one had yet seen fit to impart to us the way in which to wield our ceremonial cutlery so that it didn't look like a fish slice.

At Buller one frosty morning, this omission was rectified.

All four of us - the ex-Mons subalterns - were duly ordered to assemble on the square at 07.00, our Wilkinsons gird about our loins, eagerly awaiting the arrival of the RSM to instruct us in the esoteric art.

Resplendent in his gleaming regalia, the Great Man hove-to.

He was brief in his introduction.

147

"Good morning, gentlemen. I understand that none of you has ever done sword drill before - is that correct?"

"No, RSM," we chorused.

He looked baffled.

"Do you mean I have been misinformed?"

"No, RSM," I explained. "We were merely agreeing with you, that none of us has."

"I see." The RSM was relieved.

"Actually, I rather believe I might have done some," Richard interjected from the back with a languid drawl.

"Is that so, sir," smiled the RSM, one eyebrow raised, wise to the ways of subalterns. "In that case, perhaps you'd care to give us a short demonstration, would you?"

"Certainly," said Richard. "Delighted. Would you like me to start now?"

"Whenever you're ready, sir."

"We were delighted, too. This was kudos for our course, which had not got off to a good start. There were several characters and strong personalities among us, so collectively we had not yet endeared ourselves to our instructors.

Richard dressed elegantly forward, maladroitly tugging his sword from its scabbard like a twelve-year old struggling to draw a man's revolver.

This charade over, he went into a short, passably good display of basic sword drill movements.

We were impressed.

After a few more flourishes he performed a deft sweep, like a drum major halting his band with the staff, and returned his sword to the 'carry' position.

We had all enjoyed his short lived 'Scaramouche' bit, but had he now exhausted his repertoire?

Not so, it seemed.

Savouring the moment he dropped quickly to his right knee, placed his sword carefully but swiftly upon the tarmac, released his scabbard and placed it across his sword, sprang adroitly to attention again as though in a PT class, took one pace to the rear, flung both arms asunder like a hook-fingered

Balinese temple dancer, and broke promptly into an inspired Highland sword dance.

The RSM tried not to find it terribly funny.

Doubled-up with highly appreciative laughter the rest of us couldn't help feeling it was hysterical.

With one exception nothing very exciting seemed to happen during the rather tedious three months we spent at Buller.

The exception occurred in the November of that year.

We had been 'touring' Britain in a convoy of trucks, on a training exercise called *Long Haul*.

On the evening of Friday 22nd a group of us was quaffing mugs of tea and smoking, squatting in a tent in a wooded glade somewhere in Norfolk, when Richard Powell strolled in to inform us it had just come over the radio that President Kennedy had been shot.

"*Piss* off," we retorted, obviously completely disbelieving such a shocking and unlikely report.

Formed up in the glade on first parade next morning, the tragedy of JFK's assassination was then confirmed beyond doubt when our Course Instructor duly extended our condolences to the still stunned American exchange officer who was 'along for the ride' with us on that phase of the course.

When the course finished, in December, I found that my first proper army posting was to be to 48 Supply Company, at Bulford Camp, near Amesbury, on Salisbury Plain.

Hardly Horse Guards or Luneburg Heath, but it would do.

First of all I had to buy myself a car to get there though.

During the course of my life I was going to own a pink Vauxhall Cresta, a grey Opel Kapitan, a silver Opel Rekord, a blue Mercedes 280 SE 3.5 V8 Coupe, a silver Jaguar, a bronze Ford Granada, a red Renault, two red Rover 800s, and then another (navy blue) Mercedes, but in December 1963 I handed over a hard-saved £280 for a dark green MG Magnet saloon.

Married Quarters at this time, as always, were still in short supply, and one had to go onto a waiting list to get one. In the interim I was able to find a 'hiring' at 4, Upper Street, in West Harnham, a suburb of Salisbury itself. This was a pleasant enough little bungalow beside the River Avon, owned by a civilian who rented it out to the army.

Rachel and Natalia arrived from Gibraltar in January, and two days later, leaving Rachel to start sorting out our new home, I drove the ten miles up the A345 to Amesbury, and then onto the A303 along to the Bulford Barracks turn-off.

Major Mike Robertson-Young was the OC of 48 Supply Company; Captain Peter Gray the second-in-command, and I was their new admin officer, working in a second world war hut as usual, along with Warrant Officer Jack Smith and a couple of clerks.

Madison Avenue, it wasn't.

In an attempt to allay some of the tedium, when one of our corporals, an old soldier called 'Doc' Doyle who been apprehended committing some misdemeanour or other asked me if I would act as his Defending Officer at his upcoming court martial, eager for the experience I leapt at the chance, and, amazingly, thanks to my theatrically presented plea in mitigation, which rather took the staid and pedestrian court president unawares, I managed to get him off.

When I got back to my office in the hut that afternoon, it was to find that the nameplate on my desk had been changed by the clerks to *2/Lt Perry Mason,* a popular fictional American TV lawyer at the time.

A few nights later the president of the court, Major Ted Swaine and his wife, invited Rachel and me round to their quarter for dinner.

Things were starting to look up a bit.

However, the ongoing, never ending rationalisation, downsizing and reorganisation of the Army that had kicked in a few years before, was still going full pelt.

General Mcleod's 1964 reimplementation of the 'Q' Services was in full swing, and the upshot of it was that the RASC was to specialise purely in transport and become the RCT (Royal Corps of Transport) while the Quartermaster aspects of its previous role were to be relinquished and absorbed by the Royal Army Ordnance Corps (RAOC.)

This meant 48 Supply Company.

I did not fancy this idea very much at all, so hearing they were short staffed I went off and had an interview to join The South Staffordshire Regiment, then stationed at Dover Castle.

I had no connection with or affiliation to Staffordshire, in fact I don't think I'd even been there, but the regiment had a nice Staffordshire knot cap badge, and it seemed like a good idea at the time.

Everything went well and their CO invited me to go along and join them for a probationary period, but then I heard they were due for a bachelor tour, carrying out jungle patrols along the Belize-Guatemalan border, whereas over the grapevine I also heard that if I stayed with the RAOC I might soon be sent to Germany, so I withdrew my transfer application in favour of hanging on for a new Mercedes.

One day in the summer of 1965 48 Supply Company had its re-badging ceremony, where we removed our garter-star and EIIR-cypher RASC badges from our headgear, to be replaced with the triple cannon and three cannon-balls badge of the RAOC with its *Sua Tela Tonanti* motto (To The Warrior His Arms), before marching past a bemedalled Brigadier H.T. May on his dais, who took the salute in validation.

Amongst all the other guests attending the parade that day were my mother, an extremely pregnant Rachel, and my three-year old daughter, Natalia, all standing there watching from a grassy knoll.

The most memorable part occurred just as I was drawing abreast of them at the head of the company, the sun glinting off my drawn sword, when above the crunch of marching feet the whole parade heard the piercing cry of my overexcited little girl gleefully call out: "That's my daddy there. *(Pause for thought.)* When *I* grow up *I'm* going to be a soldier's woman." Like breeze ruffling a cornfield a tangible wave of appreciative mirth could be seen rippling through the ranks. It was the highlight tale at the curry lunch in the Mess afterwards, and I wasn't to live it down for days.

Shortly afterwards, Rachel, now eight months pregnant with our second child, flew back to Gibraltar with Natalia for her confinement.

A couple of weeks after that, I was in Turkey.

48 Supply Company's role in life was to provide troops in the field with their victuals.

Romantic?

Not very - no.

Important?

Absolutely - yes - essential.

With the west still at the height of the Cold War, concern for the vulnerability of the extreme flanks of NATO to pressure from the Soviet Union, in particular in northern Norway and Greek Thrace, had resulted in the formation of the Allied Command Europe (ACE) Mobile Force, comprising land, sea and air force elements of several NATO nations under the command of Britain's Major-General Lord Michael Fitzalan-Howard, GCVO, CB, CBE, MC, late Scots Guards. The aim was not to assemble a force capable of repelling a Soviet incursion on an exposed flank, but rather to demonstrate Alliance solidarity and determination in the face of any menacing Soviet move.

The Force insignia was a mailed fist, grasping a flash of lightning. It was a meaty enough badge to which to owe allegiance, but with some of the things that occurred I sometimes felt that Mickey Mouse with egg on his face might have been more appropriate.

This ACE Mobile Force of ours was a multi-national organisation comprised of US armour, Italian artillery, Belgian parachutists, Norwegian and Turkish infantry, a German field medical station and British logistic support, all controlled from Force HQ, at Heidelburg.

Flying out from RAF Lyneham in a C-130 transport aircraft, I found my companion for the trip was none other than the 54-year old (now 100 and living in Hong Kong) Claire Hollingworth, the renowned war correspondent.

On 31 August 1939, she had been working as a journalist for less than a week for the *Daily Telegraph* when she found herself at the Polish-German border reporting on worsening tensions in Europe. Driving alone on a fact-finding mission, she saw a massive build-up of Nazi German troops, tanks and armoured cars facing Poland. The following morning she called the British embassy in Warsaw to report the German invasion of that country. To convince the doubtful embassy officials, she had to hold the telephone out the window for them to hear the rumblings of a *Blitzkrieg* commencing. Her eyewitness account was the first report the British Foreign and Commonwealth Office had about the invasion of Poland. If I had known at the time who I was sitting next to on our flight to Turkey it would either have inhibited conversation, or inspired it.

The force was camped alongside Turkey's principal military airstrip at Diyabakir. This was the American-Turkish Pirinçlik Air Force Base that housed sensitive electronic intelligence-gathering systems for monitoring activity in the Middle East, the Caucasus and Russia. It was eventually to be closed on 30 September 1997 as a result of the general drawdown of US bases in Europe and improvement in space surveillance technology, but in the meantime . . .

We were to be there on a month long exercise, called *Eastern Express.*

Situated north of the Mesopotamian Plain in eastern Anatolia, on the right bank of the River Tigris and 100 miles north of the Syrian border, Diyarbakir itself is the largest city in SE Turkey. The new Diyarbakir lies without, but the old city is surrounded by an intact five-mile set of black basalt ramparts and walls, the second largest and best preserved in the world after the Great Wall of China. They have four gates and eighty-two watchtowers, built between 349-375 by the Roman Emperors Constantin and Valentinian.

Down the centuries Diyarbakir had been home to the Assyrians, Romans, Persians, Armenians and then the Arabs, before becoming subsumed as part of the Ottoman Empire in the sixteenth-century.

Today its population is 2.5 million, consisting mostly of Kurds, and is renowned for its culture, folklore and watermelons.

When we arrived there in 1965 it was a dirty, dung-piled, rickety-bussed, pong-infested rat-hole of a place whose 130,000 inhabitants, their forbears at least, must have seen few white men since Richard The Lionheart.

Our NATO force was camped under canvas, in depth, either side of the airstrip. The British lines covered a frontage of about half-a-mile, the other forces a similar frontage each. Despite NATO's standardisation programme for common user arms, ammunition, supplies and equipment, national pride and problems were still rife. Interpreters and liaison officers - romantic sounding appointments though they were - had the very devil of a job, and at any given time of the day or night were never short of a migraine or two.

One morning, a few days after our arrival there, I was standing down on the airstrip chewing the fat with some of the boys, when again we heard the almighty roar of the sky being ripped apart above us as another of the enormous US Hercules freighters came in to land.

Seconds after it had taxied to a standstill the maw of its tail-end gaped, ramps appeared, and its cargo of tanks was disgorged to roll off onto the airstrip.

It was an impressive sight.

"That thar plane is the premier air freight, long range transport aircraft in the world today," drawled a big black gum-chewing, cigar-chomping US master sergeant, leaning against a nearby oil drum.

Britain's aerial workhorse at the time was the Beverley Freighter, which seemed to be about one third the size of the Hercules.

There were three of these little Beverleys drawn up on the airstrip in front of us.

"Yup, sho is a beefy plane," grinned the American, with a justifiable pride that was nevertheless just beginning to get up the nostrils of some of the British soldiers he was addressing.

"Sho beats the hell outta those three l'il ol' Beverleys of yourn, don' it", he said mockingly.

"Sure does," piped up L/Cpl Squires in his cockney voice, studiedly continuing to roll a cigarette before adding after a beautifully timed pause - "but you should see the one we got what brought those three out 'ere."

One of the Americans attached to our unit as Logistics Liaison Officer, was Lootenant Franklin D. Rideout.

Frank had never met the British before.

On Day One it was plain to see that he was a trifle dubious about his role among us, and how he should play things.

By Day Three he was sweeping aside the flap of our Mess tent with considerable panache at 17.00, to enquire, "I say, chaps - is tea ready yet?"

My job there in Turkey was Local Procurement Officer.

It made me sound like some sort of pimp, but had more to do with Frank and me scouring the countryside with my amiable good friend Charles Brooker, the paymaster, to source and purchase locally available natural produce with which to supplement the force's dry rations.

One day I sensed that Frank was working up to asking something.

Perhaps one of us Brits had inadvertently offended some American sensibility or other, and he felt obliged to straighten us out about it.

There are those who would suggest that despite our common language, the respective American and British takes on certain aspects of life can be as alien to each other as they would be with any other foreigners.

The machinery of war apart, those who waged it were still human, and all sprang from different cultural backgrounds. This fact was never more clearly illustrated to me than it was one morning when I had occasion to upbraid one of my NCOs for some apparent misdemeanour or other.

"Cor, knock it off, sir," he retorted, wiping an oily rag across his brow and stubbing a cigarette out underfoot. "We've been up 'alf the bleedin' night, tryin' to fix this 'effin' thing."

We were all under strain. I let the matter rest.

Then I had to drive across to Movement Control to find out if the battery chargers I had been waiting for had arrived.

I clambered into my Land Rover and set off along the edge of the airstrip.

It was a clear, crisp, sunny morning.

Passing the Turkish lines I waved to Hassan, a charming twenty-seven-year old captain who had been allocated to us as our interpreter and liaison officer; he had elected to learn his English in Chicago, for some reason, yet still spoke it quite well.

Hassan was standing outside his tent in shirtsleeves, indolently flicking his fawn-breeched legs with a riding crop. He had one foot placed on a small step to enable an orderly to lace up and buff his boots for him. His face was half covered with shaving foam through which another orderly was painstakingly dragging a cutthroat razor. Something in their coordinated teamwork must then have slipped because the normally genial Hassan suddenly lashed out with his crop across the neck of his boot man, and then slapped the face, twice, very hard, of the man shaving him, sending him staggering back reeling. What had happened, I have no idea. Order was soon restored and the ceremony of getting Hassan ready for the day continued, but such an occurrence in the British Army would have been front page stuff and an instant court martial for whichever unfortunate officer it was whose brain had snapped.

So what was it Frank Rideout had been working up to ask me?

"Mike," he said hesitantly, shuffling his calf-length black lace-up boots in the dust and grinning sheepishly as he played with the fluff in one pocket of his green fatigue dress trousers while holding his peaked field service cap in his other hand and scratching the back of his shaved neck with his thumb. "How would I go about having a few of my guys over to visit the British Mess tent one night?"

"I'm not quite with you, Frank."

"Waaal, y'see, it's like this, Mike," he drawled. "It's the first time a lot of our Armour boys have ever been outside the States. Their fathers served with the British in the war, and have told them that even if they gotta move heaven and earth to do so they just *gotta* get themselves invited along to a British Mess tent to see how . . . well . . . to see . . ."

"How things are done properly?"

"Yeah, I guess. Right."

"I see no problem, Frank." I laughed. "I'll speak to the Colonel. I'm sure he'll agree that we should be delighted to have you all over."

"Gee; you think so? Really? Gee, that'd be really great, Mike. Thanks. I surely do appreciate this." He pumped my hand several times, spun on his heel in the dust and strode off to report back.

Mission accomplished.

One happy Yank.

Splendiferous images flashed to mind of the renowned Royal Artillery Messes at Larkhill and Woolwich, groaning with their magnificent displays of silver and military impedimenta. There were historic regimental artefacts and accoutrements still in most British Messes sufficient to blow the minds of any but the most rabidly rebellious visitor. Some of the antique cannon mounted at their entrances might have had their teeth drawn, but who was to know those bulldogs could no longer sustain their bite? Well groomed, they still looked good and impressive. A formal regimental Mess night at any one of these august establishments, with the services of immaculate and punctilious Mess staff still beholden to the system - occasions such as these would have made God himself feel inferior, if he wasn't (which he reputedly is of course) already a member, holding the honorary rank of Field Marshal.

The scarlet and the gold: the glinting and jingling of the spurs: the candlelight reflecting from the ebony gloss of creaking Mess wellingtons - this was more the sort of scene I am sure Frank had in mind, rather than the three adjoining and windblown 180 lb marquees which constituted our field Mess out there in Turkey.

Anyone passing by outside at night, hearing the raucous laughter from within and seeing the larger than life shadows flickering and darting about on the canvas walls by the light of our Tilly-lamps, had probably allowed their imagination to run riot with visions of mythical cabalistic Mess ceremonies taking place inside, which - of course - was simply not the case . . . unless you counted the occasional debagging.

The reality was that after a dissatisfactory dinner of compo stew and prunes we would sit round the stove in our muddy boots and combat dress telling dirty stories, talking rugger and swigging NAAFI beer.

However - if this would not disillusion our American brothers too much, who were we to deny them the hospitality they craved?

Given their natural generosity and largesse, the only reason we had not done so to date was from a possible feeling of our own social inadequacy.

I spoke to the Colonel.

He agreed it was a good idea and no less than should be expected of us, so we would entertain three American officers a night.

I relayed this dictum to a joyous Frank who accepted it with humble gratitude and scurried back to the US lines to start dealing places on the Guest List.

In the Mess tent that night, sitting round the stove in our muddy boots and combat dress as usual, we ruminated on what we had done.

"I mean, we can't just let them *come*, can we?" asked one of the more aware young subalterns. "Surely, they'll just sit and gawp at us all night, won't they? It'll be awfully inhibiting to conversation."

"Normal conversation's not what they'll be expecting," opined the sagacious Charles Norseworthy, a trendy young major who really wanted to be an actor and had done quite a lot of amateur dramatics back in Camberley. "They'll be turning up expecting to find the place imbued with some indescribable ethos that will permeate their marrow and which, over the years, will become exaggerated in the telling as it is told and retold over American dinner tables until long after the guy's a retired general. Either that, or they'll expect something outlandish. In any case, it's up to us to give it to 'em."

"Do you have something in mind, Charles?" the Colonel enquired, tamping his briar, smiling, a knowing twinkle in his eye.

"It's rather funny you should say that, sir. As a matter of fact, I have."

"Let's hear it, then," we all insisted, leaning towards the stove and lending our ears to his ploy.

"Geoff Banks is flying back to UK tomorrow night - aren't you, Geoff?" Geoff nodded. He had been recalled to give evidence at a court martial in Aldershot.

"Okay, then," said Charles. "This is what I propose we should do . . ."

There is a tradition in the Army that when a newly commissioned subaltern joins his regiment, the officers arrange a 'reception surprise' for him. Full of bonhomie and exaggerated fraternal affection on the surface, it is designed to test the young man's mettle to the full. He, understandably nervous, is on his best behaviour, keeping his head down, maintaining as low a profile as possible, listening and learning, terrified lest inadvertently he should commit some awful gaffe that would damn his career from the outset.

Having arrived, and had thrust into his hand in the first five minutes, with the expectation that he will consume it, more gin than he's seen in his lifetime, his known world then proceeds to be turned upside down. The chap who keeps insisting that this is a hard drinking regiment and if he wants to make anything of his life in it he will have to keep up - is the Padre; only it is not really the Padre at all, but the Adjutant with a dog collar on. The Padre will probably have donned a mess waiter's livery and is busily dispensing alcohol at the bar. The resident, hoary bachelor major will be addressed by everyone as 'Brigadier', and hamming it up like mad will spend the

159

entire evening of our young chap's initiation barking out the most inane gibberish, with which everyone else will heartily agree and say what a splendid fellow he is. A downy faced subaltern will then enter to be greeted by everyone generally rising to their feet, intoning respectfully: "Good evening, Colonel." Our newly joined subaltern, upon being introduced to his 'Colonel', only to be told by this nineteen-year old that he thinks the newcomer is a very 'ugly' officer, might now just begin to realise that he is being 'had' - but which way does he turn? Just as he is going under for the third time he might feel a soft hand placed gently atop his own, and whip round to find a gorgeous woman smiling warmly at him.

"Hallo," she'll purr sexily. "Are they giving you a hard time of it? I'm Eloise. I'm sort of, well . . . Mistress to the Regiment, I suppose. Would you like to come upstairs and relax with me for a little while?"

To the loud and general acclaim of the room at large, our new boy will stagger off grinning on the arm of the well-briefed, game young wife of some junior major, who then promptly contrives to push and lock him in the broom cupboard for the night.

Next morning everything will have returned to normal once more: for everyone except our bemused subaltern that is, who can spend several days trying to find out who is really who.

A watered down version of this ghastly ceremony is what we thought we'd lay on for the Americans.

When Frank pulled back the flap of our marquee next evening and nervously led his three lambs in to their slaughter, they were all tugging anxiously at their clasped caps and calling everyone 'Sir'. The scene could not have been better staged if some Hollywood production luminary had been on strength.

Like some Victorian aquatint of the Crimea, a dozen British officers were lolling languorously about the stove, each assuming a posture that he felt best suited his *alter ego*. The sartorial accoutrements hastily rustled up from God knows where, were proof positive of the ingenuity of our island race.

Despite living out of a dufflebag in the middle of Turkey, Peter Galsworth had somehow managed to acquire for himself a monocle and an ivory cigarette holder. Lounging effetely in a green, canvas-backed camp chair he toyed idly with the cord of one whilst nonchalantly exhaling the most exquisite smoke rings from the mouthpiece of the other. As each ring broke and dissolved, Richard Jefferson would then bow gracefully forward to inhale its unfurling smoke expertly up his own right nostril. Economy at its best. One fag between two. Watching this, one of our three young American visitors quickly withdrew the soggy, rum-soaked King Edward cigar butt from his mouth and dropped it into the stove. We all thought it an awful waste, but couldn't spoil our tableau by saying so, and mentally willed our junior subaltern not to leap forward to grope for it. We merely raised eyebrows to each other instead. Our observant guests misunderstood this reflex action. Blushing to the roots of his crewcut the discarded stub's chompee was nudged to stammer: "Gee, I'm real sorry, gen'lemen. Maybe I shouldn't a done that, huh?"

"That's quite alright," I assured him solicitously. "My name's Mike. How do you do? Now, what can I get you to drink?"

"A beer would do just fine, for all of us, I think; thanks."

I was relieved. For one dreadful moment I thought he might have asked for mead.

When I came back and handed them their beers I was thanked more profusely than ever before or since for anything I had ever done for anyone, short of saving their life perhaps.

All I had managed to muster for myself in the props department had been an old school choker. This oily maroon rag now sat about my neck like a technicolour cast. From somewhere else Roger Daley had dug up a creased, moth-eaten blazer with three of its twelve buttons missing, while the Colonel, God bless him, had donned plus-fours, set off to especial advantage by his army boots, and the rather colourful pair of rugger socks he'd chosen to wear with them. Geoff Banks - soon to be our star turn of the evening - lay curled in the foetal position, shivering, beneath a grey army blanket on the dirt floor over in the far corner, as though on a heroin withdrawal course. We had seen each of the Americans cast a wary eye in his direction, but they were too polite to ask who Geoff was, or what was his predicament. Every time one of them stole a further glance at him, Geoff would emit a heart rending groan and summon up yet another almighty shudder.

The next time the Mess steward came in to tend the stove, the Colonel called across: "Smith, just be a good chap and give Mister Banks another dousing, will you please?"

"Certainly, sir," Smith replied, relishing every moment, and without a flicker of a smile or batting an eyelid he crossed the floor and bent to pick up a fire bucket, full of dirty water and fag ends, which he then hurled in a mighty deluge over poor old Geoff.

"I'll just go and refill the bucket, sir," he said to the Colonel, who was trying to appear otherwise engaged, re-tamping his pipe.

"What's that? Oh, yes, if you wouldn't mind please, Smith. Thank you," he said, without glancing up from what he was doing while the rest of us contrived to carry on talking amongst ourselves, ignoring the incident completely.

It didn't take long.

"Say . . . er . . . excuse me, sir, but . . . but . . . whadhedodatfor?" blurted out one of our flabbergasted guests.

"I'm so sorry, but - what-did-who-do-what-for?" Roger Daley asked, shuffling a pack of cards he'd just removed from the moleskin lined pocket of his blazer.

"Whadid that guy there throw that bucket of dirty water over that guy there for?" almost *demanded* the American, indicating with his chin to which of the parties he referred.

"I, sir," retorted the retreating, wised-up steward, Smith, "threw this bucket of water over Mister Banks because the Colonel told me to, sir."

"And I told him to do so because poor old Geoff has gone and copped a most dreadful bout of malaria again," the Colonel explained. "I say, do any of you chaps play bridge, by any chance?"

They didn't.

They declined, politely, saying they would prefer to watch, please.

We gave them each another beer and then roped Geoff up from the floor to come and sit beside us in his sodden blanket to make up a four. The rubber commenced. Contrived and desultory chatter meandered around the smoke filled tent. Periodically Smith would reappear to poke the stove and collect and recharge any empties, before wafting back out again to his own little domain round by the refuse bins. Outlandish war stories, yarns and anecdotes were exchanged with our trio of eager Americans, who really were very nice guys, and with their guards down were now finding us not quite so strange as we'd set out to be. But then the mood suddenly changed again.

Three American necks cracked to interpret it.

"I'm sorry, Geoff," Roger Daley drawled, "I know you're a bit under the weather, but nevertheless I'm afraid I have to say that I think you are cheating."

"I *beg* your pardon, I most certainly am *not* cheating," Geoff retorted hotly, "and I resent your imputation that I am, *most* strongly."

He was sitting close to the stove, his reeking blanket giving off clouds of steam.

"You may have contracted malaria again, Geoffrey," Roger continued, "and I am very sorry for you, but that still does not allow you to cheat and expect to get away with it. There is a code, you know."

"I was *not* - cheating," Geoff insisted vehemently, thumping his cards down on the upturned NAAFI box.

"And I insist that you were," Roger riposted, blandly.

"I wasn't," snapped Geoffrey.

"Were."

"Wasn't."

"Were."

"Wasn't."

"Sir, I beseech you?" Roger turned dramatically, imploring the Colonel for his intervention. "Geoffrey was cheating. Surely you're not going to sit there and condone it, are you, sir?"

The Colonel pursed his lips, tapped a finger against them in pensive adjudication, and nodded his head once or twice before deliberating. Then he said, "Look, I really am most awfully sorry, Geoffrey old chap, but I do rather think that Roger's right, y'know. Don't you agree?"

"Oh, very well, sir," Geoff said, hanging his head in shame. "Perhaps I was then; just a little bit."

Askance as a *Mikado* chorus line, we all looked at each other, and tutted.

Still wrapped in his sopping blanket, Geoff arose, seeking sympathy from each of us, but found that everyone's gaze was conveniently averted, like some arms-folded, chin jutting, grand operatic rejection scene. He then tried proffering his hand; which nobody took. Next he turned to the Colonel, who, sadly, shook his head also. You could almost hear the Americans whimper. With a wan little smile, Geoff then turned and offered his hand hopefully to each of them. They didn't quite know what to do, but hesitantly at first, and then one by one they each shook his hand, and said: "Good night, sir; it's been . . . er . . . a pleasurable experience. We hope that you are soon recovered from your malaria."

I stepped forward to place an arm round Geoff's hunched shoulders and led him across to the flap of the marquee. Turning, he shrugged off his stinking blanket, pulled himself erect (so to speak), saluted, and swept from the tent.

Inside, you could have heard a pin drop.

Only a few moments later there came the crash of a single shot from behind the latrines.

"*JEEEEZUS* H. *Christ,*" the first American gasped, leaping from his chair as if someone had shoved a red hot poker up his arse.

"HOLY SHIT, I don't *believe* it," cried the second American.

"We'd like to thank you for a most interesting evening - er, sir," said the third American, who had quickly got up and thrust out his hand to the Colonel, "but if you don't mind I'm

164

afraid we really better be getting back to our own lines now. Gentlemen . . .?"

And they were gone.

Hot on their heels, Franklin D. Rideout, somewhat hurt and embarrassed, but with realisation slowly beginning to dawn on him, paused at the tent flap, turned round looking puzzled and saw us all beaming fondly at him. His face suddenly breaking into a grin, he clicked his fingers and slowly swept our assembly left-to-right with a wagging and all-encompassing index finger. "Okay . . . YOU-SONS-OF-*BITCHES* - begging your pardon, Colonel: - we *owe* ya."

And *he* was gone.

Quickly cleaning up and getting into some dry clothes, Geoff Banks was on the plane back to Lyneham at midnight.

Next evening the entrance to our Mess tent was jam-packed with Americans clamouring to gain entry.

SIXTEEN

AFTER A STAY IN TURKEY, on 6 October 1970 a twenty-two-year old American citizen named Billy Hayes was arrested by the police, who were on extremely attentive high alert at Istanbul Airport at the time because of terrorist attacks, just as he was about to fly out of the country back to the States with his girlfriend.

After being found with several bricks of hashish taped to his body, about two kilograms in total, he was sentenced to four years and two months' imprisonment on the charge of drug possession.

He was sent to Sağmalcilar prison (today transformed to a Four Seasons Hotel) to serve out his sentence.

In 1974, after a prosecution appeal (which originally wished to have Hayes found guilty, not of possession, but of smuggling), his original four-year sentence was overturned by the High Court in Ankara, and increased to a staggering 30-years.

His prison stay became a living hell: terrifying and unbearable scenes of physical and mental torture followed one another, where bribery, violence and insanity ruled the establishment. Monstrous wardens cruelly forced the prisoners to undergo the worst brutalities imaginable. Some prisoners worked for the prison administration as 'informers'. In a fit of madness, Billy bit off the tongue of one of these informants who had notified the warden of his escape plan. In 1975, after being committed to the prison's insane asylum, Billy again tried to escape, this time by attempting to bribe the warden-in-

166

chief. He ended up accidentally killing the warden, because the latter wanted to rape him. Billy put on an officer's uniform and managed his escape by walking out of the front door. From his epilogue, it was explained that on the night of 4 October 1975 he successfully crossed the border to Greece, and arrived home three weeks later.

This was the synopsis of Oliver Stone's 1978 film adaptation of Billy Hayes's true story *Midnight Express.* It was a disturbing movie that took many liberties with Hayes's original book, and caused great disturbance with its erroneous portrayal of Turkish brutality.

But there is another prison in Turkey that *is* considered to rank among the world's worst, and that is Diyarbakir.

In the 19th century, Diyarbakir prison gained infamy throughout the Ottoman Empire as a site where political prisoners from the enslaved Balkan ethnicities were sent to serve harsh sentences for speaking out or fighting for national freedom. More recently, too, this infamous penitentiary has been cited for its human rights violations, which are thought to have crossed the line into true atrocity. From 1981 to 1984, 34 prisoners lost their lives there because of excessive instances of torture, both mental and physical. This prison is notorious for the sexual abuse of its inmates, and its unliveable conditions. Prisoners have attempted hunger strikes, set themselves on fire in protest about prison conditions, and committed suicide in order to escape the horrors of this Turkish facility. Diyarbakir is known to incarcerate mere children for sentences of life imprisonment, and its 'crimes against humanity' make it one of the word's most sadistic and forbidding penal institutions.

I've been there.

Not as an inmate of course, but a visitor.

One evening Hassan, our Turkish liaison officer who'd been free and easy with his riding crop, arranged for a small group of us to meet him outside Diyarbakir Officers' Club at 23.00 for a 'night on the town', whatever that meant. His only stipulation had been that we should not wear uniform.

At 22.45 two mud-bespattered British Army Land Rovers could be seen nudging their way like dodgems through the unfamiliar downtown streets of Diyarbakir.

The Officers' Club was a fairly imposing building, situated about where Swann and Edgar would be if this had been London. Bumping our vehicles up against the steep kerb outside, we cut their motors and clambered out like an ill-clad Russian rugby team on tour. Fully cognisant of the implication of Hassan's stipulation on dress we had stripped ourselves of all badges of rank and donned the motliest selection of sartorial garbage imagineable. By UK standards we resembled a gang of meths drinkers skulking round a railway station goods yard in winter. Rest assured - downtown Diyarbakir was not the West End. We were smart.

Hassan was waiting for us.

He cast a slightly surprised look at our apparel and was unable to prevent the involuntary raising of one eyebrow. With a barely perceptible shrug of resignation he then ushered us genteely into a sidestreet behind the Officers' Club where beneath a cluster of dusty trees three horse-drawn cabs were already parked up waiting for us. Gamely clambering aboard these we set off at a leisurely clip-clopping pace into the deepest back streets of old Diyarbakir. Within ten minutes we had hit the outskirts. A full moon shone over the wall against a clear night sky and the open plain beyond. It felt like the year 1500. All I lacked was my sword. The narrow, cobbled road was flanked by dark, hulking, shuttered warehouses and moonlit medieval buildings of indeterminate purpose. There was not even a mangy dog to disturb the stillness, and the stench of stale urine pervaded the air from the open sewers. The street became narrower and narrower until it felt as if we were disappearing down a pencil sharpener. Just as it seemed we could go no further without becoming wedged, our lead cabbie manoeuvred his barouche around the corner of a building that looked as though it might have last been renovated about the year 1347. We swung into a large, deserted cobbled square.

And there before us stood *The Compound.*

Its gates were open.

Wall-mounted, mosquito-encrusted bulbs cast pools of eerie light over the duo of armed Turkish soldiers posted to check all comers at its portals. Today only a Covent Garden stage set could invoke for me that scene of a medieval Holloway. I so easily imagined an orchestra tuning up in the pit to herald the first burst of sound from the villainous bass-baritone as he and his magnificent voice surged across stage, being adroitly counterpointed by some glorious mezzo-soprano in the turret and the lead tenor warming up in the wings. But the ball game that awaited us was hardly so cultural.

Why?

What was *The Compound?*

It was the women's wing of Diyarbakir Prison.

As Hassan explained it to us, if Fatima Blogget lifted a pound of spuds, bashed Abdul Blogget or otherwise created a nonsense, that's where she would go to serve out her sentence. Any gypsy pedlar, a doctor's erring wife or recalcitrant whore who fell prey to Turkish law, could find themselves popped inside for a while. During her period of incarceration, she would work, for which labour she would receive remuneration. A quarter of her wages would go to her husband or dependants, and the remaining three-quarters into the state coffers. It was quite interesting work that was taken to more readily by some than by others, especially if one was a fantasist, but if you happened to be a Turk who was quite fond of his wife or girlfriend and she got nabbed, you would tear your hair out.

The women didn't break rocks, as such.

The Compound was a state operated brothel . . .

. . . staffed by the inmates, as part of their sentence.

Hassan paid off our three cabbies and we shuffled across towards the gates like a school crocodile about to visit the Tower of London. The Turkish guards stepped forward to frisk us, and nodded OK. We went through the gates and there was my imagined stage set again. The hookers who stand in their windows in Amsterdam's red light district and Hamburg's

169

Herbertsrasse are well known. Diyarbakir's *Compound* had been built an aeon ago and seemingly for the same purpose. It was like a small village in there except that the little gingerbread style shops which might have sold cream teas, fancy scones, home made fudge and copperware were given over instead to sullied beds and cushions that displayed more earthy wares - at least it was crumpet, not just cake - behind their flyblown sills. Such was the scene that the occasional goat, chickens, and even a cow or two wandering about the place would not have seemed incongruous. Apart from one or two of the 'attractions' who wore 1950s stilettos, the only apparent sop to 20th century fashion was the Turkish pop music that blared discordantly out of the myriad of transistor sets perched on shelves, steps and dresser tops.

We roamed curiously about from building to building. Some of them were single-floored, ground-level cottages. Others were crudely constructed, three-storey apartment blocks with sparse canteen rooms. There were about thirty women in all (the local crime rate might have been in decline) who were either reclining, flicking through magazines, or strolling about the place in various modes of attire and stages of undress. Some of them came up to us completely naked and began acting with paranoiac coquettishness. It was suggested that these might have been vicars' wives making the best of it while they had the chance. Others of them would loll indolently about, completely indifferent to attracting any custom at all: professional whores on the outside who were enjoying a busman's holiday, perhaps. Of the thirty, sad to say, none possessed what was our perception of an attractive structure. The best of them resembled some woman down the street caught unawares in her bathroom. However, in an attempt to accommodate their nation's NATO allies the majority of them besieged us with a charm offensive second to none. For a thousand odd years their role in life had been to service the camel trains (not these girls; the ones before) and now all of a sudden here was the cream of the Western Alliance fetching up on their doorstep. There was obviously a certain novelty value attached to us, and we represented

170

potentially big business. Those of the women who managed to stay the pace over that month we were in Turkey, must have done quite well for themselves. And for the state coffers. Thirty women? Fifteen thousand men? In one month alone they could have cleaned up the equivalent of a ten year stretch. One of our Belgian officers decided to try one on for size. It cost him the equivalent of 75p, for 'a quickie'.

When he emerged from the lady's room re-zipping his fly scant minutes later, leaving her leaning against her door jamb coyly waving him *au revoir*, he was grinning from ear to ear.

"This," he said, "must be why they call it *Eastern Express.*"

When *Eastern Express* finished, always an hour late and a dollar short I just happened to be the last person to board the final transport plane out of Turkey.

It was a strange feeling to be left standing there on Diyarbakir airfield, now denuded of its concentration of alien canvas, equipment and polyglot militaria, and to watch the great heavily laden aircraft go lumbering up into the sky to drone their complements in varying shades of khaki back to their respective homelands, hearths and debriefs.

Like battlefield pillagers, stray dogs were already abroad sniffing all the strange smells left behind, timorously lifting their forepaws and curiously twitching snouts about the flattened grass, retrieving discarded tit-bits.

It was 14.00.

The sun flashed out of an ice blue sky and although now warm, it was obvious that the night was going to be bitter. Would I still be there to see it, I wondered? Overlooked on the passenger manifest? Would my small group of colleagues who were standing there with me, fly back to England without me, waving down from the plane's windows having left me behind like Robinson Crusoe on the darkening airfield with my hexamine burner, toothbrush, spare socks and a biscuit to make my own way back on foot as best I could next day? No, of course they wouldn't.

171

The final plane came shimmering in out of the western haze, landed, swung around and taxied over towards us, dropped its steps, and up we filed into its body. Glancing back over my shoulder for the last time at Diyarbakir, I half expected to see some crazed and despotic war-lord break out of the surrounding plain and come clattering down onto the airstrip with his ponies, brigands, machine-guns, bandoliers and angrily raised swords, just in time to swarm all over us and make us take our trousers down to enable his rabble to perform all manner of horrible, gory and undignified things upon us with their primeval hand-beaten cutlery. From the warmth and security of their homes our already departed NATO allies would read about us in disbelief in the world's press on the morrow, while their American, German, Italian, Belgian or Norwegian wives affectionately fondled those precious parts of their anatomy of which we so cruelly and savagely would have been deprived and gagged with just prior to our disembowelment. Our own wives and girlfriends would receive stunned notification of our fate from a team of ill-prepared officers lucklessly appointed to the task. Short-lived national commiseration would follow and after a protracted appeal some small financial compensation (some years later), and then the infamous Diyarbakir Massacre would all but be forgotten. But if you've had a reasonable run, enjoyed a few bevvies and flung the woo about a bit, getting hacked to pieces with a rusty sword on foreign soil, even in error, could make for a more telling family history, perhaps, than contracting pleurisy or falling victim to a bus.

Unsurprisingly the crazed tribesman of my fevered imagination never did materialise.

Our plane took off; hip flasks were opened, and playing cards and dice produced.

At 21.00 that evening we landed back at Lyneham to set foot once more on English soil. A convoy of chartered coaches stood drawn up outside to convey our various sub-units back to their respective locations.

But first we had to go through Customs.

HM Customs officers at RAF airports operate the same way they do elsewhere, in tax inspector/parking meter attendant/Gestapo mode with their black composition shoes, Woolworths socks, shiny blue uniform trousers and stale BO. We had been heavily engaged on NATO manoeuvres in the heart of Turkey, not on some package tour junket to a fleshpot. A few brass baubles was the extent of our booty. We'd had no time, inclination or know-how to raid a poppy field and process the stuff. I was reminded of a colleague who had been signaled to return from operations in Aden back to UK once in a hurry. He had dashed back to base from operations, hastily thrown together some of his belongings in a grip, ripped the battlefield morphine ampoules from about his neck and chucked them unthinkingly into the grip along with a syringe and some loose ammunition from one of his pouches - you can see it coming, can't you - and hurried through Customs at home, without a moment's thought. A*ha*; gotcha.

Wrong.

On that occasion he got through alright.

It was only unpacking his things at Hereford later that he was hit by the possible difficulty he might have encountered, and his explanation, that sure as eggs are eggs would have been disbelieved.

We were bushed, hungry and had a long way still to travel. The majority of bored customs guys screwed the bobbin that night and fed the lot of us through with only cursory checks and comments.

Except one.

A new boy, keen to flex his muscles.

He was a lean, mean, pinched, sallow faced little weasel of an individual, the type who would emit high pitched putrid pongs into the sump of his already soiled Y-fronts for days on end without thinking about it.

One of my soldiers was a gentle Shropshire farm lad called Tymon, still innocent to the ways of the world and the machinations of mankind. It was not alliteration alone that had made him affectionately become known to us all as 'Timple'.

"Anything to declare?" the obnoxious little customs person asked Tymon as he went through.

"No," said Timple, shuffling uncomfortably from the scrutiny. "Well . . . I've got me two-hundred fags like, but that's all."

"I see," said Blue-Job, sneering with malice and obvious doubt. "Perhaps we'd better have a look and make sure then, had we?" Apparently he didn't like the healthy young boys in the Army at all; we obviously got right up his bunged nostril.

"Yeah, sure," said Timple with obliging trust, opening the worn catches of his battered Army suitcase to reveal a pile of dirty washing, his toilet tackle, one pungent green towel, a couple of pulp-novel paperbacks, his second pair of boots - and 200 cigarettes. Blue-Job probed these contents with the delicacy of a starving Masai rifling a gazelle's entrails.

"A*ha*," he leered, triumphant, tipping an open packet containing 17 Rothmans out of one of Timple's boots. "What have we *here*, then?"

"Packet of fags," said Timple, grinning. "Sorry, I forgot they was there."

"Sorry you very well may be, lad," said Blue-Job, who was roughly about the same age. His beady little eyes glinted with malevolent ecstasy behind his NHS glasses. "I shall have to ask you to step into this room over here, please."

Timple started to look embarrassed. The rest of us had finished being processed and he knew we were all eager to get onto our coaches and away. A groan of collective disbelief and dislike rumbled round the customs hall. Angrily I stepped forward, sporting a tan, a glint and the beginning of a Wyatt Earp moustache, started in Anatolia. A Smith and Wesson was belted to my hip.

"Do you really want to go through with this, Officer?" I enquired politely. "You can see these boys are all rather tired and hungry and still have a long way to travel. They've been stuck out in the bundu for weeks. The coach drivers have been waiting hours for us to get here. They are getting restless outside while being paid overtime by the tax payer. You're holding up one hundred people for a case of dirty washing and

174

seventeen bent fags. Is it really necessary?" I smiled. It was no use. There was to be no reasoning. My approach had not doused but fuelled his little fire.

"This is a fairly flagrant contravention of regulations, I would say. This man clearly denied having anything to declare, and yet I discovered . . . these." He proudly held up the crumpled packet of 17 Rothmans. "For all I know he may be concealing all sorts of things elsewhere about his person.

"The only things he's likely to be concealing are a few lice and a tide mark," I replied.

"Well, we'll soon find out about that, won't we," he said, closing Timple's suitcase and taking hold of the handle. What a glorious future lay ahead for this little fellow. Every organisation's got them. Their task complete his older, wiser colleagues were standing about in groups with their arms folded waiting for us to leave so that they could all go home as well. Occasionally they flickered a glance at their young brother's charade of powerplay, but made no effort to intervene. Knowing there was no more I could do to stop the nonsense, I thought I would indulge myself a little longer.

"You've not been in the Army, ever, have you Laddie?" I enquired, feeling like pistol-whipping the little shit.

"I don't see what that's got to do with anything," he said, "but no, I haven't."

"I didn't think you had. From the look of you you'd have probably failed the medical anyway. Still, you've got a much nicer uniform than ours to wear now, haven't you, and it's nice and warm and cosy in this nice big shed doing this super job of yours. Drink anywhere near here, do you sunshine? Got a favourite pub where we can find you sometime, perhaps . . .?"

It didn't do any good. It was a lame, childish and empty ploy, but I felt a tad better for doing it, and who knew, it might just have given him something to think about.

They took 20-minutes going over Tymon's body, before allowing him to keep his 200 and reluctantly releasing him - after first having confiscated his 17 bent additional cigarettes of course.

Back at Bulford Camp at last I stumbled into the Mess, gathered my mail from the letter rack and ripped my way eagerly through it. There were a couple from Rachel in Gibraltar saying that she now felt eleven months pregnant, and ready to pod a bull calf - and a Posting Order.

Posting Orders arrived like exam results, in an instantly recognisable brown MoD envelope with an oval red date and departmental stamp in the bottom corner. They were torn open quickly, as though from Hitler in the dark days, recalling one to Berlin to answer for some heinous perpetration about which one thought one knew nothing but now finds he has become the prime suspect and official scapegoat. It was now December. My masters at MoD's AG9 Branch, those captains of my fate and rulers of my future destiny were not sending me to Hong Kong, Jamaica, Barbados, Washington, or even as Britain's Military Attaché to Rio de Janeiro - no - apparently my personal career plan now decreed that in January 1966 I would be going to command 31 Army Youth Team at Bicester, in Oxford.

I had a drink to sleep on it and then another one, without sleeping, so chewed the fat with the boys in the Mess about all the local scandal since I'd been away, which local scrubber on heat had been putting out on the grass behind the NAAFI for the boys, and anything else that had transpired in the unit during our absence. Then I wandered across the lawn to my room in the bungalow block, unpacked my kit into various piles for burning, blancoing, hosing down, dinsinfecting, cleaning, washing and polishing, stripped off and stood beneath a hot shower for ten minutes, felt better, dressed and went back to the Mess bar for one more drink, or six, and then at 03.00 my body and I finally took ourselves off to bed for thirty-six hours.

But it was not to be.

At 07.30 I was woken up by Sinclair, one of our white-jacketed Mess stewards who shook my shoulder and leaned down flashing a silver salver in my face.

"Congratulations, sir," he said, sticking the salver under my nose.

"Why? What have I done? Won the bloody thing?"

"Signal's just been phoned through from Comcen, sir. From Fortress Headquarters in Gibraltar. Confirmatory copy to follow. I wrote it all down for you, sir. Here it is."

I grabbed the piece of paper from his tray, swiped the sleepers from my eyes, missed, knocked over my bedside light and tried to focus. He had scrawled the message in pencil on a bar chit, across the top of which I was encouraged to drink Courage Beer while the Babycham Bambi pranced prettily in a cloud of bubbles up one of the margins. It was a fitting medium upon which to read *Fine bouncing boy. Congratulations. 9lbs 4oz. Mother wears surprised expression of enormous relief. Grinning a lot, too.*

"Thank you, Sinclair, I said, beaming a bit at the edges myself. "I've no plans for him yet. Don't know what he'll be. Probably prime minister, or something. My head hurts. Put a crate of champagne on ice for me for lunch, will you? Spread the word, and make sure you wake me at noon."

"Certainly, sir," he grinned, tip-toeing from the room and letting the door bang. He reopened it to apologise and dropped his tray. Didn't matter. The Congolese Army Band countermarching around my cranial parade ground didn't matter either. Nothing mattered at all really. I had a son. A boy of my very own to bring up, educate, mould, advise, bollock and be proud of, to share happiness with and launch into the world of grown men with his chest filled and head held high to carry our family name on to fame, glory and the bed of some other beautiful woman wherefrom to extend our dynastic line even further. I just hoped he didn't have a hangover when he did it.

There was never any question of him not turning out to be a boy of course. A bull-calf perhaps, yes, but essentially a boy. Yet from the outset there had been a grey area in the production line. What should he be called? *Timothy* and *Nigel* were regulation Army issue names at that time, but possibly slightly passé I thought, with all due respect to my good friends de Foubert, Knocker, Smellie and Sharp who each received their Nigel appellations in mint condition and still wear them well.

Clint was rugged enough, but essentially lower deck stuff. He might do well and become a peer of the realm someday, so we couldn't call him *Fred* either. During all but his conception and the initial incubation period I had not been present, so Rachel and I had been unable to have those cosy little fireside chats where we would have bandied about every name from A to Z, discarding most of them and coming up with a short list of 27 to fight over. Little Native Americans (in my day more affectionately known as Red Indians) were always easily named. At the moment their first squawk hit the prairie the proud pappy would quickly pull back the flap of his tepee to clock what was going on outside and then name his son after the event. Hence many a brave warrior grew to manhood saddled with such nomenclature as *One Bear Sniffs*; *Long Snake Wriggles* or *Two Dogs Peeing*. A novel system, I'd agree, but not so easy over here. Imagine '"Allow me to introduce to you my son, *Number Nine Bus Passing.*"'

Rachel and I now had to name our 9lbs-plus papoose by proxy. She would send me copious missives from Gibraltar containing lists of mediocre suggestions culled from or submitted by relatives for consideration, which I would derisively dismiss before penning a serious list of far more stirring, durable, resounding, worthwhile and meaningful names such as Vulcan, Roy, Reuben, Gervaise - names with which a man could be proud to sign a Declaration of War, of Independence or of any damn' thing he liked really - none of which, for some reason, Rachel seemed to like very much. At one stage we almost settled for giving him just a number, which because he had been preceded by his sister, Natalia, would have to have been Two. Silly name. Then I saw *Mutiny On The Bounty* and was reawakened to the possibility of naming him Christian. This stuck, and so we then had to work out a middle name, because it was something we had never got around to doing for our single named daughter Natalia. Somehow or other *Alexis* came out of the hat. Not boy; not girl; not anything in between; neither Greek nor Russian, but a name by which he could stand alone, despite his grandmother suggesting that it sounded more like an Oriental breakfast food or laxative. So now fully named, Christian Alexis George kicked and squirted happily in his crib in Gibraltar's Royal Naval Hospital, next waiting to be circumcised.

His mother, who was Jewish, wanted it done. The Royal Navy, who had brought him into the world, had no practitioner versed in the art, so the local rabii was asked along to oblige. He came at the appointed hour, laid out his implements as though preparing to dissect a pork sausage, did his job nicely and neatly, made the predictable crack about performing the task for a lad called Christian, accepted a bottle of whisky from Rachel for his trouble (her normal barter currency) (I'm pleased to say) and went whistling on his merry way.

Since then he has never been called Christian once.

He was always Alexis; Lex; Alex, or Butch. And sometimes we even called him Jennifer, but this was just to make him cross when he'd been naughty.

The following week I went out and traded in my MG Magnet for a second-hand pink and grey Vauxhall Cresta, and then started to pack my belongings to go to Bicester.

In January I drove the heavily laden car from Bulford to Oxfordshire to take over our new married quarter at 26, Langtun Avenue. Two days later I collected Rachel, Natalia and the new boy from the airport, drove them to our new home, got them bedded down, lovingly stroked Rachel's now empty tummy and promptly refilled it, although by mutual consent we agreed that our sprogging days were now over and we would remain a two-child family, therefore it was time one of us ought to think about getting ourself neuteured. Turned out it was to be me of course, but that's another story.

Next day I reported to work.

One day at school in the early 1950s we received an address from an Army Schools Liaison Officer. These SLOs were trendy and presentable guys - what today is called 'cool'. After completing a little bit of real-time soldiering somewhere, these 'dudes' were sent out for a spell on a recruiting binge, spreading the gospel about a career-at-arms being a worthwhile calling for any lad of gumption. Because we all had to do National Service back then anyway we would be taking a compulsory bite of the cherry whether we liked it or not, so the role of the SLO might be deemed to have been superfluous, going round our schools proselytizing militarism. But it was a rainy afternoon and we were allowed to miss Latin to pile into our main assembly hall to listen to this dashing Royal Tank Regiment captain, resplendent in his immaculate service dress and gleaming black Sam Browne belt, recount to us what fun he and his squadron had beating about the north German Plain in their great lumps of tracked heavy-duty armour. The message was that rather than going into accountancy, the Church or local shopkeeping we might care to consider the possibility of becoming proper, lifelong, professional soldiers instead. These SLOs (in 2007 they were to become renamed Army Careers Advisors) aimed to attract incomers to the Officer Corps.

A sister organisation, the Army Youth Teams (AYTs), were geared more to enticing fresh soldiery to the ranks. The teams were first formed in 1964, eventually totalling 79 in number. They were manned solely by Service personnel, of whom there were 395 nationwide. Their annual running cost was approximately £2.7 million. The rôle of the teams was to contact young people and encourage those of the right calibre to join the Army by assisting them in character building activities and demonstrating Army skills and methods. An AYT consisted of a subaltern commander; a staff sergeant; a couple of satisfied, going places corporals, and a L/Cpl who thought he was. They had an office in the barracks, a minibus, a film projector and a parish. For administrative purposes they were attached to one of the local Army Recruiting Offices in their area. By appointment, most evenings and weekends they travelled the surrounding counties visiting various youth clubs, which were obvious sources of potential recruitment. They did not recruit directly, but were required merely to create a military awareness and sow the seeds of possible interest, so that of their own volition, hopefully, the youth of the country would come flocking to all the Recruiting Offices down the high streets of Britain, to sign on.

In order to reduce recruiting expenditure and release Service manpower for higher priority tasks, in 1978 these Youth Teams were disbanded, but in 1966 they were still going strong and my tour of duty commanding 31 AYT at Bicester was to last for a year.

How many recruits were directly attributable to our efforts that year there was no way of telling, but we must have netted a few - and had a lot of fun doing so.

Let's find out about some of it, shall we . . .?

SEVENTEEN

IT WAS 10.00 a.m. on a Monday.

Dressed in my best bib and tucker I had just wheeled out after paying my respects to Lt Col Ted Darley, the firm, fair and friendly CO of 16 Battalion RAOC at St George's Barracks, Bicester, and was now following the Adjutant, Captain Geoff Doyle's direction across to my new office.

The door was ajar.

They were expecting me.

With trepidation.

What was I going to be like, they wondered?

I went in, and saw for the first time the four members of my team, each wearing his best uniform for the occasion. We weighed each other up warily. We would be working together for the next twelve months as a close knit unit. It was important that we gelled.

Sergeant Bragg called them up to attention, and saluted.

"Sergeant Bragg, sir, Good morning, sir. Welcome to 31 AYT, sir." He grinned a lopsided and naughty grin that had got him into and out of more scrapes than hot dinners, and stepped forward to shake my outstretched hand.

"Good morning," I said, including all of them. "And who exactly *is* 31 AYT, Sergeant? Perhaps you'd like to introduce me?"

"Certainly, sir. This reprobate here, I'm afraid, sir, is your namesake sir, and I feel quite sure that you're not related in any manner, shape or form whatsoever, sir: Corporal Dick George, sir."

A strong looking, lantern jawed man with glasses shook my hand, nearly crushing my fingers as he did so. He looked a solid, dependable sort to have around in a tricky situation. Beside him there stood a clean, smart, good looking young NCO with a healthy complexion and a twinkle to his eye.

"Corporal Guy Adams, sir," he said, introducing himself.

"How do you do," I said, and moved on to meet L/Cpl Brown. He shuffled a bit, seemed affable enough, but along with Sergeant Bragg had now done his time with the team and was shortly to be posted.

"How do you like your coffee, sir?" Corporal Adams asked. A kettle had just started steaming over in the corner. They were getting things off to a good start. I felt I might be able to rub along with this lot alright.

The rest of the morning was taken up with reading myself in: familiarising myself with the files, taking stock of my equipment inventory and being force-fed the ethos of a youth team; well, this one at any rate - and yet the whole time my attention kept being distracted by 24 items of soiled equipment that I could see piled lopsidedly in a toppling stack alongside the far wall of the office.

"Okay," I said, "I've read the files. I'm in the picture with forthcoming events and commitments. I've seen a run down of the special interest films we show. Now . . . I'm almost afraid to ask . . . we're not an extension of the bedding store and I can't believe we operate a field knocking-shop, so - tell me - what are all those peed mattresses in aid of, festering away by the wall over there with half their ticking hanging out?"

"They're our mats, sir," explained Sergeant Bragg.

"Course they are. How silly of me." I sipped some cold coffee, lit a cigarette and offered the pack around. "So those are our mats, are they. I see. Here's my next silly question. Just what the **** do we use 'em for?"

"Judo, sir," they chorused together.

"We can't afford proper judo mats, you see sir," Sergeant Bragg explained, "so the QM issued us with those US mattresses to use instead. They're better in a way, really, than proper mats. They're easier to load into the minibus."

"Judo," I said.

"It's the mainstay of our display, sir," Sergeant Bragg looked slightly puzzled. "We give a demonstration at every club we go to. We're all judo trained, sir. Surely you're judo trained as well, aren't you, sir? Black Belt? Third Dan? It's an absolute prerequisite for the job."

"Er . . . I don't think I am - no."

There was an embarrassed silence, as if they'd discovered a virgin madam had been sent in to run their cat-house.

"Well - don't you worry, sir," Corporal Adams piped up perkily. "We'll soon teach you."

They jolly well did, too.

That evening we went to Banbury and I saw the unit in operation for the first time.

With Guy Adams at the wheel our green minibus roared through the gates and screeched to a stop outside the appointed youth club. Groups of gum-chewing teenagers, yobs and mollettes lounged about on the stairway listening to transistorised pop music. Leaping from the cab Dick George called out to them as he strode round to fling open the vehicle's rear door: "Righty-ho, all you lovely people," he cried. "Let us be having you now, please. Come-*on*-come-*on*-come-*ON*. Start forming a chain and get these mattresses unloaded. Take them in and lay them out on the floor."

We hit them like a S.W.A.T. team.

Dick could emanate a menacing presence, no doubt enhanced by the army combat suit that he wore. School masters, club leaders and the Police these kids could handle. Dick they weren't so sure about. They quickly rallied round and humped in the mattresses. I soon discovered that our arrival at these clubs, where we moved in and took over *Go-Go-Go-Go-GO,* constituted the most organised and disciplined aspect of these young people's lives. They got swept up in the enthusiastic flow we generated, and all loved every minute of it.

It took us three minutes to lay out our 'judo mats' to form a square in the centre of the youth club floor, while Guy Adams quietly got on with assembling and setting up our film projector and screen. Sergeant Bragg and Dick George disappeared behind the scenes and came back shortly afterwards wearing their white cotton *judogi*, a pair of drawstring pants, and to withstand the stresses of grappling and throwing, thickly quilted, heavy weave cotton jackets, fastened by their respective coloured judo rank belts.

We stood around casually chatting to the members while awaiting the late arrival of their harassed club leader. As soon as she had come faffing in, all of an apologetic lather, readjusted her stays and straightened her bonnet, we ran our two films. These were both MoD sponsored technicolour productions, one showing a swashbuckling unit on operation in the Middle East, engaged in a fictional incident concerning the quelling of an insurrection of dissident tribesman with mortar fire, artillery and an airstrike, and the other a rescue operation on Kilimanjaro, carrying down a crashed pilot, designed to show the youngsters the sort of adventurous capers they could be getting up to if they joined the Army. When the lights went up Sergeant Bragg and Dick George then got a bit beastly hurling each other about on the mats for a few minutes, we had a cup of coffee, answered some questions, and then went home.

A year of it, I thought, could become tedious.

We covered clubs in Oxfordshire, Northamptonshire, Buckinghamshire, Berkshire and Hertfordshire.

After a couple of weeks I realised that the number of recruits we were likely to attract, if any, in no way justified the expense of running the youth teams. It might be a nice little swan for a year, cabbying about the shires, showing films and putting on a judo display, but I needed more of a challenge than that, and knew I would have to devise some way of finding one.

It didn't take long.

For a couple of weeks Dick George had been taking me on the mat in the gymnasium to teach me basic break falls. After the first week I could hardly move, so with some massage-like pummelling he unravelled my joints, and then during the second week showed me some holds and throws. I was sleeping well, but could scarcely get out of bed each morning. I had seized up so much that all he could do was toss me about like a stiffly hinged plank, eliciting no retaliation whatsoever; satisfying for him: demeaning, but still character building for me. By the second Friday he told me I had reached the black belt stage. This was utter crap of course, but it added a morale lifting fillip to my already whet appetite. I now knew where my challenge lay, and how I intended to improve 31 AYT's public persona.

Bragg, George and Adams were all good judo men.

Judo is all well and good, but it can become a tad boring to watch after a while. With the team's willing participation therefore, I intended to adapt their skills and devise a proper Unarmed Combat Display pure and simple; or - better yet - evil and complex. But before I could mould their expertise to this end I had to earn the right to do so.

I had to get myself through the Army's crash Unarmed Combat course at the then Army School of PT at Blandford Forum, in Dorset.

Sergeant Bragg left us the following week to become a Royal Marine Commando. He was replaced by a Staff Sergeant Robin Sider who was more serious, more discipline-oriented, and initially seemed a little out of sorts at the prospect of having to become an integral and pivotal part of such a one-man-and-his-dog outfit. However, he soon bit the bullet and joined in with the spirit of everything, bought himself a tracksuit and adapted to his new way of life, like a monk cast among sinners who'd been told to get on with things to his usual high standard because it was his Lord's wish and decree that he should do so.

Much to S/Sgt Sider's chagrin, I amended it to two vacancies on the Unarmed Combat course.

Breakfast at Blandford was from 08.00-08.30.

Reinforced on Day One with lashings of egg, toast and coffee I strolled nonchalantly into the gym at 08.35.

At 08.50 I dashed right back out again to be violently sick.

186

Judo is a sport. It keeps one fit, active and alert, all factors which when combined with an acquired knowledge about how to take advantage of an opponent's loss of balance, stands one in very good stead in a fight. But how many fights does the average, well balanced adult get himself into in a lifetime? How many fights have *you* had in, say, the past . . . 20 years? Any at all?

Aided initially by the late Bruce Lee, a whole chain of previously fairly obscure martial arts have either been dragged out and resurrected, or else newly invented and plopped into the evening class circuit, but rather like the chap who took his harp to a party and no one asked him to play, it is not practical to lug your judo mat down the high street with you on a Saturday night just on the offchance that someone is going to leap out of a Dolcis' shop doorway to have a go at your throat.

Any degree of proficiency at judo or its siblings takes time and dedication to acquire. If the aim of doing so is purely self defence in the event of being attacked, I would rather settle for a good straight left or a standing start record for the 100-metres dash. Or a piece of lead pipe. Or use the training time to make lots of money and hire a bodyguard instead, then I could continue to enjoy my excesses and keep my typing finger intact.

I will not deny that a demonstration of crowd clearance by one man can be pretty impressive stuff though.

Major Graham 'Black Mac' Macdonald, a friend of mine who spent some time in Japan with the SIB (the Royal Military Police Special Investigation Branch) was a Judo Black Belt 3rd Dan, as well as being an international judo referee.

Much myth surrounds these esoteric practitioners.

One Saturday night at Bicester, I was witness to the myth being proven as fact.

Mac was Duty Officer.

At 23.00 a call came through from the Guard Room to the Mess that there was one mean fracas underway at the NAAFI dance. Mac placed his half finished tumbler of whisky resignedly on the bar, went out and climbed into the duty

187

vehicle and drove down to the NAAFI to assess the situation. Because I had nothing else to do I went with him.

When we arrived there the dance hall was a riot of mayhem and broken glass, smashed chairs and tables, all because a gang of lads from the neighbouring Royal Pioneer Corps camp up at Graven Hill had come down and tried to move in on one of our own particularly juicy WRAC girls, renowned for being favourably disposed to the physical attraction of men at large generally, whatever their cap badge. Rumour had it that even one or two officers had managed to have a go on her at certain times. It was the prevailing opinion that she would make someone an extremely interesting wife, but at that time no one could imagine who that someone could possibly be.

Mac right ended one of the upturned chairs, stood on it and with his stentorian Scottish roar bellowed out across the seething assembly: "Now LISTEN UP ALL OF YOUS. I AM THE DUTY OFFICER. *I shall return in ten minutes, and when I do I shall expect to see this whole place cleared and empty. You all read me? . . .* OKAY."

He stood where he was a moment longer so that they could all see him, and absorb his message. Everyone knew 'Black Mac'. Adjusting his service dress and Sam Browne he then stepped down from his little rostrum. Back in the vehicle outside he glanced at his watch, offered me a cigarette, we lit up - and waited.

No more than five minutes had elapsed before there was a crash of breaking glass and a chair came sailing out through the NAAFI window, closely followed by a badly cut corporal.

They were at it again.

Mac appeared to take no notice. He smoked quietly on until the ten minutes were up. Then he opened the car door, stubbed his second cigarette out underfoot, and unstrapped his Sam Browne belt.

"Haven't had a good workout for weeks," he chuckled. "And these buggers have asked for it."

When we went back in, the NAAFI was in uproar.

Mac stood there unperturbed for a minute to allow awareness of his presence to permeate. One or two peripheral belligerents who saw him did drift uneasily aside, but the body of the kirk rioted on unchecked, swept up on a tide of blood lust and frenetic abuse. One burly participant, hurled out by the scrum, unavoidably cannonaded backwards into Mac. Scarcely seeming to raise his wrist Mac dropped the man neatly to the floor by a nice little tap on the back of his neck.

One down; 35 to go; or so.

"I don't care if you *are* a bloody officer," hollered another bleary-eyed hulk, lurching towards Mac with increasing momentum, brandishing a broken bottle aloft in his right fist, "but yon Jocko there you've just hit's a mate o' mine."

His slurred voice became a dull thump as neatly aided by the tip of Mac's toecap and an adroitly executed body-flick, he founds himself sailing through the already broken window to land in the bushes outside.

"F'Chrissake who *is* this fucker" yapped a demented little Pioneer Corps pugilist, roaring out of the throng and swinging wildly in all directions but mainly at the immovable human on the edge of the floor. Mac caught the man's first blow judderingly on the outstretched palm of his left hand and in a trice reduced him to a whimpering heap who knelt before him clutching at the sinew and ripped ligaments of his freshly torn shoulder blade.

Three more of the sweating soldiery detached themselves and shambled menacingly towards Mac, intent on putting paid to his persistent and aggravating interruption of their Saturday night dose of culture. Each of them made a grab at him and all four subsided in a slowly flailing huddle to the floor. Mac got up again. The others didn't.

The centre of the fight still continued to rage. Mac strolled slowly across towards it and started to work methodically through each cluster of combatants. In three minutes he had masterfully rendered the entire hall *hors de combat*.

We left and went back out to our vehicle.

"I suppose there'll be hell to pay over this, won't there?" Mac grinned. "But wasn't it worth it?"

The only injury he sustained was unexpected. With her lipstick smudged, half of one large tit adrift somewhere down around her navel and her hair awry, the WRAC girl it had all been about emerged all of a flurry and came rushing up to him with her arms flung wide.

"Oh, well;" Mac grinned, puckering up his knight-errant lips for their just reward.

He was wrong, and had a bruise on his face for a week where she clocked him with her handbag.

At the hands of a past master the art of Judo certainly has its uses when fire hoses and riot police are not to hand, and for walking round Shanghai waterfront bars alone at night it would be comforting to have a bit of it tucked under your belt too - although I think I'd still prefer a gun.

My reason for being at Blandford was not to learn how to carve a swathe of destruction through society at large. I just wanted to get sufficient knowledge to enable me to stage a theatrically impressive unarmed combat display with 31 AYT.

It was my intention to put us on the map.

Leaving my breakfast to solidify behind the dustbins, I returned queasily back inside the gym once more. I was wounded - pride, and tum - but I was still determined to learn how to chop up at least one house brick before the week was out.

By 12.15 I was breathing hard.

I decided to forego lunch.

At 15.15 I was perspiring profusely and by 16.30 I was creased.

The majority of sporting endeavours last about an hour. But an army course, compressing as it does a lifetime's experience into one week, lasts continuously from 08.30 Monday until 17.00 Friday.

Judo jackets are made from tough, heavily stitched quilted cotton. When the lilywhite hands of the penpusher are unexpectedly called upon to emulate the gnarled fists of a

190

lumberjack and must repetitiously strive to upend and hurl a 15-stone opponent onto the mat, the knucklebones soon begin to appear through the flayed skin of each finger. Raw rubbed knuckles bleed. By 10.00 that first Monday morning our dozen previously pristine white jackets had become incarnadined. The romance of the sport was fast disappearing. I now understood what Churchill meant by 'blood, sweat and tears'. However . . .

. . . we soon transcended the vale of misery in which we found ourselves, when our latent survival and killer instincts began to emerge. Our instructors saw this transformation regularly of course, but they were still delighted. It meant once again that they were successfully achieving their aim. Our knucklebones shrugged their shoulders and accepted their lot and our addled brains settled down to being sloshed around our skulls like boxers rebounding from the ropes. We swiped the red mist from our eyes and carried on.

That evening a dozen shattered warriors dozed in their pre-dinner baths and later slept the sleep of the dead. Even the pangs of cramp gave up and crept away, defeated by the depth of their victims' sleep. We hurt pretty bad.

It was agony climbing into our encrusted judo suits each morning and dragging ourselves achingly across to the gym, feeling like PoWs reporting for duty on the Burma Railway. But we were learning. By God, were we learning. By the Thursday some of us were even becoming quite cocky with our newly acquired skills and wanted to sneak down into the village to start beating people up. To nip any such misplaced confidence in the bud, the senior instructor called for silence.

He waited.

We waited.

Then he slowly smiled an assassin's smile and dramatically mouthed one terrifying word: *"Randoori."*

A chill permeated the gym.

The word hung suspended in the air like a muffled clapper's death knell. *Randoori*. The judo term for a free-for-all. It was like waking up to find your house surrounded by police when you're guilty but thought you'd got away with it.

There were twelve of us. Each one had to take on each of the others in turn until the best man won. One hundred and forty-four quick fire bouts. The sweat froze on our friction burned bodies . . .

I'd like to say that I was the last man standing, but I seem to recall that I was the third to be sent skidding out the ring to end up with my chipped teeth wrapped round a firebucket.

Then came Friday at last.

The final day of the course.

The instructors divided us into four three-man teams and told us to spend the rest of the morning devising and rehearsing a short routine to perform before the Commandant as a form of passing-out ceremony that afternoon.

S/Sgt Sider and I - who needed all the help we could get - were landed with rather an unimaginative young Gunner called Hoskins, who hadn't wanted to come on the course in the first place. The three of us undoubtedly constituted the weakest team, which became steadily more apparent as the morning wore on. We could see the other three teams each perfecting their realistic little scenarios in which a rebel sentry was guarding an ammunition dump in a jungle clearing. A relief sentry was asleep nearby and a British soldier armed with nought but a cosh and a knife had to dispose of them both. Each of our presentations was meant to be a variation of this theme and at final rehearsal three out of the four teams' efforts looked very impressive. Bodies bounced and thudded across the mats and there ensued unarmed combat sequences that would have made the real James Bond resemble a big girl's blouse. We kidded ourselves as much anyway.

Except in our case.

Hoots of jocular derision greeted our ineptitude as we tripped, fell, got it all snarled up, lost our pants in the mêlée and made what appeared to be a contrived hash of the whole thing rather à la Marx Brothers. The instructors were not amused. Their Commandant would obviously glower at them later that afternoon and imply they had not worked hard enough on us.

A tactical reappraisal was needed.

S/Sgt Robin Sider and I, the only officer, a lieutenant, were the two most senior ranks on the course. We had to pull something out of the bag. We dispensed with lunch and along with Gunner Hoskins, our whingeing third team member, we went into a huddle. Ideas were bandied about, considered and rejected. I glanced at Robin, slumped there dejectedly beside me in his dirty white judo suit, and had an idea. Clad as we were we couldn't have looked less like a British patrol if we'd tried.

Judo is of Japanese origin.

The answer was simple.

We'd turn the whole thing into a period piece.

"Got it," I beamed, sitting upright and snapping my fingers.

"What's that, sir?" Robin asked, looking up from resting his chin dejectedly in his palm.

"I'll tell you. Now listen - Hoskins . . . you can be an innocent Japanese maiden guarding her flock by night . . ."

"Yer, *what* sir? I don't wanna be no innocent Japanese maiden, I . . ."

"Hoskins," Robin snarled. "If my sir says you're going to be an innocent Japanese maiden, then by Christ Hoskins, you'll be a fucking innocent Japanese maiden. Is that CLEAR?"

"Spose so, grumbled the morose and bleeding Hoskins.

It was 14.00.

The Commandant of the APTC School took his seat in the gym.

He warmly applauded the first three displays of agility, skill and simulated blood lust.

The instructors beamed.

Then it was our turn.

There was an embarrassed silence.

Careerwise, the senior instructor had obviously thought it politic to pre-warn the Commandant that one of the groups had not quite turned out to the usual standard.

This was wonderful.

We'd take them by surprise.

Hoskins came wandering vacuously into view from behind the toilet door and shambled across to take up his position on the mats, a broom handle clasped in one hand. He adopted a stance with his other hand placed limp-wristed on his hip, and gazed sexily at the door of the changing rooms. S/Sgt Sider was crouched menacingly in the undergrowth beneath the vaulting horse waiting to leap out and rape him, while Lieutenant George (as might be expected, I was playing a self appointed hero, with an MC already in the bag) placed himself precariously upon a wobbly bench.

"Gentlemen, good afternoon," I said, bowing to the Commandant and nearly toppling from the wretched thing. "You have been privileged to witness three superb displays of prowess at Unarmed Combat . . ."

"Hear, hear," came great cries of agreement, accompanied by a further derisory ripple of applause. They didn't think we stood a chance.

"Well, you are now about to witness another . . ."

"Ha, ha, ha," they guffawed in unison.

The instructors looked anxiously at the Commandant and were reassured to notice that he was smiling, which enabled them to relax a bit.

I continued.

"Unarmed Combat has its ancestry in various ancient Japanese forms of self defence. I would ask you now to imagine that this bloodstained mat you see before you is a jungle clearing on the island of Okinawa. The time is the early seventeenth century. Genghis Khan and his warring Mongol hordes have swept through the island . . . no I don't suppose it could have been Genghis Khan really, could it: look, on reflection it better not be Genghis Khan but, anyway, some equally fearsome warlord and his boys have been ravaging and pillaging the villages hereabouts and now he and his barbarian warriors are camped up there behind the wall bars (would you believe, some of them actually turned their heads to look) counting their ill gotten gains and drinking cups of horses' blood for tea. Sated with *saki* and beset with still unassuaged lust they require the services of a woman - stop fidgeting, Hoskins; your turn will come - so they have dispatched one of the more sober of their number to acquire a ripe young - stand *still*, Hoskins - virgin for their use. You see him now, leering out from over there behind the vaulting horse. Not Hoskins, the virgin: Staff Sergeant Sider, the forager in quest of Hoskins's body . . ."

Hoskins visibly clenched his buttocks beneath his judo pants. My spiel was getting to them. The Commandant, still a relatively young man, looked positively lascivious and kept crossing and uncrossing his legs and tapping his foot excitedly, while with a glazed expression the tattooed senior instructor seemed to be viewing Hoskins in something of a new light. He even looked as though he might be about to rush the young Gunner himself, which wasabsurd because he and his wife lived just down the road and he'd only been home for his lunch half-an-hour ago.

"Before you now, then, is an innocent young Japanese maiden guarding her flock by night . . . shut *up* Hoskins, we've already been through all that . . . unaware of the furtive figure drooling saliva down his chin over there and fondling himself in the brush. Let us now . . ."

Everyone cast a furtive glance at the Commandant, mistakenly thinking it was him I was referring to him, so Robin quickly picked up on this and kicked-in with some exaggerated drooling and fondling to draw their attention back to himself.

"Let us now see what happens . . .," I cried, snapping my fingers for Robin to leap into action. He shot from his position beneath the vaulting horse and promptly rolled over, clutching his left leg in anguish.

"Ayeeeee," he screamed.

It was very good and got their attention all right, but wasn't what we'd rehearsed. I realised I'd been talking so long that he'd got cramp. Fortunately it was only a momentary attack. He quickly rubbed his calf, stretched his prehensile toes a couple of times to twang the struts back into true, smiled a weak apology at me and then scurried off crabwise across the

195

mat to ravish the 'unsuspecting' Hoskins, who glanced distastefully over half a shoulder like a frightened rabbit and was already hunched in readiness for the surprise assault. Awaking from his slumber beside a medicine ball Yours Truly, Defender of the Faith then leapt onto the mat to intercept, but in doing so I turned my ankle and stubbed my big toe on the mat's wooden framework.

"Yarooooooo," I yelled, hopping about on one leg clutching my foot. (Would that I could do as much today).

Robin *Yaroooooood* back at me and lunged with his samurai sword (a piece of firewood we'd found on the floor of the changing room). I grabbed the razor sharp blade of this and divested him of it. From there on our display went without a hitch. We brought in and executed all the throws we'd been taught during the week. Hoskins was never actually raped - although for most people's money perhaps he should have been. Everybody loved us. The Commandant voted us the best, and after a cold shower Robin and I drove back to Bicester to sleep the weekend away with embrocation.

Mind you - God help anyone who'd tried to attack us on the way.

They wouldn't have stood an earthly!

EIGHTEEN

WHEN S/SGT SIDER and I limped back into the office on Monday morning, there was a newcomer present.

L/Cpl Brown had been posted to Germany a fortnight before. Now a frail looking, red headed young Yorkshireman who had especially asked if his next posting could be to a Youth Team, had arrived to take his place.

How deceiving some first impressions can be.

L/Cpl Dave Tate was going to turn out to be one of the grittiest, toughest, most robust, gutsiest, able and versatile individuals I have ever known.

I didn't realise it at the time, but formed up before me I now had the makings of one of the finest Unarmed Combat display teams in the country.

"Ever done judo before, C'orl Tate?"

"No sir, I haven't."

"I see," I said, pursing my lips and musing, "only we're a judo unit here, y'see." From the corner of my eye I could see Dick George and Guy Adams smile at each other. "It's pretty well our stock in trade, you know. Would you be prepared to have a stab at some?"

"Course I would, sir," he replied pleasantly, seemingly quite enthusiastically.

"Good: well what I suggest we do is that you and Corporal George use the gym each morning this week. Let him teach you the basics and put you through a few throws and things, then I'll come along and look at it all on Friday to see how you've been getting on. How's that sound?"

Dammit: if S/Sgt Sider and I had left shovelsful of spinal chippings strewn across the mat at Blandford, this youngster was jolly well going to go through the initiation mill as well.

It was now going to be a recognised and obligatory rite of passage before access to 31 AYT would be granted.

"Sounds great, sir. Can't wait to start."

He and Dick George promptly fell out to go and get themselves started in the gym, Guy Adams set to stripping and cleaning his film projector, and S/Sgt Sider strolled across to the NAAFI to purchase that day's supply of his essential support system - a Lyon's fruit pie, while I sat at my desk to draw up a few ideas I had for our new presentation.

Glancing through the diary I saw that Friday two weeks hence had been circled in red.

It was the Corps Boxing Championship that night, traditionally held there at Bicester each year.

31 AYT had been asked to put on a small judo display in the ring just before the interval.

Marvellous!

Two weeks.

Just the deadline and incentive we needed.

What a début it was going to be!

On Friday Robin Sider, Guy Adams and I went down to the gym to see how our L/Cpl Tate had been faring under Dick George's tutelage.

"He's a natural, sir," Dick George beamed. "We've had a terrific week. I've known people not learn so much in a year. Wait until you see this . . .!"

The two of them then launched themselves into an impressive three-minute workout that left me in no doubt whatsoever that our new boy was absolute mustard.

He had been sent to us by fate.

I was over the moon.

With this team I was absolutely confident that I could produce a really impressive display.

I was delighted.

"Right, now gather round and listen-in," I told them. "We've got just four days in which to get this new show together. I plan to have it ready for the Boxing Championship on Friday night." They all looked slightly askance. "Don't worry," I said. "With your skills and one or two ideas of my own, we can't fail. Now - I shall want you to acquire a few bits of kit as soon as possible. Here's the list: a bayonet; a .38 revolver with blank ammunition; capsules of theatrical blood; one black leather glove; an eye patch; a briefcase; a cudgel and some items of clothing I shall tell you about in due course. And one other thing before you go. There are only five people in the entire British Army with the surname George. I know that, because I've checked. It is bloody ridiculous that two of them should be serving here in the same five-man unit together, and I'm sick of wondering who's addressing who in this place . . . C'orl George . . .?"

"Sir?"

"For the remainder of our tour here you, my ol' buddy, will henceforth and hereinafter be affectionately known as Number Two. Alright?"

"Right, sir," he laughed. "Good idea."

"Of course it is," I said. "I thought of it . . . All of you back here at 14.00 then, please. We shall be rehearsing all afternoon, so don't have beans for lunch."

Army boxing is probably more rife with tradition even than fox hunting. Officers wear mess kit, smoke cigars and quaff brandy while their charges slug it out with each other like pit bulls in the garishly illuminated ring.

It is blood sport impure and simple.

I was sitting next to Major Bob Hoy on one of the tiered seats specially constructed for the event on the stage of the Graven Hill Theatre, looking down at the ring that had been erected in the well.

Stretching back towards the entrances at the rear, the theatre's normal seats were enveloped in a pall of blue tobacco smoke slowly wafting in spiralling eddies of wandering contentment. Despite the extractor fans in the roof the heads of the senior ranks and soldiers sitting there were still shrouded, as if they were a field of mushrooms in a low lying mist, but not quite so fresh.

It was a stag evening.

A male rite.

Perhaps a naked sex goddess slipping astride a glistening Nubian stud on the canvas beneath the floodlights to the beat of tom-toms would not have gone amiss, but the presence of any other woman, be it even the Colonel's lady, would have been more out of place than an uncircumcised Christian in a Jewish harem.

As it happened there *was* a glistening black stud on the canvas. L/Cpl Thomas from the Regimental Depot had just been put there by Pte Walonsky of the Ammunition Depot at Bramley in the middle of their third round. Thomas was out for the count, but he had gone down fighting. Walonskey's face was a shiny mask of blood from the heavy cut he had received above his left eye. He was declared the winner, was sponged down and skipped deftly out of the ring, waving his clenched fists in the air and joshing with his mates along the aisles to the changing rooms.

The ring was now clear.

It was the interval.

Our turn.

31 AYT was on.

Rachel always told me I looked gorgeous in my mess kit and spurs. It was one of her turn-ons. (Seeing me in it, that is; not telling me about it).

In 1965 I had been serving with the RASC.

In July that year the Mcleod reorganisation of the Q services decreed that certain aspects of RASC/RAOC should be merged, transferred or taken over.

I was one of those aspects.

I had received a letter asking me if I would like to go across to RAOC or remain with the newly formed RCT (Royal Corps of Transport).

I opted for the latter, only to receive another letter saying that my application for transfer to the RAOC had been approved.

Deciding it would not be politic to kick up more fuss, I did as I was told for once.

Unfortunately it meant relinquishing my silver spurs, they not being a feature of the RAOC's dress regulations. Rachel missed my spurs too, but the bum-hugging, thigh-clinging, red-striped overalls still seemed to work her juices quite well.

As I stood up from my seat and walked carefully down the steps towards the ring it was impossible to be adjudged especially elegant by my peers. All of us being in the same regimental boat and clad in the same kit would have required a matchless feat for any of our number to have stood out or overly impressed any of the others. After all, this was Bicester - not Berlin. In Berlin we used to wear mess kit to go beyond the Wall to the East German side to attend the opera. Our regalia on those memorable gala evenings would blow the East German mind something rotten. It made *us* feel pretty good too. There was no way anything like that was going to happen tonight though.

A REME major had one of his elegantly tapered legs crossed over the other as I passed the bottom aisle. The mirror-like gloss on his Mess wellingtons gleamed heroically in the artificial glare. Darts of light flashed from his right spur rowel as he revolved it indolently with the toe of his left boot and flicked cigar ash onto the matting beside him. Bloody REME, I thought to myself as I passed. Shouldn't be allowed to wear spurs. Should wear spokes.

Reaching the ring I climbed up its three stumpy steps to clamber beneath the ropes. Several people glanced afresh at their programmes to see if it told them why Mike George had suddenly decided to appear in the ring like this. Oh yes - says it here, look - a judo display? In his mess kit? Daft pillock. Give me a light please, Charles, there's a good chap; bloody thing keeps going out.

The microphone hung before me, suspended on a wire from heaven. I reached up and drew it down to my face like an overhead electric shaver. If anything went wrong and the boys fouled up, the next five minutes could turn out to be the worst of my life so far.

"Brigadier; gentlemen - good evening," I said, but conversation continued unabated. How rude of them. No one was taking a blind bit of notice of me. I know I was still only a subaltern, but *toujours la politesse* just the same. I flushed and felt cross and silly, shuffled a bit and then noticed the pressel switch on the mic. My fault: I'd forgotten to press it. *"Thank God,"* I whispered, and my voice boomed out over the auditorium.

That got their attention alright.

"What's this then, a revivalist meeting?" someone yelled from the swaying mass surrounding me on all sides.

"Brigadier; gentlemen - good evening," I said, cracking on. Gosh - I sounded like Richard Burton in a paddy in Notre Dame. This could get good. Conversation had stilled to a silence. They were all sitting up and paying attention now. I was being taken seriously. Life had become quite fun all of a sudden.

"We have just witnessed five magnificent bouts with the gloves gentlemen, but although traditionally British, boxing, as you will be aware, is not the only form of aggression or self defence that one can employ. Your programme will show that in contrast you are about to enjoy a short display of judo. In fact you are not . . ."

"Bring on the dancing girls then!"

It was the same damned anonymous voice from over on the left somewhere. I'd kill the funny bastard if only I knew who he was, but I flashed a false smile round the assembly to show I could take that kind of thing and that it was water off a duck's back.

"No, there is no cancellation gentlemen, nor I'm afraid do we have any dancing girls for my fruity friend down there. What we do have for you instead though is a breathtaking display of unarmed combat . . ." I paused to allow a sigh of collective ecstasy to rent the air. None came, so I pressed on: "so who *are* these Bicester exponents of the impressive and

202

lethal art of unarmed combat? I'll tell you gentlemen, shall I? It is the men of 31 Army Youth Team . . . in other words . . . it is MEN - *SUCH AS THESE!"*

A pre-zeroed spotlight leapt to life and glaringly pinned Dick George crouched like Spiderman 30-feet up in the eaves beneath the roof of the theatre, dressed completely in black and wearing an eyepatch, with a diamanté-free black leather glove on his left hand. As he launched himself into space and came plunging down the previously rigged death slide to land in the ring beside me, every speaker in the house burst to life with the opening bars of the resounding James Bond theme.

So far so good.

Everything was going impressively to plan.

The music quieted and I continued my award winning introductory spiel.

"I would ask you now to imagine that this is no longer a boxing ring you see before you here. It is now, in fact, the slimy, slippery deck of a hostile submarine that has just surfaced off the coast of Iceland. On board there are two unsuspecting Eastern Bloc agents who will be emerging from below deck at any moment to row ashore and destroy the new atomic plant at Reykjavik. Unbeknown to them, however, they are to be foiled. Why? How? Because just winched down by helicopter beside me now is that fearless British agent *extraordinaire*, Corporal Dick 'Sailor'-'One-Eye'-'Black Hand' George - my Number Two. Gentlemen . . . *LET BATTLE COMMENCE."*

The James Bond theme smashed into the auditorium once more before fading. I let myself quickly out beneath the ropes, and dressed in their best 'commies going ashore in Iceland' rig Guy Adams and Dave Tate skipped into the ring from below deck and started piling into Dick George. Revolver blanks were fired; bayonet thrusts deflected; cudgel blows warded off; theatrical blood sacks were scrunched between gnashing teeth to burst nauseatingly by the pint down each of their chins. This exquisite ballet of mock death unfurled with thudding body blows, excruciating arm locks and terrifying overhead launches effected by grabbing the opponent's lapels, placing one foot in his groin and toppling over backwards, taking him with you while kicking upwards and releasing him to send him hurling on overhead in what in the trade is commonly known as a Flying Mare. Then the speakers crackled to life once more and the eager voice of S/Sgt Robin Sider (until then contentedly munching mouthfuls of his favourite Lyons fruit pie up in the box) bellowed in an atrocious Bronx accent from out of the darkness: "Okay yous guys. Knock it off, I say. This is the CIA. Put up your hands. We've got you covered by satellite from up here. If you don' wanna be 'nylated just pick up your toys, climb down off that submarine and make your way quickly to the toilets situated at the back of the theatre. We thank you, gen'lemen. The show is now over."

They applauded.

We were launched.

For the remainder of that year we spent most of our time demonstrating unarmed combat everywhere.

Very quickly, though, I realised that I would have to devise another programme, for our open air performances.

The Boy Scout Jamboree had been underway for a week, camped alongside an airfield 'somewhere in southern England'.

It was Sunday.

The final day.

31 AYT had just rolled up in our vehicles to give our now renowned demonstration of Unarmed Combat, which was to be the *pièce de résistance* of the whole jamboree. (C'mon; weren't you a boy once?)

Seventy-five square yards of grass had been roped off to accommodate us.

We lay a quarter-of-a-mile off, engines idling behind some bushes.

"LADIES AND GENTLEMEN . . ." the speakers boomed out round the scout-thronged airfield. *"May I have your attention please? An urgent message has just been received from Scotland Yard's Special Branch . . ."* We knew the whole crowd of spectators would be grinning eagerly from ear to ear

31 AYT, Bicester, Oxon – 1966 L-R **L/Cpl Dave Tate;**
Cpl Guy Adams; **L/Cpl Dick 'Black Hand' George;**
Sgt Chandler; **S/Sgt Robin Sider;** Author

APTC Judo/Unarmed Combat
Course, Blandford Camp, Dorset
– 1966. Author second from left,
middle row; S/Sgt Sider, fourth
from left, middle row. Pte
Hoskins, first rear left

'Black Hand' 'does' for
Dave Tate's nose

'Black Hand'
smashes Tate

Author – making to rip out
'Black Hand's' black heart

as my recorded tape played over the speakers. My taped voice continued: "An extremely dangerous Eastern Bloc spy has just escaped from London with a briefcase containing top secret documents vital to the security of this nation. He is reported to be heading in this direction, closely pursued by a multi-rigged spy-busting unit. *Aha* - here they come now."

The familiar James Bond theme burst across the airfield and 31 AYT was 'on' once more.

Wearing a brown trilby, sunglasses and a dark suit I switched on the headlights to full beam, gunned my shocking pink Vauxhall Cresta with its joke bullet holes stuck across the windscreen forwards to bucket out from behind some trees and across the field towards the crowds circling our arena, closely followed by our minibus (*sans* mattresses in the back) careening in hot pursuit with Guy Adams hanging onto the roof rack for dear life with one hand while with the other loosing off a blaze of 7.62 rifle blanks at my fleeing exhaust. Skidding to a carefully contrived stop at the far side of the roped off area I leapt from my car, crouched behind its open door and let off a hail of revolver shots at the minibus as it slewed round and braked. Dick 'Black Hand' George, Guy Adams and Dave Tate piled out of it led by Robin Sider clutching a megaphone. Robin commanded the crowd not to be alarmed and instructed me, the infamous communist spy Dickybar Tomski, to lay down my arms and surrender, in response to which I hurled a thunderflash at him, the power of which should never be underestimated. Those things go off with more force than a thousand bangers in one lump. A small hole appeared in the ground, the smoke cleared, dogs howled and a mean *Randoori* then ensued.

Robin Sider was a well built chap. He was the tallest member of our team. After the general shenanigan of throwing each other about on the grass for a bit, he meaningfully (implied menace, you see) stripped off his shirt, hurled it aside, and then switching open the glinting blade of a very large flick knife, moved purposefully towards me for the kill as I lay there wounded and twitching in the grass. I *was* twitching, too; that bastard Tate had thrown me right into the middle of a nettle patch just as I'd been in the process of happily breaking his neck, Adams's back and George's skull in three fell swoops.

It was not just for the pleasure of seeing the hair on Sider's pectorals that we'd persuaded him to do his Burt Reynolds bit. As he drew back his arm to hurl the knife to embed it in my body, I let rip our final salvo of small arms blank into his gut.

"Ahaaaaaaaaaaaaa," he screamed (just like he did at Blandford the day he'd got cramp) dropping the knife and clawing both hands to his stomach while frantically trying to burst ten blood capsules in his fists, so that a scarlet deluge flooded him in a gory finale. The *real* reason he'd taken his shirt off was simply because his wife Jeanette had refused to wash them any more.

He keeled over beside me, and the show was done.

Applause rippled round the arena like a *feu de joie*. Everyone was delighted; all except one little boy: he cried when we all stood up and he realised we'd been cheating.

Little sod.

Hadn't even had to pay to get in.

When we'd cleaned ourselves up with grass to wipe the blood away, we strolled across to the main marquee where the Scout Commissioner had invited us for tea. To get there we walked across the airstrip, along the edge of which the scouts had pitched their tents in smart regimental lines. Running equidistant the length of the runway was a series of black and yellow striped steel cone markers. I had been wiping off the blood and cleaning the blade of the flick knife as we walked. This complete I closed it and dropped it into the thigh pocket of my trousers, and realised I had a thunderflash left.

"Fellahs - we've still got a thunderflash," I said. Gleefully, irresponsibly, and completely without thinking I pulled its striker tab and popped it under one of the steel cones as we passed.

Oh, would that I had thought about it first.

I kept forgetting just how powerful those damn things were.

They are not fireworks.

They're for real.

207

"Christ," said Sider.

"Oh, shit," said Adams.

"Keep walking," said Tate.

"Too late," said Number Two.

The explosion, when it came, was frightening.

Accentuated by the steel cone it made our ears ring horrendously.

Not only that, but it whanged the steel cone flat as a sheet and sent it soaring forcefully 40-feet up into the wide blue yonder, where it seemed to hover like a shining UFO for a few seconds to attract everyone's attention before commencing its lethal descent. It came slicing back down sideways like a stray guillotine blade despatched by catapult.

It couldn't have thudded harmlessly into a grass tuft, could it?

Nor even clatter noisily onto the airstrip.

Admittedly, it didn't decapitate anyone, and I was extremely grateful for that, but it taught me one hell of a lesson.

It completely wiped out a tent.

Cut right through it.

Demolished it.

"That's my tent. Look what you've done to my tent," wailed a justifiably distressed and indignant Queen's Scout who had come rushing across all of a tremble, a little hesitant about complaining because he didn't know if it had been meant to have been done on purpose because we were the heroes of the hour and could do no wrong.

It must have been like discovering your favourite film star's a shit.

"Okay, old lad," I grinned placatingly, trying to sound less concerned and more cheerful than I was. "Don't you worry; we'll sort out it for you."

"Somehow."

"Shut up, Tate," I growled, scowling at him, but smiling reassuringly once more to the palpitating Queen's Scout, grubbing about inspecting his desecrated piece of canvas that looked like an air-smash in a wood. Apparently the tent had been a birthday present from his hard working dad only the previous week.

Okay. I felt bad about it.

Right?

"That was quite an impressive display you gave us." the Commissioner smiled as he passed the sugar.

"Yes; I'm sorry about the tent," I said. "But I assure you'll we'll make it good. We'll get him a new one."

"Oh, I'm sure you will," said the kindly old scouter. "But I was referring solely to your display of unarmed combat of course."

I'm sure there was a twinkle in his eye.

It took a fortnight of concentrated wrangling to convince the Claims Commission that it had been an accident, but we did eventually manage to get the good old Queen's Scout a nice new tent.

Because it was my own independent command 31 AYT was probably one of the best postings I ever had in the Army. They were a great bunch of lads and we got along famously together. When my tour with them came to an end I was next sent to Hanover, in Germany. For the next 40 years (and to date) the first Christmas card I receive each year is from Robin Sider. He went on to be commissioned and finished his military life as a major. Later on he was to enter local politics, where he lives, at Shepperton, and although it sounds like the name of a TV series he then became the Mayor of Spelthorne.

The other lads spread to the four winds, but then . . .

. . . one Saturday morning, in 1994, when my then second wife, Diane, and I were living in Torquay, I was turning the pages of the *Daily Mail* only to came across the happy smiling faces of the now 50-year old David and Sandra Tate, accompanying a half page article about them both - and then I remembered . . .

One day back in 1966 David had come into the office, saluted smartly, as he always did, and said: "There y'go, sir; what do you think of that?" and handing me a five-inch high fibre resin model he'd made the previous night of one of the

Queen's Beasts, the ten heraldic statues depicting the genealogy of Queen Elizabeth II commissioned by the Ministry of Works from the sculptor James Woodford RA, to stand in front of the temporary annexe to Westminster Abbey for the Coronation, in 1953.

The original Beasts were some six-foot high and the sculptor was paid the sum of £2,750. They were cast in plaster and could not therefore be left in the open air.

After the Coronation they were removed to the Great Hall in Hampton Court Palace, and in 1957 were relocated to St George's Hall at Windsor Castle.

The Beasts were taken into storage in April 1958 whilst their future was considered.

It was eventually decided to offer them to the Commonwealth Governments, and Canada being the senior nation was offered them first.

In June 1959 Canada accepted the Beasts and they were shipped there in July.

Originally the only part of the statues to be coloured was their heraldic shields, but for the celebrations of the Canadian federation in 1967 the Beasts were painted in their heraldic colours.

They are now in the care of the Canadian Museum of Civilisation in Ottawa.

In 1958 Sir Henry Ross, Chairman of the Distillers Company, Edinburgh paid for Portland stone replicas of these statues, which are on display outside the Palm House at Kew Gardens.

What *are* these Beasts?

The Lion of England; the Griffin of Edward III; the Falcon of the Plantagenets; The Black Bull of Clarence; The Yale of Beaufort (the yale was a mythical beast, said to be white in colour and covered with gold spots. Its peculiar characteristic was that it could swivel each of its horns independently. It descends to the Queen through Henry VII, who inherited it from his mother, Lady Margaret Beaufort); the White Lion of Mortimer; The White Greyhound of Richmond; The Red

Dragon of Wales; The Unicorn of Scotland - and the White Horse of Hanover.

The beasts have been commemorated in bone china figurines, cups and saucers, glass tray sets, plaster models, porcelain candlesticks, British postage stamps issued in 1998, silver tea spoons and tea towels.

One of them, the Griffin of Edward III, is a legendary creature with the body of a lion and the head and often wings of an eagle. As the lion was traditionally considered the king of the beasts and the eagle the king of the birds, the griffin was thought to be an especially powerful and majestic creature. Griffins are normally known for guarding treasure. In antiquity it was a symbol of divine power and a guardian of the divine.

It was a five-inch model of Edward III's Griffin that David had made, and, appropriately, I now realise, in view of this provenance and symbolism, which both of us were completely unaware of at the time, asked if *I* would like to keep.

"Corporal Tate, I'd *love* to," I said. "I think this is excellent. You really ought to do more of these."

Although at the time I had no idea that he would do so, apparently he must have taken me at my word.

The 1994 *Daily Mail* article I was reading in Torquay?

It reported that David had just sold his company - *Lilliput Lane* - to an American outfit, for £37m.

Based at Penrith, in Cumbria, and founded by him in 1982, cast in Amorphite from wax and silicone moulds, David's was the company that produced (and still does) those exquisitely detailed miniature hand painted cottages and historic buildings you can buy at H. Samuel the jeweller, and many other outlets.

I was over the moon with excitement when I read it.

The boy done good.

I promptly sat down and wrote him a letter:

Dear David; About that fiver you owe me . . .

He sent me a charming reply (no fiver) and eight years later, when I drove up to Penrith for my niece's wedding there, I was able to stay with David and Sandra at their beautiful Garth House in nearby Brampton, when we embraced like long

211

lost brothers, and are now both firmly back on each other's Christmas list.

And that original five-inch griffin?

It still sits beside me now, on my desk, as it has always done, since 1966.

NINETEEN

STEPHEN WATTS WAS a six-foot-three Royal Marine Commando who adored climbing things.

I was a five-foot-eight logistician who didn't.

One weekend he asked if I would care to join him.

This time, it was Mount Snowdon.

"Id rather go to the pictures?" I said.

That was not to be.

Stephen was a great big hairy honky.

He got his kicks from stretched, wet, damp, creaking bones, humping overweight back-packs up cliff faces, and the possibility of death. 'S alright, I thought: it'll be character building and good for my soul: I'll go.

With Stephen you didn't just *go* to Snowdon.

It was none of your jeans and an anorak, trainers and a flask, with sandwiches.

It was Everest revisited.

We trained for three weeks.

WE TRAINED FOR THREE WEEKS . . .

. . . every night we could be seen sloshing through cowpats around the byways of Ambrosden, he well to the fore, me shuffling along trying to keep up at the rear. I was fit; but Stephen was supra-fit: or perhaps he was just really fit, and I wasn't.

The third Friday of the month dawned, and after work that afternoon - we went.

We took a Land Rover.

We had loaded all our kit into this vehicle the night before, and by 18.00 were drive-shafting our way up the left-hand side of England. We stopped at the Junior Leaders' Regiment Mess at Oswestry for dinner that night, and then continued left into Welsh Wales.

Stephen was a member of some climbing club that owned a cottage in Bethesda.

It sounded fun; scones and a log fire with a Blodwyn harping, but this was not to be.

The cottage was a stone-built, dripping wet, green-slimed stag-pad, the sort in which sodden and starving PoWs escaping over the hills from Bulgaria would have been pleased to seek refuge.

Open market value?

£137.50.

Plenty of fresh running water though.

We arrived at 22.30.

Unpacking a couple of cans of the Army compo rations we had brought with us, we smashed them open on a bayonet and heated them up, sausage and beans, on one of the hexamine cookers.

After a night in our sleeping bags on bare bedsprings, we left the cottage at 07.00 next morning and drove to the foot of Snowdon, where we parked the Land Rover at the Pen-y-gwryd Hotel and set off.

It was a crystal clear day.

Like John Cleese attacking foothills, Stephen leapt long-leggedly off to the fore, placed his size-13 boot into one small toe-hold and heaved himself effortlessly up by a fingertip.

I followed suit, and broke a nail.

By the time I'd quelled my shock wave, sucked the end of my finger and carefully got ready for the next step, I saw Stephen already proudly poised on an overhanging bluff from where he peered down at me like some curious mountain goat silhouetted against the cerulean sky, and hailed me heartily from his position up there in seventh heaven:

"You all right, Mike?"

"Never better: just broke a nail though."

"Is that all? *Shaaaame.* Come on then, shake a leg or we'll never get started."

I batted one eyelid, and he was gone. A moment later I heard him round a corner hammering pitons into the rock face with the speed of a rivet gun. By the time I'd laboriously made my way up to that first bluff I could see him 100-feet above me acknowledging a small eagle that had emerged curiously from its eyrie.

"You all right?" he cried back jovially again. Sadistic bastard. He must have known I wasn't. He must have known that I was already sweating and sore, that my woollen shirt was chafing my shoulder blades and I was feeling nauseous.

"Fine, thanks," I hollered.

Perhaps if I fell and killed myself he'd be sorry and it might prey on his mind and spoil the rest of his day.

I banged one of my own pitons in, and hit my thumb.

At 11.00 I wearily crested an overhang to find Stephen perched above it on a small slab of rock enjoying an al fresco coffee morning with four robust girls who had obviously ascended via another route.

"Hi, Mike: have a Kit Kat," he cried, his mouth full of chocolate wafer.

"In a moment, thanks. Let me get my breath back first."

What I craved more than anything was a cigarette.

Fumbling in my breast pocket I withdrew one from the pack.

This was what TV adverts were about.

What a heroic dash I must have cut, squatting casually up there half way on top of the world, rugged and ready for a drag.

"Cigarette?" I asked, proffering the pack to everyone.

There was stunned silence.

They each looked at each other, amazed, and tried to edge away.

"No thank you," said the prettiest of them, with slightly uncalled for disdain I thought.

"Disgusting habit," another added.

Oh, well; wrong again, Mike. Shrugging my shoulders I struck a match. In the clear mountain air the sulphur whanged right up everyone's nostrils, nearly lifting the tops of their heads off.

"It's time for us to be getting along I think," said Girl Leader commandingly, and stood up just as I exhaled my first waft of lung-warping blue smoke, the possible cause of a passing buzzard suddenly falling from the sky on collapsed wings.

"Why did you have to go and do that?" Stephen asked, miffed.

"Don't be ridiculous. It was someone down there in the valley, with an airgun."

"I mean the women. Why scare them off like that?"

"Never you mind," I assured him. "Two strides and you can be up there waiting for them at the top, straddling the summit with legs akimbo and hands on hips like the Jolly Green Giant, can't you."

"Guess so," he said, thinking I meant it. With a surge of rattling equipment resettling itself in his pack he moved off on another fast ascent, soon disappearing from view again.

When eventually I caught up with him I found him with a wizened old mountain man, and together they were swinging a third party round a buttress on the end of a piece of rope.

"Hi," I called, coming abreast. "It's me."

Stephen's sweating brow was furrowed with the effort of trying to prevent the reckless mid-air dangler from plummeting to a mushy demise down Snowdon's most jagged side.

"Aha," cackled the old mountain man, spinning round to acknowledge my arrival. "The rest of the Army."

"How d'y'do," I said, bowing slightly.

"Mike, belay yourself to Sydney," Stephen shouted without glancing from his task. "We're going to absail down to that lower edge, and then go round and upwards from there."

"Sorry; y'what . . .?"

"I must say," Sydney interjected, "it's jolly reassuring to come across both you well trained, fit and able young Army chaps up here - especially on such a tricky stretch as this."

I gulped. What, sir? Me, sir? No, sir!

"Come along Mike, for Pete's sake shake a leg." Stephen was now back in the perpendicular, knots falling out of his fingers while he tied sheep-shanks and bow-lines in a hawser with the dexterity and speed of a woman knitting.

"Are we in some sort of hurry?" I asked, naively.

"Bloody right we are," he snapped huffily.

"'Fraid so," said Sydney. "Perhaps you've not heard, but we're expecting a sudden drop in temperature and some heavy snow."

"Oh, shit," I said.

"Pardon?" said Sydney.

"Er . . . nothing: what's it you want me to do, Stephen?"

It started to snow.

My fingers all went numb.

I became cold and miserable.

Stephen's challenge, and that of Sydney and his dangly friend Johnathon, was to reach the summit.

Mine was survival.

Against all the odds we each achieved our respective goals and at 16.00 finally heaved ourselves exhausted on to Snowdon's highest point.

"Aha - isn't that *marvellous*," Sydney sighed, inhaling great drafts of pure clean air which he exhaled with an equally beatific expression suffusing his glowing countenance.

"It most certainly is," his friend Johnathon agreed. "Just look at that magnificent view."

Stephen wasn't interested. He'd seen it before and was coiling rope like an overworked cowboy sorting lariats, while I hugged myself like some kid busting for a pee.

View?

There were two views.

There were the grey sky, snow, sleet and a Welsh valley far below, out of which we'd so doggedly been climbing all day, and then fifty yards behind us there was a tea chalet with people gathered round it; gaily clad girls; a tarmac road . . . and a railway.

I'd been conned.

"I say . . . Stephen?" I tugged lightly at his busily bobbing sleeve, "Have you seen, over there are . . ."

"We civilians don't get the same opportunities you Army chaps do to enjoy all this good, clean, healthy fresh air life," Sydney boomed, slipping off his rucksack and fumbling with its straps. "Well -? What say we have a brew and something to eat now, shall we?"

"Good idea," we agreed.

Eagerly I took five steps towards the road and the tea chalet and the girls before realising that no one was following me.

Stephen was taking a hexamine cooker out of his rucksack and breaking hardtack biscuits into a mess tin, over which he was pouring meat balls and gravy from a compo tin, while Sydney and Johnathon were similarly engaged with their own little burner, brewing up some evil looking tea with tinned milk in it while using their bodies to shield the spluttering flames from the wind.

This was fun?

They certainly seemed to think so.

It has been said that the sort of people who win gallantry awards are usually those with the least imagination.

They did not even see the small outpost of civilisation fifty yards ahead, or if they did it had as much substance as a mirage.

Not for me though.

"There's a tea wagon over there." I pointed out hopefully.

Sydney nodded, deigning to cast it a glance. "Poor soft-bellied buggers, eh. Bet they wish they were more like us."

"Rugged," said Johnathon.

"Buggered," I put in, for the lightheaded hell of it.

"Exactly," said Stephen, not hearing. "Still, we mustn't mock. It's not their fault. We should feel sorry for them."

It was happening, this conversation.

They were serious.

They believed every word they uttered, hunkered on that blasted slab of windswept rock, pairing their nails and digging out calluses with a blunt bayonet.

What was I to do?

Join them?

Or beat them?

I was cold, damp, tired and miserable.

I'd had enough.

I wanted to go down on that little railway train, have a mug of hot, sweet tea and a bath, a Swedish massage, and a feather bed.

Fat chance.

My heroic trio were probably awaiting nightfall when we could all lower each other down by rope in the dark.

Or jump.

What *was* I?

A man, or a mouse?

No, I was *me*, dammit: a person of my own, and this wasn't my scene.

I would make my stand.

"If you fellows don't mind I think I'm just going to nip across to get myself a sticky bun or something."

They stopped what they were doing and stared at me, puzzled.

I edged away, turned my back and walked quickly across towards the warmth of human companionship, with each step expecting to feel myself dragged back to the cliff edge by my ankles on the end of a piece of coarse rope and told: "Mike, you don't seem to understand the rules."

Either that, or have an unerringly aimed piton thud between my shoulder blades to bring me to heel.

I purchased my bun and hot drink and turned from the chalet to see people climbing aboard the little mountain train, getting ready for its return trip to the bottom.

To firm my resolve I bought myself a ticket and went back to tell the others what I was doing.

"Hurry up, Mike," Stephen called as I got near. "We're going to start our descent."

They must have turned chicken.

It wasn't even dark yet.

"Stephen . . ." I said, having devised a good and cowardly way to do this. "I didn't want to mention it to you, but on the way up I was having a bit of trouble with my knee. Rather than hold any of you up on the return, I've decided it would be better if I went down on the train."

"Gosh Mike; what a noble gesture." He smiled. "I'd noticed you lagging a bit and wondered if there might be something wrong that you were keeping from us. But we can't let you sacrifice yourself like that. Heavens, no. We'll take it in turns to carry you."

Christ, I thought: was there *no* getting away from it with this lot?

"Stephen, no - it simply wouldn't be fair. I appreciate your offer, really I do, but I'd feel much better doing it my way."

"Alright Mike, if you insist - we'll see you back at the Land Rover in a couple of hours then. Our descent should be fairly fast. If you're going on that little train though, you'd better hurry. It looks as if it's just leaving."

It was too.

God - more than my life was worth to miss it.

Effecting a hastily contrived limp, I hurried as fast as I dared to the railway and managed to clamber aboard just in time.

From the step I turned to wave, but they had their stooped backs to me, re-buckling their ruck-sacks.

They resembled three well-intentioned Manchurian shamans cloaked in the rites of some mythical cult of hardship, carving a pilgrims' way across the tall, frozen places of the Earth.

Down from the mountaintop at last, the lights of the Pen-y-gwryd Hotel beckoned me like those of a caravanserai, but the warmth, relief, succour and gluwein of the twentieth century bettered one-hundredfold the yaks' milk curd that earlier travellers might have enjoyed at just such an establishment.

When Stephen, Johnathon and Sydney reappeared some indeterminate time later, tired, drawn and weary, they found me stretched out supine and mellow on a banquette in the Alpine Room, contemplating the glass covered

Hunt/Hillary/Tensing signatures scrawled across the ceiling from when they'd trained at Snowdonia back in the early 1950s, prior to their epic Everest achievement.

That evening we all went out to sample the pub delights of Bethesda, and then turned in early.

During the night I dreamed I was on a rack in a dungeon being stretched and pummelled by three malevolent mountaineers. My subconscious computer was sifting, rifting and taking stock, giving me an all over body check. It was something we had been promising ourself all day, me, myself and I, that when rest came that night we would carry out this arithmetic of ills. In the morning I would awaken to be presented with the bill and be magisterially told what compensation was due for the misuse and abuse to which the whole machine had been so rudely subjected.

Ironically, it was my right knee.

Swollen like a football.

The whole of me was so stiff I was all but locked rigid, but when I swung my right leg to the floor it felt like a loose pendulum seeking purchase in a quagmire.

It had no intention of soldiering that morning.

I tried to stand, but it was no use.

The knee felt like a wet lump of *papier mâché* pulp that had been living in a drain and then encased in chicken wire, stuffed into an old sock and been bashed against an outhouse wall.

I fell against the six-foot table in the middle of the cottage's communal sleeping room, and groaned.

"Wassup?" Stephen asked, drying shaving soap from his ears with a smelly green towel as he came up the back steps from having washed in the cold mountain stream outside.

"Leg's packed up," I muttered, prodding gently at the mush beneath the tautened skin.

"Mmmmm; doesn't look too good, does it," Stephen agreed, bending over to look while vigorously drying his crew-cut with his towel. "Doesn't look like *you'll* be doing any climbing today, old chum."

I had to agree with him.

"I'm sorry, Stephen. I really seem to have ballsed up the weekend for you."

"Not at all." He grinned. "We always make provision for casualties in this game, y'know. You managed the best part of yesterday and enjoyed that all right."

"Oh, yes," I said. "I did. It was splendid. Enjoyed it immensely."

The rest of that Sunday I spent huddled in the Land Rover reading Harold Robbins, while in concert with other like-minded people to whom circumstance had introduced him, Stephen stopped the vehicle and volunteered to take part in a mountain rescue operation that was underway.

While he was up there strapping some other luckless sod to a stretcher, I had opportunity to appraise my ills.

I knew it wasn't solely Snowdon that had floored me.

Ever since Korea I had suffered a certain weakness in my knees. I was convinced it had been acquired in my late teens, living a physically demanding military existence, lugging ammo boxes up beleaguered mountain passes, sleeping in damp clothing in snow-filled trenches in sub-zero temperatures, and eating too many biscuits. Despite the resilience of youth, some things had inevitably been compromised whilst in the very process of developing. In my case? My Achilles' knees. They were my weak spot, and Snowdon had now got to one of them.

Eventually Stephen returned and we were able to hit the road back to Bicester. We got home at 23.00 and my God that Bath and that Bed were so beautiful. Rachel was a bit choked that all that throbbed was my leg, but she understood, bless her, and allowed me to fall asleep immediately.

Ever since then I've contented myself with hill walking in the shallow end.

TWENTY

"YES, IT DOES LOOK A BIT 'iffy' doesn't it," Lionel Henderson, the unit MO said next morning, prodding the oedema that was my knee. "We'll send you over to Princess Mary's, the RAF hospital at Halton and let them give you some physio for it."

Three mornings a week for the next month I was to drive across to RAF Halton, at Wendover, near Aylesbury.

Three mornings a week I was strapped up, wired up, heated up and made to lift bricks with my toes in what soon transpired to have been a vain endeavour to avert the knife.

A month after we'd started, the physio admitted defeat, the surgeon rubbed his hands, and I shrugged.

I simply wanted to get the bloody thing sorted.

I was admitted.

As wards go it wasn't at all bad.

In fact compared with mixed NHS wards today, it was *The Ritz*.

Nodding introductory greetings to those who were present and awake as I limped past, I found the bed that had been allocated to me half way down on the right hand side and dumped my grip on its neatly tautened cover. Apart from slippers, toothbrush and a comb, all I seemed to have brought with me was two ballpoint pens and a ream of paper.

"What is your mission, sir? To rewrite *War and Peace?*"

I spun round to find a pretty little Canadian nurse offering me a bottle and nodding at the loo, thereby instantly putting the mockers on any further romance between us.

"Sample, please," she said. "Hurry up and I'll shake it for you."

"That'd be nice."

"Your bedcover, sir. And when you've done your Jimmy Riddle I would be grateful if you'd put that cumbersome grip of yours into the cupboard over there, please? This is a hospital, not a troopship. I'll be back to take your temperature in a minute."

Holding the tiddly widdle-bottle gently between my forefinger and thumb I set off towards the lavatory.

"Hallo."

Stopping in mid stride to see who had spoken, my gaze traversed an apparition. A hospital bed is a hospital bed and the Hammersmith Flyover, then under construction, was the Hammersmith Flyover, but somehow or other the two together had produced a hybrid progeny that stood before me now in all its glory . . .

In the top right hand corner . . .

Up by the Day Room of Ward 7, in the RAF Hospital at Halton, near Ayelesbury, Buckinghamshire, in November 1966.

And the sight of it caused my mind to flash back . . .

When we'd been living in Salisbury two years previously, Rachel had befriended a nearby farmer called Harry Packet who kept his dairy herd just opposite our home beside the River Avon.

Harry and I used to sink the occasional jar together, and it was during one of our sessions that he told me about an RAF friend of his called Tony Svensson.

Apparently Tony had been the light of Harry's service years and the original gay blade before the meaning of the word was changed.

He was forever relating to me tales of Tony's happy-go-lucky lifestyle.

One yarn he told was the occasion Tony had been thrown from his horse, which had then galloped off towards Cornwall. Roaring back to Boscombe Down, Tony had got himself

224

airborne and gone jet-hopping the hedgerows of Wiltshire in search of his wayward steed, while maintaining air-to-ground radio-relay with his friends in the pursuing horse box.

"I'd love you both to meet each other one day," Harry said. "You'd get on like a house on fire."

"Where is he now?"

"Last time I heard? Australia. He was test flying the new French *Mirage* out there . . ."

"Hallo," I said. "What the hell happened to you then? Smack into the moon?"

It looked as if a foraging patrol had gone round to each building site in the area to knock-off scaffolding, clamps and pipe welding equipment and then got Heath Robinson to build the contraption at which I was now gazing with such incredulity.

They'd then put a bronzed, cheerful, good looking basket case right in the middle of it and tipped the contents of a dustbin over him.

He was sitting up in this bed surrounded by apple cores, winches, and empty Mackeson bottles; pullies, a portable typewriter, a small scattered pile of soft-porn magazines strewn about, and some other things far too horrible to mention in an area where ladies may have dared to be sauntering unannounced.

"Name's Mike George," I said, unconsciously offering him my widdle-bottle before noticing he had a much bigger one of his own slurping into the half empty fruit bowl, chokker with sweet wrappers.

"I'm Tony Svensson."

Whereupon he shifted on one buttock to let a fart rip into his bedding like torn silk and cordite. "I'm so sorry; please forgive me. Nothing personal, I assure you. Being confined to bed for a long period like this with hospital food plays havoc with one's intestinal tract, you know. Stand back a bit, if you like. It'll clear in a minute," he said, flapping me away with his wrist. "Oh, and perhaps you'd open the window while you're there would you, then I can get rid of these."

Ferreting in the crumpled bedcovers he retrieved and chucked out of the window three of his brown apple chogs, which action was followed by three dull, wet, metallic thuds from below. Easing my nose above the sill I saw a staff car driver looking daggers up at me just as his charge, an Air Commodore, came striding towards him down the hospital steps.

"Harry Packet," I exclaimed, snapping my fingers with realisation, whirling back to my new acquaintance now engaged fluffing up his bedclothes to fan in cool air.

"What?"

"Harry Packet."

"Don't be vulgar. What do you mean, Hurry Pucket?"

"Harry Packet," I said again. "A farmer in Salisbury. Used to serve with you. He told me about you looking for your lost horse from a jet plane once. Said I ought to meet you one day. That you were in Australia."

"Well yes, those bits are right, I was. How about that, eh? Old Harry Packet. No – sorry; can't say I remember him." He leaned on his elbow. "I think you'd better move round this side again now," he suggested . . . "I'm about to do another."

He did.

After it had rolled away and its reverberations stopped rattling the superstructure of his amazing bed, he grinned. "Actually, yes - I *do* remember Harry Packet. Always a tremendous tit man, I recall."

"Figures. He's got his own dairy herd now. Fancy meeting you like this though. Seriously, what *did* happen?"

"In a nutshell?"

"If you like."

"Broke my leg."

"And the rest?"

"Most of that too, actually. Want to hear about it?"

"Yes," I said. "I shall be here for a week or two, and so far all I've been given to do is fill this sample bottle, so do fire away . . .

"I was commissioned from Cranwell in 1949," Tony told me. "From there I went to Oakington on jet conversion training, where as well as learning to fly fast I met and married my wife, Pam. In 1957 I completed a test flying course at Farnborough and then spent the next sixteen months with the Bloodhound ground to air missile. For the next six years I traveled about from place to place, until in 1963 I was selected to go out to Australia on an exchange posting. The RAAF was in the process of converting from their Avon *Sabre* jets to the new £1¼m French *Mirage,* which was capable of speeds in excess of 1,400mph. One-hundred of these had been ordered from France . . ."

"One of which you pranged, I suppose?"

"More or less, yes . . . well - no, I mean . . . too bloody right I did, actually; drove it into the ground at 900mph."

"And you're still able to sit here telling me about it? How come?"

"Because I bailed out of the bloody thing, three seconds before impact. I used to be five-foot-ten; now I'm five-eight. But I'm alive, and I suppose I shouldn't be really."

"Phew." I shook my fingers like a Frenchman who'd burned them.

"We'd been over there in Australia for about fifteen months, and I'd already had several flights in the *Mirage,*" Tony went on. "Funnily enough I was a bit accident prone at that time. Just before we left England I drove my Triumph TR into a brick wall at 70mph and walked away unscathed, and then as if that wasn't enough we had another close shave in Australia, soon after we'd arrived. Pam and I were driving our VW up a steep mountain road when a caravan ahead of us sheered off from its tow bar and came careering back towards us. There was nothing we could do except gasp."

"What the hell happened?"

"It hit us, of course, and pushed us over the cliff. The caravan went all the way to the bottom which spoiled its owners' holiday a bit, but our VW's chassis miraculously hooked onto the cliff-edge so we were able to climb out and manhandle it back onto the road. We were shaken up, though.

227

After that caper, flying the *Mirage* for fifteen months without incident, with my track record, I suppose I was about due another shunt."

He grinned, and contentedly farted into his bedclothes once again.

"Go on," I said. "Don't keep me in suspense."

"Well, I was stationed at Laverton Air Base. I shall always remember - it was 1.30 p.m. on Monday 7th December 1964. Pam told me afterwards that she had been hanging out the washing on the line and our eight-year old son Mark was sitting in his classroom at school while his dad was streaking across the Australian sky in his *Mirage*. The usual family scene don't y'know." He grinned again. "Actually I had been testing that particular plane a dozen times that morning. Number A-31, it was. I'd just finished a picnic lunch on the grass alongside the airstrip. A-31 stood shimmering on the tarmac in the hot mid-day sun. It was time to take it up for its final test. Strangely enough, you know, it later transpired that it was my thirteenth flight that day. Anyway, I picked up my flying helmet and walked across the tarmac to the plane. Just as I climbed into the cockpit and snicked the canopy shut a member of the ground crew rushed up waving my Mae West at me. I'd left it behind on the grass. Another omen? Maybe - I don't know. I'm not normally the superstitious type. Anyway, I taxied out onto the runway, got air traffic clearance to roll, opened wide the throttle and within seconds was slicing through the sky 36,000-feet above Victoria.

"Just as Pam was pegging up my shirts and pants a sonic boom rent the air. She smiled knowingly. You see it was the third time that day that I'd gone through the Sound Barrier, but what Pam didn't know was that *this* sonic boom was not a normal one. It had been caused by my fantastic rate of descent as I managed the controls in an effort to right the uncontrollable plane as it plummeted us both earthwards. Seconds later Pam froze with horror as a pall of black smoke presaged the ghastly sound waves of the *Mirage* disintegrating into the ground."

"Christ," I murmured, aware that my palms were sweating. "What happened?"

"The manoeuvre I was performing resulted in temporary loss of control of the plane. I knew it was going to happen because it was meant to, and I should have been able to counter it readily enough. I had already done the same thing successfully eight times in the previous twenty minutes, but this time when I attempted it the plane unaccountably started a violently gyration. I took immediate spin recovery action, which for some reason only exacerbated the problem. The plane continued diving towards the ground, rapidly accelerating to 750 knots, which is about 900mph. The earth appeared as a swiftly spinning disc before my eyes. Within seconds I became completely disoriented and powerless to do anything. The instrument panel was a meaningless blur. It was only with the utmost concentration that I was able to focus on the rapidly unwinding altimeter. It showed 9,000-feet. Well, the minimum safety height for ejection from a spin is 10,000-feet. It later transpired that I was not in a spin at all, but a very rapid, vertical, spiral dive, a far graver situation from which I should have ejected at a much higher altitude still. Anyway, I finally pulled the blind on the Martin-Baker ejector seat at 7,000-feet. The moment the canopy shot away the 900mph airstream slammed into me like a brick wall. The seat cartridge fired a second later and hurled me out senseless into the supersonic slipstream. A-31 meanwhile screamed down towards the ground like a banshee in torment. Three seconds later all that was left of one £1¾m test aircraft was a 25-foot by 45-foot crater in the Australian topsoil, and the great pall of black smoke seen by a thunderstruck Pam from our garden twenty miles away."

"Where the hell were *you*? Sitting on a cloud?"

"More or less." Tony laughed. "As the ejector seat and I were hurled out, the impact of the slipstream was so severe that both my arms were flung asunder - like ripping the legs off a boiled chicken. My right arm was fractured and I dislocated my left shoulder. The wind-blast whipped away my oxygen mask and 'bone dome' lacerating my face horribly in

229

the process. When one's parachute is normally deployed it pulls the occupant clear of the ejector seat and the harness and leg restraining straps automatically fall away. In my case one leg restraining strap was left secured. This meant the speed of descent, combined with the force of the opening parachute - at least *that* worked - with the additional weight of the still present ejector seat, together exerted a breaking strain of about 1,300 lbs on my right leg. I don't know the breaking point of the human shinbone, but those 1,300 lbs made quite a good job of mine. It sheered apart completely below the kneejoint. My wedding tackle was duffed up a bit too. You can imagine, can't you, 1,300 lbs of webbing ripping into your credentials . . .?"

I could. And I did. And I winced and crossed my legs as Tony continued to relate his amazing tale.

"As soon as my parachute canopy snapped open it did so with such force that with the weight of the ejector seat still hanging from my leg the canvas harness split me right up the middle. Onlookers rushing to the scene could see my inert form hanging limply from its harness as I dropped. Thank God it was an utterly still day, otherwise the left to right oscillation of my uncontrolled descent would have been more severe than it was. I crumpled to earth eventually in a paddock about three-hundred-yards from the plane's main point of impact and the still smouldering crater it had made, but in doing so the ever increasing pendulum arc of my swing had become so great that when I did finally thud into the ground at forty-five degrees the inside of my left foot connected so violently with that part of Australia that the left leg and hip bone were completely shattered. My face was a bloody mask and my limbs grotesquely distorted, but this, thank God, was the extent of my immediate injuries. And at least I was alive. It later transpired that I was the only man ever to bail out from a plane at such a high speed and such a dangerously low altitude and live.

"Wind blast during the fall ripped my gloves inside out and off my hands. One tightly laced flying boot was also deftly removed. My flying suit and Mae West were flayed to shreds and my Rolex watch sprang from my wrist. All of these items

230

were later found widely dispersed on the ground over an area of some five-thousand square yards. The watch, funnily enough, was picked up personally by the officer in charge of the cleanup operation. He'd gone for a pee behind a bush only to find he was spraying his tinkle all over my Rolex, still ticking merrily and telling the right time. When I was fully compos mentis again, a couple of years later, it occurred to me that an appreciative letter to Rolex would be in order. I wrote to them from beneath clean white sheets to tell them I had found their product to be both shockproof and waterproof . . ."

"New watch?"

"You're joking. My nurse removed my bedpan and in doing so knocked the watch off the cabinet onto the floor. Bloody thing's never worked properly since. But let me tell you about the second miracle of that day. As if still being alive wasn't enough, cruising along the road half-a-mile away - and you're going to have to believe this - there was a mini-van with six doctors in. The coast was just a mile to the south of us you see, where they used to load and unload all sorts of explosive materiel from a large jetty complex there. Once a year a team of doctors used to go there to lecture. I just happen to have picked the day that coincided with their annual visit. There was very little they could do of course, until an ambulance arrived from Avalon, but at least nothing untoward was practised on me by any well meaning amateurs in the meantime. By then I had regained consciousness, but I didn't actually recall anything that happened for at least the next ten days. They eased me gently onto a stretcher and from then until we arrived at Laverton Base Hospital twenty miles away I kept chattering fifteen-to-the-dozen. Obviously severe shock was setting in; probably at the thought of having to tell Pam I'd lost the watch she'd bought me. I kept repeating 'What a bloody way to earn a living'. Remember, I had taken off at 13.30. It was now 14.30 and I was being admitted to hospital. Quite a lot had happened to me during that hour. My injuries were such that an intensive care team was rushed from Melbourne expressly to 'save my life'. It wasn't until later that the orthopaedic boys started their long, gruelling flog to reassemble and pin my bits and bring me as nearly as possible back to normal. All this took place two years ago you see, and I'm still in hospital. I am now two inches shorter and my limbs look as if they're done up with zip fasteners, but when I think of what nearly happened you can bet your bottom dollar I thank my lucky stars for modern medical technology."

"What an incredible story. What is the extent of your injuries now? I mean, where on earth did they begin to put you together again?"

"Well, I'll tell you," he said. "The day after the crash I lapsed into unconsciousness again. The doctors diagnosed the necessity for a brain operation. A surgeon was flown in from the Royal Melbourne Hospital especially to do the job. In the event he didn't perform the operation after all, but he told Pam not to hold on to any false hopes for my survival. Fifty-fifty was all he would offer. I am still not too clear about what happened over that period exactly, but it was something to do with fat embolism forming on the brain. I had to have my skull shaved and a hole drilled on each side. I don't know if it was to let fresh air in or steam out, but in order to disperse the fat formations I had to be intravenously injected with neat alcohol. I then embarked upon one glorious uncontrolled bender for four days and nights. In this comatose, tiddled and bemused state my befuddled brain leapt from one hallucination to another. I sang bawdy RAF songs. My bed became a Seine riverboat. I couldn't understand why the broad Australian orderlies didn't have French accents. My bed then turned into the cockpit of a new aeroplane and those same white-coated orderlies were its ground crew. I remember a source of great annoyance to me was the Thomas's splint on my left foot. Like a fractious child in its pram trying to pull off a sock I was always trying to wriggle out of this block of wood. Then I dreamed I was in the bowels of a German ship and the splint became vital to my sabotage mission. Night Sister's torch indicated the enemy was coming and then as soon as her check was over I would resume pushing and pulling the thing. One night I was successful, and dislodged it. I gave a cry of triumph and promptly informed the ward at large that they could sell the bloody thing to the Africans for a plough share. Unfortunately its violent removal caused the steel shaft in my thigh to bend, so I had to have another operation to put in a new one.

"The neat alcohol in my bloodstream had been doing its work though. After ten days the pressure on my brain subsided, and I awoke.

"I was over the hump - but a long way from the finish.

"As a Christmas present that year I was taken off the blessed painkilling drugs. Physios came and started manipulating my legs. One day the casts were removed. The stubble on my head was turning from bristle to silk once more. I began to hold semi-intelligent conversations again. The doctors worked hard and I worked hard. And then finally, after seven months, I was discharged and was flown to Singapore on the first leg of my journey back to UK. When I arrived in England I went to the RAF's rehabilitation unit at Headley Court in Surrey for seven months. And then still on crutches I swung out of the gates one day to temporary freedom. Obviously I was medically downgraded so there was no question of my resuming active flying duties, so they found me a post instead as a ground instructor at the Empire Test Pilots' School at Farnborough. My legs and joints were still full of screws and steel shafts of course. In January the right leg had to be rebroken and straightened. In August they removed one of the pins from the left leg, but it wasn't quite ready for it and wouldn't take the strain. It collapsed. And that, my friend, is why you find me here talking to you today. They've now had to rebreak it yet again and do some sort of bone graft or something. So that's my story. Now tell me about yours. Bilharzia? Brain surgery? Open heart op? Spine . . .?"

"Water on the knee," I said, turning and limping off to the loo with my bottle.

At 16.00 next afternoon it began in earnest.

"What do they want with me?" I asked, standing nervously beside my bed but instinctively edging towards Tony, reaching out to clutch a corner of his bedspread.

Two burly RAF medical orderlies were advancing purposefully towards me down the ward bearing with them a silver tray and various accoutrements. Stopping beside me they wordlessly drew the curtained screen around us, looked me in the eye and patted my blanket.

"Come along, sir. Up you jump," said one of them, smiling at me like a Mengele henchman. "It won't hurt," he added, not in the least reassuringly.

"What? Tell me. Tell me what won't hurt?" I asked, like a fretful sheep rolling its eyes with fearful anticipation in an ammonia-pervaded abattoir, just before the earmuffs are clamped on and it is electrically stunned before the adroit slitting of its throat and dispatch to the great big pasture in the sky.

One of the two orderlies was brandishing a razor.

"You're not going to do it. Are you? *Are* you? I want a proper doctor. It's my favourite leg. I want it done properly."

"It's nothing to worry about. We're only going to shave it for you."

"Like hell you are," I protested defiantly. "Shave what?"

"Your leg, sir. We've got to shave all the hair off your leg. It's standard practice before any operation."

"Oh, I see. Okay. Very well then, that's different."

I wriggled hesitantly out of my tracksuit pants and climbed up onto my bed. Before I could say 'knife', with one deft sweep of his implement, from groin to ankle the razor merchant laid bare a pristine strip of leg like the first swathe from a new-mown lawn.

"Sheeeeish," I exclaimed. Albeit a dry shave it had not been painful, but a surprise nonetheless. The ever increasing pinkness of skin as he smoothly planed away the hair seemed to reveal a commensurate reduction in masculinity; one of the reasons I'd never become a professional cyclist. Worse was the severed droppings that had wriggled beneath my bum and felt like itching powder.

The duo of demon Sweenies soon finished, retrieved their tools, patted my sheer, sheer thigh and calf, and departed.

"I should have a bath now, if I was you," one of them suggested as he left. "Wash away all the scratchy bits."

They hadn't bothered to remove the screen from round the bed, so I sat for a moment comparing legs.

First I considered the hirsute and masculine item on the left, then switched my gaze to its seemingly feminine counterpart, which looked like the sort of thing I might have had if I'd been my sister.

Not a bad looking leg really.

Surreptitiously I slipped my hand inside my shirt to check my pecs, desperately hoping I wasn't suddenly going to find them shaping up and turning soft in sympathy, but they were still in good order so I returned my attention to the legs.

On impulse I pulled the bedcover across to cover the hairy left one, and then languidly arching the silky smooth right one I tucked my tackle and stuff down out of the way and sat on them, to see what it looked like being a girl for a moment.

It felt the same, but as if I might have been a transvestite, which wasn't me at all, so having frightened myself once, I stopped.

"Y'alright in there?" Tony called through the screen.

"Yeah, fine; just picking my nose."

"Well take your bloody screen down; I can't see you."

"I don't want to be seen," I intoned balefully. "I joost want to be alone . . ."

"Why?"

"Because they've scarred me," I cried. "Scarred me for life. Marred my beauty."

"You shouldn't have taken your beauty in there with you in the first place then, should you," someone yelled across from another bed.

"Removed my masculinity, they have," I groaned.

"Why? Did the razor slip?" guffawed a pilot officer with a broken back from one of the beds across the room. I'd give him broken back . . .

"Ladies and gentlemen . . .," I cried, leaping from my bed and standing behind the screen. "You have seen Gypsy Rose Lee and Phyllis Dixey. You have seen Marlene Dietrich. Now

235

- for your delectation and delight Ward Seven proudly presents on this one and only occasion *the* delectable, *the* desirable, *the* one and only right leg of renowned international cabaret artiste . . . *Michaela George.*"

Discordantly bellowing *The Stripper's* bump-and-grind music I lifted my right leg and stuck it as provocatively as I could through a gap in the screen.

There was stunned silence.

It must have looked good.

Either that or there was no one there.

I stuck my head through for a look, grinned, and was immediately pelted with a shower of grapes, apple-cores, match boxes, cat-calls and abuse.

Grabbing my soap and towel I fled laughingly up the ward to the wash room where I ran myself a quick bath to get rid of the bits.

Toweling myself dry afterwards I went back to my bedside and clambered into my tracksuit again, noticing as I did so that one of the chaps on the other side of the ward was giving me rather a strange and intense look.

"What's up with him?" I asked Tony quietly, nodding with my chin.

"I think your daft little cabaret upset him a bit."

"Why?"

"He's been here almost a year. His wife's let him down, and stopped coming to see him about six months ago. He's getting divorced fairly soon. As you can imagine, apart from the occasional bit of innuendo from the nurses he's had no opportunity to develop any sort of relationship with anyone else."

"So what's that got to do with me?"

"Nothing, really. It's just the way your shaved leg came poking through the screen like that. It shocked all of us a bit, but I think it got to him more than the others."

"Shocked him? Why on earth should it shock him?" I blustered, taking a monumental bite out of one of Tony's apples.

"Gave him a hard-on," he said.

236

The surgeon was digging the fingers of one hand under my kneecap, pressing down from above with the other and telling me to tense. I did so once, before realising how much it hurt. He seemed to find this funny, so asked me to do it again.

"Come on. It's only a small pain. How do you expect me to find out what's wrong with you if you won't let me test its reactions?"

"Dammit, Doc," I said. "It's *me* that hurts. When you dig your fingers in like that, it won't tense. I get a message that says 'pain - so don't tense.'"

"You're a coward."

"I'll go along with that."

"All right, then. We'll have a go at it tomorrow for you. No breakfast though - okay?"

"You're not going to take it out on me like that Doc, are you? Surely not."

"No one going under anaesthetic has any food or drink beforehand. Simple as that. You'd throw up and choke."

"Right: but, Doc, it's going to be a heavy day tomorrow. I shall *need* my breakfast."

"No breakfast," he said, patting my thigh. "Hey - that's quite a nice piece of leg you've got there, isn't it," he added, and grinned. "Got it insured?"

Oh, Christ, I groaned, slumping back onto my bed.

Not another one.

I could get hooked on pre-meds.

I love 'em.

Washed and scrubbed, been toilet, you sit up in bed wearing just your open-up-the-back green theatre gown and surgical socks, looking like a virgin waiting to be taken off to a sacrificial altar somewhere. Along comes a chirpy little nurse who dabs your forearm with spirit, and with official Government and Medical Council sanction then whops in a trickle of happy-juice that wafts you gently off to where bluebirds play. All about you has a hollow tread as you lie beatifically back and smile like an opium addict in mid-flight. The drug is intended to relax your muscles and ease tension so that you have no worries about people in masks and rubber gloves pulling back flaps of your skin, slicing up raw red meat and tissue and honing slimy white bone ends with Victorian shaped surgical steel instruments.

"We're going to lift you off your bed now and put you onto a trolley," one of the nurses explained.

"Yes, a'right, I'd be delighted. Thank you very much indeed," I mumbled through my chemically parched lips.

I sensed myself being skilfully shovelled onto canvas, then like the flick of a deftly executed judo throw I was transferred from bed to gurney, staring at highly arched corridor ceilings while being trundled silently along on shock-absorbing tyres from Ward 7 out into the hospital's main arterial concourse, powerless to do ought but trust in my orderlies' adroitness as we took our place in the mainstream of traffic *en route* to theatre.

I felt like a dressed turbot on a lunch trolley being wheeled up to the Directors' Dining Room.

My tail-end orderly crashed me feet first through two overlapping yellowed plastic doorflaps, wherein we paused in some sort of ante chamber.

With a subdued clattering of dishes I could hear the first course being wheeled out into the Recovery Room, and then it was my turn.

I was pushed through to the serving hatch and one of the principal luncheon guests wandered across to take a peek at me. He took the menu from the foot of my tray and scanned it to see what I was, then peered down to have a closer look and just a quick sniff.

"I'm not ganger . . . I'm not. " I licked my lips to try once more. "I'm not gangrenous."

"No, and I hope you never will be; at least not in here," someone said behind me. "You'll just feel a slight little prick in your arm now, and before you can say 'knife' you'll find yourself waking up in your bed back in the ward again. Okay?"

"Wasn'a goin' a say 'knife'," I mumbled. *Sheeit.* One; two; three; four . . . *whoops* - an enormous invisible express train suddenly rushed up out of nowhere and enveloped me.

I wish I could get a hold of some of that stuff.

"Nuuuuurse . . .

"Nurse - I think he's waking up," I heard Tony's voice cry out.

"Hal*lo*," cooed my favourite fragrant blonde number a few seconds later, standing crisply, cleanly and serenely there beside me, smoothing my brow and twinkling her big blue eyes.

No wonder so many of us married them.

It was in order to reassert our masculinity when we're back on our own terms once more, whole, intact and fully functioning, using grown up urinals instead of bottles and able to wash and dry our own bottoms again. We want to show them what we're really made of.

"How are you feeling?"

We also do it as an expression of deeply sincere appreciation for the TLC they spread about when we're distressfully bedded down in their care on one of their wards - unless it's with tertiary syphilis, when we may as well bring along our own sandwiches: or so I've been told.

"I'd kill for a cup of sweet tea, if that would be all right please?"

"I think we could do a bit better than that for you," she said, spinning angelically and crackling off with a swish and a swirl of starched vestments.

"How d'y'feel, mate?"

Leaning up on one elbow, it was Tony, grinning down at me from his own bed four-feet away.

"Not bad, I suppose. Bit woozie . . . but, hey . . . *Bloody Hell*: what's *this,* chrissake? Oh, *no* . . . they haven't gone and chopped the fucking thing *off,* have they? That *bloody* doctor. I *knew* he had it in for me. I'll sue the bastard, I will. I'll bloody *sue* him, just you see if I don't . . ."

An enormous cage straddled my bed to keep the bedclothes from my stump.

My *stump?*

My *God.*

I quickly struggled to inveigle my right hand down inside the bedclothes for an anxious feel.

Phew . . . thank the Lord for that.

The temporarily missing limb seemed to be still there.

At least *some*thing was, and had been lagged in a bulbous swathe of surgical swaddling.

I had a test-wiggle on my toes, which responded; so at least the main tube down the middle worked okay.

That was that then.

Job done.

I'd be home in a few days; playing squash again by the weekend.

"Here we are then. Do you think you can sit yourself up or would you like me to spoon feed you?"

"Yes please."

The delectable Florence had come back with a teapot, cup, saucer, silver spoon, sugar in a bowl, milk in a dinky little jug and slivers of cucumber and tomato in a brown bread sandwich on a plate on a tray with a fresh doily. I could have married her. Or worse.

"Which?"

"Marriage," I blurted: "Oh, sorry, I mean yes . . . I'll sit myself up, and yes I'd like you to spoon feed me as well, if you would please."

"Come along then." She smiled. "Sit up and get yourself organised, and then I must leave you. You're not the only patient on this ward, you know."

"I know, but I'm the nicest; although I do know that poor old Tony here craves your attention and lusts after you almost as much as I do."

"I think Squadron Leader Svensson is quite capable of looking after himself," she retorted hotly, turned, and flounced off back to the office, obviously more than just a little in love with the swine.

240

I grimaced at Tony, who grinned back.

He spent a lot of time grinning, actually.

That, and keeping the nurses amused with his good looks.

It was then I threw up.

"Whatever's the matter, you big baby. *Surely* you could have called out for a basin or something?" Florence had come dashing back all mock-stroppy, fussing efficiently, doing the necessary and volubly talking the while to cover my embarrassment. I didn't know which I wanted most: her - or some more of that wonderful happy-juice.

"I would've if I could've," I groaned. "This is so humiliating. One minute I was fine and then suddenly it all came over me. I don't know what to say. I'm really sorry."

"It's all right," she sighed, finalising the mopping up operation and standing beside me for a moment. "It's my own fault. I knew I shouldn't have given you that food and drink so soon. Oh, well - at least you'll enjoy your supper more now, won't you."

I slept.

Ten minutes later I woke up again.

The fuss, the novelty and Florence's pretty little pot of tea had been a short lived interlude.

Now the pain was kicking in.

There was a gnawing and pulsing sensation deep within my knee, like some distant miner coming up a shaft, clawing out lumps of yellow pain, like sonar soundings that were bursting on the surface and fanning along my thigh beneath its constrictive mass of bandages. I was in the throes of deep-knife trauma, unable to arrange myself in any position that allowed relief,

I groaned.

Once again dear Florence was quick off the mark.

She couldn't have fancied me: drawn; pallid; hollow-eyed and post-operatively tousle-headed, with a slimy sheen of sweat across my brow and down the runnels of my nose where my exuding sugar excess usually foregathered in a juicily squeezable encampment of blackheads pickled in spiralling cigarette smoke.

No, she must just have been incredibly good and dedicated at her job, so I suppressed and forgot the man/woman thing for a moment, content to lie back and accept her professional ministrations, with no more lip from me other than politeness and appreciation.

"Beginning to hurt, is it?"

I nodded.

"I expect we can find you something for that, then."

"Aspirin?"

"Cynic." She giggled and deftly snapped a disposable syringe from the goodies-trolley she'd wheeled across. Lifting the sheet she gently stuck the needle into my left thigh.

"There you are," she said, briskly rubbing the point of entry before covering me up again. "That won't take long to do its stuff, and then you can get some sleep. I'm about to go off shift, so I'll see you again in the morning - okay? Try to behave yourself and I'll say nighty-night for now."

I laid back and enjoyed 'the happening'.

I'd had the pre-med; the big dose; the knife; the job; the sealing up and stitching afterwards; the bandaging; the subsequent awakening; the tea and sympathy and my unfortunate unpleasant reaction to it, the dulling of the anaesthetic and now the insistent emergence of post-operative pain. To combat this, I'd just been given a painkiller. Its balm was now flowing across the red beaches of my internal tissues, ushering out the alien pain and driving it down my leg and away, out of my toes and over the lip of the mattress to disappear across the floor and out of the door. Come to think of it, that's not a bad ad for toilet cleanser.

This time I slept right through.

"My *God*; it looks *terrible.*"

"Laser surgery's not been invented yet Sunshine, and you can't cut a cake through a keyhole," my surgeon prodding gingerly about his now uncovered handiwork told me.

It was three days later.

242

The mass of bandages, gauze, lint and gubbins had been unravelled like a surgical puttee from my leg, and re-wound for Oxfam.

And there it was.

The knee my parents had given me.

Back from its adventure.

Shaved, sullied, sliced and stitched; white, tight and swollen as hell, it now had a livid purple scar running from the top of the shinbone right round the inside of the knee to the thigh.

It looked as though he had used a Saracen sword instead of a scalpel, and thrown a tea party inside while he was there.

They also seemed to have run out of the right surgical thread.

I had been stitched by a wolf cub with 15-feet of left over hawser to dispose of.

He hadn't cracked his reef-knots too well, either; grannies abounded.

I continued to stare at my leg in fascination, going off surgery in a big way.

It would be homeopathy for me from now on; and clean living.

The surgeon placed his cool hand over the steaming mound that resembled a suet pudding come straight off the stove.

"Hmmmm," he murmured. "I don't like the look of this swelling at all, I'm afraid. I think we'll have to aspirate it. We'll have him down this afternoon, sister."

"Whassaspirate?" I asked.

"Nothing to worry about, old lad. We just stick a needle in and drain off the accumulation of fluid, that's all."

"Gee, thanks," I chuckled as he turned away to continue his rounds, attended by his entourage.

No lunch.

More happy-juice. (Whoopee).

It was back onto the gurney and another trundle down to the theatre.

Tony had been given a pair of crutches during the day and been told to test drive his new pins.

He had been stamping and clattering about the ward determinedly on them all evening.

His wife, Pam, had been in to visit him.

"How are you doing, darling?"

"All right, I guess; although they seem to think I'm still a bit unstable."

"Unstable? Darling, they don't know the half of it. You're a raving lunatic."

My aspiration done and the swelling reduced, I slept fitfully that night.

Snatches of conversation from around the ward pervaded my semi-consciousness.

All of us were tossing and turning in our beds because of the grampus-like snores of a deeply sedated post-operative pilot keeping us awake.

After 15-minutes of rattling adenoids he shifted his head slightly, grunted, smacked his lips and a blessed silence descended.

None of us stirred, fearful lest he should start up his dreadful racket all over again.

"I think he's died," said a voice from the dark.

Then from the far corner of the ward came the sudden crash and tinkle of broken glass.

"Oh *Gawd*, not *again*," a chorus of distraught voices wailed. *"Sister"* one of them yelled. "You'd better come quick, love. Wing Commander's on another of his bombing runs."

One of the little night nurses came scurrying down the ward to the bedside of a retired, cantankerous old bushy-moustached Wingco who had started regressing to second childhood only the previous week. Tonight - as on other nights, not an irregular occurrence - he had found himself reliving a mission over the Ruhr. Caught in his eagle-eyed glare he had seen an unsuspecting spider crawling across the ward floor and unleashed a bomb on it . . . the bomb being his well aimed, well filled bed-bottle.

"Right, mate," said the physio next morning. "It's about time we got this leg started up and working again. You don't want to be spending the rest of your natural in here, do you? Now then - when I say 'tense', tense. All right? Tense."

I tensed.

Nothing.

I gave it my all, nearly shat myself with the effort, and then tensed again.

My brain shrieked *"TENSE"*.

Still nothing.

My cables hummed the message down the communications chain with extreme urgency, but again . . .

Absolute zilch.

I was reminded of the difference between Fear and Panic; fear being the first time you can't get it up the second time, and panic, the second time you can't get it up the first time.

"Come along now," said my physio with a degree of asperity. "Try and make a proper effort this time. *Tense.*"

I tensed. Oh, so good and so hard and so determinedly did I tense.

Again - nothing.

My knee simply didn't want to know.

My buttocks quivered from the effort; my toes clawed and pinged; my abdominals rippled, pectorals lifted and fell, and my deltoids and scapulae writhed while my eyeballs protruded with a manic stare, but still my kneecap sat there as motionless as a bleached pebble atop its landmass.

With the load being sent coursing through it my thigh did respond with an occasional judder, but still the kneecap refused to budge.

Worse, it was swelling up again.

"We've done just about all we can with that swelling," said one of the doctors. "All we can do now is fix a tap and washer to it."

I was a point of interest.

A stop-off on the tourist route.

All manner of people called by to have a look, to prod, poke and offer their suggestion for re-starting a knee that was defying medical science and in the process of doing so was slowly beginning to atrophy.

My thigh was already reduced to the size of Twiggy's forearm.

"Right," said the Chief Physio, whom they'd summoned from Auschwitz on special assignment. "I shall get that thing working by tomorrow. You may not know it yet my friend, but you are going on the Black Box."

Leaving me to ponder this announcement he shambled back up the ward on his knuckles to go break more rocks.

Black Box?

I shook my head, stupefied.

What had I done to deserve this?

I had entrusted myself to their professional care for a simple operation to have a small flange of extraneous bone shaved off my patella, to stop the knee clicking and painfully locking.

It wasn't my fault they'd fouled up.

They were behaving as if I was deliberately trying to be difficult; but I wasn't.

Try as hard as I could I couldn't get my leg to work, and that was that.

They must have snipped a wrong wire or something.

"Florence," I called when she came flouncing past with a replenished bowl of fruit for someone. "What's this Black Box thing they say they're . . .?"

An orange bounced to the floor as she skidded in her tracks and flung her hand up to her mouth.

"The Black Box," she gasped, hurrying to my bedside."Oh; oh, no; you poor dear. Surely they're not putting you onto the Black Box? Oh, please say they're not. For my sake."

Hey, I thought: this Black Box must be really something.

"Yup," I told her. Tomorrow morning apparently."

"Oh, no," she groaned. "Look, couldn't you *please* try to get your poor knee to work before then? Concentrate as hard as you can for the rest of the day. If you can possibly avoid the Black Box you must do so at all costs."

Until then I had secretly thought they'd been winding me up, but now I wasn't so sure - so I spent the next few hours flexing and tensing until I was awash with sweat, but still to no avail.

Not even a hint of a budge.

Although spared another bombing run that night (the poor old Wingco had been removed to a private room) I slept fitfully again.

At 09.00 next morning there was a flurry of activity at the door.

Word had got round and now every eye in the ward strained to see what was in store for me.

The Black Box was about to arrive.

Two alert nurses had come rushing ahead to draw the screens round my bed to prevent me seeing the item's progression up the ward, like a portable guillotine being trundled into place by tumbril.

I imagined muffled drum beats, but apart from the occasional *ooh* and *ahhh* and a *phew* or two, the rest of the patients remained respectfully silent.

A gap in the screen was slowly drawn apart, and Florence slipped in.

"It's here," she said, giving me a wan little smile.

"I know."

"You've got to try to be ever so brave now, won't you," she said, swiping a compassionate tear that had sprung to one periwinkle blue eye. Hers, not mine.

"I will," I promised, begining to quiver like a frightened filly.

"RIGHT" boomed the Auschwitz Physio with a fanfare of trumpets and dramatic beating of tenor drums, sweeping back the screen with both arms and hurling a Mephistophelian glare at me as his minions wheeled in a trolley like a mobile music centre.

"LET'S BE HAVING YOU. But *first* let me introduce you," he intoned, and with a theatrical flourish from which only a scarlet-lined cape and black goatee were missing, cried: *"THIS* . . . is THE *BLACK BOX."*

It was a black box.

Like a doctor's medicine bag sitting atop a trolley.

The Chief Physio dismissed his minions and slowly opened the box's lid, savouring each flicker of expression as I peered nervously inside.

It resembled some sort of sophisticated battery charger.

"What's it do?" I croaked.

"What's it do? What's it DO, you ask? *Surely* you must have worked out already for yourself, haven't you, that what it does is - why . . . IT *ELECTROCUTES*, of course," he roared.

God what a ham, but one who certainly enjoyed his work.

Bending over and reaching down beneath the trolley he took out two cushioned steel plates, one of which he promptly clamped to each side of my thigh like the brake-shoes of an armoured car. He plugged one set of leads into the box and another into the mains plug beneath my bed, stood up, and then doused the plates with water.

"I am *now* . . .," he announced, with feeling and a serious amount of gravitas: "going to switch it on."

I didn't know *what* was going to happen, but I was concerned lest I was about to disappear in a puff of smoke and smouldering bedclothes. I didn't think they would kill me on purpose. I was sure they weren't allowed to do that. But I was not so trusting that I could discount the thought of his negligently allowing some fault or other to occur.

He switched on.

Nothing happened.

I relaxed.

This was a doddle.

Then like a car seat heater doing its stuff I felt the plates slowly begin to warm up.

Mephisto adjusted his box's knobs and dials to fine tune it, splashed more water at me and generally warmed to his theme. The box purred and started to hum. I wouldn't have been surprised if it had emitted sparks.

Was I going to wake up in the year 3000?

Chief Physio hunched cackling over his machine.

He glanced over his shoulder once at me with a satanic glint to his eye, raised his fist and applied it to a lever.

"*Right,*" he shouted. "Let us now make your leg aware of its existence."

The plates clutched at my thigh.

And the plates clutched at my thigh.

And they clutched at my thigh.

And *clutched* and *clutched* and *clutched* and *clutched* and *clutched* and *clutched* and *clutched* at my thigh.

The electrically induced muscular spasms contracted the quadracep and released it; contracted it and released it; contracted it and released it until - lo - when the wonderful Mephisto cried *"Enough . . .",* beamed triumphantly, turned off his confounded machine and deftly removed the plates, I was able to continue the motion on my own, unaided.

I'd had a kick-start.

I cackled with glee. "Hey - how *about* that?" I giggled, twanging my quad like a dog wagging its tail at tea-time. My left thigh, not wanting to be left out, started up as well in sympathetic concert until both patellae looked like a couple of hep peaches bouncing out an intricate Hawaiian war dance on a tom-tom.

"Thank you very much indeed," I said. "I'm most grateful."

"Not at all. Don't mention it. You're welcome, he replied," and paged his minions to come back and fetch the Black Box to trundle off to do its stuff in some other ward.

After lunch Sister arrived with one of her henchpeople, brandishing tweezers and a surgical dish.

"Oh, Gawd," I groaned. "Is there no end to my misery? What is it this time?"

I think the idea was to pluck out my darning, neatly, one at a time, but when she picked at the ugly little black end of the first stitch and tugged, it wasn't just the stitch that came out, but the whole scabby scar and half the accompanying knee came away with it, like a zip fastener ripped from its moorings.

"*Ooch,*" I hissed, wincing.

"S'truth," Sister cursed, blanching.

"Oh, Sister," her henchperson groaned, looking round furtively. "I promise not to tell anyone if you won't."

"Quiet, Phoebe."

"I'd quite like some of my knee back though, if I may, please?"

"Yes, of course," Sister said nervously, trying to retain her cool. She glanced quickly over her shoulder, then prised the pie-crust and half the filler off the end of her tweezers, and with the edge of her palm tried repacking it back into place like Plasticine into the side of my knee.

"There," she said. "I expect it should take all right." And with that they were gone; back to her room to talk about it.

The ripped scab stung a bit, but, as predicted, soon re-took; probably something to do with all the oranges I ate as a child.

I continued to receive physio twice a day and after ten days I was told it was time to start walking again.

Crutches were produced.

With much mirthful encouragement from Tony and the rest of the ward I was eased out onto the highly polished floor and told to get on with it.

I couldn't.

I stood there like a splay-legged fledgling and quivered.

My buttocks twitched and wobbled like blancmanges.

I felt queasy wavelets ripple through me to burst as spots before my eyes.

My head turned from side to side like a Dalek with a blown fuse.

Then my trousers fell down.

I had lost weight.

Unable to find their normal purchase they lay crumpled round my ankles just as some fool student nurse chose that moment to throw open the doors to let in our visitors.

"Good afternoon," I carolled to one gorgeous young wife come to visit her husband at the far end of the ward. The sight of me could have put her off sex for life, but broad minded, been around, not offended, she smiled and went on her way; bless her.

Florence, bless her too, had seen my plight and came hurrying across to my rescue.

She knelt down, swiftly pulled up my breeks, tucked me in like a mother with a kindergarten child, took in all the extra with a pin she produced from thin air, and smiled a smile which made me glad I had them back on again.

"Come along, Gorgeous," she said sweetly, taking my arm as gently as a jewel-encrusted sword and guiding me. "We've got to get you walking properly again. All right?"

All that was missing was the appropriate organ music as we progressed in regal slow time up the centre aisle of Ward 7.

Beauty and the Beast.

Prince Kor the Deformed and Princess Karina.

Me and Florence.

And my crutches.

She soon got me walking again.

Within two weeks I had painfully managed to achieve the requisite 90-degree bend in the knee that they insisted upon before sanctioning discharge.

I was also told I would never ski, that within two years the other knee would have to be done as well, and that within six years they would in all probability both have to be locked with steel pins.

Absolute rubbish!

A few weeks later, after Tony, too, had been discharged and was sent home for rehabilitation, Rachel and I drove over from Bicester to his RAF married quarter at Halton to have tea with him and Pam. They were a lovely couple who instead of a car kept a pony and trap in their garage.

In April 1967 Tony and the myriad surgeons, doctors, nurses *et al* who had fought him back to normalcy received the greatest recognition for their achievement.

After a four-hour examination, consultation and deliberation, a RAF Central Medical Board classified Tony as fit to resume flying duty.

I should like us to have remained lifelong friends, but our paths diverged and we each of us moved on in different directions.

In writing this account and realising, with horror, that he must now be aged 78, I was moved to check out Tony's name on Google where, distressingly, I found this:

Christie's Sale 1281
Orders, decorations, campaign medals and militaria
25 September 2001
Spink London
Lot 731
CATERPILLAR CLUB BADGE: gold pin-backed badge, the reverse inscribed: 'S/Ldr Svensson': extremely fine, in card box of issue by Mappin & Webb, interior inscribed: *Presented by Irvin Air Chute of Gt. Britain Ltd.*
Estimate
£180 - £220
Price Realized
£552
Lot Notes: Sold with newspaper cuttings relating to the incident for which the recipient was awarded the above Badge.

Since its inception in 1922 there have been more than 100,000 members of the Caterpillar Club, among whom can be counted Charles Lindbergh and the astronaut John Glenn.

A tiny gold lapel pin of a caterpillar with amethyst eyes is presented to anyone whose life has been saved by bailing out of a disabled plane by parachute, the significance being that the canopies were made of silk.

A caterpillar climbs out of its cocoon before flying away.

That's how I learned that my devil-may-care old hospital chum, Tony, had been killed in a car crash just a few years before.

TWENTY-ONE

THAT CHRISTMAS EVE I got lockjaw.

I had neither cut my thumb nor sat on a rusty nail, but still I couldn't get my mouth open.

I grimaced.

I pushed and I pulled.

I relaxed and tried to forget about it, then leapt up on it unexpectedly . . . but all to no avail.

My jaw remained firmly clenched.

My trap was shut.

It was as if I had been successfully hypnotised.

I had a raging temperature and was sitting up in bed sipping turkey soup through a straw.

"Must have been those RAF surgeons," moaned Rachel. "Dirty knife. Has to be a connection."

I had only been home from RAF Halton three weeks since my knee operation - my crutches still downstairs in the hall - and now this.

"I don't think it can have been that," I reasoned. "They were very nice and clean in there. This is just some psychosomatically induced aversion to Christmas. You know I don't like it."

"It's a pain in the butt," Rachel complained. "You did exactly the same thing last year, when you got that stinking cold, remember?"

I remembered.

One way or another I always seem to get mildly crocked at Christmas.

Rachel was convinced I did it on purpose, but I didn't. Honestly. It just always seemed to *happen* to me.

Be that as it may, Christmas 1966 was now a 'write-off' in the George household.

Christmas Day proper I sucked two bowls of turkey soup through a straw.

Boxing Day I'd 'had' turkey soup, so tried blancmange, but this clogged my straw so I gave up, rolled over and went to sleep.

Tuesday 27th I awoke, beaming from ear to ear, sang an aria in the bath that morning and was back to normal again by lunchtime.

"You did, you see; you *did*," Rachel screeched. "You did it absolutely on purpose, just because you don't like Christmas. You have to be the focal point of attention the whole time don't you, even if it means ruining other people's pleasure. What sort if Christmas do you think this has been for the kids, eh? Having to keep quiet the whole time and tip-toe past the bedroom door . . ."

"No, you didn't have lockjaw," said the dental officer at ten-o'clock next morning, after I'd managed to crank my mouth open far enough for him to look inside. "Nor do you have rabies or pyrrohea. What you *do* have is quite simply the nastiest pair of impacted and inflamed wisdom teeth I've ever seen. I'm afraid it's a major extraction job for you, my boy."

"So *soon* already," I groaned, slumping into his chair, but then perking up quickly at the prospect of again being able to get lashed on the medics' pre-med happy-juice.

This time I was sent to the Cambridge Military Hospital at Aldershot.

There were four of us in our little corner of the ward.

One was a Kenyan officer cadet from Mons who had contracted frostbite whilst stuck up Kilimanjaro on leave.

Another was an RAOC colleague of mine, Graham Gerdes, who was also there to have his wisdom teeth removed.

There was me.

And there was 'John the Circ'.

It does not obtain so much today, when few things do, much, any more, but back then the Army liked its junior officers to try to remain single until they had attained the age of twenty-five.

This meant they could be sent off on night exercises with their platoons, to learn the basics of their trade without some woman kicking up.

'John the Circ' had decided to do things differently.

Not heeding the Army's preference one jot, at the tender age of twenty he had taken unto himself a bride.

She was a gorgeous looking woman and well worth taking unto upon, but in his eagerness he had taken her unto himself so often and so hard that a design fault had appeared.

He looked quite disconsolate and sore, lying there in his bed watching me unpack my stuff and shove it into the bedside locker next to his own.

"What's the problem then?" I asked cheerily.

"Circumcision," he grumbled, managing something of a sheepish grin.

"Tough," I said. "Painful?"

"Believe it." He shifted position, wincing to prove his point. "It's a bastard actually; especially now, at my time of life."

"What time's that?" I laughed.

"I just got married," he told me. "Three weeks ago to be exact."

"Tough shit," I grinned. "I can see your problem. What does your wife think about it? Relief at her momentary respite?"

"Actually, no; she loves it and's missing it like hell. I'd just got her threshing nicely, when this had to go and happen. Bloody nuisance. Angela's nearly going up the wall with it; without it. You'll meet her. It's visiting time. She'll be here in a minute."

"Surely you'll be home again in a couple of days though, won't you?"

"Not if she keeps insisting on visiting me like this, I won't" he said. "I should have been discharged last Tuesday, but the bloody thing won't heal."

"Why's that?"

"Stitches keep bursting."

Just then the doors opened to let the first visitors of the evening come trickling into the ward.

Angela, the obvious and unmistakable bride of three weeks eagerly edged herself to the fore.

Blushing she may recently have been, but now she was flushed.

A luscious redhead and undoubted scorcher, she came bouncing in bra-less and proud, click-clacking quickly up the ward on a vertiginous pair of stilettos, head held high, green eyes all of a-sparkle, tacky red lips parting in readiness.

"Hallo Darling," she cooed.

She jiggled in anticipation and broke into a little flurry of hair patting and coat removal as she neared her husband's bed.

I glanced at John.

He wore a glazed expression.

Adoring.

Besotted.

He opened his mouth.

Gritted his teeth.

Sweat broke out across his brow.

"Hallo my Darling*aaaaaaaaaaaaaaaaaaaaaaaaaaaghhh.*"

It was then that I understood his problem.

She was a stitch-buster all right.

Continue like this, he might never get well.

I didn't even *have* any stitches, and mine had nearly burst also.

The Royal Army Dental Corps' Colonel David Fang (true) had steel grey hair and told me that in all his twenty-five-years as a dentist he had never seen wisdom teeth like mine.

"You're going to have a fair bit of swelling there, I'm afraid," he told me, smiling.

They operated.

At 14.30 the following afternoon I struggled back to consciousness to see a circle of concerned and inquisitive faces peering down at me.

Lifting one arm free from beneath the sheets I placed the pads of my fingertips gingerly against my face.

The whole area felt swollen.

My pillow was soaked with blood and dribble, but one thing worried me most of all.

The two teeth meant to have been taken out were on the right, but my largest swelling was on the left.

It wasn't an arm or a leg, but all the same . . .

"You've taken out the wrong bloody teeth," I blurted through carmine spittal.

"Took out everything I could lay my hands on," said the Colonel. "They were just as impacted on the other side and would have flared up pretty soon, so I thought it best to whip 'em out along with the others. It was like trying to tug buckled iron bars out of concrete. They were brutes. Here, take a look at yourself."

He passed me a hand-mirror, grinning as I craned my head forward to peer into it.

My face resembled an under-inflated football left underfoot in the rush-hour; or a pomegranate launched from a mortar at an oncoming tank; or a tomato used by Joe DiMaggio for baseball practice.

It was bruised to buggery.

Graham Gerdes, wheeled down for the same operation as me only ten minutes before, was now sitting up in bed opposite happily grinning and munching an apple.

I bet he came top at school in everything too.

He would obviously be home and back on the range by tea-time, while I lingered there in discomfort for days.

"Give him a hundred mgs of Pcxohythlikymine and two of ferrous oxide," said the Colonel to a hovering nurse, patting the side of my bed as he got up to go. "We'll try to get you out of here by Saturday."

Saturday came.

"Quite honestly, I'm a bit worried," he said. "I shouldn't let you home at all yet. You're still drugged to the eyeballs. Apart from which you *look* so dreadful. You'll be getting the hospital a bad name. However . . ."

All I remember of my drive home from Aldershot to Bicester, via Henley, that Saturday morning was three lanes of swiftly converging traffic and me choosing the middle one. If it had happened today, and I'd had a prang . . .? but things were different back then.

More by luck than judgment I arrived home without incident, pulled the big Vauxhall Cresta into our drive, and shut the engine.

The front door was almost flung off its hinges as Natalia rushed out to greet her daddy.

My happy heart surged with joy as I climbed out of the car and bent down to sweep my little girl into my arms.

"Daddy, daddy, daddy," she cried, but then seeing my face she skidded in her tracks, turned and hurried off in a nervously whimpering retreat back to Mummy.

Rachel took one look at me, pointed at the stairs, and said "Bed."

I couldn't imagine she had that in mind, but I was too pooped to care.

While I had been driving back from the hospital and then languishing in bed at home with my swollen face later that weekend, I got to thinking a bit about 'John the Circ', his stunning young wife Angela and the trials and tribulations that can beset testosterone soaked subalterns in pursuit of their burgeoning sex lives.

When one is institutionalised, be that establishment one of HM prisons or a military barracks, one has to be more circumspect than normal in the pursuit and acquisition of sexual fulfilment.

Although the occasional riotous party did take place, an Officers' Mess was not perceived as being a night club.

Many of our young officers felt that because they were obliged to pay accommodation charges for their rooms and were told that the Mess was their home, they should be allowed to bring through its doors whoever they chose, whenever they chose to do so, especially if they happened to be 'up for it' girls, so there were rules in place to prevent the upper reaches and private rooms of one's Mess from becoming the setting for nightly enactments of a French farce.

These days standards are so loose that they've mostly dropped off, but back then we had to wear ties after six-o'clock, and suits to dinner except on Wednesdays, when a sports jacket was allowed.

We railed against the inconvenience at times, but at least a sense of 'occasion' was always maintained, of which very little seems to be left in the informality of modern life.

Arriving at an event improperly dressed would be highly embarrassing and a cardinal offence career-wise.

Today some invitations request Smart Casual, but I have often rung hostesses to enquire "What's the dress?" only to have them sound surprised, and ask "Y'what?" - or "Well, whatever you feel most comfortable in, I suppose."

Ladies' roles in Mess life were obviously recognised and catered to.

Most Messes had a comfortable Ladies' Room (other than the loo) with flower arrangements and copies of *Country Life* where they could meet together, drink tea and feel safe.

There were also Ladies' Dinner Nights held once or twice a year when, resplendent in mess kit, their menfolk danced attendance upon them as in the days of yore.

As in the days of yore, too, after the port had been passed, with the senior lady setting the example and announcing "Ladies - I think the time has come for us to leave the gentlemen to their brandy and cigars," they were all traditionally expected to arise together like an elegant flock of birds, and withdraw to powder their noses, so that we men could let our conversation revert to its usual risqué-ness for a while, before rejoining them.

It was all very nice and worked well, although naturally there would soon emerge a burgeoning breed of younger wives, those who hated to miss a trick, who failed to see why they shouldn't be allowed to stay behind with the chaps and talk dirty.

Up until the Crimea, after which it was stopped, a certain percentage of wives were even allowed to accompany their husbands to war, sharing the risk, the rigour and tented accommodation with them alongside the other men.

They foraged, cooked, washed, sewed, dressed wounds, soothed fevered brows and provided a quick and comforting leg over when asked to - and there were several bairns rudely born in some of those expediently erected Crimean huts, its tents and snow-filled ditches.

Nowadays we have uniformed womenfolk actually flying fighter planes and serving on the front line, but at the time of which I write they were treated more . . . genteely.

So with Mess rules proscribing the use of its facilities as a locale for the assuagement of mutual concupiscence, where was a young officer to take his catch for the kill when returning from a successful Oat Patrol?

It could be argued that she was unlikely to make a successful future general's wife if she agreed to be courted in the icy sludge of Aldershot's renowned Long Valley tank and infantry training area, but a subaltern then didn't earn enough to cough up for a hotel room every time a lady's libido matched his own after a strenuous game of tennis or squash together, which being young, fit and active and on a good healthy diet it was often wont to do - thank God, otherwise from where would today's officer class have sprung?

Sex with a woman, whilst cloistered within one's constricted khaki purlieus, was at once encouraged and applauded by one's peers, yet impeded.

Do it; tell us how well you're doing at it; let us guffaw alongside you with the telling of its antics, but other than an engagement ring it would be better if you didn't let us see proof of it.

If a red-blooded twenty-year old civilian Caucasian male lures twenty maidens a month to his one-room lair above the off-licence in the high street, he's an OK guy.

But heaven help his commissioned twin brother, Rodney, if he should smuggle even one bird a tour into his room in the Mess, and is caught atop her, and word leaks out.

That would attract instant opprobrium and censorial chastisement from his seniors.

Dammit, the wretched creature might even disturb the dogs - *and* if *I'm* not currently getting it, then *he's* obviously getting more than his fair share!

But it used to happen; of course it did. It used to happen all the time.

The ingenuity needed to pre-plan and execute such an operation successfully, was excellent training for other things as well.

The expertise required to smuggle a girl into and then sooner or later out of one's room up on the top floor landing while the Brigadier's holding a formal cocktail party in the ante room downstairs, was commendable.

Running such a gauntlet was a pretty good bird-assessor too.

Her reaction under duress, and her cool if confronted at 06.00 on the morrow by one's batman coming in and drawing back the curtains, was a pretty good indication how she might fare in support of one later in life, if proposed to.

A sort of one-woman pre-selection board in a way.

Picture the scene:

"Good morning, Bloggins. I thought you were off today?"

"So it would seem, sir."

"This lady's my sister."

"Very good, sir; just as sir wishes. Will it be one cup or two this morning?"

Or, if really pushed:

"Bloggins, I don't think you're going to believe this for a moment, but last night this young lady fell out of an aeroplane and landed on the Mess roof. Amazing, what?"

"Almost too amazing to be true, sir."

"What's more Bloggins, her clothes were all torn off in the descent. Dashed bad luck, what!"

"Dashed bad, sir; but 'er cloves is cluttered in disarray all abart the room, sir."

"Ah, yes Bloggins, but you see . . . they just happened to float in piecemeal through the window afterwards"!

It mattered not.

The Blogginses of this world usually liked their 'sirs' to be one of the boys, being past masters at the game themselves, and many a young lady's blushes have been spared over the years by generations of Blogginses considerately enquiring: "Will it be both you gentlemen taking tea this morning?"

There was once a subaltern in a Mess of mine called James, a good looking dago with a penchant for practical jokes, such as putting a half dissected rat into a polythene bag and shoving it under someone's bedclothes.

He found this hilarious.

One of his victims, Neil, lived in the next room to James.

Having just completed four nights tactical fieldwork on a local hairdresser, Neil was going to press home Phase Five of his strategy that night.

He had successfully overcome the lady's understandable reticence, and together he and his adrenalin had smuggled her up to his room where to his horror he discovered that the door, which in order to facilitate a smooth entry he had earlier left ajar, was now locked, with a note pinned to the lintel which read *LOOK IN YOUR LETTER RACK.*

Furiously vowing eternal damnation on the incorrigible prankster James, Neil whispered vague and hurried reassurances to his confused amour before hurtling back down four landings to retrieve his key from the letter rack in the hall.

Only to find it wasn't there.

Instead he found another little note which read *LOOK IN MOUTH OF CANNON.*

Becoming weak and quite white at this stage, Neil thudded across the moonlit square outside, which at that moment was under a deluge of rain.

Sheets of it sliced into the concrete.

The ground about the ceremonial cannon was ankle deep in mud, but skidding and sloshing to a halt beside it Neil gingerly inserted his finger down the barrel to extract - not what he so eagerly sought, his key - but another note, a soggy one, which read *YOU'LL FIND YOUR KEY UNDER MAT OUTSIDE YOUR DOOR.*

Neil and his ladyfriend never did make it.

During his worrying absence she stood patiently clutching her handbag, shifting from foot to foot like girls do with that nervous pre-sex bladder problem they have, while four subalterns, a major, and the resident retired colonel, all in their dressing gowns and carrying sponge bags on the way to and from their nocturnal ablutions, paid her their polite respects.

When she and Neil at last managed to attain the sanctuary of his illicit MoD boudoir, he hurriedly commenced trying to make amends, wooing her anew with soft music and gentle caresses, until, judging the time to be right, he pulled back his bedcovers to ease her semi-seduced form between the sheets.

Seconds after she'd discovered James's dead rat, there was a fire alarm.

The whole Mess had to pile out in the rain to form up on the assembly area by the cannon to be accounted for.

Neil attracted seven extra duties for that caper, while the happily grinning James got away with the whole episode scot free.

He was never a particularly popular chap, so I am sure he eventually got his come-uppance somewhere along the line.

When boy meets girl and he invites her up to see his things, that's usually, initially, exactly what he means.

He has photographs; his rugger ball and squash racquet to show her; the cup he won for ping-pong, and his course photo.

Girls like to see these things, to help them assess 'mateworthiness'.

The way Mess Rules stood though, a young officer was expected to ship out his toys in a suitcase.

What sort of idiot did he feel, sitting over dinner at Bagshot's *Pennyhill Park Hotel* with a valise of souvenirs open between them. "This is the shell case I brought home from Borneo. It usually stands beside my washbasin . . ."

Anyone with an ounce of initiative got his lass up the back stairs, and damn the consequence.

Romance could then move on from the shell case to more combustible pyrotechnics.

Unless the Army was content for the lower echelons of its officer corps to become a race of celibates, it needed to recognise and accept that once a chap's voice had broken and the first vain sprouting of hair appeared on his upper lip, there was much more to follow.

Concealing willing wenches about one's person, with a view to fornication, by inviting them up to see the panoramic vista of Pirbright by moonlight from one's window on the top floor landing next to the batmen's room, didn't have to be a hanging offence, and yet the occasional apprehension by an official eye that refused to turn blind, did sometimes used to result in the premature damning of an otherwise excellent young officer's career.

The Officers' Mess should never have been allowed to become a bordello, but there was no reason why one's ladyfriend should not have been allowed to enter and leave by the front door for those tacit purposes other than their annual supper, and flower arranging.

It would have been a far more seemly arrangement than expecting the young people to conduct their loving in the back seat of his banger on some nearby bomb site.

Another gripe was haircuts.

Whether it has to do with mobile phones, tight pants or their declining sperm count, the majority of young men today appear either to be follicly challenged, or else have deliberately shaved their heads to the bone to make them look that way. Whatever the reason, the effect suggests either homosexuality, lice, or aggressiveness - especially with the compulsorily accompanying tattoos, three-days' worth of stubble, and nose studs.

Being reasonably hirsute, I do periodically get the zany idea that it might be nice to have a spring clean of my own sometime, so that I could see what the naked configuration of my skull looks like at least once before it's ground to ash.

Why don't I?

Because whenever I investigate my scalp with a tentative exploratory scratch, usually during *News At Ten*, my nails get caught up on things like bumps, concavities and various indeterminable excrescences; solar keratoses, bullet ricochets, embedded pieces of long ago grit, and old bits of shrapnel - so if all was laid bare I am fearful that it would not at all be a pretty sight.

But it was not to make her soldiers look threatening that paragraph 36 of that red-backed military Koran, Queen's Regulations, stated: *The hair on the head is to be kept well cut and trimmed.*

The reason for this is to prevent one's hair getting caught up in the breach-blocks of one's weapons: oh, and to deter aforemementioned lice too, of course.

In Iraq and Afghanistan it is obviously sensible to have short hair because of the heat, dirt, dust and sand, the flies, and water shortage

It is also meant to look uniformly smarter that way.

Even though the Army swears by it, there are drawbacks to short back and sides though.

Most people love a military parade: the glinting blades of the swords and bayonets, the fluttering of Colours, the beat of the big bass drum and blare of brass, the stirring of one's blood at the sight of ramrod straight, fearless, gravel crunching young warriors and the sound of their marching feet.

Phew.

So woe betide any luckless squaddie who drops his rifle, feels sick, keels over or can't help making a rude noise just as the inspecting general comes clanking past to inspect their standard of turnout, and yet . . .

. . . not so much as an eyelid is batted - especially in a high wind - when 500 soldiers effect an immaculate about turn that because of the lack of purchase afforded by their short back and sides, leaves the peaks of the navy-blue Number One Dress hats of 200 of them still facing the way they've just come from. The results are four-fold:

1. 5,000 spectators pretend nothing untoward has happened.

2. 200 soldiers find themselves unable to keep a straight face or give the parade their undivided attention, knowing that they now resemble Foreign Legionnaires in peakless *kepis* wearing black plastic sunshields down their necks.

3. The same 200 soldiers suffer public indignity as they stiff-neck-edly try to retain a hat which should have fallen off, whilst surreptitiously trying to jerk and wiggle it back into its rightful position once more.

4. The normally immaculate Advance in Review Order looks more like Napoleon's retreat from Moscow.

5. The CO will subsequently say to his Adjutant or the Adjutant will say to the RSM or the Company Commander will say to his CSM "We really must get these Number One hats sorted out . . ." and yet still no one seems able to have done so.

One Monday morning in Germany, the CO told a fashionable fellow officer friend of mine that he really did think it was time he thought about getting his hair cut again.

"Yes Colonel, I agree," said Charles, who saluted and left the office.

Charles wasn't at lunch that day.

Missed dinner, too.

Nor was he at breakfast on Tuesday, or anywhere to be found all day.

We were becoming quite worried and started to make serious enquiries as to his whereabouts.

When there was no sign of him on Wednesday either, we had to post him 'missing' and AWOL.

Then all of a sudden, just as though nothing had happened he reappeared back in the Mess for lunch on Thursday.

"*Charles,*" cried the Colonel and the rest of us with relief. "Where on earth have you been?"

Charles seemed surprised.

"But Colonel; you told me to get my haircut."

"Yes, I did," said the Colonel. "But that was on Monday."

"But Colonel, I thought you knew. My barber's in London."

TWENTY-TWO

A GUITAR IS A CUMBERSOME item to carry without its case when you are transporting other things at the same time, such as your family.

We were on a plane over to Germany where I had been posted to take up a two-year appointment as second-in-command of a unit in Hanover.

My happy time with 31 AYT had come to a close.

We had packed up our quarter at 26, Langtun Avenue in Ambrosden, and that's when I realised that without a case the only way I was going to get my classical Spanish guitar to come with us - so be it - was under my arm.

It had been accepted as cabin baggage at Heathrow and spent the journey slithering about the floor beneath my seat.

The plane was now banking in preparation for landing at Hanover's *Langenhagen* Airport.

Fortunately I was not wearing uniform, or even I might have been embarrassed at the incongruity of arriving in BAOR looking like some lone ENSA artist, toting an oversize banjo along instead of a sword.

It was mid-winter nevertheless, and so my British warm overcoat still proclaimed my status.

Nor had I had much chance of a haircut, what with the time taken writing about them, two shortly interspersed stays in hospital, handing over the Youth Team to my successor, one Mike Jiggins, and then packing up and handing over our quarter in Bicester prior to this German move.

The result was that my older, childless, rather more strait-laced and traditional predecessor, waiting there courteously to greet us with a unit vehicle at the airport entrance, was slightly taken aback to see his relief appear from customs and come limping into view with a wife, two kids, long hair, and a guitar slung loosely across his shoulders.

Rachel was whey-faced from airsickness, and Natalia and her pram-borne, bubble-blowing baby brother Lex were each alternating between sulks and fractiousness.

Our trolley was laden to toppling with battered suitcases and shopping baskets bulging with excess oddments that we'd been unable to pack.

I thought our soldier/driver looked quite encouraged at the shape of things to come, but as far as George Dillon was concerned, ours was not an auspicious arrival.

Once he had ascertained for sure that his luck was out and I really was me, he grudgingly shook my hand, smiled frostily at Rachel and the children, saw our goods and chattels and us into the green minibus, and then made good his escape to hot foot it back to the unit to report to the others there that in his opinion all did not bode well for the future.

He told me later that he had never seen anyone travel with quite so much luggage before, but then upon reflection remembered that he had seen the Cameroninas leave Berlin once.

Rachel and I were married aged nineteen and twenty-one respectively, so our carefree 20s never happened. While all our friends whooped it up and had fun, we were being happy but flat-bound and responsible young parents.

Later, when our children were at boarding school, we would be able to travel with a nice set of luggage and a leather briefcase containing a crisp current copy of *Country Life* and a gold Sheaffers pen instead of disposable nappies and a chewed biro, while our colleagues, who married later in life, would be wresting with all that poo, goo and boo-hoo stuff.

Hanover, in the meantime, was a beautiful city.

Temporary accommodation had been arranged for us in *Seelhorstrasse.*

Marie Rummey, the OC's wife, had stocked the fridge with a well thought out 24-hour ration pack of domestic comestibles, and her husband, Charles, with whom I was to work for the next 12-months, till he was posted, had made sure there was a carton of stubby Amstel beers waiting chilled for instant consumption.

Although there was snow on the ground outside, within minutes of our arrival Rachel was padding about in just her bra and knickers asking how long it would be before England was going to discover central heating.

At 09.00 precisely next morning, the doorbell rang.

Rachel was feeding Lex, and Natalia was putting marmalade on her dress, so it was me who answered it.

"Guten Morgen, Herr Hauptmann."

Christ.

They'd come for me already.

Anton Diffring's younger brother stood on the threshhold in a gleaming, black leather, ankle-length trench coat, lips parted in a travesty of a smile, gold teeth and black-booted heels together, waist slightly bowed . . . .

Tick-tock.

"Mein Name ist Harry Mewers. I haf brought wiz me a unit feehicle for your disposal and I am instructed to act as your guide around ze town should you vish it; plis."

I wound up treading on Natalia, who'd been standing just behind me as I stepped back.

There have been two formations named British Army of the Rhine (BAOR).

Both were originally occupation forces in Germany, one after World War I, and the other after World War II.

The second British Army of the Rhine was formed on 25 August 1945, from 21st Army Group, under Field Marshal Montgomery.

Its original function was to control the corps districts which were running the military government of the British zone of occupied Germany.

After the assumption of government by civilians, it became the command formation for the troops in Germany only, rather than being responsible for administration as well.

The 1993 Options for Change defence cuts then resulted in BAOR being replaced by the 25,000 strong British Forces Germany (BFG) in 1994. However -

. . . it was now 1967, and Harry Mewers was one of those thousands of German civilians employed by the British Army in a myriad of clerical and industrial capacities.

The majority of them had never fought the British of course, all having been engaged on the Russian Front - and Harry Mewers had been one of these, naturally; although when I got to know him better over a beer one day he did let slip having taken a pot-shot at a stray American one afternoon in the Ardennes.

Leaving Lex happily digesting breakfast in his cot, Rachel and Natalia waved me off at the front door and watched me climb into one of our unit's vehicles beside Harry Mewers, who then gave me the Ritz tour of Hanover while wending our way indirectly to the bank.

Inside the imposing *Commerzbank* building I was introduced to Herr Hemerding, the Under Manager, who opened an account there for me on the spot, issued me with my Konto (account) number and presented me with a small yellow envelope of loose-leaf cheques to use. All I now needed to do was notify the Chief Army Paymaster at Ashton-Under-Lyne in Lancashire of my Konto number, and my monthly pay would be credited to me automatically in *Deutschmarks* in my new account there in Hanover.

My business complete, Mewers then took me for a coffee at the *Opern-Konditorei* in *Georgstrasse,* one of those superb German salons where the coffee and cake and the quality of smartly dressed ladies sitting about in the middle of the day waiting to see, to be seen and to make new acquaintances, beat anything one could ever find down an English high street, where *Molly Brown's Black Cat Cosy Tea Room & Eaterie* was usually about the best to be had, and they closed at 4.30 p.m.

After that day's 'shopping' and getting myself oriented, I reported next morning to my new unit, 5CSSD.

The Army loves its initials.

There was SOE (Special Operations Executive) in the war: the SAS (Special Air Service) and SBS (Special Boat Service) - and now here was I about to become Second-in-Command of BAOR's CSSD.

Commando Squad Special Division?

Er, no: CSSD stood for Camp Stores Sub Depot, and had nothing to do with pink frilly things for sexually disoriented soldiers, but dealt instead with tons and tons of dirty green canvas marquees and tents.

The British Army in Germany was spending most of its time training for an expected war, a war that was to be fought keeping the Russians back where they belonged, on the other side of the River Weser.

Wars are fought in the open, so an army needs tents in which to live, train and operate from.

Number 281 *Schulenburger Landstrasse* in the *Vinnhorst* district of Hanover was the location of an impressive *Wehrmacht* barracks we Brits had taken over after WWII. These were now home to 5CSSD, where a dozen British soldiers and 300 German civilians processed unit demands, and received, refurbished and reissued all the canvas and camping equipment required for use by the whole of BAOR.

At the end of their respective manoeuvres unit convoys would come rumbling through our gates to return all the manky, mud-caked stuff for refurbishment. Once it had been cleaned, and processed through our canvas stitching bays, the repaired kit was taken by forklifts to be stacked on wooden pallets from stone floor to ceiling in vast, hangar-like storage bays, until yet another convoy of trucks would arrive, to borrow some more of it for a couple of weeks, to go and erect their encampment somewhere out on the *Teutoburger Wald* or *Lüneburg Heath*.

Just a small quadrant of 5CSSD, *Schulenberger Landstrasse,*
Hanover – 1967

Stack upon stack, row upon row, floor above floor of canvas
tentage awaiting loan issue to BAOR in the field for annual
manoeuvres

273

Having paid my respects to the OC, Major Charles Rummey, Captain George Dillon, whom I was there to relieve, then took me round the depot to meet everyone.

Herr Eschke was the HR Manager, assisted by a gorgeous little blonde item called Susie Glüfke.

Herr Rehman, a WWII Panzer driver and his sidekick, Albert with his black pork-pie hat and foul smelling cigars, ran the traffic office.

Herr Arnim von Bayer, one of Rommel's staff officers in the *Afrika Korps*, and a Herr Pietsch were responsible for all the repair workshops.

A Russian woman called Elvira, like a medieval Romany, spent her life in an outhouse sorting tent pegs, and a marvellous little jack-of-all-trades who could fix/make absolutely anything, Willi Andressen, and his helpers crashed and banged about all day in the metal workshop.

Herr Rischek and his team operated the tailor's shop, where as a sideline we manufactured the navy blue uniforms for the British Frontier Service who patrolled the border with East Germany, which is why sometime later I managed to acquire for myself rather a nice navy blue overcoat knocked up on the cheap.

All that lot were below stairs.

Above stairs, up in the executive suite, we had general dogsbody and Mr Fixit, Harry Mewers, whom we've already met; Herr Winterstein, a charming old school gentleman draughtsman with exquisite penmanship who singlehandedly operated our planning department; the processing office, where a dozen German ladies prepared all the unit applications under the eagle eye of WO1 Terry Faulkner; the Orderly Room, where the Chief Clerk, S/Sgt Davies, ran the Brit side of things; and then there was my office.

My office was vast, with a small adjoining sub-office wherein sat my two secretaries, Waltraud 'Traudchen' Obermann and Siegried 'Siggy' Ziegenbein, who both fell in love with me in no time at all and like puppies with slippers would bring me in special pieces of cake and all sorts of other goodies each day with my coffee.

Having said goodbye to the outgoing George Dillon, who I seem to recall had been posted to Singapore, and rearranged my new office to my liking, I had just filled my fountain pen and straightened my ruler when Siggy came in with the mail.

"There's one on top that you might find interesting," she said with a smile.

I had only been in the unit two hours, and yet here was an Order just arrived from HQ at Rheindahlen sending me off the very next day to attend a fortnight's Colloquial German Course, being held at the RAEC centre in Celle, a pretty little town half-an-hour to the north-east of Hanover.

I spoke schoolboy French and a similar smattering of Spanish, but as yet no German. It was a language that had always appealed to me, and so this seemed like a heaven sent opportunity to do something about it. With a substantial German civilian staff working there at the depot, although the majority of them spoke English, it would be no bad thing for me to acquire a few new linguistic ground rules, which is why I didn't quibble over this Order, and starting next day every weekday morning for the next two weeks I drove along the girl-lined Route 3 to Celle.

Girls?

Everywhere I looked in Germany I seemed to see girls presenting their wares on a commercial stall. Especially along most of the length of Route 3, where they stood flashily and scantily clad beside their cars parked on the verges, waiting for horny passing lorry drivers, or anyone else who happened to be in the mood, to pull in and avail himself of their excellent continental roadside service.

The next two weeks in Celle were spent sitting in the RAEC's language laboratory with a dozen other BAOR newcomers, listening to tape recordings in German and trying to understand the subtleties of advertisements in *Stern, Quick, Neu Revue, Bünte* and several other colourful weekly picture publications.

Our final test, at close-of-play on the last Friday, was to describe-in-German the route we would take driving from Celle to Hanover, on the map pinned to the wall.

Most of us managed to scrape a 'pass' out of this exercise, although the course's token Brigadier didn't do quite as well as the rest of us.

"Right, very well," he hurrumphed, making his way up to the map. "So let me get this straight; you want me to describe the route taken from Hanover, all the way here to Celle, is that right?"

"Yes, Brigadier, if that's what you'd like to do, sir; just like everybody else, but in reverse" the RAEC captain affirmed.

"In German!"

"That's it, Brigadier, you've got the idea. In German, if you'd care to give it a shot, sir."

"Yes, right, very well then . . . we'd better see about this then, hadn't we! Now -." With his left hand on his hip, rubbing his chin with his right, he considered the task.

"But they all speak English so damn' well out here, don't they!" he remarked, half turning his head from the map, one eyebrow raised appealingly to the instructor.

"Brigadier . . .?"

"*Dam*mit; oh, very well then, if I must play act . . . I believe that *heute mussen wir in unsere Wagen fahren* from Hanover - *hier* (finger jab) *nach Celle - hier* (finger jab) along *dieser Strasse* I think it is, you know - where you get to see all those pretty young girls lounging about near the bushes by the side of the road. Totty, we used to call it in my day. *Naturlich wir mussen nicht stoppen, weil sie sind* not very nice girls apparently, *und ich bin* happily *verhairatet*, although *memsahib's* not averse to a spot of that sort of hanky-panky stuff herself *de temps en temps*, but perhaps I'd better not say too much about that – what! So - *hier ist ein Ausfahrt*. I always think that's such a lovely word, don't you? If you didn't know it meant *Departure* it could be so dreadfully suggestive . . . *und dann* we drive just a little bit farther down until we *reachen diesen* language *Schule* just *hier* . . ."

Final finger jab and the heave of one massive sigh of relief.

The RAEC instructor was aware that in one's best career interests it was probably advisable never to 'fail' a brigadier!

After those two weeks I felt sufficiently buoyed and confident to be able to voice and discuss German proposals before a NATO summit meeting, but there was no time for that sort of malarkey.

I had to get back to my tents.

The OC was off on a fortnight's skiing holiday the following week, so I needed to acquire a proper working grasp of things before then.

By the time I'd seen him off the premises a week later, I'd cracked it.

I could have run the establishment standing on my head, and could hardly wait to get started. While the cat was away skiing, this German-speaking mouse was really going to rift the place with his new broom.

After lunch that afternoon the Chief Clerk came to my office with a signal that had just arrived from HQ, which read:

From Hildesheim: Subject AGR Course 5-11 Feb 67. 1 x vacancy to be filled Capt M.A. George (474405). Joining instrs follow.

Dammit!

The course was due to form up in two days' time, on Sunday evening.

The OC was away.

I was the only officer left to run the place.

I had been in the chair only five days and here they were sending me off yet again at short notice to fill a vacancy on some wretched AGR course, whatever an AGR course was.

I didn't even know what it meant.

To cap it all I would have to come all the way in to the unit the following day, Saturday, just to pick up the joining instructions.

When I got there at 10.30 the Chief Clerk had already sorted the mail.

"Your joining instructions have arrived, sir." He grinned. (Little shit.) "I've put them on your desk."

A solitary piece of paper was propped against a glass weight in the middle of my desk. Sweeping it up in my fist, I

277

read: . . . *will attend Anglo-German Relations Course,
Logistikschule der Bundeswehr, Blankanese, Hamburg 5-11
Feb 67 . . .*

WOW!

I was being sent on a week's Anglo-German Relations
Course.

In HAMBURG.

I felt like a Muslim given an all expenses found trip to
Mecca.

I could hardly believe it.

Hamburg.

City of cities.

And the Anglo-German Relations Course - one of the best
fun courses in the British Army.

Thank God I'd already got my two weeks' colloquial
German course under my belt.

What perfect timing.

I dashed off home to tell Rachel the amazing news.

At 19.00 on Sunday 5 February 1967 the Hanover-Hamburg
train rumbled across the bridge over the River Elbe and I gazed
for the first time upon the winter night lights of that magical
city.

Hamburg: a City State.

It has been said that if Germany ever went to war again,
Hamburg may decide to do so as well.

During the closing phases of WWII, when the rubble that
was Hamburg was being occupied, the cellars of the famed
Four Seasons Hotel were found to have been the studio for the
infamous Lord Haw-Haw's transmitting equipment and
wartime broadcasts.

The Allied Commission adapted this facility to send out the
first British Forces Broadcasting programmes in Germany,
before BFBS moved to their Cologne studio.

German radio broadcasting was controlled and restricted in
the post war years.

The VHF waveband was relatively unexploited in those
days and so it was that one which was given to the Germans to

play with. This they did effectively, and so developed their techniques that Germany's stereophonic broadcasts soon became of an unsurpassed quality and crystal clarity.

Another British officer was travelling with me on the train, attending the same course.

Outside the *Hauptbahnof* we got a taxi to the *Logistikschule der Bundeswehr* at *Blankenese*, going via *St Pauli* and the *Reeperbahn*.

Entering the traffic flow converging at the top of the *Reeperbahn* was like jostling to gaze in wonder down the craterous mouth of just about the largest helter-skelter, hurdy-gurdy, fun palace adventure playground in the world. When our taxi's tyres *thrummed* over the glistening, garishly neon-lit reflections in the wet cobblestones, my head was like a Wimbledon spectator's in fast replay.

Our taxi driver chuckled to himself while my fellow passenger and I sat in stunned and silent awe.

Raw sex ran with the beer and the frankfurters and hamburgers in every gutter in *St Pauli*.

The motherlode of all lust was compressed into this one square mile.

Thousands of scantily dressed 'ladies of the night' were lolling around its drainpipes, lamp-posts and door knockers.

Clad only in the barest essentials, thousands more hassled their asses enticingly up and down the pavements.

A car-borne cavalcade of them were cruising slowly around with their boobs flopped on the dashboards for appraisal.

There were girls in thigh-high slashed leather skirts and pussy-pelmets straddling bar stools, sitting cross legged in cafés, clubs and restaurants and even gathered round the entrances to the gents' loos.

It was disgusting!

Sodom and Gomorrah revisited.

I *liked* Hamburg.

Blankanese was a select residential suburb to the west of the city, a little way out along the north bank of the Elbe.

The German Army's School of Logistics was a grey, efficient, purpose-built complex that suited us fine; after all, we couldn't expect to be on the *Reeperbahn* the *whole* time.

The aim of the course was to help further the cause of Anglo-German relations by an introduction to German political, economic, social and cultural life through lectures, discussion and personal contact.

That's what it said in the handout.

The British Army seldom offered this many perks; I just happened to have got lucky in being nominated for this one.

The most interesting aspect of the course was the visits.

On the Monday evening we were given a cocktail party reception at the British Consulate.

Afterwards, we stopped off at the *Reeperbahn*.

This meant that few of us got back to the *Logistikschule* until 06.00, where we stood beneath cold showers nursing our hangovers and lewd thoughts while dreaming of a good English breakfast, and some kip - neither of which was forthcoming.

We had forgone our sleep, and breakfast consisted of cold rollmop herring and gooseberry jam on bread rolls with crusts so sharp that they sliced our gums.

Red-eyed and with our stomachs rumbling we debouched from our bus at 09.30 outside Hamburg's *Heeresoffizierschule* (officer cadet school).

All I recalled of that morning was how impressed I was upon entering one of the classrooms to hear that the lesson on Tactical Doctrine was being given entirely in English, when the complexities of this subject at Sandhurst are difficult enough for some British cadets to grasp even in their own language. The Germans were obviously taking the NATO Alliance seriously.

After lunch we went on to Studio Hamburg to be given a talk about German television by a Herr Meyer-Hanel, while unbeknown to us we were being televised for the six-o'clock news.

That evening we were dined by the Hamburg branch of the Royal British Legion (no, I never knew they had one there either) and filing into their bar for pre-dinner drinks I just happened to glance up at the News on their TV wall-mounted screen, only to see myself striding towards the camera staring like a lost sheep, filmed mounting the steps of Studio Hamburg earlier that afternoon.

Our Royal British Legion dinner was a riot.

It was a prearranged affair, so we had done what was expected of us - and attended. Our surprise can be imagined when half way through the soup course a little WWI British retainer came trundling round clad in a grubby white jacket bearing a bus conductor's bag slung round his neck, asking if we would pay for our dinner. We had not been told about this, someone's crossed wires etc., but paid up graciously nevertheless; but *not* right in the middle of our leek soup like that: shocking bad form.

On our way home again several of us stopped off at the *Reeperbahn.*

Correction: some of us returned to barracks.

Next afternoon we visited the *Rathaus* for talks, coffee and cigars with representatives of the main political parties.

That evening we all went off for some light relaxation to Hamburg's famous music hall, the *Hansa-Theatre,* the long running vaudeville venue founded in the St Georgi red light district in 1894, in *Steindamm* - and then on the way back to barracks some of the others stopped off at the *Reeperbahn* once more. It was purely a question of availing oneself of a facility when it was there.

After Thursday morning's lectures we were taken by ferry to visit and have a very fine lunch at the BP refinery on the Elbe, after which a bracing launch trip round Hamburg Harbour blew the cobwebs away.

This enabled us to remain awake when we dropped by later that afternoon to *Springer-Haus*, the main office of the German press baron, Axel Springer.

A swish lift swept us up to the Picasso-lined top floor reception lounge where one of his *avant-garde* editors entertained us to canapés, stiff gins and some wisecracks.

"Hamburg is a very progressive city," he explained in a thick Bronx he'd thought it pretty clever to acquire. "I'll tell ya, we've even got a Jewish mayor, an' y'caint get more progressive than that - especially here, in Goimany."

We stopped off at the *Reeperbahn* once more on the way back.

Next day we all went home.

It was Friday.

Rachel took one look at me, and grimaced - offering the opinion that she'd never imagined the course would be *quite* such a harrowing ordeal!

After we had been living in the *Seelhorstrasse* dormitory area for a few months, I was at last fortunate enough to be offered an apartment in the much sought-after, and posher, long-term officers' residential district in *Wallmodenstrasse*.

As luck would have it the outgoing tenant had been living on the top floor; Block 47, Flat 13.

The Royal Engineer officer and his wife who lived below us, in Flat 47/11, rejoiced in the letterhead they'd had printed: 47/11 - *Der Kolnischerwasser Wohnung* (the Cologne water residence) whereas up there in our penthouse suite we referred to ourselves simply as *The Hanover House of George.*

We loved it.

Stepping out of the lift we opened our front door onto a vast, green-carpeted bowling alley of vestibule and hallway.

The view from our lounge/diner was a magnificent one of the whole of Hanover, a fairytale vista of green copper domes and steeply sloping red-roofed houses poking above the treetops.

Those other parts of this beautiful city that didn't quite fit our full frontal 300-degree panorama, could be seen from the side and rear windows.

Standing there with a fully charged whisky tumbler in the middle of a thunderstorm I felt like Thor himself, safely riding the heart of the holocaust, protected by torrents of wind-lashed outriders crashing against the windows and brickwork, which made the building sway on its foundations, whilst within we remained omnipotent and impregnable.

When it snowed we felt we were perched atop the Eiger, with all mod cons.

In summer it was wonderful standing on the balcony with a G&T enjoying the view, although frustrating that it was too small to stretch out full length in the sun and get one's kit off.

I tried it once; got my feet tangled up in the wrought ironwork, and was crapped on by pigeons.

It was just large enough to sit out after dinner and enjoy a good cigar, or if the budget was tight that month, an indifferent one.

One evening I was out there with Stuart Craven, a friend of ours, enjoying our coffee and brandy in style.

No sooner had Stuart raised his goblet to his lips than the park below erupted into a magnificently timed and beautiful ten-minute firework display.

"Thank you," said Stuart, toasting me. "I'm most impressed."

Our son Lex was nearly two by now, and showing an inordinate degree of interest in German lavatories.

German loos have a ledge, pan or shelf in them as a sort of temporary detainee transit camp to allow the post-operative inspection of one's droppings (if so desired) prior to their disposal.

This final inspection facility allows depositors to have a quick shufti, just to ensure they haven't lost a collar stud, any small change, or a piece of carrot they might have grown particularly fond of, before flushing.

For some reason, if ever he was missing, Lex could usually be found kneeling on the loo floor with the seat up, splashing about with his toy submarine in the previously mentioned ceramic cavity's ambient water.

As far as I know he doesn't do it so much now that he's in his 40s, when I'm sure he's developed some more acceptable even if similarly fanciful fetish, but right up till his teens he could be relied upon to seek any excuse to inspect the host's plumbing, and having done so would return beaming to the assembly at large with the unabashed announcement to an embarrassed Rachel, "They've got a lovely toilet here, Mum."

It was like having our own resident health inspector on the team.

My best friends in Hanover were David and Vivienne Arthur. David was the Clerical, Medical & General's European representative. He and Viv lived in a flat in *Berrenbostel,* just outside the city, on the edge of the countryside.

Most Friday nights David and I would go to the *Löwenbrau* to sink a few bevies together.

The *Löwenbrau* was Hanover's popular beer hall in *Georgstrasse,* just a few doors along from the *Opern Konditorei* coffee, cake and crumpet pick-up joint opposite the Opera House. It had an *Oompah* band, scrubbed tables and benches, and great gleaming kegs of beer from which busty, bowlegged barmaids in flowery Bavarian *dirndls* dispensed copious flagons of steaming brew to shifts of thousands.

They did sausages too.

Resembling the dining hall of Nottingham Castle at the time of Robin Hood, the *Löwenbrau's* timber walls and balconies were festooned with all the flags, pennants and armorial bunting relating to Teutonic land ownership and scar-faced chivalry, so . . .

One Friday night David and I decided we would form a British Club.

We enjoyed the establishment so much, and had fallen in love with so many of its barmaids and waitresses, and were so crazy about *Löwenbrau* beer and so knocked out by the *Gemütlichkeit* of the place, which by comparison made an English pub seem like a piss-hole in Piccadilly Underground, that we decided we would frequent it regularly.

Weekly.

Every Friday night, in fact.

Religiously.

Without fail.

Forever.

So we bought ourselves a little Union Jack on a stick and having told Rachel and Vivienne we were going to the British Club, would ceremonially unfurl our little flag in the centre of the table, order our first round and set up shop.

What we'd set shop up as, we didn't really know, much less did we care, but within minutes we would be joined by others, mostly German, all grinning and asking if we wanted a girlfriend a-piece, beer, friendship, or a fight, whereas most of the other Brits there, by and large, seemed to ignore us.

Perhaps they were shy.

Then one night after a Tupperware party Rachel and Vivienne walked in.

Our cover was blown.

The place was packed, as usual.

Beer was flowing and the crowd singing, surging and swaying to the band's Black Forest and yodel music *oompahing* out from their raised stage in the centre.

The last thing we wanted in the middle of all this merriment was hassle, but it looked like we'd got it.

The girls had decided we should leave.

Almost leading us by our ears the four of us edged through the crowd towards the exit, but on the way out I noticed that the band had stopped playing and was fiddling with its music sheets. This was not unusual. It happened whenever somebody with a funny cardboard student's hat on his head staggered up from the body of the kirk to buy the band a drink, take the conductor's baton and lead them through a few crazily conducted bars of his choice: it was an outlet for people's previously unrealised musical ambition, and despite this the obliging band usually managed to carry on playing somewhere along the right track, whatever the drunken nut with the baton was doing indulging his musical fantasy.

This time was different though.

A well dressed man in his 40s wearing a grey business suit had slipped up onto the stage and was conferring with the band's leader. The musicians were leaning forward and each lending an ear, and were now rearranging the music on their stands. The smartly dressed man turned, and stepped forward a pace to face the Friday night revellers, whose hubbub was deafening.

Their hubbub was deafening.

Until he started to sing.

That's right: you've got it.

He had assumed the classic stance of the operatic tenor in mid-aria - and that's exactly what he was: the lead tenor from the Opera House opposite who had slipped in briefly to quench his thirst and have a warm up before getting changed for that evening's performance.

His voice rose, swelled and rang to the rafters as he socked to us the aria's sustained and glass-shattering final high note. He cut it off with a downward snap of his hands, threw us all a half salute, shook hands with the musicians, jumped down from the stage and was half way to the door before the applause erupted like an avalanche around him. He was beseeched, tugged at and implored to sing again, but he knew his business, declined, waved once more, and was gone.

God - what a memorable interlude.

It was good to be alive when things like that happened.

TWENTY-THREE

THE BIG CRY in any specialist or technical branch of the army has always been that one should be a soldier first; a tradesman second.

Officers were expected to be on top of a disparate range of subjects, to keep abreast of developments in certain areas and to remain at all times physically and militarily ready, willing, able and up to it, when more often than not the concerted specialist nature, demanding requirement and expectations of some people's work prevented them, time-wise, from being able to keep up to date with these criteria. Periodically therefore, if he is sensible, such an officer would arrange for himself a short 'infantry attachment' to become refamiliarised with the basic rudiment of his vocation, which was . . .

Khaki?

Killing people.

The prerequisite to being allowed to sit the three-day Captain to Major written examination, the passing of which was critical to promotion, was to pass the one day practical promotion examination first.

The one-day practical promotion examination consisted entirely of teeth-arm tactics; map-reading, signals, radio voice-procedure, administration and morale - all hairy battlefield warfare stuff, none of your dilettantish poodle-faking.

Because I would soon be taking both these exams I knew the time had now come for me to get out from behind my desk and go 'back into the field' for a bit. To do this I arranged for myself a week's attachment to a BAOR infantry regiment on one of its training exercises.

My request was duly approved and processed, but when my joining instructions arrived from Rheindahlen HQ they were a-typically not very specific. I was merely ordered to report, ruggedly accoutred, at 15.00 the following Sunday to a grid reference in the middle of a small wood on *Lüneburg Heath.* But I had no idea to whom I was reporting.

Rachel stoked me full of stodge that Sunday lunchtime, giggled while watching me wrestle unaccustomedly with my camp-kit, and then she, Natalia and Lex all waved sweetly from our balcony as I roared off northward in my Land Rover.

An hour later I turned off the Hanover-Hamburg *Autobahn,* drove through a village, bumped across open fields and dragged my vehicle's sump along a rutted woodland trail towards, I hoped, the RV-point with my host unit.

Swinging the mud smothered vehicle onto a mossy mound, I switched off the ignition, humped my gear out of the back and ploughed my way on foot across the remaining 100-metres of gorse and bracken to the camp site.

Straightening up from my final assault through a bramble bush, I found the camp in a clearing right ahead of me.

I couldn't believe it.

It was a mirage.

A miracle.

I was in a time warp.

It was like turning up in heaven and finding your deceased father, sitting there in his old armchair in the drawing room waiting for you, with no intervening years between.

Standing on a grassy knoll to my fore like a khaki-clad Red Indian chieftain, stood the CSM . . .

. . . Whom I knew.

It was Corporal Len Hart, then of 'A' Company 1st Battalion The Royal Sussex Regiment in Korea - my old outfit - and now apparently CSM of 'A' Company 3 Queens (the Regiment's new title since its amalgamation) who with prior notification of my arrival was standing there waiting to greet me on *Lüneburg Heath,* Germany, exactly one decade later.

"Good after*noon,* **sir,**" he said, throwing up a quivering salute while managing to keep his tremendous jaw line from quivering as well. "Your tent awaits you and is ready for occupation, **sir**."

"Thank you S'arnt Major. How very kind of you."

"Yes, **sir;** wasn't it," he replied, and grinned.

"You old *bastard,*" I roared, both of us dropping any further pretence as we stepped forward to pump each other's hand vigorously. "Christ, this is a surprise, Len. I had no idea the mob was here, or that it was you I was going to be attached to. And my old Company too, no less. Shiny 'A'. This is too much. Who's in command?"

"You're never going to believe it," he grinned, cocking one bushy black eyebrow mischievously.

"Who?"

"Nigel."

"Nigel Knocker? The Adjutant?"

"The same."

"You're kidding. Has he mellowed?"

"Yeah, he's alright," Len chuckled. "Not a bad bloke, actually. He knows you're here and is quite looking forward to seeing you again; I think."

As soon as I had shaken down my kit and drunk the traditional earthenware jar of rich, thick tea brimful with dollops of condensed milk and ladlesful of white sugar, I made my way up to the higher-class end of the glade to scratch on Major Nigel Knocker's tent flap and pay my respects.

Ten years had elapsed since I had left the regiment, and him, in Gibraltar, but right now there was only time to chat briefly about the old days and what had happened since, because he was about to hold his 'O' (Orders) Group for the next day, which as an officer on attachment to the company I was invited to attend; this is when the OC gives a run-down and debrief on the day's events to the company's 'management' staff, for them to relay later to everyone else, and issues his plans for the morrow.

Several six-foot tables had been placed together to form a square around which sat the 2i/c, the three platoon commanders, the CSM, CQMS, platoon sergeants and me, all men of varying inclinations and abilities on benches, idly chatting between ourselves while awaiting the boss's arrival. With the snap of a twig and a flurry of dry leaves Nigel then duly appeared over the crest of a gully. We all stood as he arrived to take his patriarchal place at the head of table.

"Thank you; sit down please. Good evening. Right - well I'd like to start this evening's session by informing you about and extending a very warm welcome to Captain Mike George, who served with the regiment in Korea and Gibraltar and is now attached to us for a week to try to freshen up on what he's forgotten in the meantime. It's nice to have you back with us again, Mike. Welcome home."

Gosh.

To say I had a lump in my throat would be understating it a bit.

Next day I went out with 1 Platoon (my old platoon) but instead of footslogging and manpacking our kit - as we used to, through the swirling Korean dust of some passing American convoy - this time *we* were motorised as well.

Life in the British infantry had certainly developed a pace in the past decade. The AFVs 432 (Armoured Fighting Vehicles, also known as APCs, or Armoured Personnel Carriers) had transformed the ground pounders into a newer and faster ball-game; but I wasn't altogether sure I didn't still prefer horses.

At 11.00 we had lagered up briefly in a dustbowl to receive some incoming radio messages and plan our redeployment, when my attention was suddenly caught by a rapidly approaching spiral of dust, like a small twister with something heavy in the middle of it tearing towards us from the horizon like a bucketing road-runner. It was an APC with a filthy white pennant snapping from one of its antennae.

"Who the hell's *this*," I asked, "churning along like a bat out of hell?"

"Chief Umpire," my host subaltern informed me.

"He's certainly shifting," I said. "You'd think he'd got a supercharger on that thing."

"Yup; Major Ellwood's certainly no slouch," he replied.

"Did you say *Ell*wood? *Steve* Ellwood . . .?"

The APC was moving fast to some location beyond, and passed by 15-metres in front of us, powering like a freshly landed meteorite bouncing across the Gobi. Despite his beret, earphones and yellow-tinted dust goggles, I couldn't fail but recognise immediately the strong, tanned features of its commander. It was him alright. Steve Ellwood. My boyhood hero from Korea days who, among other things, had once force marched 'A' Company to oblivion and back to ensure that we all passed our physical efficiency tests.

"Morning," he cried, thrusting one *Sieg Heil*-ish arm out in salutation as he went roaring by on dust-flaying tracks.

Gosh this was fun.

I felt sure I must have died and gone to heaven, and it was still only Monday.

Thus the week unfolded.

I got hungry, dirty and tired.

I must admit that from preference I'm probably more at home sliding round a drawing room carpet in glossy pumps than the North German Plain in a small tank, but my profession demanded that I did both, so both I had to do. But it was certainly a terrific load of fun being back with my own old parent regiment again. At the end of the week, though, I was not sorry to get home to our flat in Hanover for a good clean-up, nosh and sleep, and be able to tell Rachel all about it - but then the following Monday I would again have to face my office chair, which after a gung-ho week tearing around with the old crowd, was going to seem even more humdrum and sedentary than ever it did before.

TWENTY-FOUR

THE HANOVER FAIRGROUND (*Messegelände Hannover*) is an exhibition area in the *Mittelfeld* district. Featuring 496,000 m² (5.3 million sq.ft.) of covered indoor space, 58,000 m² (624,306 sq ft) of open-air space, 27 halls and pavilions and a convention centre with 35 function rooms, it is the largest exhibition ground in the world.

Originally the area of the fairground was an aircraft works. After World War II, in which Hanover was badly damaged, the British military government of occupied Germany wanted to hold a trade fair and sought for a good place, since Leipzig, the traditional fairground of Germany, was unavailable, being in the Soviet occupation zone.

The hangars in *Laatzen,* south of Hanover, were deemed suitable for this purpose, and so the Hanover Fair, then named *Exportmesse 1947* was first held. The concept proved to be successful, and so a permanent fairground was established, growing over the years.

In 1961 the *Exportmesse,* held on the last ten days of April, became renamed the *Hanover Messe.*

Hotels were filled.

B&Bs made a killing, and with the probability of traffic congestion, and worse, the Police had their work cut out as well.

To help launch Britain's endeavours at the show and to show that we were officially aware of what was taking place around us, the British Consul in Hanover became traditionally beholden to throw a cocktail party that week for the fair's contingent of British contributors.

This was held in our Garrison Officers' Mess in *Heiligengeistrasse.*

Happy to do our bit for Queen and Country, we handed our Mess facilities over to the British Consul for the evening, for him to utilise our staff, import some extras of his own, and lay the event on as he wished. We all received invitations to the 'do', as a courteous expectation that we would act as the Consul's (*ergo* Britain's) hosts to the visiting Britons - because the Consulate staff proper was only three strong.

Along with our friends and colleagues, Rachel and I paraded at the appointed hour, collected our luke warm gin and tonics from the tray held by one of the passed-over but seemingly still willing waitresses at the door, and sidled forward to join the discreet mêlée within, there to mingle and inconspicuously help keep things flowing.

To highlight the punch-line of this anecdote I should outline to those readers who may not be aware, one of the cardinal codes of conduct in a British Army Officers' Mess.

It is dress.

In those days an army officer was blessed with thirteen different forms of dress. These ranged from Number One Dress - the high collared blues jacket and tight overall trousers worn on ceremonial occasions - down to Number 13 Dress itself, which I seem to recall was either PT shorts and plimsoles, or else an item of tropical white garb or something, with all manner of other kit and caboodle between. Not all of us possessed every form of dress all the time of course, but most of us over the years, as the need arose, did manage to accumulate a fair proportion of several of them.

Those ever invited to a military function will recall that the expected Order of Dress for the occasion was clearly indicated on their invitation: and woe betide defaulters or anyone deciding not to comply, or deciding to 'make an alternative statement'. The Army was very dress conscious, and the expectation of being correctly attired at all times extended especially to civilian dress, where one could score inestimable points if one was of the band-box brigade, but foul-up hopelessly on sharp rocks if sartorially inept.

293

There are different 'in house' rules applied to the 'bending' of Dress Regulations on parade. For example, should one be feeling slightly under-the-weather and experience difficulty getting dressed that morning, staggering onto parade minus one collar-dog, with a pip askew or an upside down lanyard, the usual penalty would be having to stand everyone a round of drinks in the bar later, and embarrassment alone was usually sufficient to prevent any recurrence. If an officer showed up improperly attired he was made to feel as much 'out of it' as a woman in a short skirt when the others were swishing about in long.

As mentioned elsewhere, one was generally expected to wear a lounge suit, collar and tie in the public rooms of a Mess, and for dinner on Mondays, Tuesdays and Thursdays. Wednesdays were deemed to be an extension of sports afternoon, so sports jacket and flannels were acceptable on those evenings, as they were on Fridays, Saturdays and Sundays. In the Mess bar almost any form of dress was permissible up to 19.00. This enabled the squash players to down their shandies before the stiff collar brigade came in for its pre-dinner gins, when post 19.00 frowns and comments could be severe enough to deter any remaining improperly attired scruff from dallying.

There were anomalies.

I have heard the latest dress peccadilloes discussed at Mess Meetings as being the most important item on the agenda. Trying to keep abreast of the times, at one such meeting it was suggested that leather jackets could be acceptable as long as they were *nice* leather jackets. Most of us knew what that meant, but what price the duly appointed arbiter of good taste when confronting a 15-stone officer clad in some multi-fringed Afghan monstrosity who insisted that *he* considered it was *perfectly* 'nice', thank you very much?

I have seen an extremely clean-cut, smart and pleasant looking captain (it was me, actually) in new suede shoes, neatly tapered cavalry twill trousers, freshly laundered Turnbull and Asser shirt, choker and navy blue cashmere sweater ordered to leave the Mess for being improperly dressed because I was not wearing a jacket and tie. By whom? By a scruffy looking major wearing sandals, baggy flannels in which he'd been under the car all day, a filthy old sports jacket with a fishing-fly in its lapel, and a hank of necktie which must previously have doubled as a pyjama cord in his PoW camp, yet within the letter of Mess Rules he was the one properly and acceptably attired.

On one occasion I was duty officer over Christmas, and as far as I knew the only person left in the Mess, everyone else having departed for the holiday. At 01.00 on Christmas morning there I was curled up comfortably in front of the Mess TV when the door opened and in walked Lt Col Derek Fanshawe, one of our dress-sticklers, a retired officer whose role there in Hanover was Permanent President of Courts Martial.

"Good Lord, I thought you'd gone home for Christmas, Colonel," I blurted, rising to my feet.

"So I see. I'd be obliged if you would tighten your tie and jacket for me if you would, please? You have your top button undone and are improperly dressed."

At one-o'clock on Christmas morning? Alone?

Bollocks!

There was seldom any leeway.

Except - one might have thought - where our British civilian guests who were to attend the British Consul's cocktail party were concerned.

Although it was our Mess, having lent it to the Consul to entertain our country's trade exhibitors, that evening we were to be guests in our own home.

One of the exhibitors I got into conversation with, Greg Peterson, resembled a polished and convivial Oliver Reed. He was spear-heading an enormous export drive of British goods to Europe, and this Hanover Trade Fair was his tub-thumping, Hyde Park show case. He was accompanied by a bevy of extraordinarily presentable, personable and luscious young ladies, all of whom were lending considerable sparkle and charm to the occasion.

"I was in Canada last year and just a couple of months back, in Japan," he was telling the small group of us who had gathered round. "There is a real undercurrent of movement in Britain's exports at the moment. Why, only the other day I met a Brit who was speaking proper French." We smiled. "I predict great stuff for the future and feel quite confident the country is soon going to start swinging back with a vengeance . . ."

While he spoke I glimpsed Colonel Fanshawe sniffing about, sidling up in his navy blue pinstripe, to hover on the periphery, toying with his sherry and appearing slightly ill at ease, as if wanting to join in, but too shy to do so. I resented his intrusion, it was distracting when I was particularly interested in hearing what my new Trade Hero, Greg, was saying. I knew little or nothing about exports. In fact, in common with many army officers I knew little or nothing about anything much, but had acquired the knack of looking intelligent. I did want to know what Greg exported though, so asked him. It was something transistorised that went into sub-marine construction plants, but I never found out what exactly because no sooner had he started to explain than bloody Fanshawe pounced, and let us all know what it was that had been on his tiny mind the whole time. He didn't have a clue what our conversation was about, and couldn't have cared less, but had merely been waiting for a lull to enable him to break in.

"You'll excuse me butting in," he said, addressing Greg, "but I'm afraid I shall have to ask you to leave. I consider the brightness and brashness of your necktie renders you improperly attired to be in an Officers' Mess."

I was stunned.

He wasn't even pissed.

The man was a quite unnecessary embarrassment.

Deranged.

Greg raised one eyebrow. "I'm so sorry you don't like it," he said, stroking the knot. "Actually, I rather do. Unlike that rather scruffy old cricket club job you're wearing, this one cost a fortune, you know. Bought it in Milan. Oh, well - your gin is warm and your presence tedious, so if you're quite serious then

I guess it *is* time for us to be moving along." He placed his half empty glass gently on a table, and shook hands with me. "It was thoroughly nice talking with you," he said. "Sorry I can't say the same about your rather weird friend here though. How much are we taxpayers forking out to keep the likes of him on, I wonder? Come along ladies; apparently it's time for us to be leaving," he commanded masterfully.

"We only just got here," one of the darlings trilled, puzzled, not yet having caught the drift. "Why are we leaving so soon?"

"My dear," I said, wanly, squeezing her arm: "hopefully you'll never know; and even if you did, you would never understand."

"Hey fellahs, Greg and the girls are leaving," cried a voice from across the room.

There was an immediate evacuation of ten charming and perplexed people, all because of that benighted, bigoted, stupid, hideously mannered old colonel and his antediluvian ideas, of whom there were many still serving in the army in those days.

They walked among us.

Mind you, it must be said that since their long overdue demise, standards *have* rather dropped a bit!

A few months later - still on the subject of dress - the Senior British Liaison Officer (another retired colonel; but a nice one, and one I could do business with) collared me in the Mess corridor one day, and said: "Mike, next week is British Week here in Hanover. I've been approached by a local gents' outfitter who wants to tart up his window a bit. He's asked if I can track down a few items of a British Army officer's uniform to help him do it with. What do you think? Can you sling a few items my way?"

"No problem at all, Colonel. It will be done."

Perhaps I shouldn't have been so ready to oblige.

The following week when I was walking along *Georgstrasse* I was horriefied to see the most garish apparition imaginable. Bold as brass, in the middle of the city's premier gents' outfitter's cinemascopic window, there stood a life size mannequin centrepiece for all the world to see, displaying the most bizarre agglomeration of military garb culled from the lot I'd loaned to them. Looking like something from the chorus line of some Ruritanian musical, the mannequin was adorned in my mess kit - but they had tucked the overalls *into* the mess wellingtons, which was all very pretty, but as military fashion had gone out over a century before. My Sam Browne belt and sword had been arranged upside down round the middle of this model, and then they'd gone and stuck my beret on top of its bald head. Adding insult to injury was a placard leaning against the mannequin's left leg, which proclaimed:

BRITISH OFFICER - GALA KIT

I'll say!
Looked more like Benny Hill.
Averting my gaze and hoping not to be recognised, I hurried away, wincing.

TWENTY-FIVE

"DO YOU REALLY THINK that's a nice thing to do?"

"Perhaps not really, no sir; but I believe that both Churchill and Eisenhower did it in the Rhine once."

"That was under completely different circumstances," retorted the haughty Greenjacket major, who had unexpectedly appeared out of the mist behind me. "That was in 1945 and they were justifiably pleased with the Allies' achievements. Then it was a fitting and symbolic gesture."

I rezipped the heavy-duty fly of my combat trousers, readjusted my headdress, and stepped back into the fog bank shrouding the River Weser that chill March morn.

My father had always told me that I should know my man.

The next phase of my career might well depend on this Greenjacket chap.

Possibly I could jeopardise it if I further offended the man's obvious susceptibilities.

He obviously had a thing about peeing in other people's rivers.

His mother must have told him it wasn't nice, so it had to do with his potty training: most things to do with the male psyche usually were.

To hell with all the oil barges and coal lighters ploughing up and down, people swam there in summer.

Duly chastised, I stood corrected.

It was the day of the Captain to Major Practical Promotion Examination.

Since eschewing all other professions but Arms, I was finding that not everything was brasso, bugles, bullshit and bunting - but that at various junctures along the line hard core bullets, bayonets, bomb blasts and British belligerence had to come into the equation as well, and an expected mastery of same.

Not once since being awarded my coveted pips had the desk jobs or paperwork ever seemed to ease up.

By keeping my nose clean and doing what was expected of me I had managed to earn my recommendation to lieutenant, but then found that I had to study and consolidate all I knew for this next hurdle, the practical examination for promotion to captain, which is why I had engineered my attachment with my old regiment, The Royal Sussex, a few months earlier at Lemgo.

The exam always had to do with a battleground scenario, which was the Infantry's, the Cavalry's and the Gunners' daily stock in trade.

This is what the Teeth Arm boys did as a matter of course, to earn their crust.

They didn't have to bone up on the Support Arm's working practices in order to pass the exam, but we still had to bone up on theirs.

Arguably, therefore, the exam was a tad more difficult for us.

However, it was fully understood that our military specialisms were secondary to the fact that first and foremost we were meant to be soldiers, skilled in attacking or repelling enemy hordes, should the - in truth unlikely - need to do so ever arise, so we were obliged to put our noses to the grindstones and swat like buggery to pass this essential Teeth Arm exam.

Pigs would fly before any one of us ever got to command an infantry battalion, but in theory we were meant to be able to do so, and were examined in that light.

It was simply a fact of life.

Successive generations of subalterns had insisted that it was a totally unnecessary test, until having finally passed it they then found themselves tacitly agreeing that there was now no reason why their successors shouldn't suffer the same prolonged misery they had done.

Hence, in perpetuity, annually, clusters of subalterns from all over the place would foregather at remote grid references in desolate areas from Salisbury Plain to Soltau to reveal their hastily acquired ability to appear to be able to command some particular phase of some hypothetical battle, if not for the edification of their examiners, then at least, usually, for their disbelief and amusement.

The previous autumn I had defended (to little avail) a farmhouse in Berkshire.

In the summer I had managed to annihilate an entire mechanised combat team on Luneburg Heath.

Now, at 09.15 on a Thursday morning in March I, my packed lunch, other hopefuls and their various accoutrements, were timorously poised for yet another exciting, action packed, make believe day doing something other than urinating in and around the River Weser, at Hamlin.

An officer's practical promotion examination impedimenta, traditionally consisted of the following:
1. Binoculars, compass, protractor and cotton for map reading.
2. A map of the area, to read.
3. A map board and talc to put it on and write over
4. Coloured wax crayons with which to mark the tactical disposition of Redland (the enemy) and Blueland (own side) forces on the map board/talc.
5. A notebook and pencil(s).
6. An orders card.

Before any battle, its commanders make 'an appreciation of the situation' confronting them. In reality this is usually done in their heads. For the examination, however, it has to be put down in the notebook (with one of the pencils detailed in para 5 above.)

Having appreciated the situation, and with true British phlegm refused to accept (or realise) that it is probably a hopeless one, they formulate their plan.

It is then no earthly use keeping this plan to themselves. They have to convey it to their subordinates, who will be expected to 'execute' the plan. This way everyone gets in on the act.

This passing on of the plan is done by the medium of an 'O' or 'Orders Group'.

The company runner is despatched to run round first with a 'Warning Order'.

A warning order warns everyone to get ready for an Orders Group and at what time and where it will be held.

This is usually in a wooded dell some 15-minutes later, where chipped and filthy enamel mugs of pine needle-filled tea are served, while shot and shell come slicing out of the air above.

'O' Groups have been known to get fairly hairy.

Specially if your pencil breaks, or it starts to rain.

The commanders give their orders and their subordinates jot down all the information they require before, in turn, going back to their own individual little plots of land to disseminate the intelligence to *their* subordinates.

This is usually done in droll and very clipped English.

Even in some Scottish regiments.

Unless this rigid formula for plan giving/taking was adhered to at all levels, people got missed out, or pointed their gun in the wrong direction when all the noise started, and then the battle could go awfully wrong.

To assist commanders to remember each item heading of the various little bits of concurrent activity they were expected to initiate before the battle kicked off, the School of Infantry's All Arms Wing at Warminster in Wiltshire periodically produced a small green card, not unlike a fixtures list, called a Company Operations Orders Card, which measured 4" x 7" and was designed to fit snugly into one's heavily stitched map pocket, situated on the left thigh.

In other pockets it became crumpled, and difficult to read in the dark.

Or after a year of heavy use.

From time to time, in its wisdom, and in the light of new

knowledge, the School of Infantry's 'think tank' would revise little bits of the Army's tactical doctrine, and then updated Orders Cards were issued.

Each new edition of the card superseded its predecessor, but there was usually an overlap in distribution.

This meant that unless units kept a weather eye open for each newly amended printing of the Orders Card they could very well find themselves conducting their particular part of the battle off a different hymn sheet to everybody else, thereby adding to the fog of war.

Only that morning one of the aspirants on my exam by the Weser had come scuffling in his galoshes across the muddy carpark at the RV waving in the air a buff coloured Orders Card, crying *"Wadi? Wadi?* For Christ's sake, what's a *wadi?"* A cursory glance revealed that he was still using his father's 1940's card from North Africa. Loosely the format was the same, but there had been changes.

Those phases of War covered by an Orders Card in the 1970s, were as follows:

1. Attack.
2. Defence.
3. Withdrawal (always tactical; never anything else; anything else might be quite sensible under the circumstances, but would be classified as panic.)
4. Assault River Crossing.
5. Relief in the Battle Area. (Nothing to do with bordellos, or peeing in the Weser.)
6. Short Radio Orders.
7. Patrols.
8. Ambush.
9. Warning Orders.
10. Helicopter Operations.

So you see, military commanders have quite enough to think about when the pressure is on.

It's not all cocktail parties and polo.

In the same way that we all believe we could conduct an orchestra, every schoolboy probably feels himself well able to carry out an exemplary attack, and win the day by tea time.

303

"Up lads and at 'em. Line abreast. Pennants flying. Bags of smoke. Thunder up the hill in fine array and sweep the enemy from his foxholes at the top. Why is that machine-gun still firing at us? Christ - it's one of mine. I forgot to coordinate its activity."

The friendly if wayward machine-gun could be the least of the young commander's problems.

Confidence is one thing.

Unjustified overconfidence is another, and can be dangerous.

Enemies dug-in on hilltops have been known to refuse to budge.

They can also mete out terrible reprisals and send a routed attacking force scurrying quickly away to rub their bottoms and have a rethink. Have you, as commander, told your force where to regroup in the case of such an eventuality?

Even in its simplest form, any phase of war can become a complex matter.

It is for this reason that lieutenants and captains are occasionally expected to forsake the beer and skittles of Army life and go out to reveal what they have learned of their craft. If they have applied themselves and learned enough, they might get promoted.

If they haven't, they won't.

It seemed fair.

If we were to liken the Army to an insurance policy, it would be very easy to put it into a security box and carry on with life's ceaseless round, happy in the knowledge that in the event of an armed outbreak we had the wherewithal to cover ourselves.

However, no one should expect his policy to cover every eventuality that might arise.

Today the Army is stretched beyond belief with both Gulf Wars, the present winding down situation in Iraq, and the ongoing conflagration in Afghanistan, but in the '60s and '70s, apart from Northern Ireland and the outbreak of various brush fires, the Army needed to keep 'practising'.

In Germany, especially, it turned out *en masse* to go on training exercises once a year.

The equipment with which it was able to train though, was in short supply.

It was short on bullets.

Short on gasoline.

Our armoured regiments had a governmentally imposed restrictive practice called 'track limitation', whereby once their vehicles had completed their quota of miles, they had to pack up and go home.

Each exercise season the likeness to verisimilitude became less and less.

Seasoned BAOR commanders were almost able to dispense with their Orders Card and give them verbatim from memory, simply by recalling the previous year's exercise.

Plus c'est la même chose.

Meanwhile, we soldiered on.

The recognised kit an officer wore to attend the practical promotion exam, was combat kit.

The DPM suit (Disruptive Pattern Material, i.e. intermingled squiggly shades of black and green with dark brown undertones, designed to resemble European countryside, and act as camouflage) was introduced in the '60s to replace its plainer green forebear.

When it first hit the quartermasters' shelves it became known as the 'Can't See Me Suit'. Some were so ill-shapen that the observation was not far off the mark. The majority of officers and soldiers took theirs to be tailored.

This was 'illegal'.

The only way to tailor the voluminous trousers properly was to remove their waterproof liners.

This reduced their battle-worthiness, and gave one haemorrhoids.

Piles, if one was a soldier.

It made a smarter soldier (the tailoring) and towards this end the 'illegality' tacitly became overlooked.

Just as an informative aside - so long as one is wearing clean boots there is a simple army way to cure piles.

When naked, don a pair of tightly laced *steel*-heeled ammunition boots, drop down smartly into the squat position, catch breath, click both heels firmly together, and then stand up again.

Quickly.

It doesn't always work, is sometimes accompanied by a tearing sound and waves of excrutiating pain, and is not for the faint-hearted, but if your ointment hasn't worked and you're courageous enough, it could be worth a try.

There were thirty combat-suited officers on the muddy bluff overlooking the River Weser that Thursday morning in March of which I write; myself, the cavalryman with his father's buff coloured Orders Card, and 28 others of assorted size, shape and cap badge.

There was no way I was going to pass this exam.

I was no prancing Cavalier used to hurling squadrons of tanks with *élan* through the farmyards of northern Germany.

I was no Gunner, versed in firepower capability.

I was no hairy Para, turned on by jumping out of aeroplanes onto enemy objectives, and in the process of doing so repetitiously, completely buggering-up his spine for retirement.

I was no masochistic Marine Commando skilled at survival.

I was no Combat Engineer used to lobbing portable bridges across crocodile infested chasms in the midst of heavy bombardment . . . Dammit . . . to compound my depression my eyes had fallen on two men standing motionless beneath a dripping spruce, well away from the rest of us, stoney-faced, rugged, immovable, suffused in myth, the army's Samurai: *Christ,* I thought, my heart sinking into my belly like the sun dropping into the sea - *they've even got the SAS here. What possible chance is there now?*

SAS.

Britain's renowned Special Air Service.

The Army's 007s.

The MoD's own Underground Theatre Players.

They of the winged dagger cap badge and *Who Dares - Wins* motto.

I had dared, to report here at the appointed time, but I had few illusions about winning.

How could I compete with these guys?

They were Teeth Arm professionals who did this sort of thing for a living. All the time. All year round. Summer and winter. It was their bread and butter.

I was now in the RAOC, a technical corps which dealt with computers and civilians; logistics, resupply, provisions, petrol, aircraft and motor transport spares; food, biscuits, coffins; boot laces, blankets, bullets and bomb disposal.

When was I ever going to be called upon or expected to launch a combat team assault?

No one was ever going to let me *near* a combat assault team.

It was laughable.

When the war came I would be back at base accounting for straw.

I could scarcely imagine a freshly bayoneted Major Sammy Parkes, my then OC, crawling in ashen-faced one day during the fighting, gasping: "Mike - 1st Royal Anglian are having a sticky time of it outside Hildesheim. They want you to take your Orders Card up there straight away and bail 'em out. They need you to put in a combat team attack. Don't worry about your blankets. I'll get Corporal Smith to stack them for you while you're away. You'd better be off right away - okay?"

Pigs might fly, of course, but it did seem unlikely.

My promotion to major depended upon me passing this exam though, an exam which seemed to have little or no bearing on my job.

Paras and Marines weren't examined on Ordnance procedures, were they?

Secretly of course, I suspected that if I was examined on Ordnance procedures I might be a bit pushed as well.

"I should try to stop chuntering if I was you, Mike," the Adjutant had said to me only the previous day. "You've got to expect to be examined occasionally on *some*thing, y'know. Your whole life doesn't begin and end in your pit. You'd better get used to the idea of knocking off this promotion exam. It's got to be done. We've all had to do it. Now it's your turn. I know it's a drag, but we are soldiers first in the RAOC, and specialists second. There was a famous incident in the Second World War you know, when a Dental Corps officer in a remote medical outpost way behind the front line was surprised by a Japanese patrol. Quick as a flash he downed his drill, rounded up the sick, lame and lazy, the cooks and the bottle washers, and because he knew *how* to, he was able to repel the attack. Got rather a nice medal for that, he did. He didn't cry out: 'Stop, don't shoot, I'm only a dentist.' He got stuck in and did something about it."

"Yes - I heard." I grinned back at him. "Both Japs were scared shitless."

"I'm not sure that I approve of your attitude, Mike." He stared at me, thin-lipped and with a steely glint in his pale blue eyes. "You've had plenty of time to study for this exam. We've given you all week to bone up on map reading, signals, voice procedure and tactics. There's only that and the admin question to worry about, and you ought to know more about admin than the Teeth Arm people, so what's your problem?"

"I don't enjoy working at something that is hypothesis pure and simple," I said; " something which I need just in order to pass one day's exam and will never need or use again. It has no bearing whatsoever on my work. The whole thing is pointless."

"You're in the Army. You've joined it of your own free will and are free to leave whenever you want. You are in the RAOC. The motto of the RAOC is *Sua Tela Tonanti*. I assume you know what that means, Mike, do you?"

"Of course I do: *To The Warrior His Arms*."

"Precisely. And if you don't know where the warrior is, what he's doing, what he needs, what he wants it for, or how to find it to give it to him, and what quantity he'll want it in when you get there, then you're no fucking good to man or beast, *or* the RAOC, are you?"

"In that order, sir?" I grinned.

"Don't be facetious," he roared, losing his rag big time and thumping the desk till his watch flew off. "You will pass that examination tomorrow, or I shall expect a thoroughly good explanation in writing why you didn't. And I know the Colonel will, as well. Now get out."

I winced, saluted and left his office. Pompous twit. Mind you, everything he'd said was perfectly true of course. It was just that his officer management was so appalling that I delighted in riling him. Other officers in other mobs, I knew, received telegrams from their COs wishing them the best of luck before their exams.

Somehow I didn't think I'd be getting one from my lot.

"You will be delighted to know . . ." the jovial brigadier directing the examination was giving his opening address . . . "that until this wretched fog lifts the map reading and tactics questions are somewhat in jeopardy."

His remarks were greeted with a shuffling of booted feet in the slush, wry grins and a miniscule lessening of tension: about a third of a notch in the gut string. Bonuses such as this were hard come by in military affairs.

There was invariably a catch.

"However - the weather people assure us that it will have lifted by mid-morning. Meanwhile we shall kick off with the Admin and Voice Procedure questions. It just means that we shall be a bit later than planned in packing up this evening."

Even in jest afterwards I never said anything about it to anyone, but to me it was as clear as day that they must have got the results mixed up.

At 17.00 that evening I was cold, wet and miserable when I was ushered into the brigadier's tent to be told my fate.

"Third attempt, wasn't it?" he asked, craggy eyebrows raised in query.

"Yessir, 'fraid so."

"Mmmmm. Well, you've made it at last. Well done. It's understandably a bit more difficult for you non teeth-arm chaps . . ."

"You mean . . . you mean . . . I've *passed*, sir?"

"I believe so, apparently, yes . . . that's what it says here, on this list. You sound surprised. Don't you think you should have done?"

"Oh, of *course*, sir," I said, swiftly realigning my marbles: "but . . . are you absolutely *sure?*"

"Yes, I'm absolutely sure. Now perhaps you'd like to send in the next one, will you please: goodnight to you."

"Thank you, sir. Goodnight," I said, remembering to salute (smartly) before staggering out into a cowpat, uncaring in my moment of personal triumph.

I couldn't believe I'd finally passed the wretched thing.

I was certain I'd made a complete Horlicks of the whole affair.

They *must* have got the results mixed up.

Some thrusting careerist Para ADC, on being told he'd failed, would demand a recheck and have it upheld. I would be notified of the error by post in a few days and have to go through the whole bloody nausea all over again. In the meantime I would have to suppress all jubilation and keep a low profile. That was the trouble with being one of life's also-rans, never geared for success, on one of the rare occasions it came my way I couldn't even enjoy it in case it was a mistake. Oh, well- at least it would get the Adjutant off my back for a couple of days.

Pompous twit.

I slung my gear in the boot, climbed into the car and headed back to camp.

Like sirens on the Lorelei, a cup of tea and a long hot bath beckoned welcomingly.

TWENTY-SIX

ON ARRIVAL IN HANOVER the previous year I had bought a great big second-hand Opel Kapitan saloon, from Dick Morse, the Garrison's education officer.

It was in dull thud grey, with fully reclining seats that collapsed into a king size bed, and drove like a smooth running battleship.

In August 1968 Rachel took the children home to Gibraltar to holiday with her family. I drove them to the airport at Gütersloh to see them off on the first part of their journey, and got myself back to Hanover at midnight.

Knowing that after a few days without them I would become fractious, I had planned a trip of my own.

I was setting off the very next morning to drive to the south of France.

After a good night's sleep I showered, shaved, dressed, made myself some breakfast, and went outside to start loading up the car.

It was gone.

My first reaction was disbelief, and the assumption that although I knew I'd parked it there last night, the same as I had every other night for the past year, perhaps last night I'd had a brainstorm and parked it somewhere else for a change, just to give my brain this jolt, and a kick start.

I then thought I must have been the victim of a practical joke.

Some of my friends had arrived home piddled and thought it would be amusing to manhandle my car into the back of someone's garden perhaps.

In any case, with everyone else still a-bed there I was at 06.00 on a sunny Sunday morning wandering around *Wallmodenstrasse* trying to find my car.

It had been stolen.

"If we don't find it abandoned in a field by three-o'clock this afternoon, you can forget about it," said the Police. "It'll have been painted blue and driven to Italy."

At 15.00 that afternoon they found it abandoned in a field 30-miles to the north east, with a broken quarter-light where it had been broken in to, and a broken clutch cable where the miscreants had run out of luck. A couple of drunken German teenagers had crossed its wires and gone for a joy ride. Although they had been reported whooping it up roaring through one of the villages at 02.00, they were never caught.

Lady Luck had been kind, pre-warning me of a dodgy clutch cable which would probably have given out on me when I was crossing the Alps, or something.

Next morning, after everything had been fixed, I loaded the boot with a box of compo foodstuff, hexamine burners, three jerry cans of duty-free petrol, a crate of beer, a blanket, two towels, a pair of flip-flops and a road map, and set off on my great journey south.

I didn't rush, but enjoyed the drive to Munich and then across Switzerland and down into France. It was hot and I drove bare-buff, swigging the occasional warm beer, kidding myself I was having a whale of a time.

That leg took a couple of days, before I fetched up in Monaco and slept in the car, parked there on Monte Carlo's immaculate esplanade.

About 01.00 a Monagesque policeman popped his head through the window to see if I was dead, drunk, dead drunk, or a drug addict, but, satisfied, quickly withdrew.

Why France?

I should have gone to Spain. I loved Spain, but I had 'done' it ten years before and now wanted to clock up some new experience.

France's Côte d'Azure and the Riviera were still the holiday haunts of the rich, where one met a better class of skin, so that's where I wanted to get that year's quality tan.

I was thirty-years old and as a serving army officer relatively impecunious.

The Army gave us the chance to visit all these exotic places, but with not enough money to enjoy them fully when we got there.

Off duty, we travelled steerage.

But I'd still decided to hit the south of France, if nothing else just to sniff the same air they sniffed, to see if some of it rubbed off.

I wanted to catch the glint of their sea, which seemed to have more of a 24-carat glint to it than ours, but doing so was like trying to carve out a piece of the action with a penknife: a cup of coffee only in St Tropez; an overpriced hamburger at Menton; sleeping on the waterfront in the car; shaving in Nice railway station and showering on the beach at Cavalaire.

It was hardly 'Hey - Big Spender.'

Travelling alone, I always seemed to be on the edge of things, never being invited to 'join in the scene'.

I was an observer.

A people watcher.

Possibly short on some of the charismatic wherewithal needed to attract attention, I skulked enviously like a hyena outside the camp circles of the chosen.

No gorgeous St Tropez starlet showed any inclination to try me on for size.

No wealthy playboy took me under his wing to drive us to wild parties in his Ferrari.

Still, I was a trail-blazer - even if only a little trail-blazer, and all my trails had already been blazed many times before by other people, and were only rough little tracks anyway. So what, if I ate out of a billy-can - at least I was where it was 'at', even if I hadn't been asked 'in'.

For years I used to go to the Earls Court Motor Show with the forlorn hope that someone would produce a plushly appointed 140 mph dream car that no one else had noticed, the hire purchase of which my shallow pocket might be stretched to meet.

No such vehicle ever appeared.

But at least I could *sit* in the floodlit Jaguars for a moment or two, and dream that I was streaming across the Camargue with some legendary blonde raking her talons along my tautly denimed thigh, before being edged off the stand to make way for someone who seriously did intend buying the car, and had the wherewithal to do so.

In due course Rachel and I managed to buy our first house. Then a new car. Not a big one. A little one. In 1976 we went to Tenerife for a week on a winter holiday together when everyone else was working, and felt deliciously decadent. We didn't sleep in the car on the waterfront that time, subsist on beef-burgers or ablute in public conveniences, but stayed in a hotel. We were able to pay our way, and claim our rightful place at the hotel pool. If our money was stolen, we were insured, or I could use one of my credit cards - but none of this grown up stuff seemed to kick in much before I was thirty-eight.

Meanwhile, there I was, still only thirty, stretched out asleep on the flattened down seats of my old Opel Kapitan on Monte Carlo seafront in 1968.

Next morning I swam out my sleepers in the Med, curled myself round a coffee and croissant and then set out along the coast westward to St Tropez.

St Tropez.

Brigitte Bardot and bare tits: if only I could find my way to the colony's famed Tahiti Beach, which I did, by instinct, quite soon.

Parking the car beneath a bamboo lean-to, I hit the lavender scented strand where the warm sea plopped torpidly along its water line and the whole place was weighed down with ennui and a heavy film of sun oil.

Transistorised music drifted in the sluggish air and the fragrance of charcoal-grilled squid wafted from the Polynesian-style beach bars.

The beautiful people were sprawled about languorously in hammocks and *les minimums* and their smooth olive skin, the men dark, svelte and muscular with black, hairy chests, their gold-chained, perfumed girls high-stepping slowly through the hot sand like panthers on slender shanks and slinky thighs, barely clad in various itsy-bitsy items of kit that were that era's precursor to the modern thong . . . body piercing and tattooed spines and buttocks not having arrived yet.

It was a hundred metres or more west, just out of aroma-shot of the younger set's more fashionable beach bars, that I stumbled upon my first pair of bare breasts.

Free, big, brown, firm and juicy they jutted proudly towards north Africa, with their owner posing splay-legged on the hot sand, her arms flung out in support behind her.

This was still 1968, hence the delicious shock factor of seeing a woman even topless for the first time, let alone completely naked.

Ten yards farther along there was another one.

And yet another.

(All in matching sets, of course.)

My poor little heart was thumping fifteen to the dozen by now, while my neck performed its usual overexcited Wimbledon trick.

When I felt my heart suddenly grab and try to claw its way out of my chest to come up and have a look of its own, I sensed we were drawing close to divining something big.

We were.

Over there, to the left, beneath that multi-coloured sun-shade thing stuck in the sand . . .

. . . A stunningly attractive girl's beautifully pert and peach-shaped bottom – *absolutely and unmistakably __bare__* - signifying . . .

. . . that she was sunbathing there – COMPLETELY IN THE NUDE.

Oh; glory – and ***Vive** la France!*

This particular honey-bunch was her own self-appointed picket line post, beyond which everyone I came across

315

thereafter was romping about or lying around and simply strolling in and out of the sea completely and utterly starkers.

It was my Damascene moment.

Instant convert.

Since then (as with pyjamas) I have never (unless obliged to) worn swimming trunks.

I can quite understand those who believe they might find it ludicrously offensive to see a varicose-veined old coot of seventy flashing his dong and flaccid buttocks about at Blackpool, accompanied by his stooped wife dredging her droopy boobs through rock pools and dislodging the molluscs, but most naturists do wonder why we in Britain have to accept some unqualified arbiter's presumption to dictate that 88.8% of female breasts may be exposed without fear of prosecution, and 98.6% of the male torso, but the other little bits and pieces without which none of us would be here, are not fit to be seen? The Continent's more liberated and universally accepted attitude is much better; that if they *are* to be seen, then they're much nicer done lightly grilled.

One summer, years later, I was parading my all-over charred husk along the shoreline of Spain's Costa Natura beach, when with mounting mirth I realised that I knew the similarly unattired couple obliviously striding out hand-in-hand towards me with body parts all a-go-go.

Perhaps I should have taken evasive action, but the opportunity was too good to miss.

Turning to face the sea I stood to attention and saluted as they drew abreast of me to pass.

"Good afternoon, Brigadier," I said.

You've never seen a more flustered pair in your life.

After that, back at camp in UK, my everyday existence was to become pretty good for a while – until that brigadier was posted, and was replaced by a christian philatelist.

With a whole lot of gurgling and revving, the motor yacht *Scherazade* out of Panama was reversing, trying to park her stern parallel with the other gin-palaces up against the quay.

316

The equivalent of a top-of-the-range, sea-going Mercedes, she was a large, powerful, gleaming white, teak and chrome vessel with a lot of glossy dross aboard her.

These guests and hangers-on were like nine-year olds at a stage school, engaged in pathetic endeavours to appear as though they were doing something useful in order to impress the awestruck groups of eager to be impressed onlookers, all gawping enviously at them from the quayside.

Like cherubs on a frieze they minced about in a paroxysm of delight, thrilled by all the attention they were getting and assuming that those ashore were assuming that they were each someone famous.

The games people play.

Some of them picked up pieces of rope and half coiled them before dropping them back on deck again, as though by doing so they had contributed something grand and useful and were an irreplaceable part of the ship's complement, without whom it couldn't function.

She was without doubt a beautiful vessel.

Her owner, whose fuel was being expended to stage this ego trip, stood aloof in the wheel-house, grinning at the false hilarity of his guests, his body language implying that he was not really terribly amused by the antics of this consignment and hoped they wouldn't be too surprised not to be invited again. At the moment his main concern was to get his expensive yacht properly moored. It was fairly apparent that he didn't really know how to do this, although he obviously wanted it to appear as though he did.

One of the unsuspecting rent-a-crowd on the quay was suddenly caught unawares by a salt-bleached leader rope being thrown to him by one of the bona fide Panamanian deckhands standing in the stern.

The rope caught the man across his mouth, raising a welt on his lip.

Instinctively he made a grab to catch it, but missed, and like an escaping python it slithered off the quay and slapped back into the water.

A newcomer had now appeared in the wheel-house.

The professional hired help.

With his hands masterfully on the controls he glanced back over his shoulder towards the quay.

He pressed a couple of switches, dexterously revved the throttle and with the engines making Vosper-Thorneycroft Sherman tank and gargling salt-water exhaust pipe noises, backed *Scherazade* skilfully into her pre-paid parking lot there on the Côte d'Azure, cut engines, tied up and flung back the remains of a nearby Martini before going off to wash his hands and change his T-shirt.

It was an enjoyable performance, from which I decided that should I ever own a similar piece of kit I would employ ex RN personnel to man her, and amongst all the on-board Paris Hilton-type totty decorating the place, would be included a disciplined selection of attractive ex-Wrens.

I had parked the car further along the coast at Le Levandou, packed my pup-tent and a single grip and boarded a small ferry no larger than a fishing smack for the trip across to the Ile du Levant.

Most passengers wore shorts, T-shirts and sandals, but there was one more formally attired young couple, slightly aloof and detached, who struck me as probably being Italian newlyweds.

The crossing was not a calm one. We were all soaked by splashing waves. I smiled at the young couple, they smiled back, and we exchanged a few banal remarks in English.

When we arrived, the ferry didn't dock, it simply bumped against the jetty wall a few times and groups of us would jump ashore like amphibious commandos. My Italian newlyweds went one way, and I trudged off round the island to pitch my one-man tent somewhere and baste my buttocks in a bay.

After sundown, smarting deliciously from salt, sand and sunburn, I sat myself gently down at the only vacant table in one of the island's more popular restaurants. No sooner had I picked up the menu than my newlyweds came in, gazing about forlornly for somewhere to sit. Their eyes lit on the two vacant chairs beside me and widened hopefully. With half suppressed smiles of enquiry playing around their mouths they made their way towards me. The girl was just about to ask, when I preempted her: "Of course, I'd be delighted if you would join me," I said, rising to pull back both empty chairs.

In fact I'd wanted to read my book, but I knew there'd be little chance of that. They were going to sit with me anyway, so it may as well be at my request.

"That's so kind of you, thank you," the girl said in faultless English. "Please allow us to introduce ourselves. I am Maria-Lucia and this is my husband Sergio Lopes."

"Mike George," I said, shaking their hands. "Tell me, you are Italian and recently married - yes?"

"Good heavens, no," they shrieked. "We're Brazilian and we've been married four years. We live in Rio de Janeiro, where I teach English and Sergio runs his refrigeration business installing air-conditioning plant in marine traffic. We have been over here in Europe for a few weeks, making our 'tour'."

They were charming company; intelligent, witty, knowledgable and urbane. Maria-Lucia especially had an insatiable curiosity and thirst for knowledge. Travelling mostly by train they were scheduled to be spending six months in Europe. Their immediate programme was to work their way back along the coast to Genoa to collect their luggage, awaiting them there after its arrival by sea from Brazil, before heading inland to stay with Sergio's brother, their country's UN representative in Geneva.

"That's pretty much the route I shall be taking back to Germany," I told them. "Why not let me give you a lift?"

"You can't be serious. You hardly know us."

"I'd be pleased for the company. You're both pretty people and smell nice, so where's the problem?"

And so we drove along the Corniche to Genoa and Geneva together.

Next day we only got as far as Nice, though. It was such a priceless pearl of a day that it had to be spent on the beach. The pebbles on the beach at Nice weren't very nice; they're nasty, large, grey, metallic and uncomfortable flints, but the heat they radiated and the configurations they adopted enabled one to flake out across them, floating in a shimmering haze and squinting through oily eyelids at the high, green tide that deeply lapped the shoreline.

Sergio and I awoke from our half slumber as a shadow fell across our faces. It was Maria-Lucia. The angel had gone off up onto the promenade above and now stood before us clutching three frosted beer bottles and three scrumptious looking open sandwiches with lettuce, cucumber and tomatoes trailing out their sides.

"Come along, you men," she said, squatting beside us in her wisp of a tanga. "Eat, drink, and let's get a move on, eh?"

We swigged our beer, devoured our sandwiches, showered at the communal freshwater showerhead set in one of the groynes, returned to the car and set off for Italy.

At 19.00 we stopped for a spaghetti supper and then continued our drive on to Genoa. It was midnight when we came shooting out of a mountain tunnel to see the port glinting below us. There was no point entering a strange city at that time of night to find accommodation. That day's sunblasting and the night drive had exhausted us, so we pulled in to a lay-by and slept where we were in the car until daybreak.

That morning, early, we dropped down into Genoa and headed straight for the railway station for a wash and brush up and then to collect the Lopes family's luggage.

It was a good thing I was travelling light and the Opel was big!

Leaving Genoa as soon as we could, we headed north for Turin, through the Aosta valley to the foot of Mont Blanc, through the recently opened road tunnel beneath it, and on to Geneva, where I dropped a grateful and appreciative couple at their relative's luxurious apartment there. It was late. We had already exchanged addresses and so bade each other our farewells, and parted - they, straight to bed, and me to drive on through the night back to Hanover.

It was not to be the last I would hear of the Lopes.

Rachel returned with our children from their holiday in Gibraltar, I returned to work, and within a week we started to receive postcards and letters from Maria-Lucia and Sergio as they progressed up and down and around Europe. Then, one day at the beginning of December, there arrived a mock note plaintively enquiring: 'What is to become of two lonely Brazilian people miles from home with nowhere to lay their heads as Christmas comes . . .?'

The upshot was that they came to live with us in Hanover for a month, using us as a base for their stay and our cellar as a depository for their luggage. They were sweet, fun people, Maria-Lucia especially possessing a wit, intelligence, awareness and empathy such as I have seldom experienced.

One day she expressed a desire to experience a bit of Hamburg's infamous nightlife.

Knowing what this entailed, Rachel and I were hesitant to agree, although Rachel had never been there herself and was reacting on hearsay and the condition she'd seen me in whenever I'd returned from a trip there. Nevertheless, Maria-Lucia got her way as usual, and so off we all went to Hamburg.

The first club we went to was far too tame for her.

"More," she demanded, grinning and thumping her little fist prettily on the table top.

And so we progressed through the hairy, hairier and hairiest of clubs.

"Maria-Lucia, I'm shocked at you," Rachel upbraided her. "I thought you were such a nice girl."

"Oh, but I am; I am," was her reply, "but I was born with naughty genes. What's the point of going down a coalmine unless it's the deepest and dirtiest coalmine there is?"

Leaving the naughty clubs behind we went to the *Zillertal* on the *Reeperbahn* for a refreshing beer, and sat at a table just inside the door. Everyone who came in had to pass by us, and I noticed that Maria-Lucia was slowly becoming more detached from our conversation as a puzzled expression etched its way across her face.

"You know," she said, turning to us suddenly, "I know most of these people who are coming in."

I thought she'd flipped, but just then two more stunning girls walked past and smiled and nodded to us.

"They're all Brazilian," Maria-Lucia told us excitedly. "I recognise some of them, from Copacabana, honestly. Please excuse me, but I have to find out why they're here."

Pushing back her chair, she smoothed her dress and was gone.

"Is she serious?" I asked Sergio, who for a Latin was always fairly relaxed.

"I'm not sure. I'll find out," he said, and went after his wife.

A moment later a great cheer rent the air, followed by an increasing and incessant babbling in Portuguese. Maria-Lucia had made contact. Suddenly the *Oompah* band leader found himself peremptorily deprived of his baton by a wild eyed young man who had leapt up onto the stage beside him. The band was quickly led to understand that some sort of South American rhythm was now called for. They obliged, and the floor erupted as a writhing conga of deliriously happy Brazilians started dancing about, singing, and for some reason bearing Maria-Lucia and Sergio aloft as they did so. Rachel and I were soon hailed and dragged into this mêlée as well, and within a minute the entire *Zillertal* was reverberating to a frenzied Copacabana beat. That week there had been a student conference held in Hamburg for all European-based Brazilians, culminating in this Saturday night get-together at the *Zillertal*. Maria-Lucia was flushed and ecstatic, her brown eyes flashing diamonds of joy.

"But why were they carrying you about on their shoulders like that?" we asked afterwards, back at our table.

"Well . . .," she hesitated, and if she hadn't already been flushed might have blushed a little. "We - well, we're not altogether unknown in Brazil, you see. Sergio's father is the mayor of our capital, Brasilia, so I suppose . . ."

Sergio threw his head back and laughed.

"Nonsense, darling. You're very flattering, but the real reason we were fêted is even more flattering to me," he said.

"Why's that?" I asked.

"Well Mike, I'll tell you. That little girl there, who married me, used to wear a bikini in such a way and waggle her bottom in such a way that one day Antonio Carlos Jobim couldn't resist writing a song about her.

"Which song was that?" I smiled, pretty sure I knew what the answer was going to be.

"Let me just tell you that for some years we lived in a place called Ipanema."

Much as she could have been I didn't think Maria-Lucia really *had* been the inspiration behind *The Girl From Ipanema*, but it made a nice little story.

After Maria-Lucia and Sergio had returned to Brazil we found the postal services within that country to be so unreliable that after a while it became pointless trying to maintain correspondence with each other, despite Maria-Lucia and me being prolific correspondents. Eventually I became tired of dispatching carefully addressed sheafs which never reached their destination. Then one day I was sitting on a beach in Yugoslavia talking to a violinist from the Vienna Philharmonic Orchestra, who worked in the Post Office by day.

"The majority of your letters must have been arriving on a Friday, then," he said.

"What would that have to do with it?"

"Brazilians being Brazilians, any letters that are still undelivered or unsorted at close of play on Fridays have all their pretty stamps taken off them and are then are swept into a great big pile in the middle of the floor and burned."

"I don't believe it."

"Believe it," he said. "I used to work there. I know."

After that I sent my letters c/o The British Embassy in Rio with a polite covering letter explaining the position and asking if one of their young men might feel disposed to deliver my letter personally, enjoy a G&T with Maria-Lucia and gain an entry to Brazilian society's upper echelons for his trouble.

They obliged, and this novel system worked quite well for a while, but it then began to wear thin, and was stopped.

Since then all contact with the Lopes family fizzled out and we lost touch, although while writing this, now that we are in the technological age, I looked up Maria-Lucia Lopes on

Google, and came across a Facebook entry and photograph that could very well be her 40-years on, which I am still wondering whether to pursue.

You don't *really* think they burn those letters, do you?

TWENTY-SEVEN

"HOW MUCH LONGER do you think I'll be staying in Germany, Colonel?"

"Another year at least, definitely."

"So it would be alright if I got a new car?"

"Of course, absolutely."

The significance of my question and having a twelve month window to play with was that the car could then be taken back to UK tax free. Anything less than a year, and whopping amounts of money would have to be paid to HM Customs and Excise at Dover.

What prompted my enquiry?

Thirty-kms northwest of Hanover lies the small town of Steinhude, adjoining a glacial lake known as Steinhuder Meer (sea). This 8-km long, 4.5km wide, 3-metre deep inland lake is part of the glacial landscape that was formed 18,000 years ago, after the recession of the glaciers during the last ice age. It has long since been a natural recreational area for watersports, picnicking and enjoying family fun.

Driving my family along the Autobahn one hot Saturday to spend the day there, suddenly we heard the most awful noise behind us.

It felt as though we were a wildebeest been brought down by a lion.

We had dropped a big one alright, and continued showering a trail of sparks for a hundred yards or so down the road before the car ran out of impetus.

We were like a Flying Fortress dragging its prolapsed undercarriage, bomb load and toolbox along the tarmac, but I saw a miraculously located garage just off to our right and was

325

able to clatter into its forecourt with an enormous sigh of relief before everything about us expired in hot oily smoke.

The car now resembled a giant mechanical wasp which had had something horrid happen to its sting. Guts and long bits of chewed up and smouldering wire seemed to be trailing behind us everywhere.

It was the last of our rear axle.

Fortunately this all happened bang opposite our destination, the Steinhuder Meer, so the day wasn't a complete loss. We unloaded everything from the boot, crossed the road, and went off for our swim as planned.

That evening we cadged a lift back to Hanover.

Next day, having asked the CO how long I could expect to be remaining there in Germany, I returned with a breakdown truck to tow the car back to my regular garage. I authorised the renewal of the rear axle with a replacement second-hand one from a cannibalised Opel, and having done so - much to the garage owner's delight - then ordered a new Opel Rekord Coupé from him, a sexy looking fastback phallic symbol, priced at £800 (about £20,000 today.)

It took courage.

Most of my colleagues drove British cars, except for NAAFI staff. They drove round in Volkswagens with *BUY BRITISH* stickers on the back, until someone more sensible pointed this out to them one day, and the stickers were removed.

The lines of the Rekord had appealed to me very much for a long time. I thought it was the most attractive car on the road. Mine was ordered in metallic silver with black upholstery, and five weeks later I was notified that it was ready for collection from Opel's factory at Rüsselsheim, near Frankfurt.

On Friday 16 November 1968 I travelled down by train to collect it. I spent that night in Frankfurt, and then next morning took a taxi out to the Opel factory.

Snow lay on the ground.

Fully tanked up and ready to go, my shiny new car awaited me on the massive forecourt of the Opel clearing site. All I had to do was sign a collection receipt while they bolted on

DE630B, the BFG (British Forces Germany) number plates I'd taken with me, and I was free to drive home to Hanover.

I climbed in, switched on, drove off and knew the car was going to prove to be one of the best investments I had ever made. She looked good, handled well and felt right. I stopped at Wiesbaden to buy her a set of floor mats from Karstadt and then set off for Bonn, where I spent the night at a hotel on the Rhine.

Next morning, Sunday, I drove slowly back to Hanover, arriving there at 19.00.

A mile from home I stopped at a petrol station to tank up, and the car wouldn't restart.

The electrics had cut out.

The petrol pump attendant gave me a push to get going, and then next morning Rachel did the same. I drove straight to the garage where I'd ordered it and they tightened the car's alternator which had come adrift, and also kept it for the day to give it a thorough overhaul, degrease and polish.

When I collected it that evening, I was a proud and happy man, but then . . .

. . . just as though they knew . . .

. . . like a squawking seagull that craps gleefully on your car's bonnet when you've just finished washing and polishing it . . .

. . . the very next day at work . . . *I received a posting order back to the UK.*

The Army did things like that.

All the time.

They must have derived a perverse pleasure from the massive personal inconvenience it caused.

Five months later, my ready-to-move date, I packed Rachel and the children back to Gibraltar again, sadly handed over our lovely Hanover apartment, loaded the new car to the gunwales with gear, and with sufficient hard-won money stashed in my hip pocket to pay the tax, I set off reluctantly for Bremerhaven and the overnight ferry to Harwich and Blighty.

My civilian Clerical, Medical and General insurance friend, David Arthur, was returning by the same boat on a business trip, so I couldn't have had better company to buoy up my spirits. I had been having such a wonderful time in Germany that I didn't really want to return to England at all with its filth, fog, strikes, bloody-mindedness and rudeness; its attitude, apathy and declining standards – and this was 1969.

What was happening to my country?

Why was it lagging so far behind Europe?

Why was it so hell-bent on slipping into the sea and leaving nothing but sadness, memories and a pile of flotsam on the surface of the Channel?

Was it the people?

The politicians?

The weather?

Had all of these elements cumulatively seeped corrosively through to the national marrow? And this was before the sagely long foreseen but ignored effects of Immigration and militant Islamism taking their cancerous holds on the place. Even then there didn't seem to be *anyone* of sufficient charisma or moral stature who could rally us, and once more cry: *'Rise: Stand: for Elizabeth, England and Saint George.'*

On arrival at Harwich David and I slapped each other affectionately on the back and set off reluctantly on our separate ways. We were never to see each other again. He was going up north to attend an insurance course for two weeks before going back to Germany, while I drove south along the cherry-blossomed highway to Colchester, on through London and down through Kent and Sussex to my father's new home in St Leonards.

The car?

Much to the frustration of HM Customs at Harwich, when they checked everything it transpired that for some obscure reason I was legally entitled to keep it in the country for a whole year before any excise duty would be due.

328

The reason for my UK-posting was to attend a six months Ordnance Officers' Course at our depot in Deepcut, near Camberley, in Surrey.

I was due to report there in June, which meant that I now had three weeks leave.

Nice as it was to see dad again, I didn't really want to spend three whole weeks under his wheels; it would hardly have been fair on his wife, Sue.

What did I do?

Booked a package holiday to Estartit, on Spain's Costa Brava.

By train.

To get there I had to report to Victoria Station at 09.00 one morning in May to catch the designated train to Dover, embark, cross the Channel, continue to Paris where we crossed from Gare du Nord to Gare d'Austerlitz to board an enormous train that soared above the platform like some 1929 military seige machine, malevolently *hissing* and *pissing* like the greatest of mechanical beasts imaginable. We were scheduled to depart from there at 21.00 to travel through the night, reaching the Spanish border next morning. Hot, sticky, uncomfortable and tired, I felt like a member of the International Brigade in 1936, returning to fight. The thought of a good night's sleep now appealed to me, but as the train was full and I'd made no reservation, there was little chance of that.

"Excuse me," I heard a nice English voice say beside me, "I wonder if you'd be interested in a sleeper for the night? I seem to have overbooked for my party and find I have one ticket left."

If I'd been French I would have kissed him.

"I certainly would," I said, handing him the money. "And thank you very much indeed."

"All aboard," cried one of a dynamic duo in French, while his colleague stomped along the platform chopping off fingers slamming doors. At the front of the train the engine gave an enormous *hiss* like the biggest pressure cooking experiment in

329

the world, and in his singlet and shorts Michael George climbed aboard.

Ridiculous.

What must I be thinking?

Steam went out with the Ark.

My memory's been playing tricks with me.

All that *hissing* and *pissing* stuff was a figment of my imagination. For *hissing* and *pissing,* please now read *throbbing.*

The thing was a diesel train, of course.

There was a sexy blonde in the carriage, and a negro with a guitar and lots of *Gauloises.* We started talking and they were such fun there was no reason for us to stop enjoying each other's company until 02.00, when she fell asleep with her head in his lap and one little hand curled surreptitiously out of sight. Man!

"I'll see you," I said, rising to my feet and sliding open the door to the corridor. "I'm off now to find my *couchette.*"

"You'll be lucky," said the blues singer through a haze of smoke. "All the interlocking vestibules were secured at eleven-o'clock. You're stuck here with us for the night."

Turned out he was right.

I walked to the end of the corridor just to check. Through the window, on the top bunk of the *wagon lit* in the next carriage, I could see my grip where I'd left it earlier, just after I'd bought the spare ticket from my fellow Brit. Now there was a locked door between us.

Emergency communication cord?

I returned to settle down for the night with the black man and his blonde.

When I awoke at 06.00 I could see the dramatic medieval walls of Carcassonne silhouetted palely proud on the dawn's horizon. Not long after that the train pulled in to Port Bou, Spain's crossing point with France where we all grottily clambered off to be cleared through customs.

"*Achtung: Achtung,*" the station tannoys crackled in German for some reason. I don't quite know why; but it sounded impressive. This was a *holiday?* I was *paying* for it? It made me feel more like a refugee than a freedom fighter. However, with nothing to declare I shuffled through the shed and out the other side into the early morning sun, where beneath a dusty olive tree I found a waiting coach with the name of my hotel painted garishly along its flanks. I climbed aboard, tried not to smell myself too much, sat on one of the seats at the back, and waited. After a few minutes a big-boned, loose-jointed, ham fisted fellow flopped up the steps in his sandals and started to reel off a roll-call.

"Mr and Mrs Smith? Mr and Mrs Jones? Mr and Mrs . . .?"

I'd goofed. There were no Misses.

"Mr and Mrs Thompson, Sarah and Rodney -?"

Finally, after a pause and a curious look around . . . "and - Captain George?"

They all turned to look at me. The courier beamed.

"So *you're* the one," he cried with satisfaction.

"Why? What have I done?"

"The whole hotel has been wondering who you might be. There's a famous Spanish TV character called *The Captain*, you see. Half the hotel staff thought you might be him. I must admit, I wasn't sure myself whether you'd be Royal Navy or BEA."

I smiled, too tired and washed out to enlighten him. Besides, I was embarrassed. Professor George? Doctor George? Father George? I'd booked the holiday over the phone and unthinkingly used my rank as a daily matter-of-course, but if it was going to generate this sort of curiosity outside the military environment, I would need to become plain Mister again.

The bus was now drawing in to the hotel's palm-treed parking lot. It was 09.30. I booked in and straight away went up to my room to lie on my bed to 'catch up'. At lunchtime I showered, shaved, put on clean clothes and went down for some lunch.

There was only one other unattached male staying at the hotel. Norman was a seventy-year old retired train driver. We were put at the same wobbly table together for meals.

What was I doing there?

331

"You've arrived two weeks too soon, that's all," Bob the courier told me. "This is the first week of the season. Another fortnight and the whole place will be buzzing with life. I wish you would stay. I could use you."

Now I'm afraid I can't remember the point of the story.

After two weeks of boredom I flew home again with an absolutely indescribably gorgeous all-over tan, and went to commence my six months course.

TWENTY-EIGHT

THE NEXT SIX MONTHS were to be the worst of my life.

Other than having route canal treatment, 70 OO's (Ordnance Officers') Course, held from June to November 1969, was one of the most gruelling periods of time I have ever had to endure.

There were eighteen of us on the course, all of whom became bonded as long term acquaintances, three of whom - Lawrence Williams, Rob Sinclair-Lee and Ian Coppock were to become close lifelong friends, although after 1985, when he went to live in Australia, Ian unfortunately decided to sever contact for some reason, and 'dropped out'.

The Infantry infanteered; the Gunners gunned; Signallers signalled; Caterers cooked, Sappers built bridges and roads, and Commandos commandeered beach-heads: every arm or corps had its own esoteric range of specialist in-house skills at which its practitioners needed to become proficient. But over the years the RAOC seemed to have acquired for itself an even greater gallimaufry of commitments and responsibilities than most, covering the entire gamut of provision and supply, bomb disposal and ammunition, in addition to a whole host of other ancilliary support services. Its officers needed to be jacks of all trades and masters of several. As might reasonably be expected, in order to assimilate a general overview of this massive Corps' activities, and get a pretty in depth working knowledge of everything it did, somewhere at the outset of our careers we quite rightly had to attend this concentrated course, of which two were held annually.

Unfortunately I was to find that I loathed the School of Ordnance, its staff and the subject matter it purported to convey. If truth be known I would have been far better suited and happier bouncing across the north German Plain in an armoured car or crawling through the undergrowth with a bayonet between my teeth than expected to get excited by being the military equivalent of some Marks and Spencer warehouse manager, but changing direction at this stage would have been too tricky for words.

The course was divided into phases, each phase covering the different tasks an Ordnance officer might be called upon to perform, such as Field Force Replenishment, or getting the right goods to the right place in the right quantity at the right time: Provisioning: Work Study: Ammunition: Design for Storage Facilities and Structures etc. And so on. God it was tedious. I am not slow to record my disapproval of rubbish, and that course – then - in my opinion, was rubbish. We had to attend it, undergo it and pass it to get the required tick in our box for having done so, but I found the subject matter so boring and the lecturers so bad that I could scarcely prevent myself collapsing in slumber over my desk, and my desk was slap-bang in the front row. My 'attitude' was soon noted of course, and knives were drawn. 'The name of today's lesson every day for the next six months, is Get George'! They nearly did at times, too; it became a close run thing. Because I was the oldest attendee and had a little bit of service under my belt, I was expected to come top in everything, whereas in reality I was coming bottom, so they assumed I was taking the piss. I wasn't. It was just that I found great difficulty reconciling the theory they were expounding from their prepared notes, with the actual practice I had encountered in the field, so when it came to the exams I had a tendency to write 'real' answers to the questions, rather than the text book ones they expected. For example, as luck would have it (or not) one of the instructors on one of the phases was George Dillon, the very chap whose job I had taken over in Hanover, and had been doing satisfactorily and innovatively updating for the past two years. I was up-to-date with what actually happened on the ground,

70 OO'S (ORDNANCE OFFICERS') COURSE

School of Ordnance – Deepcut, Camberley. Surrey, May – Nov 1969

Rear L-R: David Moore; **Eddie Condon;** Lawrence Williams; **Kieran O'Kelly;** Chris Murray; **Mike Weedon;** Ian Coppock; **Richard Kirby;** Frank Falle; **Des Townsend;** Rob Sinclair-Lee
Front: **Tan Pau San;** Roland Hughes; **Frank Alizzi;** Chief Instructor Lt-Col Ozzie Logan; Col Commandant Gerry Landy; **Louis John;** Author; **Mustapha bin Mansor**

The George
Boys
- Reunion -
Dad's pad,
St Leonard's
1969

the 'real' operating procedures, whereas the slightly out-of-date notes from which he operated would have us do things differently. Result? By giving the 'proper' answers I failed the exam for that phase, the phase covering the very job I'd been doing for the past two years.

One day we were required to sit a compulsory computer programmer's aptitude test, designed to assess our suitability for further training and development in that burgeoning new field. This was 1969, remember. Computers had just been invented; well – more or less they had; you know what I mean. In their infancy, say. It was all that binary stuff. I didn't understand a word of it. My name on top of the paper I got right, but then it turned out even that was incorrect, because they wanted a number and some symbol or other put there instead. A scan through the ensuing questions showed me I was definitely in the wrong room again, so I sat back, folded my arms, shrugged, and looked around at my colleagues, all of whom were scribbling away furiously, their brows furrowed with concentration. It was a three-hour test. I looked at my watch. 09.15. This was going on till noon. Sheeeit; it could turn nasty. I had another look at the questions, just in case, but it was no use; they might just as well have been written in Martian. Completely beyond me. What to do? I started to compose a ballad instead. It was about a developing love affair between two computers and the different things they got up to until the Army found out, they were court martialled, and disintegrated in a shower of tearful circuitry. It was good, There must have been thirty or more verses. I mean, dammit, I'd had nearly three hours to do it in. I handed it in with my otherwise blank answer paper afterwards, but never heard another word; either of appreciation, or of protest. But I never got sent on computers.

After I had come bottom for the fifth phase on the trot, I suppose it was only to be expected that I should be summoned before the Commandant, a silver-haired, bellicose, puce-countenanced, verbally adroit colonel with, reputedly, a terrific sense of humour: except where I was concerned.

"I do not brook nonsense," he bellowed, before I was even half way across the room.

"No, sir," I agreed.

"I don't remember inviting you to speak. How *dare* you interrupt me like that."

"Yes, sir."

"HOW *DARE* YOU, I said," he said.

"Yes, sir."

"STOP ITTTT."

I knew when it was best to keep quiet.

I switched off and had a think about the Hawaiian Islands instead, while he continued to lambast me.

"And so I will give you one ultimatum," I heard him say, and nipped quickly back from Hawaii to his office. "Either you come in the top four places at the next exam, or I shall call for your resignation."

Christ.

The wicked old sod.

That was hardly playing the game at all.

That really was a bit below the belt.

Resignation?

I was thirty-one-years of age with a wife and two children to support, but I knew he had the power to do it and would probably have relished the exercise.

It had been my first face-to-face with Mr Big, and the message was clear.

I wasn't being tipped for Head Boy.

It was definitely shape up, or ship out time.

I lurched out into the noonday sun to gather my thoughts. Be in the top four in the next phase? Impossible. The only thing I'd ever come high as fourth in before had been an egg and spoon race at kindergarten.

I was no academic; not a swot, or a military 'brain'.

Thirteenth out of 13 was about my mark.

Thirty-second in a class of 33, if one was away sick.

Five-and-a-half per cent for maths.

Mine was the sort of track record that reeled backwards to the north-east like a Red Arrow defecting.

Come fourth?

Couldn't happen.

"Hi, Mike. What was the verdict?"

Ian Coppock and Des Townsend, with whom I shared a room in the Mess, were just emerging from a nearby urinal. Nothing sinister. Just a pre-lunch pee and brush-up. They were special buddies of mine on the course, and knew of my plight. It was a plight neither of them would ever share, vying as they did with each other most of the time for top place in everything.

"It has been put to me that if I don't come in the first four in the next phase's examination, he'll be calling for my resignation."

"Christ, George," said Ian. "That's impossible. You know what the next phase is, don't you?"

That thought hadn't occurred to me. From where I sat each phase was just as bad as the next.

"It's the Ammunition Phase," Des said, in a hushed tone.

"Oh, no," I groaned, clasping my hand to my head. Traditionally the Ammunition Phase was the worst, the hardest, the most tedious and the most boring and soul destroying phase of the entire course. For a start it wasn't even done there at Deepcut. We all had to travel up to the then RAOC Central Ammunition Depot at Bramley, near Newbury, in Berkshire where we would be living in wooden huts near some woods for a fortnight. There was a thought. Perhaps I could wander out and take my life one night.

After dinner that evening I was just popping a Sweetex into my coffee and opening the *Telegraph* when Ian and Des came across to join me.

"George, we've been thinking . . .," said Ian.

"That's nice."

"And what we thought, is this: namely, that at the moment you are dispirited to the extent that you have little or no interest in your future welfare, nor even the inclination or ability to do much about it if you had. Roger so far? If you don't come fourth in this next phase, you're going to have to resign, in order to appease our sadistic Commandant. Right?

You don't want to have to resign over an issue as trite as this, George - Christ - short of *hari-kari* that's the final gesture. Save it. You may need it someday for when terms are more favourable to you. But you've still got to come in the top four, and the whole world knows there's no way George is going to do that without a whole parcel of help. So what we propose is this: that Townsend and I are going to get you through this exam. Every night we are going to cram and grill you until you become the undisputed King of Ammunition. Okay?"

"But Ian," I reposted, "why bother? It's jolly nice of you both, honestly, I must say, and I appreciate the offer enormously, but I'm never going to pass the wretched thing, so it would be unfair of me to distract you from your own best efforts."

"Bollocks. Quiet please. Defeatism will not be tolerated. It will be as I have said. You will pass. Now buy us a drink."

Good friends.

Can't buy 'em.

Gotta earn 'em.

They were as good as their word, bless them.

During class I could doodle and daydream to my heart's content, although on this occasion I did try to concentrate and take stuff in a little bit - but no sooner had we broken for tea than they would both descend on me, shackle me, strip me down to basic ingredients and then rebuild, reinstilling in me all of that day's lessons.

This pummelling process continued every night for two whole weeks.

Then dawned the day of the exam.

As we all walked in our groups across to the examination hall at 08.30, Ian and Des seemed to be trying to hold me back for some reason, while the rest of the course hurried ahead to take their seats.

"Good luck, Mike," cried each one as he went by.

"Best of luck, mate."

"Don't worry, Mike. You'll make it."

Our trio drew up last at the ominous portals and went in. The entire course was there, present and already seated. Only three places remained, adjoining each other right at the back of the hall, and I realised what had happened. Ian and Des had been lobbying. It had been rigged. The whole course were in and pulling together to ensure that I made it. They were mature, intelligent guys, each of whom had made his own assessment of the worth of our course, and found certain aspects of it wanting. Most of them were as jarred-off with it as I was and couldn't wait to get away from its schoolboy environment and back into a proper military field once more. They knew what was at stake for me at the hands of these schoolroom tacticians and were prepared and wanted to do their bit to buck the system and score a point.

The exam started.

Ian and Des had boned me up so well that for once in my life I found I actually knew the answers, and was whipping through them all like a dose of salts, but they both seemed intent on clucking over my shoulder (surreptitiously of course) and observing my every calculation to make sure I got it right. I had soon finished the paper and sat back, grinning, arms folded, confident and content that crisis had been averted, but then a small piece of card appeared at my left elbow; from Des. *Recheck number 9. I think your calculation's wrong.*

It wasn't. The calculation was right. I knew it was right. I tussled with it a bit in my mind, and then left it as it was. What had Des been fussing about? Then I felt my right elbow being nudged. It was Ian.

"You've used the wrong formula for number twelve," he whispered."

No I hadn't. It was perfectly correct. What was he fussing about?

That evening we had a monumental debrief together, piss-up and sleep.

It was great when the results were posted.

I'd come fourth.

Des had come second.

Ian had been so concerned looking after his charge that he'd inadvertently turned a double page on his question paper, missed half of them and come 15th.

It was nice while it lasted, but I couldn't keep it up.

I came bottom again in the next phase, but fortunately that was the penultimate phase of the course and the Commandant, still not sure if I was a temperamental genius or a common or garden troublemaker, couldn't think what to do about it, so gave up.

The course finished, we had a party and I was posted back to Bicester.

TWENTY-NINE

IT WAS TUESDAY 9 DECEMBER 1969.

I had collected Rachel from RAF Lyneham where she had flown back alone from Gibraltar on the previous night's flight, and we were now standing in our gloves and overcoats with the BIA (Barrack Inventory Accountant) counting cups and saucers in the kitchen of our new married quarter at 4, Glebe Close, Ambrosden, Bicester.

It was bitterly cold.

We were glad we'd decided to leave the children in Gibraltar while we prepared things for them first.

Most army quarters in Britain now have central heating, but all we had in the bedroom that freezing night we took over our new home was a completely ineffectual, wall-mounted two-bar electric heater. The ice was thick inside the windows. We couldn't believe what we'd come back to, after the warmth and luxury of those two glorious years we'd just spent in Hanover's *Wallmodenstrasse* flat, with its individual waste disposal units and central boiler house pumping out instant and constant piping hot water into every tank and radiator in the block. Why were we Brits always the poor relations in such things?

It used to be the norm for families to have to wait up to a year or more before a quarter could be made available for them in the husband's new duty station, at home or abroad. The readiness of their allocation was based on a points system. Points were awarded for years of service, length of time married, number of children, previous periods of separation, size of underpants, religion, I can't remember them all. Father would have to concentrate on his new job, pining away unaccompanied, whooping it up with the nurses in the Mess in Nicosia, Hong Kong, or Catterick, while wife and children would be eating out their hearts for the duration, living out of a suitcase with long suffering relatives in deepest Wiltshire.

"If only we had a place of our own," we'd all wail.

But what would have been the point, because we were always allocated a quarter eventually.

While we were serving Queen and Country round the globe it was our wives' chosen duty to be with us, and besides, if we had our own house, which we couldn't afford anyway, we would have to furnish it, 'let' it, and maintain it, which would all be too difficult. No, we'd get round to buying our own home eventually, with our £4,000 gratuity, after we left the Army. Sufficient unto the day . . .

Then came the housing boom.

We realised that the rent we were paying to the Army each month was the equivalent of pouring a mortgage down the drain, so we all started to get our foot into the civilian property market.

With military personnel all buying houses, those who lived in the Mess all week and were not on duty began pouring forth on Friday afternoons to disperse to their own pads around the shires of Britain for the weekend, where they were becoming known down the local, their children were settled in school and taking their exams next term, and their wives had very nice little jobs and were deliriously happy within their new community. No more 'points system' to worry about. No more packing cases to assemble, with esoteric BFPO numbers stencilled all over them cluttering up the front lawn. Britain's new Monday to Friday, 9-5 commuter-belt Army had arrived.

Result?

Nineteen-year old subalterns could get married at 16.00 and move into the quarter of their choice that evening. Whereas previously there were waiting lists of up to a year, so many vacant quarters were becoming available that those who occupied the adjoining ones were moving closer together for warmth and companionship - being Army, old habits dying hard – like circling the wagons for mutual defence in case of attack. It wasn't long before parcels of redundant army quarters were even coming up for sale on the civilian market.

So there we were, Rachel and me, back in Bicester once more, bemoaning our lot at being stuck in perma-frosted Blighty while our friends were off sunning themselves in Cyprus, Hong Kong and Singapore. Perhaps I should have worked harder on that damned OO's course and got a good chit for myself after all. The low-key administrative job to which I had been appointed was not a particularly onerous, pleasant or unpleasant one, but waiting for my name to go into the MoD's Lucky Dip postings bag again in two years time, to see where we would be going to next, would drive me mad in the meantime, unless I found a raft of extra mural activities to engage me.

I poured myself into physical activity.

If I wasn't working out with weights in the gym, I was playing squash. If I wasn't playing squash, I was cross-country running, and in this way I was at least able to keep myself fit enough to organise and run our Physical Efficiency Test programme, which every military unit required its soldiers to undergo annually. Unfortunately, being British, the wherewithal to complete these tests usually had to be improvised, so one of the first things I had to do was scour that part of Oxford looking for a suitable route. After spending one weekend trudging about the place on this quest, on the Monday morning I took my Sergeant Major, WOII Sandy McGuiness round with me, for a second opinion.

He was not impressed.

"With all due respects, sir; but just what the hell is it?"

"Nine-foot ditch, S'arnt Major."

"*Mmmmm.* Well, I mean, it's not, sir, really, is it! I mean, it's barely three-foot really, is it! Half the lads could probably step across it. Leaping a nine-foot ditch was originally intended to simulate the uninhibited hurling of one's heavily laden self across a gorge or chasm, or a snake infested, barbed-wire entangled, bamboo-staked, mine-sodden, snow-filled cess pit crawling with bilharzia right in the enemy's artillery sights while you were quite tired at the time having just schlepped a hundred miles humping seventy-pounds of uncomfortable kit and a rocket launcher over broken glass in your bare feet. All *this* little furrow has to offer is a disinterested worm and half a bent stinging nettle."

"There's a rusty bucket."

"Oh, is there, sir? Where's that, then, sir?"

"Semi-submerged, in the ditch there, S'arnt Major. Next to that upturned shopping trolley."

Oh, yes, so there is, sir. All jagged and lethal looking. That should sort the men from the boys, shouldn't it, and . . . oh, do look, sir; there's two more worms just reared their ugly heads as well. This is getting really exciting, isn't it."

"Well, there just aren't any ready made nine-foot ditches in the area, S'arnt Major. Believe me, I've looked everywhere. It's taken me three days to locate even this stagnant little trickle-riddled trench. I thought if they jumped over, and then jumped back again . . ."

" . . . They'd be heading back in the direction they'd just come from. That's a devious one, sir, I must say. Confuse them completely, that would, poor punch-drunk idiots. Why don't we get them to effect a pirouette in mid air on the way over as well, exercise their leg muscles, develop pelvic thrust?"

"Don't be facetious, S'arnt Major. It's hard enough as it is to jack these things up. Our next problem is going to be tracking down a six-foot wall, otherwise we shall have to dispense with *that* arduous little rigour again this year, as well."

"Dispense with the six-foot wall, sir? Oh, *no*, sir. You can't do that! It would be like picking your nose with your pace stick, or something. It'd be heinous. Getting the lads over the six-foot wall is a tradition, sir. It'd be sacrilege to do away with that. Why can't we do the six-foot wall, sir?"

"There isn't one."

"Isn't one? Isn't one? Course there's one. Says so in the book, sir. All ranks under the age of forty will annually scale the six-foot wall. Says so. Seen it, sir. Straight up, sir. No messing."

"Where is it, S'arnt Major?'

"In the book, sir. In the manual."

"The actual six-foot wall, S'arnt Major. Where's it at?"

"Well, I dunno, sir, exactly. It's a question of looking for one, isn't it. Must be one around here somewhere. Stands to reason, doesn't it. This is an army camp. There's always a six-foot wall in an army camp, sir. Same as there's a nick an' a gym."

"S'arnt Major, we're a detached unit, not a home based, fully equipped training establishment. I can assure you that the ever elusive six-foot wall is not to be found in these barracks, nor its environs, nor for that matter even within a seven mile radius of where we now stand. There's a three-foot wall round our Mess, which they could step over three times I suppose, and there's that twelve-foot balustrade around yours - but a six-foot wall? *Niet.* I'll concede that there's one down in the village, quite a nice one as a matter of fact, well pointed and in pretty good nick, but it's surrounding the garden of a private house, so you can imagine if . . ."

"Well, that's bloody charming, sir, isn't it. Which rotten sod's had all the available six-foot walls away, then?"

"S'arnt Major, for the best part of ten years I have annually scoured parts of the United Kingdom and a fair chunk of north west Europe in a vain quest for six-foot walls. They are in short supply. They've been superseded. There are two-foot walls, and twenty-foot walls, and everything in between *except* six-foot walls, which I am sure is why the army's chosen them as being the regulation height decreed for our chaps to scale, but there quite simply *aren't* any, and so if we insist on complying, and want one, we'll have to construct it ourselves."

"Well, can't we do that then, sir?"

"Hardly on, S'arnt Major. In their combined wisdom I think neither the PRI nor the CO's Fund would consider the purchase of six-foot's worth of bricks and mortar a justifiable expense."

347

"Don't see why not, sir. It'd be a start, wouldn't it. Good thing to have your money in, I'd say, bricks and mortar. Put it down as adventure training expenditure."

"I take your point, S'arnt Major, but it's actually a six-foot wall we're discussing, one side of which is clambered up and the other side of which is scrambled down. Once a year. Hardly a sound long term investment for regimental funds, would you say?"

"Well, why can't we indent for a proper one, sir? You know, an obstacle course, like in other units."

"Not really, S'arnt Major. They're expensive bits of kit, y'know, and as I said, we're not a training establishment. And do bear in mind, won't you, that the original 'scaling the six-foot wall' concept was to simulate the crossing whilst under duress and enemy fire, of a rugged obstacle. There's nothing in the book that says come the day all enemy walls worldwide are going to conform to the MoD's laid down six-foot standard, with a breathing space on top to let you unhook your caught-up doings from your wotsits on the way over. Oh, no. The chances are that we're going to come up against some prime eight-footers with little bits of Muscovite nail and pretty pieces of green Siberian wine bottle sticking out of them. Nor would it be advisable after you've thundered along that dewey 'no duff' course with Ivan one inch removed from the gap in your drawers-cellular and you see what you take to be a familiar six-foot wall looming up out of the early morning mist, screeching to a relieved halt and throwing your pursuer a cheeky little victory sign. He won't like it very much. Nor will you have done yourself too much good when you realise with a torrent of supercharged nausea and an adrenalin rush that the six-foot wall is now a spiked seven-foot job and your normally friendly PT instructor - him just not there this time. It could very well become politic to grin sheepishly and pretend you thought it was all some huge joke. You'll have to shake the sand and loose pebbles out of your trouser leg, wiggle your little finger agitato in your left ear and in your best Russian, say: 'Look, old chap; I seem to have made rather a Horlicks of this. Don't suppose we could count it a dry run, could we?'

No, S'arnt Major; I feel that where this PE test is concerned we've knotted our elastic. As there is no six-foot wall available and I possess neither the wit nor wherewithal to construct one, we shall have to forego the pleasure of scraping ourselves across it until one turns up sometime. But all is not lost. Let us persevere. The hundred-metre carry is still the best scheme devised by man to crease the unwary. Shall we give it a whirl, S'arnt Major? The advantages of a buckshee rehearsal are not to be scoffed at, y'know. I'll carry you from here across to that barn over there to start with . . ."

"Well, that's very kind indeed of you, sir, I'm sure, but I really think I can walk. There's no need to trouble yourself, sir, I . . . *oops* . . . oh, *sir*."

"There now, just hoik yourself up across my shoulders while I insinuate my arm in here between your legs, like this. Got rather a lot of tuck in there, haven't you S'arnt Major. There we go, good lad; wriggle it all around a bit, and . . . h'*up* she goes."

"*Not* that way, *if* you don't mind, sir. *Whorrr* . . . that's much better. Thank you very much. Makes all the difference in the world, that does, sir; little bit of adjustment. How much further have we got to go? For chrissakes, *oh, oh, oh . . .* "

"Not far, S'arnt Major. Why are you speaking in that squeaky voice?"

"Squeaky voice, sir? Me, sir? No, sir. What squeaky voice's that then, sir?"

"A sort of staccato falsetto."

"You might care to call it that, sir. I prefer putting it down to my simulated shrapnel wound. Couldn't we please forget about your bleedin' gong for a moment and you just drop me off here to die? There's a good chap. Come on now, sir. Enough's enough. I won't bubble you on it, sir. I'm sure you've got far more important things to do than just save me. There's all that paperwork waiting for you back in your office. I feel I'm impeding your progress, jostling about up here slung across your polystyrene-filled pack like a hundredweight sack trying to contain a ton of the proverbial, and . . ."

"There we are, S'arnt Major. Made it! Now it's your turn, to carry me back . . . S'arnt Major? S'arnt Major?"

"*Corrr,* do us a favour; I mean - if you'll just give me a moment or two here to reaclimatise myself; settle down; get my breath back; regroup and readjust some of my personal belongings, would you, please, sir?"

Yes, of course. This webbing equipment of ours *is* cumbersome and outdated, isn't it. I'm sure I saw my uncle going off to north Africa in the very same kit."

"No chance, sir: that would've been the new stuff he had. Now, sir: when would you like this show to hit the road? Next Wednesday?"

"Yes, I think so, don't you? Get it in Orders tomorrow; give the 'excused boots' brigade time to get their act together, and let surprise, shock and indignation permeate the hearts and minds of the rest of our brave lads, perhaps. How's C'orl Smith, by the way?"

"Still subject to auto-suggestion, sir."

"Well, suggest to him that he does it this time, S'arnt Major. Get him to come to some arrangement with his feet. Impress upon all of them that it's a great feeling, as you finish the bash and spray your target with small arms fire, to know that you have proved yourself and been adjudged physically up to it for the next twelve months. You look dubious, S'arnt Major."

"What, sir? Me, sir? Oh, no, sir."

Like all sergeant majors, Sandy McGuiness was a larger than life character with a sense of humour that would put many a professional to shame. There is a time honoured ceremony in the Army called OC's Orders. I used to hold my Orders on a Monday afternoon, which was when those soldiers awaiting punishment or wishing to see me about personal matters would form up in the corridor outside my office prior to interview. Invariably I had a grin on my face listening through the wall to Sandy vetting them all first.

"What do *you* want, lad?"

"Permission to report sick please, S'arnt Major"

350

"Stand up straight when you're talking to me, Jonhston. And what do you suppose is wrong with you this time, may I ask?"

"I think I'm going short-sighted, Sir."

"Oh no you're not. I haven't given you permission yet. First of all, what's that - out there?"

"What, sir?"

"Pay attention lad, or I shall shove the brass tip of this 'ere pace stick of mine so far up your arse you'll think you've got a gold filling. Look up there, where I'm pointing. Outside the window, you silly idiot. That bloody great expanse of blue stuff that's stretching from horizon to horizon like there's no tomorrow, as far as the eye can see."

"You mean the sky, S'arnt Major?"

"Exactly, lad. The sky. And what's that bloody great ball of shimmering fire you can see hanging there like an orange cymbal right slap bang in the middle of that mass of blue sky - eh?"

"The sun, sir?"

"That's *right,* son, it's the fuckin' *sun,* isn't it. And do you know what, son - that fuckin' sun's ninety-three million fuckin' miles away. *You're* not short-sighted, Johnston. Now fuck off. *Next.*

"What do *you* want, C'orl Scoggins?"

"To see the OC about getting married, sir."

"The OC's already married, and even if he wasn't he wouldn't marry you, you're far too ugly. Now fuck off. *Next.*"

And so it went . . .

On the previous occasion we'd been in Bicester, when I'd lain in the RAF Hospital at Halton having my right knee cut open and reassembled, friendly neighbours had run Rachel across to see me each evening, because she couldn't drive. Even she realised this was silly, so while I had been slaving away miserably on the OO's course at Deepcut and she had been living back in Gibraltar, she'd taken and passed her driving test there. I was delighted. It was lovely having my sexy wife slithering around Oxford in our slinky, silver continental coupé. After she'd been at it for eleven months though, a thought occurred to me one night:

"Darling, your year must almost be up, you know. Do you think it's about time we exchanged your Gibraltar licence for a British one?"

"Yup, good idea; d'you want to do it for me, please?"

"Gratuitous year and then exchange it, sir? What gratuitous year's that then, sir?" asked the authorities, aghast. "There's no such scheme, sir. A Gibraltar licence is only good in Gibraltar. It's not valid at all for a resident of the United Kingdom. If your wife's been driving over here on hers for a whole year then I think I would remain very, very quiet about it indeed, if I was you. She's lucky not to have been nicked. I dread to think what might have befallen you, her and anyone else involved in the event of her having had an accident. No, I'm afraid that before she can drive over here any more she'll need to get herself a proper English licence, and to do that she must first pass the test. Simple as that."

Simple it wasn't.

We applied for a provisional licence, and a test, and begrudgingly . . .

. . . bought a set of plastic L-plates from Woolworths, which made our sex-symbol car look like a thoroughbred with a bandaged gumboil on its arse. Oh, the indignity. It seemed to look back over its shoulder at the offending plastic square and wince, distaste writ large across its headlights and grille.

Then Rachel went and failed the ****** test.

The ignominy.

She had driven competently all over north Africa, Spain and Gibraltar. This test was meant to have been a mere formality, but then some appointed spode in a Harris Tweed jacket with pencils jammed in its breast pocket and a clipboard had had the temerity to fail her for 'improper use of her rearview mirror'. We always used an enormous panoramic convex mirror in all our cars, so that with just the merest flick of an eyelid the five counties and any convoy of police cars that might happen to have been receding into the distance behind us were brought into instant and effortless focus, but

Author, with his wife Rachel
and daughter Natalia at a
fellow officer's wedding;
Shrewsbury - 1965

Author and his wife – Ladies'
Dinner Night, Ambrosden
Mess, Bicester, Oxon - 1971

For all you car buffs out there: for some years the author's pride and joy, his 1972 Mercedes-Benz 280 SE 3.5 V8 Coupé

Eat your heart out, 007

that wasn't good enough for Fred Mincing, who'd never been on an Autobahn south of Dover in his life. He told Rachel that she had to move her head physically each time, so that he could see her do it.

"But sometimes I'm going too fast to do that," Rachel replied. "It would be dangerous."

"That was another thing . . ."

I knew the real reason she'd been failed. She had turned up in a slinky, left-hand-drive silver continental coupé. If it had been a rusted-up, plum coloured Morris she might have passed.

So it was back to the L-plates again, until another test could be arranged. She was advised to enrol for an expensive series of lessons with BSM in the meantime, and to attend the test in one of their vehicles, with its red and white bill-board on the roof.

This she did, and passed.

Point taken.

Our lovely car was turning out to be everything it promised to be the day I'd collected it from the Opel factory in Rüsselsheim over a year before. Fast; economical; roomy, comfortable and a looker to boot. I was growing so fond of it that when it expired I thought I would have it compressed and retain it as a cherished ornamental cube set on a monumental plinth in the garden. In the event it drove over the length and breadth of Great Britain and Northern Europe for 150,000 miles, 90,000 of those on the same set of Michelins. I wrote to tell them about it, and they replied to say they weren't surprised in the least, and to congratulate me on my driving. Drat! No complimentary set of new tyres.

In 1976 we bought my dream car of all time, a metallic blue Mercedes 280 SE 3.5 V8 Coupé with white leather upholstery, and the Opel became Rachel's property and family run-around for ferrying the kids, garden waste and bags of cement. It was thus engaged (with kids, I think) the day it finally did expire in an Eastbourne street in 1978, exactly ten years old to the day. Its bodywork looked as if it had been through the Ardennes Campaign. I sold it (weeping as I did so) for a mere £50 to a local garage owner called Barry Simpson, who patched it up and used it as a towing vehicle. A year later I saw it regularly parked outside a house and discovered an old lady had bought it go shopping. When the old lady died it disappeared, but then a year after that I saw it parked near Tunbridge Wells, and tracked down its new (fourth) owner to find that it was being used for stock car racing.

However, just at the moment it was still just over a year old and the time was almost now due for me to pay some money to HM Customs.

A year to the minute after I'd landed at Harwich, they came to visit me in my Bicester office, and to my amazement and delight told me that if I exported the car and then reimported it again, this time doing so in Rachel's name, we could get *another* year duty-free. I didn't begin to understand the complexity of all this, but for once the God of chance seemed to be on our side - so we did as they suggested, and went to Paris, just to be able to turn round and come back again.

Lawrence Williams started out life as a Gunner. I first met him when he transferred to the RAOC and we both did that wretched OO's course together. We had become good friends, so I was delighted when he and Yvonne were posted to Bicester and came to live only a few doors away from us. Yvonne was about eight months pregnant with Toby at the time.

I put the Paris proposal to them.

"We'd *love* to," squealed Yvonne.

"You mean . . . smuggling?" Lawrence asked. "Bit dicey for the old career though isn't it, mate? Dover's pretty well buttoned up now, 'cept when they're on strike. Basque country'd be different. Or Nepal. But not the Channel ports, I wouldn't have thought."

"Why don't you just shut up and listen for once in your life," I insisted. "It's all legit. Look, I've even got this confirmatory letter from Customs and Excise proposing the scheme. All I have to do is take the car out of the country and then bring it back in again, and we've got it duty free in Rachel's name for a year. Simple."

"All a bit of a palaver if you ask me," said Lawrence. "What are you achieving by it, except cluttering up the motorway to Dover and depriving some poor sod of a place on the ferry?"

"I agree," I agreed. "It's totally absurd, but I don't make the rules. It's jobs for the boys, and keeps the paperwork churning."

"So what do you want us to do? What is our role in this nefarious misdemeanour?"

"Absolutely nothing. Come with us, that's all. Companionship? We just thought we'd combine the opportunity with a trip to Paris and back. Share the cost."

"Yeah, okay," he said.

With Yvonne and her embryonic Toby in the back, the car tilted a bit to that side, but we got there alright, and I think she quite enjoyed going over the cobblestones. We went up the Eiffel Tower, ate some snails, split up for an hour after a contretemps in Montmartre, and then drove back home again next day.

That's when I nearly divorced Rachel.

On the spot.

In Calais she insisted on buying an electric fruit juicer she intended 'smuggling' back into Britain.

"Don't be so *ridiculous*," I remonstrated. You know what the whole purpose of this mission is. To clear the car for another year, in *your* name. Yet here you are prepared to jeopardise our whole operation just to smuggle in some wretched fruit-juicer which you can probably get down the high street for half the price anyway."

"I don't see the problem," she retorted tight-lipped because a) she knew I was probably right, because most of the time I almost invariably am, and b) she still wanted that particular fruit juicer. "They'll be so busy checking the car they'd never notice a tiddly little thing like this anyway."

"Listen, stupid - the whole idea is that they're not meant to notice anything untoward about the car at all."

"So what are you going to do - tuck it under your arm and go through the green channel with your fingers crossed?"

Trying to reason with a contrary woman is always fruitless and exhausting. "Everything's in order," I sighed patiently. "I have all the correct paperwork here in my breast pocket, and I don't want some anomaly such as a contraband fruit juicer to put the mockers on it. Alright? So, I'm sorry dear, but I am afraid I must insist that you unpack the fruit juicer and leave it behind. Alright"

"Good afternoon, officer," I said genially, stepping out of the car to meet him half way.

The customs officer was large and had red hair. His blue serge suit shone. I could tell he hated me already.

"Anything to declare then?" he asked with gruff matter-of-factness.

"Not a thing, officer," I carolled.

"No? What about the car then? It's wearing temporary importation plates: QQ 1819."

He couldn't be that good, could he? He'd been tipped off. Still in a spat with me, Rachel had cabled him from Calais. I bent swiftly to glance inside the car and glower at her. They were all cowering there like illegal immigrants, as if butter wouldn't melt in their mouths.

"Oh, the car," I spluttered. "What about the car?" It was a good job I'd had no mission in the Second World War more important than simply growing up. "Well, I'm not actually smuggling the car in, you understand, although as you have obviously gathered the car was the sole reason, actually, for us just having been to France and back."

I explained.

"I don't suppose you have any corroborative paperwork about your person whereby this rather spurious story can be verified, do you? Sir?"

"As a matter of fact I have," I said, and with a flourish produced two metro tickets and some old confetti . . . "somewhere."

Eventually I found it, and the moment his practised eye saw his firm's familiar crown and portcullis letterhead, he became less facetious for a moment, sucked his teeth and returned to his hutch to read it.

I grinned at Lawrence through the car window and gave the thumbs up.

I shouldn't have done.

"This letter's a load of old codswallop really, isn't it," said 'the man' shuffling back out into the daylight of the fume-laden customs hangar once more. "I don't understand how you've got hold of this at all. This law they're referring to went out last year. It's no longer applicable."

"Kingsbeam House *is* your head office, isn't it?"

"So?"

"Well, that's the letter they sent me. Our whole object in going to Paris for two days was to act in accordance with the suggestion given and recommended in that letter you're holding, from your superiors. *(Whoops)* You don't now mean to tell me they've got it wrong, do you?"

"Very likely, yes. They usually do. They don't know if they're coming or going up there half the time."

(Got that, Kingsbeam House? One of your men at Dover. Malcontent. Worse than average image. Bad teeth and an unpleasant odour. Attitude. Third hutch on the right as you're coming in from France.)

"What else you got then?" he asked, determined to exact his pound of flesh from somewhere.

"Oh, come on Squire: absolutely nothing," I assured him, becoming quite irked now. "What do you want us to do? We've got a dinner appointment at my father's house in Hastings in an hour and would quite like to be on our way, if that's okay."

"Well, I dunno about that yet, do I? By my reckoning you've still got £427 to pay on this car." I stiffened, and felt something within me start to leak. "If it wasn't for this silly letter you've produced, complicating the whole thing, that's what I would have charged you and you'd've been on your way by now. Anyway, I've rung for my superior. While we're waiting I'll just have a look at what else you've got."

As I started to empty my pockets out obligingly onto the counter he walked round to the car, opened the door and suggested to Lawrence and the girls that he would like them to get out. Warm and fug-ridden in there, they were not best pleased.

He wasn't interested in the contents of my pockets at all.

The mean spirited bastard was going for the jugular.

He was going to strip search the car.

We had packed everything so carefully around Yvonne's stomach before leaving Paris that morning, too. Oh, what fun to be a customs man. I believe in reincarnation. If next time I can't make it as a worm . . .?

The contents of the car, its boot and interior now emptied, sat forlornly about the tarmac, with nothing untoward having been discovered. Summoned from his larger, plusher hutch along the way, a more senior customs official with more flock and less gloss on his pants now wandered across to scan my letter, murmured something about it being a most irregular misunderstanding they would have to take up with Head Office, but that he would have to allow me the benefit of the doubt on this occasion. Lawrence helped me to repack the car, both of us locked in the sombre and bitter silence of the aftermath of unnecessary confrontation and frustration that must so often be played out at frontier and customs posts around the world.

"You see what I mean?" I snapped at Rachel as, thankfully, we drove off at last. "Can't you just imagine the field day he would have had if you'd brought in your blasted fruit juicer?"

"But I did," she said, opening the glove compartment to show me. "There it is. In there."

Sometimes y'just gotta laff, haven't you . . .!

A year later they called to see me at my Bicester office again. The day of final reckoning had come.

It was £227.

"Fair enough," I laughed, handing over a cheque. "We gave each other a good run for my money though, didn't we!"

We shook hands, they departed and I went about my morning's business.

At lunchtime I called in to Jack Smith's *Three Corners Garage* and asked if he would please remove my QQ 1819 numberplates under which the car had been registered for two years, and bolt on its new DVLA number BUD 207 J.

Got you at last did they, sir?"

"They did that, Jack," I said, and went home for my lunch.

Almost predictably, a week later, quite out of the blue, the Army posted me back to Germany.

There you are; they'd gone and done it again.

Do you suppose my AG9 posting's branch was in cahoots with customs and having a laugh - or what?

THIRTY

BACK TO THE GARRISON Housing Commandant went number 4, Glebe Close, Bicester; back to Gibraltar went Rachel and the children, and back to Germany went the Opel.

This time I was being sent to Münster, where there was a six-months waiting list for quarters.

I stopped off for a beer with my father in St Leonards en route and then went on to Dover to catch the midnight ferry across to Ostende. The last thing I did on English soil was rip off my road fund tax disc and pop it in the post for a rebate.

Once on board I squatted atop a bollard and tried to doze.

It was difficult.

Wide awake on an adjoining bollard was a school master in a duffel coat.

It wasn't long before he informed me that he had been on minesweepers during the war. He spent the entire crossing tamping his pipe and showering me with soggy dottle, while supping cut price rum from a plastic beaker, and regaling me with tedious recollections of early dawn moments on the night watch of his wretched minesweeper. It struck me that he was also imagining our British Rail Sealink ferry to be *Ark Royal,* and he her captain. Ever since seeing Jack Hawkins in *The Cruel Sea*, duffel coats seemed to affect people that way.

We hit the continental beach at 05.00.

After a trouble-free disembarkation I was soon on the immaculate Ostende to Antwerp autobahn, and then - driving eastward - by as soon as 05.30 I found myself having to ferret about in the glovebox for my Ray-Bans. Sometimes, admittedly, I had been known to wear them at cocktail parties,

362

and in the cinema, but this morning it was not just affectation, but for real. As the sun rose and came pouring into the car, it bathed me with the dawn's swiftly heating orange glow, making me feel like some airline pilot in a BEA TV advertisement.

Not long afterwards I became aware that oncoming lorries were letting rip with air horns, frantically flashing their lights and careening out of sight down embankments to get out of my way. I was weaving about with tiredness, so I pulled in to a lay-by and slept for two hours. If I'd carried on driving as I had been, I would have arrived in Münster as they were coming down for breakfast, rather than for high tea as planned.

Rested, I awoke at 08.30 with a crumpled collar and noticeably honking much more richly beneath each armpit. My condition might have been referred to as emanating pheremonal musk, which could have turned certain women on, but I knew was socially unacceptable: I was rank, and desperately in need of a shower.

Thus it was that I drove across the Dutch/German border to re-enter the Fatherland once more.

"Schone Guten Morgen, Herr Fritz," I carolled jovially through parched lips, gasping for a pint of chilled orange juice as the neatly bearded border guard poked his head out of the customs post window on the German side of the road. He didn't actually holler out "Hi, Mike - welcome back," but he did give a friendly enough wave and let me pass unhindered into his country.

An hour later I pulled into a *Gaststätte* car park, stretched, and went in for some lunch. *"Guten Morgen,"* I said, *"geben sie mir bitte ein Bier."* Then I clapped my hand to my mouth and almost collapsed with a fit of the giggles. I had been living this moment ever since leaving Hanover two-and-a-half years before. I ordered some lunch, simple fayre but exquisite, and knew for sure that I was back once more in good old Deutschland.

At 14.15 I drove through the gates of the White Horse Mess opposite Portsmouth Barracks in Münster, climbed from the car, stretched and whirled round as I heard a voice cry -

"Good God; Mike George. What are *you* doing here?"

Strolling out of the Mess after lunch, accompanied by his beautiful blonde German wife, Heide, was Captain Chris Beal, RCT, whom I had last seen eight years before, sitting in our tent in Norfolk the night Richard Powell burst in to inform us that President Kennedy had been shot.

The Beales and the Georges were to be next door neighbours in Münster's Igelpatt for the next year, and then - bugger me - when I left the British Army and fetched up in Muscat to join the Sultan of Oman's Forces as a mercenary ten years later, there they were again, and we served together in that part of the Middle Eastern desert for five years as well.

After that he and Heide were to run their own successful Desert Safari company out of Muscat's Al Falaj Hotel, but then Heide was sadly lost to cancer, and the last I heard of Chris he had moved to Dubai.

A mess waiter took me up to the top floor and showed me my accommodation. It was a spacious, dark, shapely room in the attic with a bed, basin, desk and a large walk-in wardrobe/cupboard affording ample space for skis, stray girls, overcoats and all sorts of other clobber.

I spent the rest of the afternoon unloading the car, unpacking and hanging up clothes and pictures, laying out books, washing kit and numerous other bits and pieces with which I always travelled if I could, and which so readily transformed a cell into a personalised sitting room within an hour of arrival. It is a good old army adage that any fool can be uncomfortable, and I was always amazed at how many chose to be, preferring their living accommodation to be a testament to Spartan minimalism. There was once a well known company commander in 3 Queens Regiment who used to carry my practice to perfection. He even went so far as to have a captain's chair bolted to the floor, a piece of Wilton carpet and a small cocktail cabinet set up in the armoured personnel carrier he used as his command vehicle.

Next door to me was a Spanish style bathroom, by which I mean a wet room. There was a bath in it, and a marble floor with a drain hole in the middle down which everything would run, including yourself if you weren't careful, straight into the North Sea. It was nothing if not practical.

Like a washpoint for bulls.

No feminine fripperies like frilly, fluffy, coloured loo seat covers.

It was a water-hole for solo studs.

I fixed a hose to the bath taps, slung the nozzle over the beam, tied it all together with a bent coathanger, string and masking tape and that way made for myself a first rate shower unit.

After my overnight sea trip, the six-hour car journey, unpacking and arranging my stuff, and the fact that it had been a blistering hot day, the shower water when I finally got under it cascaded over my exhausted body like warm golden rain from heaven.

That night there was a thunderstorm.

I adore all earth-raping, raging elements in full fury, when nature unleashes her primal forces - but especially thunderstorms.

They recharge my batteries.

I climbed between my sheets to enjoy listening to it crashing around outside, and was asleep within seconds.

Münster, as I was to discover next day, although 63% destroyed in WWII, and rebuilt in its pre-war vernacular, is a delightful old university city with deeply sloping high roofs to its gabled houses, historic stone buildings, cobbled streets and a beautiful shopping centre ranging beneath the colonnaded arcades each side of its famous *Prinzipalmarkt*.

Fashion and taste abounded in its shops, boutiques, jewellers and furniture and antiques showrooms. Crisply starched, gingham bedecked boulevard coffee tables were arranged everywhere in typical continental alfresco style. Heavily clustered wet bunches of multi-coloured flowers dazzled florists' windows. The populace, of which there was 270,000, was clean and smart, and strode about purposefully with a confident spring to their well shod step.

After the war the British Army took over and manned no fewer than 130 German barracks, twelve of which were in Münster.

One of them, Winterbourne, had been built two-kilometers from the centre of Münster, in 1938.

Closed in 1995, today the premises are used as a film company location, and have also been converted to industrial and office use, but formerly they served first as a German and then a British military supply point. With its own railway siding leading to the main rail network, on one side of the barracks' extended parking lot there are seven huge, ugly storage buildings (each 63 meters long by 12 meters wide) composed of a basement level, four upper and two attic storeys, as well as a bakery. The bakery, a plastered cement structure, two storeys high with a sloping roof, contains a work area with ten huge commercial ovens, coal bin, office rooms and a dormitory. Some of the warehouses have a four-storey-high silo.

I liked Münster a lot.

In 2004 it was voted the most liveable city in the world.

I didn't like Winterbourne Barracks at all though.

When news of my posting there, to an outfit known as 87 Supply Depot, first became known, several of my colleagues winced: "Wouldn't fancy going there myself. There's meant to be a jinx on the place."

"Nonsense," I scoffed. "It's Münster in North Rhine-Westphalia we're talking about, not some mythical Ruritanian castle steeped in mysticism. What are you on about? This is 1971."

"Actually sir, it is fairly well known throughout the Corps," I was eventually told be a senior warrant officer whose opinion I respected, "that Winterbourne Barracks does have a chain of disasters associated with it, which over the years have given rise to its having rather a bad name."

And so it proved to be.

It was a hot summer's day as I drove through the gates that first morning to report for duty, but no amount of sunshine seemed able to brighten the grim and forbidding sombreness of the place.

It was hideous.

I was to spend eighteen-months there and I grew to loathe almost every minute of it.

It became an effort to steel myself to go to work each day.

It was a horrid, detestable place.

Misery permeated from the damp face of every building.

The OC was 'strange'.

The soldiers were disgruntled and wary.

Was there a jinx?

I'll let you decide.

While I was there my father died: my six-year old son had his face scarred for life, and then smashed his arm very badly.

Going round a corner in their car my chief clerk's wife was hurled out the door, cracked her skull on the kerbside and was killed.

One of my soldiers hanged himself from a toilet cistern - and any further progression in my own military 'career' was suddenly to be brought to an abrupt end.

All this in the space of 12-months.

Sitting at my desk in the bay window of my well appointed garret in the White Horse Officers' Mess, I was compelled to spend the next four months swatting hard for the Captain to Major written examination, which, in concert with others of my age group - each of whom I imagined was infinitely more able than I - I was due to sit during the first week of December.

For the British soldier, Germany was the land of duty free goods, so I decided that I would prepare a celebration for myself, for when the exam was finally over.

All my life I had craved the proper kit upon which to play good music.

I had owned numerous wind-up gramophone boxes and heavy 78 rpm vinyl records, tins of (pre-stylus) steel needles, and boxes of wooden ones that looked like dental picks and came in book-match type envelopes - but I had still gone right through my teens and early twenties with my dream item always eluding me: a Pye Black Box - primeval man's last word in musical reproduction. Even then a Pye Black Box had become a museum piece; so what did I go for?

As soon as we set foot in Germany, and for the duration of our tour there, we received a financial award known as Local Overseas Allowance (LOA.) This LOA added almost a third to our monthly rate of pay. It was given to compensate for the difference in price structure between the German and British economies. What it in fact did was finance the frenzied purchase and repayment over two years of many of those sophisticated consumer items we'd always wanted to acquire but could never afford back home in Britain, at the top of which list Mercedes Benz motor cars and stereo equipment reigned supreme.

I went along to the Dutch Army's PX (Postal Exchange; the equivalent of our NAAFI) at outlying Handorf, and ordered a then state-of-the-art Bang & Olufsen.

Oh - and a new record to play on it.

The Captain to Major written exam had always been a source of great consternation for those who had not yet taken and passed it.

It was the major hurdle that had to be overcome before one could become eligible to mount the stairway to the stardom of military hierarchy.

It was the bridge to be crossed and the gateway to be passed through, before which nought else could happen.

Under an earlier system there had been numerous papers that had to be taken and passed: three Tactics papers, Military History, Military Science, Military Law and Current Affairs. Nor was one allowed time off to study.

After a while, more enlightened military masters realised the preparation needed to pass this vital examination was placing too much of a burden on the examinee at a time in his career when he was at his most effective, when his abilities were most needed and he was working the hardest. There was no question of doing away with the exam - every profession should have them - but it was decided to tow the cumbersome old system into touch and replace it with a more streamlined version.

The new exam consisted of War Studies, International Affairs, Administration, Man Management and Morale, and Military Law, with especial attention in this latter paper being focused on those sections dealing with Military Aid To The Civil Power, because although from time to time the natives around the old colonial world were still revolting, there was also at that time a high expectation of outbreaking civil unrest and blood being let flow down Britain's gutters and by-ways, and that would have to be dealt with effectively.

I was to be one of those who were going to sit the first of the new-style examination, there in Münster in 1971.

War Studies and International Affairs were considered to be subjects too new for army officers to be expected to study privately without receiving previous instruction, and so throughout the preceding year batches of us had been dispatched to various seats of learning for fortnightly RAEC and civilian courses about the definition of sovereignty and the principles of Clausewitz.

As part and parcel of this new learning process, soon afterwards the Junior Officers' Education Scheme (JOE) was introduced.

No sooner had a fledgling subaltern stepped forth from his commissioning ball than he, too, found himself concurrently embarked upon a decade of part-time instruction in War Studies and International Affairs, to ensure that he had a grounding and on-going preparedness for his own exam when the time came.

It seemed like a well conceived plan, but by all accounts was a bore.

Never slow to exaggerate the formidable workload placed upon them at any given time, junior officers entire lives seemed to be taken up with having to write a constant stream of political essays and sending them off to be marked.

The guys had joined the army to soldier; to perform the will and rectify the errors of politicians, not to *be* politicians.

The JOE Scheme eventually fell out of favour.

It was replaced by the Progressive Qualification Scheme (PQS) which was pretty much the same thing by another name, but by then I had moved on, fallen out of touch, and now no longer have any real idea about what the Officer Corps gets up to or is expected to achieve these days.

However - at lunchtime that first Wednesday afternoon in December 1971, the pleasure of placing the cap back onto my fountain pen and after two-and-a-half days of solid slog, handing in my last paper after the final exam, was unbounded.

A friend of mine, Howard Stevens, who had been sitting next to me, and I set off together from HQ 4 Guards Brigade at York Barracks, Gremmendorf, where the examination hall had been, and decided that instead of going straight home we would whoop it up a little in town first, to celebrate.

To do this we went to a *Bierstube* for lunch.

I had a litre of beer and a veal cutlet. Howard had the same to drink, but chose a giant *Bockwurst* banger to chew on. Funny how we remember these things. Then he had to get home to babysit because his wife, Pamela, had a dental appointment that afternoon.

Me?

I had a 14.00 collection detail to fulfill at the Dutch Army PX at Handorf, remember?

It was cold.

Early snow flurries curled about the ground.

I had parked outside the Mess with the Opel's boot and doors wide open, humping polystyrene packed cardboard boxes of Bang & Olufsen equipment upstairs into my room in the attic.

I was so excited that I was half trying to unpack and assemble the stuff as I stumbled up the stairs with it, dying to get my first record onto the turntable to hear how it sounded.

I had waited more than 20-years for this moment.

I had earned and saved the money for myself, and being duty-free I had happily paid a real and fair and reasonable and sensible and good and proper price for the kit, which made the whole pleasurable deal even more satisfying and worthwhile than if I'd had to pay through the nose for it back in rip-off Blighty.

It was a precious and memorable experience for me.

"Excuse me, sir; you're wanted on the telephone," the Mess Steward shouted down from one of the windows as I was lifting the third load off the back seat of the car.

"Tell 'em I'll ring back," I grunted, staggering with the box. "Who is it, anyway?"

"I believe it's a call from England, sir."

England? Rachel was in Gibraltar. Who would be calling me from England? "All right," I retorted, lowering the precious box I was hefting gently onto the snow. "I'm coming."

I scrunched quickly up the wide, ornamental Mess steps and went into the office. "Halloo," I said, picking the handset from the desk.

"Michael?" It was a female voice.

"Yes."

"Michael, it's Sue. I'm sorry to have to ring you with bad news like this, but I'm afraid it's your father. He's in hospital. He's had another stroke and keeled over in the street this morning. I wouldn't alarm you unnecessarily, but I think perhaps you should try to come home if you possibly can."

"Bad as that, is it Sue?"

"I think it might be, yes."

"All right, love; thank you for telephoning. I have one or two things I shall have to sort out here first, but I'll try to get back later this evening. Take care of things now, won't you. Byeee."

One thing about my Old Man, he always had a sense of occasion and impeccable timing.

Imagine if the call had come two days earlier, just as I was sitting down to the first exam paper after a year's study, with no chance to sit it again for another year? Phew. What a dilemma that would have been.

Quickly I finished unloading the car, and then drove straight to my unit.

My OC was displeased by father's indisposition because (as always) there was a heavy workload on at the depot, but he

371

was suitably polite and sympathetic and was traditionally obliged to approve my compassionate leave, fortunately the first I had applied for in eleven years of service.

Having cleared my desk I shot back to the Mess to pack, leaving my chief clerk to ring Rhine Army HQ to book me an emergency flight back to UK.

It was 15.00.

The plane was scheduled to leave Düsseldorf at 18.00.

Three hours in which to travel 62 miles.

No problem. I'd make it.

Bunging my kit onto the back seat, I pulled out of the Mess car park into the traffic, and drove . . . and as I drove I thought about dad.

Not at the height of The Blitz as one might have expected, but for some reason towards the end of the war he had evacuated us to south Wales for a short while where mother, my baby brother Tony and I stayed in a little miner's cottage in Porth with 'Aunty Bertha' - whoever she was. I never did find out exactly, but I believe she was distantly related to my paternal grandmother and had been charitable in offering us hospitality, no doubt after having been put upon quite a bit to do so.

Irresistibly one afternoon Tony and I systematically ran a pencil down the recently repapered bubbly bits in one of the corners of her 'best room'.

Left to our own devices we would have gone on to complete the other three corners, but were apprehended before doing so.

We were not popular with Aunty Bertha, but we constituted her long suffering 'bit' for the war effort.

There was an attractive and friendly local school teacher called Miss Bell living in the same house with us. I, who was nearly seven, had quite a crush on Miss Bell who used to smile at me and must have been all of, gosh - what – twenty-five at the time? There were not so many people who smiled at me in those days, which is why I remember her, she who sadly never even tried to lay an exploratory hand on me. Hell, there was a war on; I knew that. War was a serious business after all, and most of the time I was only in the way, so I never really expected anyone to go smiling at me. But it was still nice when they did.

It was there in south Wales that I saw my first ever mountain goat, while climbing my first ever mountain to drink my first ever natural spring water. And I went to school there for a term, which I loathed. It was a large, co-educational comprehensive primary school where all the children laughed at me because they had funny accents, which I didn't; much as our crowd must have ribbed father when he'd first moved to England as a boy. It crossed my mind that he might have been getting his own back through me, and that if we could only decide which side of the Severn we belonged some of us might find happiness. A little girl also showed me how to whip a spinning top, which is a wondrous feat I never mastered, and still consider it so today. Then, in no time it seemed, our Cymru sojourn was over, and we returned to Lewes.

I didn't know how long we'd been in Wales, but the garden of our house in Ferrers Road when we got back was a jungle of lush green vegetation swaying in the breeze. What with a war on, his work, and learning to cook Woolton pie for himself every evening, dad obviously hadn't had time to wield a scythe or pluck weeds, although fancifully I kidded myself that the real reason for the long grass and us being moved away to a 'safe' house in Wales was that he'd had to be sent off on some top secret war mission somewhere.

Throughout his life father had been a keen amateur thespian. Hitler put paid to this pursuit for a while, but after the cessation of hostilities he took up treading the boards again.

I remember first seeing him doing his stuff playing Peachum in *The Beggar's Opera* at Lewes Town Hall in 1949, and then again as Macduff in *Macbeth* at Lewes Little Theatre. I couldn't get over the fact that for some reason my reviled maths master at school, 'Killer' Price, a psychopathic wartime commando and unarmed combat expert had been the one invited to teach the cast the correct way to stage a realistic sword fight. He had come round to our house one evening, bearing with him a brace of horribly jagged-edged, much practised upon flat swords, with one of which he proceeded to attack dad out in the garden, as if he was a German, while with the other our slightly concerned and cornered father vainly tried to defend himself. It was like a real life duel to the death, which, watching it through our French windows, mother loved, because at that stage in their marriage she no longer liked dad very much. For days afterwards I wondered whether I would now be getting preferential consideration at exam time in what was undoubtedly my worst subject, being so bad at maths that one year I'd even got minus 3% for arithmetic for also having spelled my name wrong at the top.

In keeping with the times dad was unquestionably the ultimate arbiter in domestic affairs, but as he seemed to be away so much of the time on one activity or another, it was mother who ruled the roost on a day to day basis. That they were ill matched as a team eventually became too apparent to ignore, and in order to stop tearing each other to shreds, which neither of them liked very much, they sensibly quit. I since met numerous of dad's friends, colleagues, and even contemporaries of mine, who had both worked and played with him, all of whom testified that he was a super chap, pleasant, personable and possessed of charm in abundance. Professionally he had been Treasurer of the Eastbourne branch of the Royal National Lifeboat Institution, Secretary of the Lewes Red Cross Society, a lecturer at Barclays Bank Staff Training College at Wimbledon, and an examiner for the Institute of Bankers Examination, of which he was himself a Fellow.

But he had never been healthy.

Dad was always a smart and distinguished looking man, so much so that one would never suspect that he had already suffered two coronaries, haemorrhages and considerable discomfort. Now, in the middle of winter, a year after his early retirement from Barclays Bank and just three weeks before Christmas, he'd keeled over once again.

My plane from Düsseldorf landed at Heathrow at 18.00.

A soldier from London District was there waiting for me with a vehicle standing-by to take me to the nearest railway station.

The hour-and-a-half train journey from Victoria to St Leonards was a cold, laborious and miserable one. I arrived eventually and took a taxi up to the house.

Sue and my brother Tony were there to greet me.

They had just come back from St Helen's Hospital, where they told me that dad was as comfortable as could be expected, so there was little point in me going to disturb him that evening.

The three of us went there together next morning at 10.00.

The ward at St Helen's was light and airy. There were already cards and flowers building up beside dad's bed, in which he was sitting in his blue silk pyjamas looking very chipper, with a yellow choker round his neck and his monocle in one eye, reading that day's racing on the sports page. When he looked up and saw me he registered surprise, wariness and concern, like a trio of computer blips across his countenance.

"Hallo, Dad," I said, emanating as much simulated bonhomie as possible: "I've just nipped back from Germany to do some Christmas shopping, so I thought I'd pop in to see how you are."

He was paralysed and speechless but his bright, intelligent grey eyes spoke volumes. *Lying toad,"* they said. *"Don't think you can fool me. Nice of you to take the trouble to come though, just the same. How was your exam? How's Germany these days? Oh, God Mike, I do so wish I wasn't here. Why does this have to keep happening to me? I so wish I could speak, and entertain you properly at home. There's so much to say. Oh, well - c'est la vie I suppose; or not, as the case may be . . .".*

After the pleading and reliant eyes of one's patriarch have conveyed that sort of message to you, further conversation becomes stilted. Asssuming that because they can't speak they must also have gone deaf, we find ourselves enunciating our words with extra-ordinary clarity and unnecessarily loud, as though to some mindless retard. It must have been galling for

375

dad to have his eldest son going on like a deranged half-wit. It was certainly embarrassing for me, once Tony nudged my arm and I realised what I was doing.

The only part of his body dad could move was his left wrist, the one around which was strapped his gold watch. The whole time we were there he kept glancing at it, his eyes either enquiring what the time was or how long we could stay, or please could we think of leaving fairly soon because he wanted to try to read his paper. When he continued glancing at his wrist I wondered if perhaps he was trying to tell us the watch had stopped, so I leaned across to unstrap it and have a look. A fully automatic gold Swiss watch ticking away like a Rolls-Royce -? course it hadn't stopped. But it was a point of contact, so I made a great play of rewinding it, setting it accurately and replacing it on his wrist - this seeming to be about all I could do for him, and over those next fateful few days I did it often.

Oh - what a harrowing nine days they proved to be.

It was like watching someone lying in the desert with a broken leg, but expiring from hunger, thirst and rattler bites rather than from the compromised limb. Everything in dad was subsiding and shutting down. There were to be no more warning shots across the bow telling him it was time to stop playing rugger. Final cave-in time was upon us, and we were able to be no more effective than if sitting on a grassy bank making daisy chains, while down below us the pit props were collapsing.

I asked to speak with his doctor, a distinguished looking medical practitioner in his 50s who possessed the aura and gravitas of command about him.

"It's a general breakdown of several functions," he told me. "You know that he suffers from hypertension. He had what we call a cerebrovascular accident, or stroke, which has caused the paralysis and loss of speech. Because of this general condition he has developed bronchio-pneumonia. He also has a saddle embolus of the aorta, which means the blood isn't getting through to his lower body, so I am afraid gangrene is now forming in both his legs. By rights we should amputate, but . . . well, putting it bluntly, I'm afraid it would be a pointless exercise."

"He's dying."

He stared at me noncommittally.

His accompanying entourage looked a bit tight lipped as well.

One or two of them might have wished to step forward comfortingly, but none did.

"He doesn't stand an earthly?" I persisted.

"Not really, no," he replied, having decided I could probably be trusted not to break down, scream medical ineptitude and malpractice about the place and then sue the pants off him. "All we are really able to do now is keep him as comfortable as possible."

"For how long?"

"That I wouldn't like to say, I'm afraid. Not terribly long, I would have thought."

"A week?"

"I wouldn't have thought so, no."

"Right. Thank you. I've got the picture," I said. "If you could possibly manage to keep him pumped up to the gills so that we can see him out on a tide of happy-juice, then I think we'd all be very grateful."

He gave me just the hint of a tight lipped little smile before continuing on his rounds.

Whether he acceded to my request I don't know, but dad passed away a few days later, at 07.20 Wednesday 15 December 1971.

He was 61.

The whole of that day I spent driving round Sussex in dad's Renault.

First I went to Lewes Cemetery to secure for him a plot because for a long time he thought he would like to be cremated, but had then changed his mind again at the last moment.

Next I hot footed it round to the Borough Offices, to complain about the rusting hulk of a dumped tipper-truck that someone had discarded in the cemetery's precincts. It resembled a burned out WWII tank used for target practice. Judging from the jungle-like vegetation that had got a grip of its flat, grey, powdered tyres it must have been lying there for at least a year. Why had it not been moved? Nobody seemed to give a damn about anything any more. Within ten minutes I had raised sufficient Cain and made my case so forcefully that the hulk was removed the following day.

This job done I took from my pocket and placed on the car seat beside me a list of names and addresses I had prepared earlier. These were the haunts, homes and hideaways of dad's friends and cronies, whom I knew or had heard of over the years. Most of them I had not seen since his 50th birthday party at Eastbourne's Grand Hotel eleven years before. For all I knew he might have fallen out with one or two of them, or they with him, and this self imposed fanciful mission of mine might in some cases prove embarrassing, but still I felt compelled to inform them all personally of dad's demise. In the event some of them couldn't quite recall me, but as soon as they heard my name they sensed the purpose of my visit and each of them responded accordingly. After all, they had all at some time been inner circle members of dad's professional or social cabal.

I got back to St Leonards at midnight.

His funeral had been arranged for Monday 20 December - five days hence.

Hinkley Funeral Services made all the arrangements.

On the Sunday evening, 19 December, they brought dad back up to the house so that he could spend the last night beneath his own roof.

We put his open coffin in the piano room, where Sue lit a solitary candle.

We spent the rest of that evening watching television, because it was no use moping and there was nothing else we could do.

I went in once, to see him, just to have a little farewell natter. His chest was as cold and solid as a frozen turkey and his face in repose looked as though it had been made up for one further gentle stage appearance. He was boxed in cream satin, like Sir Ralph Richardson playing a dead prelate. He would have liked that. Old Mr Hinkley and his team had done well.

"Well, you daft bastard," I gulped, smoothing his brow and lightly boxing his chin, the bristle of which used to rasp me affectionately when wrestling with him as a boy. "Why did you have to go and bug out like this, just a week before Christmas, eh?" Then I stooped and kissed his brow, in what was probably the most affectionate gesture that had ever passed between us.

Next morning it was cold.

Dad's close friend at the time, Derek Humphries and his wife arrived to join the family party of principal mourners who were to leave from the house.

Sue, dad's 65-year old spinster sister Eryl, my brother Tony and I, the occupants of the first car, drew genteely into the snow-flurried curb outside Hastings Holy Trinity Church. I had no idea what sort of congregation would be awaiting us inside, if any, or what to expect.

"Okay Georges," I said. "On parade. Heads up. In we go."

"It's dad's funeral," Tony admonished me *sotto voce*. "We're not going over the top at Ypres you know."

And in we went.

The church was packed.

To the rafters.

Every eye within turned towards us as we trooped slowly down the aisle behind our simple oak coffin. It seemed macabre to have brought my black suit and tie with me from Germany, but it was sensible that I'd had the prescience to do so. I should hate to have seen dad off in hastily assembled vestments.

He was up there centre stage on his bier as the four of us filed into the front pew together, Eryl first, then Tony, myself and then Sue. The Reverend Dawe, the vicar, commenced the service and while the organist applied himself to the tune Crimond, the congregation started nobly in to labour its way through the 23rd Psalm.

Then Sue began to sing.

As she raised her glorious mezzo-soprano, so the rafters rang. She had decided to do-her-thing for dad, *big* time. The colours in the stained glass window picked up as snow flakes fluttered outside; the candles, taken unawares, flickered flurries of exquisite delight and the organist must have thought all his Christmases had come at once. It was a supreme effort. She was magnificent. As the last verse died away the whole congregation stood quivering as though in shock, emotionally reeling from the impact of her beautifully trained operatic voice being unleashed upon them so spontaneously under such fitting circumstances: the young widow singing her husband up to heaven and so home to his Maker. It was like a Mario Lanza movie, more bitter-sweet because it was real. Dad would have loved it. It wouldn't have surprised me to have seen his coffin wobble on its trestle as he tried to wriggle round for a better look.

He had requested burial at Lewes Cemetery and it was there that we took him now. In splendid traditional funeral fashion a sombrely suited and top-hatted Mr Hinkley personally led his motorised cortège along the road by foot a little way, a symbolic rite that was appreciated and enhanced even more by a gentleman of the old school on the pavement who paused to remove his headgear as we passed, a gesture of respect that doesn't seem to happen too much any more these days.

Then we hit a thunderstorm.

As though winter cold and snow were not enough to contend with, God was making this send-off a really memorable one.

The road from Hastings to Lewes is reasonably fast and open.

The storm rumbled down from Firle Beacon and lashed at us along the way like the Devil's coachman whipping the horses. Half our floral tributes were torn from the roof and hurled furiously about the countryside, such daemonic intervention indicative that Lucifer in a paddy was loath to relinquish dad from his potential grasp, just in order for him to gain heavenly access.

Although a Welshman by birth, Sussex was dad's adopted county. As evidenced by the size of the congregation, many of whom had been standing two deep at the back, he had been a well known and popular personage in the region, where Lewes was the principal town. It was the town in which he had lived, attended school and worked since 1924, so instead of bypassing it, historic little place that it is, all full of bottle necks and tight corners, I had arranged that his cortège should drive slowly right through the centre. It was not unfitting that we should have held up Lewes's traffic for him for just a short while. In order to top the crest past the war memorial, we pulled slowly up the frighteningly steep incline of School Hill in second gear. Once or twice I thought we might stall and make a day of it. If we had done, and had got the timing right, it would have been outside Lewes Old Bank in which dad served from 1938 to 1950, but the hearse driver knew his motor. We rumbled on along the High Street past the White Hart and County Magistrates' Court, beneath the gold hands on the black face of the clock jutting proudly from the flint walls of the Church of St Michael, and turned down Rotten Row into the narrow cemetery approach road.

The weather had become so savagely foul that it was almost impossible for us to stand upright at the graveside. Leaning into the howling gale with his ecclesiastic vestments flattened against him, the Reverend Dawe understandably raced through the committal ceremony while we sloshed about up to our ankles in mud, silently beseeching him to pray even faster. No disrespect to dad who would have been chuckling delightedly to himself, considering it quite appropriate that his Monday morning interment should have inspired the elements to such fury. We lowered him and his oak chest slowly down snugly together into the chalk and flint to commence his million year sleep in that part of Sussex. We paid our final respects fairly swiftly and then filed soggily back to the cars to return to St Leonards for a post funeral lunch at the house.

A few years before, dad had managed to re-establish contact with a long lost cousin of his called Trevor. Trevor, who had lost Gwyn, his twin, at sea in the war, was also a bank manager, in Bristol. Sue had thought to notify him of dad's demise and he and his wife had driven up from Bristol together specially. Sadly, they arrived too late for the funeral service. They had followed us on to Lewes Cemetery, but arrived there just as we were leaving. Trevor was a man in his late 50s with whom I shared a heritage and a little blood, yet had never met before. Talking to him at home over the canapés, I referred to the carpet upon which we were standing. "I remember crawling across this carpet as a child, in Lewes," I said. "I remember the night in the war when with a superhuman effort born of desperation my mother ripped it up off the floor to nail across the gaping cavity in the wall where our French windows had been, before a V2 rocket blast sucked them into oblivion. Last Christmas I took photos of my own two kids unwrapping their presents on it. I expect it might still be going strong somewhere a hundred years from now."

"It's interesting you should say that," this obscure relative then said to me, "because it wasn't until you drew my attention to it that the mists of time unfurled and suddenly I realised that this is in fact the self-same carpet upon which I, too, learned to crawl as a child in Wales, around 1914. Your grandmother was my mother's sister, so you can see the likelihood. But I'm afraid I can't account for the when or why of how it passed over from our branch of the family to yours."

It was flabbergasting: rather like discovering for the first time that your mother had had another child by another man in a previous incarnation.

A few years later I visited Lewes again. It was the first chance I'd had to see dad's headstone in place. It was a sunny morning. The cemetery was deserted, allowing me to indulge myself in a final, fearful, tearful outburst and farewell to the good old chap, pummelling the Sussex flints that covered him, and experiencing a violent exorcization of grief.

After this cleansing I felt moved to drive up to Ferrers Road for a look once more at number 10, that old homestead of so many memories in which I was born in 1938 and lived until 1950. There was my bedroom window from which I used to climb at night, down the roof onto the coal bunker to participate in some pre-arranged nocturnal prank or other with the other kids in the road. There was the gate upon which I used to swing and the tree I used to climb.

I rang the bell.

I didn't know the name of the people I was disturbing or how they would receive me, but I still rang the bell.

The door opened.

"Good morning," I said to the busy little woman who stood there. "I do hope you'll understand and forgive my intrusion, but I was born and grew up in this house. I'm home from overseas for a while and just felt I would like to ask if you might be kind enough to let me step inside for a nostalgic glimpse."

Would *you*? A bold as brass stranger fetching up on your doorstep with such an outlandish request, in these times of burglars, serial rapists and axe murderers - ?

Understandably, she looked a mite perturbed and undecided.

"May I ask who you are?" she enquired sensibly.

"Of course; I'm so sorry. My name is Michael George."

Her face relaxed. Can't think why.

"Oh, yes; I've heard people in the road speak about you. That's alright. Please come in for a moment then, will you?"

She showed me into the drawing room with its view over what in its neatness was now unrecognisable as the same back garden in which mother used to hang out our washing and Tony and I had played during the war; the garden in which we'd pitched tents, fired bows and arrows, thrown knives and rocks and lassos and which had been such an overgrown jungle when we'd returned from our evacuation to Wales - but that was to be the extent of my tour. Either she considered the rest of the house not tidy enough, or else common sense and wariness had crept in and she thought she might still be in line for some pillage, but whatever it was I was gently ushered back towards the front door and eased politely out . . .

. . . but fancy my name still being bandied about the road, 21 years after we'd left it.

We Georges must have made an impression.

But then the realisation struck me that by their length of domicility the present incumbent and her family had over twice the claim to exclusive memories of the house than we had.

The sequel to this visit occurred some years later when one Saturday afternoon I chanced to be strolling round Harrods second-hand furniture department and found myself drawn to a handsome, heavy mahogany sideboard, marked up at several thousands of pounds.

I stopped and ran my hand naturally along its burnished wood and realised suddenly that it had once been ours.

It was the family sideboard we'd had in Lewes during the war.

Mother used to stand the tea pot on the end of it, and the ring she'd made was still visible.

I dropped quickly to one knee, opened one of the doors and eagerly sought my initials, which I had carved in the top left hand corner with my sheath knife in 1947. Like my *Michael loves Susan* (whoever) and the pierced heart logo I'd inscribed on several trees around Sussex, there it was, my name and date, still clearly etched in the wood at the back of the sideboard. How had it left us? What had befallen it meanwhile? How did it come to be in Harrods? Purposefully I made no enquiries. That way madness lies.

Meanwhile, back in reality, dad's farewell party was breaking up. When everyone had gone Sue, Tony and I sat down for a proper read of his will. Some years earlier he had written to Tony and me in a vein which implied that he felt his days were shortening and so he was drawing up a will. He asked if there was any particular bequest either of us would like made. Our psychosomatically induced reaction to this - we didn't even want to entertain the *thought* of ever losing him - was to make dismissive light of such an enquiry. I asked if I could have the spare tyre from his car, and Tony said he'd rather like a cutting from one of his prize begonias. Dad took slight 'um' at our mocking his plight, a predictable prognosis from his doctor which, knowing nothing about, with unintentional hurt we were pooh-poohing. Shortly afterwards we all foregathered for lunch in London together one day when he outlined the actual proposed disposition of his estate. This time we realised that probably he really did know something about himself that we didn't, so we were more polite and respectful, and took him seriously.

Confirmation of that day's discussion now lay open before us in his last will and testament.

Down among the personal bequests I saw that he had left Tony his gold watch.

It was ironic really.

Tony had just bought one.

Mine had packed up; I needed a new one.

It would have been nice to have had dad's. I had always admired it - especially after that re-bonding little winding and setting ceremony we had enacted with it in the hospital together.

Tony caught my eye. "Why should I?" he asked. "You never let me read your comics." He strode over to the sideboard to scoop up a fistful of canapé crumbs, turned and grinned. "It's okay; it's yours," he said. I've got my new one anyway so it'd be far more practical if you were to have it, especially as you need one anyway. Besides, I'd prefer you to have it. You'll appreciate it more than I would."

The watch is still ticking merrily away on my wrist now as I write, 38 years later.

There was little left for me to do now except return to normality as soon as possible.

Two days later I flew back to Germany.

The Opel was parked in the snow where I had left it, beside a wire mesh fence at Düsseldorf Airport two weeks before. It started first go – and people ask why I prefer continental cars.

Christmas, as could only be expected, wasn't much fun that year. My OC was disgruntled that my absence had run to two weeks. He gave me the impression that he thought dad and I had milked it a bit. I felt he would have preferred a quicker, cleaner death than the one we'd been able to provide.

At last I got my precious new Bang & Olufsen wired up and played my record - *Hey Jude*. Although it was nice and I still have it and derive enormous pleasure from it today, under the circumstances governing its acquisition some of the anticipated kick was not quite there. Then again, if I hadn't had that and my few other records to distract me that Christmas, I would have been a sadder man than I was. I would have been a sad man, also, if my friends John and Maggie Marsden and Frank and Joe Butterworth hadn't rallied round to take me under their respective wings. John was then commanding 4 Ordnance Field Park based at nearby Portsmouth Barracks, and Frank was his captain. The five of us had drawn together quite naturally as friends, all only awaiting Rachel's arrival in the New Year to complete the team.

Frank and Joe didn't occupy an army quarter. Instead they had opted to live with a German family in a 'hiring'. Hirings were not exactly up to the specifications of official army quarters and so obviously had to meet certain standards before the army was prepared to take them onto the books. Frank and Joe happened to have come up with a winner. They had found a charmingly appointed top floor flat above a large German house whose resident family of owners adored them.

Frank was by way of being rather a large officer.

This, in some part, was because his extremely 'fun' wife, Joe, was something of a magnificent cordon bleu cook. That Christmas she excelled herself. I was collected by John and Maggie, we all went round to Frank's hiring and the rest of it I do not wish to recall except to say that it was wholly marvellous and I was breaking wind for days afterwards.

In January 1972 I was at last allocated a quarter of my own on a small British 'patch' a mile from the Mess in an extremely pleasant built-up area of Münster, known as Coerde. Our new address was to be 16, Igelpatt, which although sounding like a bird of prey's whoopsie, in fact means nothing more innocuous than Hedgehog Way.

As soon as I had moved my belongings from my room in the Mess to Igelpatt, I drove back to England to collect Rachel and the children who had flown back there from Gibraltar after our latest six months separation, and were staying with friends in Salisbury till I fetched them.

Driving from Dover I stopped off to stay with Sue in St Leonards for a couple of days first, just to break the journey and tie up some loose ends family-wise. I arrived there at 19.00, unpacked and had a gin and tonic, but for some reason Sue seemed to be taking an inordinate amount of time to prepare supper. She kept fussing about, delaying things, making excuses, and turning the oven on and off until, at 21.00, the doorbell rang. "Michael, answer that would you please?" she called hurriedly from the kitchen. I didn't have a clue who it might be at that time of night, so flung open the door ready to ward off a gaggle of unwanted Jehovah's Witnesses, only to find that it was my darling wife standing there. Having connived with Sue, hence the delayed supper, she had left the children in Salisbury and come down by train alone to surprise me. And what a surprise it was. With everything that had happened since we had last seen each other - my initial drive out to Münster; taking my exam; flying back for dad's death-watch and funeral; returning to Münster and moving from the Mess into quarters, and now this drive back to collect them . . . everything welled up, the banks burst, and a floodtide of released feelings burst uncontrollably forth as I reached out to clasp her to me. Sue left us alone sitting in the drawing room in a sobbing embrace for what must have been ten minutes at least, such was my need for a thorough emotional cleansing.

"I can't stretch it out any longer," Sue called from the kitchen. "Your burnt offerings are on the table if you want them."

Next morning our friends arrived with the children.

The following day we drove back to Germany.

THIRTY-ONE

NATALIA HAD TAKEN up horse-riding.

She was now ten; Alexis six.

Both children had settled well at Lincoln House, the BFES (British Forces Education Service) school in Münster.

Rachel had got our luxurious quarter in Igelpatt sorted out to her liking, and in order to escape the coffee morning clutch had taken a job at SSAFA, in their branch office at HQ 4 Guards Armoured Brigade in the Münster suburb of Gremmendorf.

I was slowly adjusting to the death of my father, but still eating my heart out with dissatisfaction as I entered my sixth month of purgatory at Winterbourne Barracks. It was not possible in the army to say 'I don't like it here at all, it's getting me down dreadfully, so please would you be so kind as to send me somewhere more to my liking?' All you could do was resign; and even that took time.

Natalia had fallen for horses.

Through our next door neighbours, Chris and Heide-Beal, we had made the acquaintance of a rather dishy twenty-eight-year old unattached German girlfriend of theirs, called Angelika Ritte, whose big thing was dressage, and the whole horse riding scene.

Angelika owned a magnificent black stallion called Carlton: cathedral-like, in my dreams he soared to forty hands as he stomped whinnying across my spread-eagled limbs with his spurred and leather booted mistress poised haughtily astride him, top-hatted and white-stocked with her crop, but in reality he was no more than a lovely horse which Angelika doted on and rode well. She stabled him at a manège 30-miles north of Münster.

One Sunday afternoon we drove out to watch them working together, and to savour the ethos of Teutonic equestrianism.

The school was a lavish set-up, boasting a large indoor arena. One of its walls was a thick plate glass partition adjoining a well appointed bar where guests, friends, admirers and all the poseurs and cowboys were able to sit in comfort to watch the horsey ones strutting their stuff round the arena.

Thus were we engaged, contentedly sipping *Steinhagers* while watching Angelika bob daintily about, prancing sideways on Carlton, practising for the German Olympic dressage team.

Natalia was enthralled, intently watching her heroine put Carlton through his paces, but Alexis was becoming a bit tired and wanted to be off somewhere throwing rocks. He was a good looking little boy; the image of his father! He had soft brown eyes, a healthy complexion, chubby cheeks and a fine build for a lad of six. It being a Sunday outing in Germany, Rachel had dressed him smartly in a little pair of suede desert boots, fawn coloured corduroys and a white roll-neck sweater. He looked gorgeous: good enough to eat.

"Daddy?" he asked, coming up to tug gently at my sleeve. "Please do you think I could have another coke?"

"I should think so, Butch, yes - go and get it yourself though will you, there's a good lad. Here's five marks."

"Thank you, Daddy," he chirruped, turning from our table and heading off towards the bar. I carried on talking to our friends, with my back to the bar, but Rachel was facing it.

Suddenly we heard a spine-snapping snarl and a short sharp wail.

Rachel's face clouded with horror and froze, ashen. She remained rooted to her chair. I whipped round, knocking over my own chair as I leapt instinctively to my feet, fearful of what I would see.

I had good reason.

389

Our shocked little son was standing there, his arms akimbo, looking down askance at his blood-soaked sweater. He lifted up his head slowly to gaze at me. "I'm sorry, Daddy," his expression conveyed. "I don't know what I've done wrong."

What happened was that half his face had been torn away by a dog, lying at the bar.

My mind was rushing.

The first thing to do was reassure him.

He must gather no hint of the urgency.

His face was a mess.

I could see teeth and bone gaping through the dark pink hollow on the inside of his mouth.

He was frightened and numb, but not yet in pain.

Nor, thank God, was he able to see his face.

No wonder his mother was stunned and his sister screaming.

"It's alright, son," I said, quickly kneeling down and petting him gently. "The silly old dog's gone and chomped you in the chops, that's all. There's no need to worry about the blood on your sweater. It looks far worse than it really is, and I promise you Mummy won't be cross. (I wish I could have reassured myself of that.) Now, I want you to stay right where you are and not move for a moment; okay? – then we'll go and get you cleaned up, there's a good boy. First I must look after the girls though. All right?"

"Yes, Daddy," he garbled, and a fresh gob of blood hissed down his poor little chin.

His right cheek looked like an over-ripe tomato that had been slashed with a razor in four places. The flesh unfurled from beneath, like sensuous lips of sausage meat. The dog that in one fell swoop had realigned my son's facial features for life, flopped disinterestedly on the floor. It was not an Alsatian or a Dobermann or any of the other breeds usually associated with slavering fangs, but an old cocker spaniel, grey of jowl and rheumy of eye. We never did find out what had provoked it to bite, but the most likely scenario seemed to be that Alexis must have accidentally trodden on its tail. But at the moment it was neither Rachel's stricken countenance, the need to stop

Natalia's hysterics, the breed of dog nor even the severity of the bite that concerned me most.

What struck fear into my marrow was the knowledge that this particular stable was right in the middle of a rabies area.

Certain parts of Europe have rabies.

In Germany the disease was tightly controlled, but the possibility of an outbreak was present at all times. If even so much as an infected stoat was discovered the immediate vicinity was considered rabid and its bounds clearly published in local military orders.

It was only a few days before that I had noted the area we were now in had been designated rabid.

Rabies: hydrophobia: it reads like Bram Stoker. Even in our medically enlightened times its horrors are evocative of Dracula, werewolves and Ruritanian castles, and here was I facing the possibility that my own innocent little boy could be in the very process of contracting it where he stood.

It was 1972 and we were a nice family.

He'd had corn flakes for breakfast that morning.

I couldn't believe this was happening.

I whipped round and addressed the bar.

"Is there a doctor in the immediate vicinity?" I asked harshly in German borne lucidly of controlled panic.

It appeared not so.

"Is this the dog that bit my son?" I demanded of the young man nervously holding the animal's lead.

"Yes."

"Are you its owner?" I snapped.

"Yes," he replied, edging backwards slightly.

"Do you have a car?" I shot at him.

"Yes," he nodded.

Then our friend, Heide, came across and intervened.

"Mike, let me help. I have already telephoned ahead to the BMH in Münster to tell them what's happened and that you'll be getting there as soon as possible. They've alerted a team to be ready for your arrival. The dog needs to be taken to a police compound where they'll call in a vet. Chris and I will go with this young man and his dog to see to that, and then we'll see you again at the hospital later. Now go – get Alexis to hospital."

I led Alexis outside by his hand, attended by both our womenfolk cooing and clucking over him, piled the three of them gently into the back seat of the car, quickly tied a white handkerchief to the aerial (a continental distress signal), took a mental note of the dog owner's car number behind me, and set out like 007 late for a date, to Münster's British Military Hospital.

Alexis thought it was almost worth being bitten, if it meant his dad could drive like I did that afternoon and get away with it. I wasn't at all sure I was going to get away with it, but I had every intention of trying. Where I thought it more expedient to mount the curb and drive swiftly along the pavement in order to bypass stationary traffic, I did so. Nor, despite the cacophony of horns from phalanxes of outraged Sunday motorists who despite my distress signal still took me for a drunken joy-rider, did I encounter a single policeman. (Only the following week I was booked doing 34 mph; but then life's like that, isn't it.)

As soon as we arrived at the BMH we all hurried through to the Casualty Department.

"Well – and what have we got here then?" enquired a perky RAMC orderly who had seen it all before.

"I had a fight with a dog," burbled Alexis . . ."and the dog won."

Good boy; he'd thought that one up for himself.

"I think I'd have to agree with you there, old fellow. Come on then, let's have you up here, shall we?" the orderly said, patting an inspection couch. "Suppose you hold tight while I go and get hold of the man with the elastoplast. Okay?"

Alexis gamely attempted a grin and looked grotesque with the effort. "I bet it's not just 'lastoplast," he gurgled, "I bet it's some iodine too."

"Do you know, funnily enough old fellow I don't somehow think they're going to be using iodine this time, to be honest.

Alexis's eyes lit hopefully, but I'd caught the orderly's glance and the way he'd grimaced.

392

"The duty MO and plastic surgeon have been waiting for you, sir," he said to me, spinning swiftly on his heel and making purposefully towards an inner office. "I'll let them know you're here." He closed the door behind him but I still had to clear my throat to prevent Alexis hearing words like 'nasty', 'awful' and 'really not very nice at all' being murmured over the telephone.

Meanwhile Alexis continued to drip blood on the lino as we waited for the duty MO. And what an opportunity it turned out to be to get to know my son. Qualities I had no idea he possessed kept leaping out at me for my delectation. Not once had he cried. There is little subterfuge in a six-year old, and he was genuinely concerned by the distress that his condition was causing his mother and sister. He was still preoccupied by the thought that his new jumper had got so bloody that his mother would have to wash it for him. He asked intelligent questions about what was going to happen, both to him and to the dog, for which he held no malice. I was delighted by his composure. My pride in him was strengthened and I felt a warm paternal glow. The experience was forging a new bond between us.

A few minutes later a young RAMC captain arrived, took one look at his face, said "Gawd, struth" and agreed it was nasty. I sensed his underlying excitement. It was this sort of thing that made weekend duties worthwhile. I was pleased we had been able to relieve his tedium. He suggested that if Alexis had been a hairy soldier he might have tackled the job himself, with hot pitch and twine. Under the circumstances though, he felt he would like to call in his Surgeon-Colonel, who arrived half-an-hour later in his gardening clothes.

"Yes," he said after the most cursory of glances. "Theatre, I think. He needs properly sowing up under anaesthetic."

Hell – I knew that.

Great play was then made sitting the little chap gently in a wheel chair. I pushed him back into the waiting room where Rachel, Natalia, and the dog's owner who had now been brought in by Heide, were all gathered expectantly. Rachel and I trundled our son into the lift and took him up to the children's ward, where his appearance and the blood and suppurations

393

were so severe that some of the other kids even glanced up from the western they were watching.

If Natalia was ever ill, we knew about it.

When she was nine-months old she developed an enormous and obviously painful boil in her groin, and, naturally, screamed the place down. Neither her mother nor I knew what to do while our new baby lay thrashing on the bed in agony, so simply leaping in-like-Flynn I squeezed the thing 'til it burst (whoosh) and her banshee wailing eventually ceased. Her adoring mother gazed at me in awe at my feat, so it had been worth it for that.

There developed a marvellous daddy/daughter bond between Natalia and me. Perhaps it was no more than any normal father/daughter relationship, but to me it seemed we had something special. Our natural interests, inclinations and reactions were similar. I had always wanted a daughter, and she was my first born.

Then when she was two we discovered she had a hole in her heart.

We took her to Southampton Children's Hospital for tests to establish the seriousness of her condition. The doctors made an insertion in her groin to allow a tube to be fed up into her heart which enabled them to determine their prognosis.

I was on Salisbury Plain in a Land Rover when the results came through, and was invited to discuss the situation with the specialist at three-o'clock that afternoon.

I left immediately, to collect Rachel from our Salisbury home, and we drove quickly down to the hospital. I was still wearing mud-bespattered combat kit and my pistol. God knows what people in the waiting room must have thought – that a military coup had taken place while they'd been out shopping? Eventually we were called, but Rachel preferred to stay in the waiting room, saying she would rather hear the news from me personally.

The specialists' consulting room resembled Mission Control at Houston, with a battery of illuminated X-ray viewing screens round the wall, each supported by a brushed steel control console. A thick, dark blue carpet covered the floor. The specialists wore white coats over their smart bits of natty civilian suiting. There were three of them. They were standing when I walked in. There was no nerve-tweaking preamble. One of them stepped forward, and came straight to the point.

"Mister George," he said, beaming and stretching out his hand to greet me before I was even half way towards him. "There isn't a single thing for you to worry about. Your lovely little daughter is as fit as a fiddle. She can climb Mount Everest tomorrow."

Subsequently, whatever ailment beset our daughter it simply was not *fair* that she should be left up there alone in bed while the whole world continued to go about its business, unapprised of her plight, and her temporary withdrawal from their midst, so if they wouldn't mind would they please not continue without her - like, *whoa* . . . hold up there, world . . . thank you – now if you wouldn't mind all sitting quietly on the end of my bed there 'til I have become better again, then when I am ready to rejoin you we can all carry on; 'kay?

Then we had Alexis . . .

. . . a fine bouncing boy who weighed-in at 9lbs 3oz, except that within a month he was in the children's ward at Churchill Hospital in Oxford, suffering from loss of weight.

The poor little chap was wasting away.

Everything that went down, came up.

He was unable to contain even a morsel, and was becoming a very smelly baby.

Turned out he was suffering from a condition known as pyloric stenosis, a ring of muscle like a tight elastic band around his central tube, which was contracting and making him throw up every time he had his dinner; and his breakfast and his lunch and his tea and his elevenses.

It was a slight mechanical defect that could be cured either by a diet strictly controlled enough to sneak past the ring while it was unaware, or if that failed . . . by a small nick to release it.

We were lucky.

Three days on the diet and he was back looking like Son of Bhudda again - an appearance that has not altered much since.

Unlike his sister, if Alexis was ill he would simply crawl quietly into his shell.

He'd catch the world up again later.

The world, of course, is so tickled by such copybook behaviour from one of its wounded cubs that it pauses, turns round and makes more fuss of him than it does of his sister, who is left threshing about unheeded and fuming in the next room.

Then again, Life would suggest that it is the squeaky wheel that gets the oil – so who knows who's right?

Now – six years later – here was Alexis back in hospital again.

We undressed him, bedded him down and appreciated anew what a brahma lad we had.

The surgeon asked that we return about 7.00 pm.

In the hurly-burly I had not actually met the dog's owner yet, or given him even a moment of my attention. I had shouted and bustled him about a bit, in maddeningly superior British fashion, back at the equestrian school, and he had done as he had been told, but, in fairness, he was only a kid. One way or another I now had to apply my mind to putting him at ease.

It should be explained that in Germany everyone insures himself against personal liability claims.

In that tickety-boo, Bristol-fashion country the first fall of snow in winter is followed by an army of broom-wielding, shovel-brandishing householders, all falling-in on the road outside to clear the stuff away from their steps and pathways, and from the stretch of pavement in front of their respective homes.

According to the rules of the Stadt it is their responsibility, the householders, to keep it clear and clean.

They know the form.

Any default and they will be banged for neglect of their civic duty.

More important, perhaps, should any member of the public slip and sprain, jar, bruise, pull, break or otherwise inconvenience any part of himself whilst traversing in an inadvertant glissade any uncleared portion of pavement deemed to be yours – you pay.

Big time, brother.

Germany is a claim conscious, claim oriented nation.

The British attitude (at this time) was very laid-back by comparison.

It was against this background that the young Medical Corps captain had looked me straight in the eye when he first saw Alexis, whistled, and said: "DM50,000, I should think." (£½M today.)

"I *beg* your pardon?" I'd asked, all innocence and light, for one ghastly moment thinking that's what he was going to charge me for stitching my son's face.

"You should be able to get at least DM50,000 for a wound like this," he repeated, and then seeing that I was still looking rather blank, said: "You *are* going to claim, aren't you?"

"The thought had never entered my mind," I replied, truthfully. "It was an accident, and the dog's owner is only a youngster . . ."

"Bloody 'ell," said the doctor. "I know I would. They'd have no compunction about banging one on you, you know. I'd have no qualms about retaliating. They expect it. They'll think no differently of you for it, and the condition your lad's face is in you've got a cast iron case. You'd probably get millions. Think of your boy. We'll do the best we can for him, naturally – of course we will – but just suppose it went sour, and in a few more years he needed expensive plastic surgery? Could you afford it? I'd bang in a claim if I was you. Honestly I would."

This was a salutary thought upon which to concentrate as I went back downstairs to the waiting room to confront the dog's young owner. I was still more concerned by the unresolved chance of rabies than I was with the fairly certain chance, so it now seemed, of being able to sue someone for DM50,000.

Even in those days I longed for a return to a more simple, frontier form of justice; the village bobby cuffing young miscreants round the ear to deter them (instead of having to shoot them a couple of years later) - or giving one of my sturdier sergeants the nod to take a soldier round the back of a barrack block and sort him out physically for some act of petty pilfering, rather than submit him to the quite unnecessary and administratively protracted nausea of a court martial.

By the same token, taking advantage of a legally installed system to sue someone because of the result of my son having sustained an accident from treading on the chap's dog's tail, seemed to me grossly opportunistic and unfair.

He was a pleasant, slightly bearded young man in his early twenties.

He stood up, respectfully but apprehensively, when I walked into the waiting room.

He had stoically accepted as his due my hitherto apparent disregard for him as a person, occasioned by my sole concern for rounding up his dog and getting Alexis to the hospital with the shortest delay.

He was obviously disconcerted, looking as if he expected the wrath of a parental beast to break about his person.

While I sympathised with his position, I also had to have regard for my own.

I noted the heel clicking Teutonic response as we shook hands.

Being German, albeit a young one, he was steeped in his country's systems, and so had understood from the outset (certainly before me) that he was almost certainly going to be stung for a big one, insurance-wise.

What he didn't know was that he was dealing with a softie called Mike George.

He told me that he had recently been invalided out of the *Bundeswehr* (army) after spending six months in hospital following an armoured car smash on the Autobahn.

Part of his hip had been removed and he was now permanently crippled.

(So far so good.)

He had no job and no money.

(Getting better.)

He had only owned the poor old second-hand dog for three weeks, and was sorry to have to inform me that it was still unlicenced – almost a shooting offence in Germany: and, furthermore, as his *pièce de résistance* he was *extreme*ly embarrassed now also to have to confess to me that he was probably the only man in the whole of Germany who possessed no personal liability insurance.

Whoops!

I didn't half pick 'em.

My feelings went out to him.

He wasn't having a very good day, really.

But I had to try to appear grim for a moment, in case he was conning me and grinning up his sleeve the while.

I took his name and address, thanked him for his cooperation, and having already made my decision anyway, told him that as long as there was no rabies concerned, I would not be pursuing the matter further.

He almost collapsed with disbelief and relief.

I then took Rachel and Natalia home for tea.

Alexis was still dopey from anaesthetic when we went back to see him at 7.00 o'clock.

His right cheek now resembled an ink-stained football bladder strung up with string.

The surgeon had made a marvellous job in neatly sowing the four slices of his face back together again.

Considering 'what might have been' helped us to adapt to the lot of our now scarfaced son.

"Another half-inch and his eye would have been torn out," we sighed.

And then, a trifle ungraciously, perhaps: "Thank God it wasn't his sister."

Next day we took him home again.

The ensuing week was like Christmas and VE Day combined, and extended.

Word got round.

Books, comics, sweets, ice cream, curious visitors and lavish concern all came the way of our little man-of-the-moment.

He received enough Lego from well-wishers to rebuild Hadrian's Wall.

It was this Lego that revealed another aspect of his nature that we had not seen before: infinite patience.

He had spent one whole morning painstakingly constructing a complex piece of kit with pullies, cords and winches.

Just as he had finished, Chris and Heide's little daughter, Natasha, came gambolling in from next door, and by the simple expedient of trampling on it (as little girls are wont to do) she reduced genius's work in seconds to a rubble of scattered components.

Perhaps it was the aftermath of his sedation, but 'genius' just sat and watched her, unperturbedly, until she had finished wreaking her havoc.

Natasha; the minx: Alexis – perhaps – the inherent gentleman.

After Natasha had gone he calmly collected the pieces together and then for the rest of the day sat contentedly reassembling them.

Or perhaps he's just an idiot where women are concerned!

Two days later – having with enormous relief received word that morning that the dog had been tested rabies-free - I had just got home from work, when the doorbell rang.

It was the dog's owner.

Laden with gifts for Alexis.

What gifts!

They endeared their bearer to Rachel as much as they would any mother under the circumstances, with an accident-prone son . . .

White Horse Mess – Münster: author's room in lower roof, far right

British Military Hospital, Munster (closed 1991) – where Alex had his facial dog bite sewn up

Garrison Officers' Mess – Bielefeld: author's room 1st floor, far right

Author's children, in Gibraltar - while he relocated to Münster

Author's son Alex, aged fifteen. After his dog bite, below
(aged six)

Alex's sister, Natalia – slightly older

. . . a dart board and darts; a bow and arrow; an air pistol – and a knife.

I stood in the background, grinning as my wife endeavoured to conceal her discomfort and Horst Bucholz shuffled from foot to foot, certain from Alexis's reaction that he must have done the right thing, but unable to reconcile this with Rachel's strained expression.

Given his confessed circumstances, the poor lad must have taken out a loan or cashed in all his savings to buy that little lot.

"It is because he thinks the Georges must be the nicest family in all the world," Heide explained to us later. "Neither he, nor any of his family and friends can believe that you have not taken him to court over what happened. He has said he will remember you with reverence for the rest of his life."

Oh, well – that was rather nice then, wasn't it!

With the resilience of youth, Alexis was deemed fit enough ten days later to go back to school.

"What happened, Lex," they all clamoured to know.

"Nothing much," he told them. "I was mauled by lion, at Heidelburg.".

Over the ensuing years the lividness of his scars gradually diminished and are only apparent now in extremes of temperature. They turn purple when he's cold and white when he's bronzed. The rest of the time they formed quite a fitting adjunct to what was to shape into quite a girl-catching countenance.

For some time, though, it was an ordeal for him to encounter dogs at all, but we worked hard to exorcise that fear, and he, bless him, responsible and aware little fellow that he was, responded superbly. Whenever we were out walking or playing in the woods and a dog appeared, he would stop kicking fir cones, or whatever it was he was doing, and without any sign of histrionics would simply nip nimbly back towards me like a slightly worried lamb, displaying just the merest hint of some concern.

"There's a dog coming, Daddy," he'd say, and I would feel his clammy little hand being slipped quietly into mine and squeezing tight, and he'd look up to see if I'd noticed.

"So there is," I'd say, as though I hadn't seen it till then. "He looks a friendly enough old fellow though, doesn't he? See how he's wagging his tail as he chases that stick? Look at his tongue flopping out. He's having a fine old time, isn't he! What sort of dog do you think he is, Alexis? Any idea?"

"I don't think so," he'd say, a little hesitantly, because he wasn't too sure if his father was conning him, or that he was genuinely unconcerned about this enormous dog that seemed to be approaching so purposefully.

"What do you say we make friends with him, shall we? He's probably a little bit frightened of us, you see, because we are so much bigger than he is. Lean forward and offer him the back of your hand to sniff, like this . . ."

"We're not bigger than him at all, Daddy," Natalia would pipe up from her balaclava and mittens, skipping along through the leaves beside us. "That one's an Alsatian and he's almost twice as big as Alexis and *I* think he could eat Alexis up whole if he wanted to, and . . ."

"You will shut *up*, Natalia," Rachel would snap, clapping her hand over her surprised daughter's mouth, nearly lifting her clear of the ground. "We'll talk to you later: *dear*."

No sooner had Alexis's face started to heal though, than he got smacked in the chops by a football, which opened the whole thing up again. Two weeks after that he then got himself snarled up in a metallic monkey-puzzle contraption in the school playground, from which the only way he could think to disentangle himself was to drop. This he did, but either he didn't realise or didn't care or didn't attach too much importance to the fact that he was upside down at the time, and the playground beneath him was concrete.

He broke his arm.

Badly.

His timing was perfect.

It was a Thursday.

The following week we were scheduled to drive down to Yugoslavia on holiday.

Having lost my father and had my son's face chewed by a dog, the little fellow couldn't possibly have had any inkling that by then falling out of those infernal climbing bars at school, and breaking his arm, it would result in his father experiencing serious and dramatic repercussions from one of the most unforseen and unpleasant chain of events in his entire life.

THIRTY-TWO

MANY BRITISH SERVICE PERSONNEL stationed in Germany used to go to Yugoslavia on holiday.

Although President Tito's enlightened 'non-alignment' policy was about as far removed from Moscow's party-line as it was possible to be, while the West's Cold War with the Eastern Bloc was still trickling to its close, certain arguably outdated security precautions still remained in place which we service personnel had to observe when travelling there, because the country was still ostensibly 'communist'.

Permission to go had to be sought and approved by HQ Security at Rheindahlen.

I had telephoned them a few weeks before to ask the form, and was told that if I applied a week in advance of travelling, it would be fine - the procedure being purely a formality whereby they sent out a flyer highlighting the sort of stuff it was inadvisable to do, such as taking photographs of military establishments etc., which was all pretty bog standard intelligence and basic common sense.

Then Junior went and fell out of his climbing frame.

He wouldn't be travelling *any*where for a while.

"You go," said Rachel with magnanimous and determined finality. "It's all arranged and paid for. You're the one who needs the break, not us. You've just lost your father; you've had the trauma of Lex's dog bite to deal with; and there was all your promotion exam study to get through, while taking on a new post and finding you loath it. You're the one twitching at the edges. We're fine; honestly we are. I can always take the

kids home to Gibraltar, later in the year. *You* go.You really must."

It did seem to be the most practical decision.

I had already applied to HQ BAOR the previous week to be sent the necessary paperwork, but when completing it I was slightly puzzled by one of the questions, which stated: This section MUST be completed.

Its question?

With whom was I travelling?

I was travelling alone, so said so, without at the time appreciating the implication.

I sent off the form, and thought no more about it.

It was the Friday afternoon before my departure next day, on the Saturday morning. The unit OC had been away all week attending an Anglo-German Relations Course, but he would be back on the Monday, so I had spent the day getting everything up-to-date and ship-shape, preparing my handover notes for him to read, when at about three-o'clock I had a sudden rush of blood to the head, realising that I had not received any bumph back from BAOR, so I picked up the telephone and called HQ Security at Rheindahlen.

The civilian who took my call then left me flabbergasted when he informed me that I could not go to Yugoslavia, and that a signal to that effect had just been despatched to my unit.

When I asked the reason for this, he said it was because I was intending to make the trip unaccompanied.

This was nonsense, so I asked him to put me on to an officer.

Briefly I explained to the Intelligence Corps officer who came on to the other end of the line, what had happened.

"Surely this can't be serious?" I said. "Why is the place designated an approved holiday destination, if we have to jump through such hoops to get there?"

My head was swimming in a haze of disbelief that at the eleventh hour this ill-fated trip could be jeopardised even further.

"Are you saying that at thirty-four years of age I've got to have my family along on holiday, to protect me?"

407

"You know it's nothing to do with that at all, old chum. It's purely a BAOR Security Instruction you're expected to comply with. Personnel are not officially allowed to travel to Yugoslavia alone; and that's it."

"So what you're saying is that if I picked up some tart at the side of the road and took her along with me, that would be alright, would it?"

"You know that's not what I'm saying at all, but technically, I suppose it would satisfy the requirement and be the case; yes. But in view of the circumstances and what you've told me, if I was you I think that at the eleventh hour like this, I'd just forget about it; quietly nip off down there, and don't mention it to anyone. I'll tear up your application at this end and forget we've had this conversation. And when the signal arrives your end, just ignore it. I hope you enjoy your trip."

"That's the obviously sensible thing to do, isn't it. Let common sense prevail. Wasn't it good old Douglas Bader once said, 'rules are for the obedience of fools and the guidance of wise men.' Thanks for your help, and the suggestion. Have a good weekend."

Relieved, I hung up.

In my anxiety, though, I had overlooked asking who it was I'd been speaking with.

That, as it later transpired, was going to turn out to have been a very big mistake indeed.

My trip was fun; it was interesting, and made just the break I'd needed, but none of it was any 'big deal'.

Day One I drove from Hanover down to Munich.

I had always wanted to see that fabled city and pay a visit to the historic *München Hofbräuhaus*, probably the best beer hall in the world. Able to seat 1,300 guests, this architecturally stunning edifice was originally built in 1592, and successive generations of big-busted, blonde Bavarian *Mädchen* in their swirling *dirndls* have been bustling back and forth there dispensing litres of delicious amber brew in sturdy *steins* ever since.

Back at home in Igelpat we had a delightful German student from Münster University lodging with us. Anton Winkelman came from the same little Bavarian town as Heide Beal, a lovely place called Geiselhöring. I had promised both Anton and Heide that I would make a detour en route, to look in on their respective parents. The town (population 5,000) had already received advance warning about my visit and been given my car's BFG number plate details, with the result that no sooner had I entered the place and was driving inquisitively down its main street than I was welcomingly besieged from all sides by Anton and Heide's back-slapping brothers, sisters, cousins and God knows who all else. Unbeknown to me, but fortuitously, the town's annual beer festival was underway at the time, in a tent, in a field, so most of what took place during the rest of that visit is conveniently erased from memory.

My next stop was Salzburg.

Strolling up London's Burlington Arcade a few years before, I had suddenly been jack-knifed into a 45-degree position of excrutiating pain, as though I'd either been smacked in the spine with a baseball bat, stunned by a cattle prod, or shot. This was my embarrassing public introduction to the onset of the periodic lower back trouble that would plague me until 1991, when with the most excrutiating pain ever, the guilty disc finally slipped. On that memorable occasion I could feel my sciatic nerve burn like a slow fuse down the back of my right leg, the foot flopped, I could no longer spread my toes, and that was it – job done – fixed; no more trouble since.

It couldn't have been in bed back in Münster, but had to be there in Salzburg, wandering enchanted round its by-ways on this once-in-a-lifetime visit, that Sod's Law chose to fell me for the second time with that rogue disc of mine, and I had no other option than to crawl back and spend precious hours in my hotel bed, overdosed on Paracetemol. And that's all I recall about Salzburg, so perhaps in better fettle I should return there for a proper, pain-free promenade again sometime.

No wonder Adolf Hitler chose the wondrous Obersalzburg region as the location for his home – the *Berghof* (Residence), near the little town of Berchesgaden, generally acknowledged as being the most scenic area in all of Germany.

The *Berghof* began as a much smaller chalet called *Haus Wachenfeld*, a holiday home built in 1916 by Otto Winter, a businessman from Buxtehude. Winter's widow rented the house to Hitler in 1928, which by 1933 he had purchased with funds he received through the sale of his political manifesto *Mein Kampf*.

The small chalet-style building was refurbished and much expanded during 1935-1936, when it was re-named *The Berghof*. The Berghof was a functioning residence for less than ten years. In late April 1945 the house was damaged by British aerial bombs, set on fire by retreating SS troops in early May, looted after Allied troops reached the area, and then demolished in 1953, but despite its grim and grisly history, when I visited in May 1972 it was a balmy spring day with oxygen more pure than from a hospital canister, and the whole of life smelled wonderful, surrounded as I was by genuine *Sound of Music* flowers and grass.

Moving on south to the crossing point at Villach, I entered the then Yugoslavia, and drove on 300 kilometres through a chain of thickly wooded green hillsides. This terrain was so evocative of some medieval landscape inhabited with witches, peasants and proles, subsisting in wood-burning huts alongside grunting wild boar, that I half expected to encounter a heavily armoured squadron of knights on leather caparisoned warhorses, clanking sternly by displaying double-headed Balkan eagle emblems on their armorial trappings, bearing broadswords, lances, and spiked ball and chain flails. But then I rounded a bend and came across a rocky cove with a Russian freighter moored just a short distance offshore in the turquoise waters of the Adriatic. None of this was any big deal, really, but it was all new stuff to me, and so quite exciting.

My destination was a place called Zadar, about a third of the way to Dubrovnik.

Zadar was a predominantly German holiday resort, but because I was living in Germany none of this was at all alien to me. The week I spent there, in my enormous room that had

410

been booked for the George family *en masse*, I was probably the only Brit within a five mile radius – or more. This was no problem, but after seven days of swimming off rock shelves and mindlessly sunning myself to a crisp, I decided it was time to start wending my way back to Europe proper.

To do this I took the ferry the 150 kilometres from Zadar across the Adriatic to Ancona, in Eastern Italy.

Half way over, there was a major earthquake in Ancona, and our ferry started plunging about like a cork in a maelstrom from the resulting tidal waves.

Those of us sitting in the restaurant at the time promptly clambered up onto the fixed tables, because the chairs were crashing about all over the place breaking legs – other people's, as well as their own.

Clutching at stanchions along the way, and avoiding the walking wounded who kept cannonading into me, I made my way carefully down to the car deck to check on my dust covered Opel, relieved when I got there to find that she was still firmly clinging to the deck, although her suspension was being tried to the limits, probably even more rigorously than on Opel's own test-bed.

Eventually the repetitious tidal waves unfurling across the Adriatic began to diminish, and after a while we were able to put in to Ancona, battered but unbowed, although Ancona itself, which had suffered severe bombardment in WWII, had now almost been brought to its knees again by this earthquake.

The air was rent with the bells, sirens and klaxons of fire, ambulance and police vehicles dashing all about the place, which resembled the activities of an ants' nest after a kettle of boiling water's been poured on it.

I spoke no Italian and knew where nothing was, so as soon as I had driven off the ferry I knew the best and only course of action was to get out of there with as much speed and dignity as I could, although it wasn't easy because some of the roads were busted and the directional signs bent – but I made it, and headed off towards the most famous seaside resort on the Adriatic Riviera – Rimini, 70 kilometres to the north, where I had dinner and spent one night.

411

Next morning I drove inland across Italy, westward, heading for Genoa, but half way there the Opel's water pump packed up, right in the middle of a small dusty village where everything was closed because it was lunchtime.

More in hope than expectation I parked alongside an historic brick wall, next to two soaring old wooden doors, above which was painted the weather-bashed word GARAGE.

My only companion was a scabrous dog flopped in the dust by my front wheel.

It was 1.30 pm, and I was aware that I could very well be sitting there until four or five-o'clock, when I would no doubt be informed with a shrug that my wait had been in vain.

However, two of the most extraordinary events then occurred.

A greasy Italian in an off-white vest and jeans emerged from the café opposite where he was in the middle of lunch, and asked why I was waiting outside his garage.

Delighted, I opened the bonnet, pointed at the water pump, and sliced my throat. *"Si, si; capisco,"* he said, and set-to opening his vast garage doors, behind which there was . . . nothing.

Just space.

And a shelf.

Hurrying across to this shelf he reached up and took down the only thing that was on it.

A box.

Hurrying back again, grinning happily from ear to ear he placed the box with a flourish on the car's wing, stood back, and bowed.

All that was missing was a fanfare of trumpets.

It was impossible to believe.

The box contained a brand new replacement Opel water pump for exactly my car.

It was magic.

An absolute miracle.

Still shaking my head with disbelief, pump installed, I paid him and was back on the road again within half-an-hour.

Just outside Genoa I found a nice looking hotel where I decided to stay for the night.

Pulling in and parking up, I humped my valise from the boot and strolled into Reception.

Whether it was my appearance, my lack of Italian or some other reason, my request for a room seemed to cause some consternation. One of the girls at reception indicated that I should wait a moment, and clattered off in heels to a back office where I could hear a brief consultation take place. She reemerged accompanied by a smartly suited under manager who gave me a quick visual once over, smiled, said *"Si, ciò è giusto,"* (yes, that's okay) and went back into his office.

The receptionist beamed at me, and the paperwork ensued, part of which was the need for me to hand over my passport.

A smart young porter took me up to my room, where within minutes I was standing beneath a glorious shower.

Drying myself on a gorgeous big fluffy white towel, I put on some clean kit and went back downstairs to the bar for a drink.

It was 8.00 pm, yet I seemed to be the only person there.

When I went through to the magnificent dining room and ordered supper, I was the only person dining, as well.

When I ordered some gorgonzola afterwards, I was brought an enormous, uncut whole one.

It was all very strange.

Having slept the sleep of the dead that night, next morning was the same; I was the only person at breakfast.

Not speaking a word of Italian, and unable to ponder the strange puzzle further, I paid my bill and set off for the French border.

Approaching the Menton frontier crossing, I opened the glove box to take out my passport, and spontaneously invented a new six-word expletive. *"Shit, fuck, bugger, damn, tiddly-balls, bum,"* I expostulated vehemently, pummelling the wheel with my palm.

I had left my passport behind, 150 kilometres away, back at the hotel.

By the time I arrived back there two hours later, it was lunchtime.

The car park was crammed full of vehicles.

Eventually I managed to find a space, but then had to fight my way through to Reception past hordes of beautifully dressed and elegant people milling about everywhere.

I realised it must be some enormous society wedding breakfast.

Fortunately the girl who had attended to me the previous evening and processed my bill that morning was at the desk. She saw me, smiled, waved, opened a drawer and took out my passport, which she waggled as she came back towards me to return it. Just then the under manager came out from his office, and said to me in passing, "I am so sorry that you have been inconvenienced: we were unable to stop you in time this morning when you left. How far did you get before you realised?"

"All the way to the French border. You speak English."

"Of course."

"Then please won't you tell me – last night and again at breakfast this morning, it seemed that I was the only person in the hotel – and yet now it is absolutely packed. Is it a big wedding, or something?"

"No – not a wedding at all. The hotel is brand new. Today is our official opening. When you arrived last night and wanted to stay here, we had to think about it for a moment, but then thought 'Why not?' Everything was ready, poised for today's big event, so we thought we would indulge you a little, while also using your presence to our advantage, as a dry run. We shouldn't really have let you cut into our presentation-piece gorgonzola like we did, but – hey – what's life all about if it isn't for having fun. I hope you enjoyed your stay. You were our hotel's very first guest."

Bowing once, he turned on his heel and went off to glad-hand the local mayor and a brace of low-slung, high-heeled movie starlets.

With a warm smile spreading across my face I shook my head, walked back to the car and headed back for France.

When my father had died five months earlier, I had made a point of driving round southern England to notify as many of his close personal friends as I could of the event personally.

There was one I had been unable to visit however, who was still unaware of dad's demise.

George Nobrega was a US naval officer whom dad had met and befriended somehow, years before. I had first met George and his English wife, Elizabeth, at their London apartment, when George had been posted to the American Embassy there. Subsequently he rejoined his beloved 6th (Mediterranean) Fleet's flagship, which until 1967 was based at Villefranche where, long since retired, he and Elizabeth now lived. I had never been there, but I had their address, and I wended my way up a tortuous, fir tree lined road to find it.

Heroes shrink, as you and they age.

I remembered George, when I'd met him in London a decade earlier, riding high in full fig and regalia, lording it over drinks in his Grosvenor Square apartment at cocktail hour. Obviously, when he'd left the Navy the $ to Franc exchange rate must have gone awry, or his naval pension hadn't been as much as anticipated, or else he'd just plain got his sums wrong. Whatever the sad reason, the gleaming hillside villa I had expected to see was, instead, a poky apartment built about 1900, alongside a row of other similar poky apartments housing artisans in vests, with tattoos. Perhaps I should have turned away and returned from whence I'd come, no-one would have been the wiser, but as I stood gazing up at the building's seedy and sun-peeled façade, George's face appeared at one of the open windows. Seeing me standing below staring up, oblivious to who I was, he called down: "Can I help you?"

I felt I had to see it through. "I'm Lyn George's son," I replied.

There was a reflective pause; a gulp, and then "Jeesus Christ – really? Well, you'd better come on up then, hadn't you."

The front door was opened by buzzer and I climbed a narrow flight of stairs which opened onto one small, shabbily equipped and furnished room with a bedroom, a bathroom and a kitchenette leading off. There was newspaper on the table and the remains of a sparse meal, a pocket transistor radio playing accordion music, and a henna-haired Elizabeth sitting there smoking a cigarette, nervously flicking ash into an overflowing butt-filled tray.

"Yes, I think I do vaguely remember meeting you at our place in London once," she said, through a spiral of smoke. "Things were a bit different then of course, as you can see . . ."

It was too late now to back out, but I kicked myself, wishing I'd been able to make a quicker snap decision earlier, retreating when I could. They must have wondered what the hell this weird young limey was doing, suddenly appearing out of nowhere, unasked and unwanted, to disturb and embarrass them during siesta time, and to observe their genteel decay. Having created the situation it was up to me to resolve it, so I set to with false bonhomie to explain myself and my mission. My sudden presence must have seemed so bizarre to them that they received the news that my father, their one-time friend had died six months previously, with complete equanimity. Thank God they were the last on my list to be notified. I didn't want to go through an experience like this again. The task had been a self appointed one I'd wanted to complete, but I did wonder in retrospect whether it had been the right thing to do - or had my fetching up at their doors unannounced been perceived by all dad's old muckers as a 'bit of a rum do'.

After the embarrassment of my meeting with George and Elizabeth, which at least would have given them something to talk about for months afterwards, to relieve the tedium of their daily lives from which it was apparent they couldn't get out from under, I decided it was time to start making tracks back to Münster.

I started out early next morning, Sunday, and drove all day, via Turin, Zurich, Heidelburg, Frankfurt, Dortmund – and home. With just a few stops, the 700 kilometre journey took me eight hours, and when I pulled in to our drive in Igelpatt, the Opel's overheated body parts were *pinging*.

That is the concise summary of my trip to Yugoslavia.

None of the events described should possibly have given cause for the completely unnecessary and horrendous aftermath that was shortly to ensue . . .

THIRTY-THREE

LESS THAN A WEEK after my return to the office an Intelligence Corps friend of mine from our Münster security detachment popped his head round my door one morning, saying "Got time for a chat?"

"Sure," I said. "Come on in. Coffee?"

He nodded, and I yelled to one of the clerks outside to produce."How are things?"

"Fine," he said. "But it's more to find out how things are with you, that I've called. I gather you've just come back from a fortnight's hols in Yugloslavia? How was it?"

"Alright," I told him. "It's a bit of a flog to get there, but all quite interesting. I wasn't actually there a fortnight. After a week I'd had enough, so I drove home across Italy and up through southern France and Germany. Why – are you thinking of going?"

"Dunno; might get around to it sometime. Tell me though, were you approached at all, while you were down there?"

"Couple of German girls at a bar one night," I smiled, then realised that he was beginning to look a bit serious. "What do you mean exactly . . . was I approached?"

"Well, you know, exactly that sort of thing: did anyone approach you in bars? Ask you anything? Try to find out what you do . . . stuff like that?"

With a hammer blow of disbelief I realised that, albeit preliminary, and being extremely ineptly and transparently conducted, this was an official interrogation.

"David, what on earth is this all about?"

418

"Well, *you* know Mike, your just having just come back from an unapproved trip on your own to Yugoslavia – it's a formality we have to observe, to debrief you and make a report. You know the form."

"No, actually I don't, David. And anyway, how do you know officially that I've just returned from a trip alone to Yugoslavia?"

We were notified by HQ Rheindahlen. They asked us to pop round to see you, just to find out if anything untoward had occurred while you were there, that's all."

"The only untoward occurrence was my nearly being drowned by a tidal wave, crossing the Adriatic by ferry after an earthquake; that, and rather a bad case of the runs on Day Three."

"Right; well, that's what I'll put then, and I don't suppose you'll hear anything more about it. Anyway – thanks for the coffee; must be on my way – other cases to see to. Catch you in the Mess later?"

"Right . . ."

As he saluted and left my office, for some reason I knew that even over something so unbelievably petty, someone, somewhere, bored and with nothing better to do except fulfill their own sense of importance, had decided there was sufficient smoke for him to set official wheels in motion that would now have to complete their inexorable journey, because there was no one in the chain with sufficient authority to cry 'Stop: Enough: This is patently absurd.' But it seemed pretty obvious that for some reason completely unknown to me, someone had contrived to 'set me up' - although I felt confident it would turn out to have been nothing more than just a coincidental little storm in a teacup. Dammit – all I'd done was drive to Yugoslavia and back.

Colonel Harry Brown was our newly arrived Commander of RAOC Corps Troops, and Captain Ray Holland his able adjutant. They were based 75 kilometres to the west of Münster, in Bielefeld, at the aptly named Brixton Barracks, which because of its depressing connotation, in 1975 became renamed Richmond Barracks.

For some reason, now lost in the mist of time, Ray Holland needed to be detached from his post for a few months, and it turned out that within our theatre I was the first choice to replace him.

One of the reasons for my name being drawn from the hat might have been my promotion exam results, where I had gained what was known as a 'staff pass', which meant my marks were sufficiently high to make me eligible for selection to attend Staff College.

This is how six months after my return from Yugoslavia - it was now November 1972 - I was posted from Münster to Bielefeld to fulfil this new 'temporary assignment'. Rachel wasn't too pleased of course, but it must be said I was delighted to be able to escape for a while from my ghastly job at Winterbourne Barracks.

With a population of 320,000, Bielefeld was fielding 50,000 more than Münster's 270,000 inhabitants, so it was a fair sized Stadt that I was going to.

I drove up on a Sunday, and found my way to the Garrison Officers' Mess, in *Crüwellstrasse*. This had at one time been the substantial family home of General Crüwell, one of Rommel's Afrika Korps Panzer Divisional Commanders. It was a lovely old house, full of character, and I was given a well appointed, front-facing room up on the first floor which suited me wonderfully.

Colonel Harry Brown was a delightful chap to work for.

My work – which (ironically, in view of what was about to transpire) occasionally involved the handling of secret and top secret 1BRCorps documents - was challenging and interesting; Mess life and personalities in Bielefeld were great, and early each Friday evening I would set off back home to Münster to spend the weekend with my family.

Life was good . . .

. . . until one fateful Thursday lunchtime in February, after I had already been in the sensitive post for three months.

Looking rather stern faced and bewildered, Colonel Harry came out of his office holding a sheet of paper, and went slowly across to close and lock our outer door. Turning back to face me, he then said: "Mike, I'm afraid I've got some surprising and rather unpleasant news I must impart to you."

"Oh," I said, slowly replacing my pen on my desk and preparing myself, naturally assuming something had happened to one of my family. "I wonder what that could be?"

The body blow, when it came, could not have been from further offside.

"I have just received a disturbing communication from The Director of Security in London," said the Colonel, indicating the letter in his hand. "I'll read it to you. *'In view of this officer's flagrant disregard of security regulations, where he is even prepared to resort to deception to overcome them by deliberately concealing a signal sent to his unit OC, and then travelling to Yugoslavia without permission, unless by his own admission he was accompanied by some female companion, having laid himself open to pressures and inducements his NV* (Normal Vetting security clearance) *is to be withdrawn immediately, and having now been identified as a threat to security he is to be repatriated to his UK depot's held strength forthwith, there to await further instructions . . .'*

"And . . . well – there it is. I'm very sorry indeed, Mike. Bit of a bummer, I'm afraid. I don't quite know what to say. I have been asked to report on your reaction and response. What's it all about? Do you want to talk to me about it?"

"All I can say, Colonel, is that the whole thing is utterly preposterous. I have never known such overkill; talk about drawing a sword to kill a mosquito . . ." and I related to him the entire sorry saga of eight months previously, which had now come home to roost in such a devastating manner.

"As for 'by my own admission being accompanied by a female companion', that's because I facetiously asked the Int Corps guy on the phone whether if I was to pick up some bird from the side of the road, that would constitute and satisfy the requirement for me to be 'accompanied', to which he agreed it probably would – but it was no more than a throwaway line,

421

for God's sake. I should have thought MI6 would have had far more important things than my ill fated holiday to worry about. What did they perceive as being the threat - that in a drunken stupor, or having allowed myself to be injected with pentothal, I might have told some Yugoslavian barmaid how many sprouts and potatoes 87 Supply Depot issues to the troops in Münster each week?"

Colonel Harry patiently heard me out whilst I railed at the absurdity of what had happened.

I was trying to remain cool, calm and rational, but the implications resulting from this incredible piece of decision-making were really quite unpleasant.

I was no more a threat to my nation's security than The Queen, but having spent the past three months dealing with secret documents, and after months of bureaucratic Whitehall deliberation, I was now suddenly deemed to be a such a risky hot potato 'spy-wise' that I needed to be thrown out of the country within twenty-four hours.

For an officer to lose his NV meant being rendered completely impotent, career-wise.

In one fell swoop MI6 had effectively hacked off my ears, burned out my eyes and cut off my balls. Even if I had known and could remember the name of the Intelligence Corps officer in Rheindahlen who had tacitly given me the go-ahead for my harmless trip, during our Friday afternoon telephone conversation nearly a year before, it would have done no good. Had he felt, on reflection, that to be on the safe side and cover his tracks he ought to record and report our conversation after all? Very probably. That was the sort of climate that prevailed among some career-minded officers. Would he know or care about the direness of the consequence of his self-serving, back stabbing duplicity? It mattered not.

It was *fait accompli*.

To all intents and purposes I was now completely and utterly fucked.

"Oh, how *lovely*," squealed Rachel, rushing to the door when she heard me pull the car into our Igelpat drive a day earlier than expected . . . then – breaking into an even more beaming smile of joy when she saw the car laden to the gunwales with all my instantly recognisable kit - "you've finished your detachment sooner than expected. You've come back home to us again darling – oh, that's so *wonderful.*"

It took me a while to explain to her the circumstances, and then she didn't even begin to understand what had really happened, or fully what it meant.

MI6?

Her husband?

Deprived of his livelihood and with his name tarnished for evermore because some pokey little Whitehall cloak-and-dagger clerk had erroneously decided to perceive him as being a threat to our nation's security . . .?

This was the nice little George family unit, in Igelpat: Hedgehog Way. Not Hollywood. It was unimagineable.

Jeez.

"Wouldn't you be better employed catching burglars," is what we are advised *not* to say to the police officer who's just booked us doing 31 mph.

It was ridiculous.

But like being hit with cancer, it had apparently befallen our turn to be struck.

Anger and disbelief were paramount.

There were next the denial, and then the acceptance phases to go through yet.

Little did I know at the time that I was to become something of a *cause célèbre* within my Corps.

For years afterwards, the general distillation of opinion amongst my professional peers and friends was to be: 'Mike was a bit of a silly boy who, sadly, was *very* harshly done by'.

My detractors – and there were a few – all loved it of course.

The OC of 87 Supply Depot couldn't have been less helpful if he'd tried.

I'd loathed being there with him, we were chemically incompatible, he had a stunningly attractive and long suffering

German wife who I fancied like crazy, and so hardly surprisingly he'd damned me with faint praise when writing my annual CR (confidential report: here I was, aged 34 and still having reports written about me by superior officers regarding the length of my hair, my lifestyle, and my performance at work - ugh) . . . but he was a tough little chap who'd done his stuff in his time, an ex Para and, funnily enough, at one time a Royal Sussex Regiment fellow too, just like me.

I believe that as a result of having crashed into the sea at some time, he'd had to have half his plumbing removed, as a result of which he used to get prettily easily pissed, on account of he no longer possessed the originally prescribed length of tubing for the stuff to filter through, so the effects of alcoholic beverages impacted sooner on him than with the rest of us, thus making him quite cheap to entertain.

Everyone knew this (with some of his staggering acts it was unavoidable) and he himself readily admitted to his condition. Half-a-pint, and he was anyone's: not literally, of course - that's just a turn of phrase.

I remember watching him talking with my sherry-sipping wife at Sunday drinks at his pad once, overbalance in slow motion, keel over, and spread eagle inelegantly across the coffee table, as if over a toppled whipping-post in readiness to receive punishment, still maintain his conversation with Rachel on the way down. He sent her sherry flying and crashing into the dhalias, while he knocked over, slopped and spilled everything else he encountered en route - and being a party there was quite a lot of stuff en route for him to encounter, knock, slop, and spill, but – hey - it was his house, so he could do what he liked in it, however much it diminished his stature.

Dutifully I dashed across to help him back to his feet, whereupon he ineffectually dabbed himself down with a colourful polka-dot snuff-rag, whipped with an adroit flourish from his Daks' jacket sleeve, shrugged me off, smiled at Rachel, and rather smoothly enquired of her with slurred speech: "I wonder if I might fetch you another glass of sherry, m'dear?"

The silly old fart certainly retained style, and for that, if little else, I admired him hugely.

But he wasn't very helpful in my repatriation.

Overnight I had suddenly become a spent force.

A done deal.

An administrative embarrassment.

The sooner I was gone the better everyone would like it. The esoteric MI6 had fingered me. There was no mode of redress, nor even a conduit for access to them.

By all accounts I was quite a talking point at the Mess bar for a couple of days, as well.

By lunchtime two days later I was half way to the Channel ports, having had no option but to leave Rachel to the vagaries of my now erstwhile unit to help her pack and move out, a major task at the best of times, for which the Master of the House should definitely have been present.

I was aggrieved by this.

I had loved the army ever since I was a little boy of four, but sometimes it pissed me off something rotten; and this was one of those times.

There was absolutely no need or justification whatsoever for me to be repatriated so swiftly, as if I had some highly contagious disease or was going to rush down to Münster town square and frantically start trying to flog off non existent secrets to uninterested passers by.

It's norra lorra fun being the impotent victim of an injustice.

In 1965 the RASC (its HQ housed at Buller Barracks, Aldershot, Hampshire) hived off the Q-Services aspect of its role to the RAOC (whose HQ was at Blackdown Barracks, Deepcut, Camberley, Surrey) but retained its transport element as the newly formed RCT (Royal Corps of Transport - still based at Buller Barracks.)

With the collapse of the Soviet Union and the Warsaw Pact, which saw the end of the Cold War, the whole face of Britain's armed forces underwent even further restructuring.

Under a scheme called Options For Change, even more of our fine old regiments were reduced and amalgamated, and on 5 April 1993 the RAOC/RCT/RPC (Pioneers)/ACC (Cooks) and the RE's Postal and Courier Service were combined to become the Royal Logistics Corps (the RLC, or Really Large Corps, with its HQ at Princess Royal Barracks, Deepcut) . . . which back in February 1973 was still called Blackdown Barracks, home of the then still extant RAOC.

This is where I now had to report.

Typically, nobody knew what to do with me when I got there.

An officer whose security clearance had been removed?

I was like a race horse with no legs.

The army had a tiered system for the security classification of documents. From the top these were **Most Secret, Secret, Confidential, Security** and **Restricted.**

I had not had occasion to be privy to **Most Secret** documents (and the likelihood now of my ever being so was non existent – unless I really *did* take up spying for a living), but I had occasionally handled **Secret** documents, and worked regularly with **Confidential, Security** and **Restricted** items.

Now disallowed from doing so, it effectively meant that I could not handle paper: except loo rolls perhaps, just so long as they didn't have secret invisible ink messages on them.

For some reason, the number of people coming to lunch on Sunday might easily become designated **Restricted** information, so I wouldn't even be allowed to take a message to that effect over the telephone.

As a result I was virtually unemployable – no earthly use to man or beast.

Private soldiers and recruits now had access to more stuff than I was allowed to see.

MI6's edict had put both the army and my Corps in a very tricky position.

It would have been far more convenient for everyone if as a result of my heinous misdemeanour I had been court martialled and dismissed the service, voluntarily resigned my commission, or been taken behind a wall and shot.

Or given a bottle of fine Malt and a pearl-handled revolver, to go and do it by myself.

But despite having had my security vetting removed, no Adverse Report had been raised against me, nor any accompanying charge, so if no offence had been committed, for what could I have been court martialled?

I confess that despite the despair, I laughed up my sleeve a bit at this aspect of my predicament, which had put everyone else in such a tizzy. Whoever had pulled the rug from under me hadn't thought through the complete implications of what they were doing.

With a 'little' help from my previous unit back in Germany, as a well trained army wife Rachel was concurrently in the process of packing up the contents of our quarter into half a dozen Granby boxes, those many times recycled, much be-stencilled, collapsible, flat-pack plywood packing crates the army used, to move their stuff about in.

These would be screwed down, banded, collected in unit transport and then shipped to a UK military storage facility through the MFO (Military Forwarding Organisation) there to await rent-free (unlike Pickfords', and others' £400 a minute storage charges) their eventual call-forth from me for jubilant unpacking and reacquaintance with our family possessions once more, be that – ultimately - as and when, and where.

Rachel and our two delightful children would then fly off to Gibraltar again, there to await the outcome of this newly beureacratically imposed 'setback' position in which our family now found itself.

In the meantime I was given a nice room in the Mess, where I unpacked my stuff and settled in for the duration.

When I reported to our Corps HQ next morning, to be interviewed by the Brigadier, my reception was mixed. Everyone knew who I was and that I was the Army's current 'hot potato', but no one knew of any precedent about how to treat a real live 'spy' in their midst, so each of them reacted differently. Some skitted and skirted around me with a quiet wariness. Others appraised me with the same curiosity they would some strange creature they'd found lurking in a crate of bananas, while still others adopted an air of exaggerated bonhomie.

Major Ernie Etherton, an erstwhile friend and neighbour of ours in Bicester, a well known and much loved Corps character, now employed as a Retired Officer so wearing a suit to work instead of khaki, was the Brigadier's PA.

"Morning, Mike; nice to see you back," he cried jovially, not in the least fazed, pumping my hand warmly. "Sorry about the circumstances; don't worry, they'll sort. I'll tell his lordship you're here."

I had not met Brigadier Burley before. Saluting, I took off my hat, stepped forward, firmly shook his hesitantly proffered hand, and took the offered chair.

"Well, Captain George; this *is* a rum do, and no mistake, he pronounced profoundly, steepling his fingers while buying time like crazy. "I've conducted some interviews in my time, but never one quite along these lines. What are we going to do with you, I wonder? Any ideas?"

"From a personal standpoint, sir, my own most pressing need is to prepare my appeal to submit to the Army Board. Not many officers get to do this in their careers, so I don't know who I can turn to for procedural advice. Add to this the fact that I am not allowed to discuss my case with anyone, and I find that I am a bit on my own out here."

"Quite so; quite so. I'm sure you are – yes. I think what we'd better do is get you to keep a low profile for a few days and start work on this appeal you're intent on doing, while the rest of us have a think over what we should do about things as well. How does that sound?"

"Perfectly reasonable, sir. Thank you."

I stood up, replaced my headgear, saluted, and left.

THIRTY-FOUR

AFTER MUCH DELIBERATION and burning of midnight oil my Appeal To The Army Board was submitted on 21 March 1973.

It consisted of a summary of my case and the fact that an anonymous Intelligence Corps officer at HQ BAOR had suggested that as the whole matter was of such little import really, I should disregard their signal refusing me permission to travel to Yugoslavia unaccompanied.

I asked the board whether in view of this mitigating fact they might consider reinstating my NV.

In the event, rather predictably, perhaps – they didn't; but I still had to wait anxiously until August, five months later, to be apprised of that decision.

Having at last had my military fate confirmed, there was another decision now to be made.

Rachel and the children were at last coming back from Gibraltar to join me there in Deepcut.

The children were about to enter boarding school, and we'd also decided that it was time we bought a house.

I had six years still left to serve before compulsory retirement at the 16 year point, and I would become eligible for a pension.

What should I do?

Because of the unjustified ignominy and constraints that had been bestowed upon me should I now, on principle – resign?

Or would that be cutting off my nose to spite my face; perceived by others as being done in a fit of the sulks?

Or should I disregard my mammoth setback, deal with the hand I'd been dealt, and for the sake of the children's education and our overall stability - soldier on?

The interests of my family came first.

Very much to the army's chagrin, I suspect, I chose the latter course.

I stayed.

Meanwhile . . .

. . . the life which was to lead up to my eventual departure, continued . . .

THIRTY-FIVE

BLACKDOWN BARRACKS, Deepcut, the then home of the RAOC, covered about a thousand acres and a multitude of sins – especially when in 1995 two recruits infamously died of gunshot wounds, another was shot and killed in 2001, and then yet another in 2002.

Known as the 'murdered' Deepcut Four, these cases were never fully resolved to everyone's satisfaction, but the consensus verdict was that each young trainee had committed suicide as a result of being bullied.

Old soldiers know, though, that although you can shoot yourself in the foot, it is very difficult to murder yourself with your own rifle. Which is why – along with a bottle of whisky, for contemplative company – officers have traditionally always been given a revolver with which to do it.

With the march of time and ever changing face of the army, along with many other such establishments across the country, now deemed to be obsolete and surplus to requirement, The Princess Royal (Blackdown) barracks are currently scheduled to be closed down in 2013, and be put on the market for purchase, demolition and development - as another housing estate no doubt - in 2014.

But back in 1973 . . .

. . . they were still a throbbing entity, and for RAOC personnel worldwide, camp followers and associated kindred spirits, no less than for those in situ there - the 'centre of everyone's universe'.

Contained within this attractive green belt site were the Corps' Central HQ, the School of Ordnance, the Training Battalion, and the Employment Training Wing.

There were barrack blocks for recruits undergoing their basic training and for returnees attending various trade courses there, others for permanent staff, and rather more nicely appointed wings with fluffy toys on their beds for the attached WRAC girls.

There were an educational centre and an MI Room, a resident Fire Service and the RCT's MT lines, where our vehicles were garaged and maintained.

There were also the Naafi, a museum, and the Sergeants' Mess.

For physical endeavours we had the gymnasium, massive playing fields, and a crucifying obstacle course up on the top field.

Cultural pursuits were accommodated in the attractive purpose built 200-seat Tela Theatre and Lecture Hall, where generals held conferences and the Blackdown Players put on *The Importance of Being Earnest* and other suchlike stuff.

Our spiritual needs were provided within St Barbara's Church, built in 1901 from corrugated iron: and there was a small accompanying graveyard exclusively for the interment of those deceased RAOC personnel and members of their families who had elected to reside in perpetuity there.

After a few weeks of preparing my 'appeal' for the Army Board, and being 'avoided', in case I jeopardised determined thrusters' career prospects through their being noticed standing too close to me - just kicking my heels about the place as OC Sweeping Up Leaves and generally keeping a low profile, I was eventually found a middling job as Administrative Officer at the Employment Training Wing.

Commanded by a Lt Col, with a 2i/c, an adjutant, several specialist officers, training NCOs, and a clerical staff, the wing was responsible for the 'trade' training of about 3,000 all-arms students annually, from all branches of the army.

It was my job to look after 'em, sorting out their accommodation, problems and general 'regimental administration'.

The task was neither onerous, nor particularly rewarding, but I had allowed myself no option other than to knuckle down and do it with as good a grace as possible.

However, realising that the tedium of this would drive me to an early grave, I knew I would need to find something more befitting my intellectual capacity as a diversion to occupy my mind . . .

Back out in Germany one muggy July evening the previous summer, Rachel and I had driven the 70-miles up the autobahn from Münster to attend a massed bands concert at Minden's Weserstadion.

There are few events so stirring as the performance of a military band to give one a sense of pride in being British: massed bands even more so.

Sitting in the stands one can wallow in the glorious heritage that was fought for, had been won, and handed down to us by generations of our past heroes.

The Germans, too, were turned on big time by these affairs, which was one of the reasons we held them.

They were particularly fond of the kilted Scots regiments too, who ever since their forefathers had been confronted by battalions of them emerging from their WWI trenches with fixed bayonets and screaming no known language, their officers brandishing drawn claymores and charged with blood lust, had always been referred to by the Germans as the Ladies from Hell.

It was so hot, wet and sticky in Minden that evening that the gnats, midges and mosquitoes were out in force, having a field day, swarming from sweaty neck to sweaty neck about the open stadium.

Everyone's face shone with a sickly yellow sheen in the bruised and thunderous ochre light.

Jungle dress would have been more appropriate attire than our ladies' prettily printed summer outfits and us men's grey suits, collars and ties, but this was a flag waving ceremony, and we were British dammit.

The army has always been able to create a sense of occasion, and by ensuring its attendees are appropriately attired, can thereby reflect and enhance the splendidness of each event.

One cannot command the required respect in jeans, T-shirt, and a baseball cap.

Esteem is not meant to be acquired easily, one has to work at it - but by God it was hot and sticky that evening in Minden.

My shirt stuck to my back and sweat trickled with a shiver down my spine.

A storm would *have* to break soon.

One had been building up all day.

The bands from eight regiments had been playing.

Each had marched and countermarched many times, and in addition to a massive miscellany of music, by popular demand had once more played *Puppet On A String* with its upbeat tempo, and been through *My Fair Lady* twice.

Making the Minden-ites' hair stand on end, the Jocks had come marching into the arena in their swirling kilts, the glorious sound of their incisive bagpipes and rattle and *thaboum* of their drums rebounding round the Weserstadion.

But the programme eventually drew to its close, and now all eight bands were massed for the finale.

Under the control of the immaculate frock-coated Royal Tank Regiment Director of Music, standing neatly be-spurred on his rostrum in his black officers' dress beret with its green, red and brown hackle, they were preparing to give us their mind-blowing rendition of the *1812 Overture*.

By now the army had got the ever-popular *1812* off to a fine art.

Not for them just the stirring content of the music, but for many years appropriate *flash-bang-wallop* fireworks, and other effects, had to be thrown in to accompany the performance as well.

There in Minden a soaring plywood castle rampart had been constructed at one end of the arena, through which each of the bands had been emerging during the course of the evening.

Behind these Disney-esque parapets and castellations the backstage crews were now letting off thunderflashes, coloured smoke, whiz-bangs and rockets like it was real war.

The arena was fast becoming a cauldron of very heavy decibels.

The gnats turned and hit the wing like fleeing dervishes, the drummers nearly went through their drums, the brass nearly burst its collective gut and the cymbalists were forging resonant bronze sounds as if on peace work.

The Director of Music was so ecstatic and had got up such a head of steam that he had eschewed all dignity and almost fallen off his rostrum from his exertions, while the cheering, stamping Germans were thinking of Wagner and Nuremburg and wondering whether it might be worth having another go.

Peak after peak of mounting crescendo roared and smashed about our ears, when . . . suddenly . . . the long awaited storm broke, and decided to join in with us.

The cathedral-like, seige-machine thunderclouds that had been forming all day had finally collided, like tectonic plates in the sky, and unleashed a crackling fork of lightning followed by an apocalyptic thunderclap.

But there was no rain.

It was just an electric storm.

But *what* a performance.

Nature outdid herself over North Rhine-Westphalia that night.

For several more stupendous minutes the heavens colluded and vied with Tchaikovsky, the massed bands, and the thunder flashes, to produce an overall tumultuous sound.

The Director of Music was beside himself.

A creature possessed.

There was no way that man born of woman could endure that sort of professional orgasm without jumping about a bit.

He flung back his head, his hat fell off, he threw wide his arms and brought the magnificent finale crashing to a breathtaking close.

Its gig complete, the thunder and lightning sped off towards Berlin.

Acrid whiffs of cordite hung heavily suspended over the pleasurably exhausted arena, and the Director of Music re-donned and adjusted his beret and put himself generally to rights.

He looked drained, still heaving with the exhilaration and inner light of The Chosen. After such divine intervention as he had just experienced, his further musical career could do nothing but soar.

He turned about, preparatory to saluting the General in the stand, thereby signifying the evening's traditional formal closure.

Breathing deeply and drawing himself to his full height in readiness for throwing one quiveringly up, when he did so, to the surprised amusement of that expectant luminary standing in readiness in his box, the salute was not directed to the General at all, but was diverted.

An expression of respect so great that it touched on worship could be seen to suffuse the Director of Music's countenance as he turned his head to gaze adoringly heavenward, high up into the dark sky above, wherein resided his Lord and Maker.

It was to Him . . . that the exultant Director of Music now reverently, with a gratitude that knew no bounds, offered his salute.

So I wrote about it.

Thus the diversion I was to create for myself, to help allay the tedium of my new life in Deepcut, became the picking up more often of my pen.

That's writer-speak.

More properly I should have said the unzipping of my portable typewriter.

I had already had two short stories published on the broadsheet back page of the *Evening News*, in existence from 1881 till 1980, when it became incorporated into the *Evening*

Standard, but in its time one of several acknowledged literary entry points for aspiring writers.

I also discovered another medium for which I could write.

Top shelf men's magazines.

Unlike today's semi-literate lads' mags, back in the seventies magazines such as *Mayfair* and *Men Only* had some good stuff in them, such as cars, wining and dining, and fashion; guns, trains and articles about Bowie knives, pistols and sport - and accounts of great historic feats, interspersed with pictures of naked or semi naked ladies.

Oh – and a regular sort of fictional romp full of *double entendres* and *bon mots,* and that's where I came in.

All my research had already been done, in bus shelters, when I was sixteen, so all I now had to do was switch-on to libidinous memory mode, and churn out the stuff off the top of my head.

Men Only was owned by Paul Raymond, the late Soho property millionaire who also owned Raymond's Revue Bar, so it was great fun visiting his offices behind the Windmill Theatre in Archer Street for the occasional editorial meeting, if only to see who I might be going up with in the lift.

Mayfair was an altogether much finer pedigree. Owned and edited by Kenneth Bound, an ex Green Jackets officer, its offices were in the far more salubrious Chancery Lane, and its content not *quite* so salacious as that in *Men Only*.

We also photographed a better class of nude.

Word soon got out of course, that a serving army officer was writing for *Mayfair* Magazine, and although the soldiers loved it – especially those on watch duty in Northern Ireland, who would await each edition with even greater keeness than a lad getting his *Beano* - and from comments I picked up along the way many officers and their wives read it too – the official response was that my activity was considered a bit infra dig for someone of the officer corps to be engaged in, even someone as discredited as I.

At a cocktail party in the Mess one evening I was tapped on the shoulder and taken aside by an avuncular retired brigadier, who said: "Just a word in the ear of the wise, dear boy: might I put it to you that the Chief of the General Staff did not rise to his pre-eminent position in life on the quill of a soft porn pen, you know."

I loved it, but refrained from pointing out to the old boy that I had reason to believe that under a suitable pseudonym even General Sir Anthony Farrar-Hockley had been known to pen the occasional piece for *Woman's Own*, and that anyway, even on a good day, I was never tipped to have become CGS.

While my more strait-laced peers were wresting with their recently acquired mortgages and suburban boredom, I think they imagined that I was zotting up to London every night with a *Mayfair* dolly on each arm and an entrée to all the best clubs. It didn't used to happen like that.

Well – not all the time, it didn't.

Whatever – I was strongly aware that many of our more died-in-the-wool Corps members fervently wished that my nib would snap.

If I had been serving with a cavalry regiment the whole thing would have been considered a great jape. In the RAOC it wasn't. I found myself being introduced as "This is the chap who writes for *Playboy*."

I wish.

Playboy would have paid me ten times what I was getting from *Mayfair;* nevertheless, what I did earn from this pleasant pastime helped pay my Mess bill each month, so I wasn't complaining.

The army is divided into the Teeth (or fighting) arms and the Support arms.

The RAOC was a support arm and by virtue of its role as an administrative 'tail' was never really able to generate quite the same *élan* as that enjoyed by the forepaws and chest, being borne with such pride and dash and all that stuff by the swash-bucklers up front, who positively revelled in their more exotic regalia, esoteric names and the charismatic machismo that goes with being a 'tooth'.

The RAOC performed an essential role, and without its existence the army would have pretty soon 'broken down' in the process of going about its daily business, but it was not perceived as ever being a particularly 'fashionable' outfit to belong to.

I had come to be part of it by circumstance rather than choice, but having done so I had still wanted to give it of my best.

I had never really entered the starting gate sufficiently equipped to get into early running for the higher echelons of a peacetime army, and so knew I shouldn't have cavilled too much at my lack of plum postings. Occasionally I would brush up against some of those who were on the inside lane, but most of the time I spent lagging round behind, on the outside track, with a lot of other very jolly fellows who made up the field, those who were soldiering for soldiering's sake and who could be relied upon, both as good chums and decent human beings.

We all kept a weather eye open to picking up the wayward main chance of course, but most of us were possessed with sufficient wit to realise that we had missed the mainstream.

I always thought that I should quite *like* to have become a brigadier, a rank and social position which I felt would have suited me rather well, with a reasonably acceptable pension afterwards, but although I spent most of my career spreading the rumour that my next appointment would be as British Military Attaché in Rio de Janeiro, nobody ever picked it up or did anything about it - so I divined pretty early on that red tabs in peace time were unlikely to be coming Mike George's way.

Basically, I concede, I was just along for the ride, and those older and wiser members of the Corps recognised this and reacted accordingly.

Unfortunately, though, I found it a constant strain having to conform to the RAOC's rather lack-lustre style and its all pervasive desire to maintain as low a profile as possible in all things.

My period of assimilation, as I acquired the ground rules of this colourless band and its low level code of conduct, was a struggle.

I was considered flamboyant and arrogant and had been told I needed to change my ways if I wanted to survive, let alone flourish or progress.

Perhaps I should have called it a day sooner, but I enjoyed the army and, unfortunately, after the RAOC there were few other branches left for one to transfer to, their social cachet in the military milieu not being of a very high order. This was a pity, because there was a host of fine and splendid chaps in the Corps, some of them my best lifelong friends. The Corps fielded green berets, maroon berets, heroic GCs and charismatic characters who could stand up and be counted anywhere, but who for various reasons also happened to have the RAOC as their parent outfit - and it was difficult to overcome the feeling that one needed to apologise, or explain one's reasons, for being in the RAOC, as opposed to the $17^{th}/21^{st}$ Lancers, for example.

I believe it had to do with our hierarchy.

When a man is promoted Lt-Col in an infantry or a cavalry regiment, he can usually be reckoned to be a pretty good all rounder. This was quite often the case in the RAOC as well, but because it was such a large corps, a regular quota of ill equipped individuals also got promoted, which inevitably perpetuated the corps' image of dowdiness. Several of them would progress to senior command and policy making appointments, where their influence could be greatly felt. Dull, grey, characterless, frightened little people in such posts inevitably had a stultifying effect on the rest of the Corps.

In some endeavour to alleviate this dullness, the good guys and the mavericks then tried to ginger things up a bit, to bring some light into their own parishes, but found they were banging their heads against an unmoveable and unsympathetic system, and so either had to wind their necks in and conform, or seek pastures new.

The RAOC was hostile ground for characters, colourful personalities, or any display of individuality – and those wishing to orchestrate their lives outside the Corps' narrow guidelines were very quickly sat upon.

Specialising, as it did, in the management sciences and with assorted areas for employment, the RAOC offered attractive alternatives and career prospects to officers who for various reasons wanted a change of scene from their parent arm but enjoyed the army sufficiently still to want to serve. Hence broken-legged but brainy Gunners, disillusioned but keen Sappers, burned out but able Infanteers, indolent but interesting Cavalrymen, and others, transferred into the RAOC, but whereas they brought with them so much which could and should have enriched and enlivened it, they were prevented by the entrenched and unyielding hierarchy from doing so.

As Britain so desperately needed another Churchill, so the RAOC in its way was crying out for a young, forceful, personable and trendy Director whose character would carry some clout at the MoD, who could reposition the RAOC on the map and stick a bayonet through its cap badge, to give it a greater sense of purpose and pride in itself, instead of being considered by the rest of the army as nothing more than a load of blanket stackers in the **R**ag **A**nd **O**il Company.

And these were my feelings *before* I'd lost my name and been sent back to England to repent at leisure.

Now here I was scuffling about Deepcut in the wasteland of my nuked career, so it was all pretty academic really.

Meanwhile, I still had a life to lead.

I hadn't been cashiered or court martialled, I was still an officer of the Queen, and as such – although deprived of much – I still enjoyed certain privileges. One of these was the entitlement to an army quarter, in which to house my family.

Rachel and the children were still living out in Gibraltar, but as I settled into life at Deepcut, so I was crawling slowly up the quarters list.

A new batch of these was under construction, and I was holding out for one of them.

Each evening before dinner I would wander across from the Mess and grope about the scaffolding, considering the merits of each new quarter, considering the view from its window frames, and picturing where I would eventually put my desk.

In my mind I settled for number 15, Aisne Road.

When they were finally finished and became ready for occupation, I was allocated number seventeen.

It was fully furnished and functional and the rent (in 1974) was £34 a month, but I knew I had reached that stage in life when I really should be buying my own home. This was a daunting prospect, for two reasons.

They were called Natalia, and Alexis.

Natalia was now aged nine and had attended seven different schools in England, Germany and Gibraltar.

She was an intelligent little girl and the constant upheaval was beginning to have a dilatory effect on her education.

I could see old Scarface's pattern would soon become a similar one too, unless I did something to arrest it.

Rachel and I agreed that it was time both children should go to boarding school.

As a boy I had lived and been educated in Eastbourne, and so rather than scour the country we put Natalia in the town's well known and respected Moira House, and Alexis into Ascham, the preparatory school for Eastbourne College.

The army would pay a fair whack of the schools' fees, but I would have to find the rest.

I wrote to East Sussex Education Authority, outlining my connection with the county and explaining my peripatetic military existence to them, asking if there was any scheme whereby they might care to consider contributing something towards my children's fees.

Apparently there wasn't.

They wrote back saying 'no', and enclosed a pamphlet extolling the merits of the Thomas Peacock Secondary Modern Comprehensive Boarding School at Rye, suggesting the kids could go there.

I wrote back thanking them very much for their pamphlet, but confirming that it had been decided said kids were going to Moira House and Ascham.

Not to be thwarted in my endeavour I then took out a load-spreading school fees insurance policy which demanded a horrendous premium that I would be paying well into my dotage but, nevertheless, in January 1974, the tight knit little George family was joyfully reunited in its new home at 17, Aisne Road, Deepcut, and a few days later Natalia and Alexis George and their new trunks full of posh new gear, were tearfully deposited at Moira House and Ascham schools respectively.

They say that to succeed, one must take risks occasionally, but - boy - knowing what I was to discover years later, was I ever chancing my arm.

Each day Rachel travelled from Deepcut's nearest railway station, Brookwood, forty-minutes up the line to Waterloo, to her job at Lincoln House Computer Services, in Old Street. Every Sunday her pronounced maternal instinct and Latin background dictated that we should drive down to Eastbourne to see that both children were eating well and not being bullied.

Two hundred miles each time?

Eastbourne seafront on a blustery afternoon?

Wimpies for lunch?

101 Dalmations at the cinema?

By Week Two I was hacked off with that old lot and decided that things would have to change.

Then quite out of the blue I received another letter from East Sussex Education Authority, informing me that for some obscure reason, which I never fully understood and didn't delve into too closely, they had very kindly reconsidered my original request for supplementary funding, changed their mind, and had now decided that they would like to help educate Natalia and Alexis a bit, after all.

This amazing development released a cash flow which I could now divert for house purchase.

But where to buy?

That was the next question.

I now impressed upon Rachel that instead of visiting the children every Sunday, we should start scouring the countryside on a property quest, seeking out the George family's new seat.

It was fun; exciting.

I saw the potential in several manor houses, vicarages and farms, most of them upwards of fifty-grand when, as Rachel pointed out to me from the car window, our ceiling was about six-and-a-half.

She then pointed out that however romantic a retreat a sweet little crofter's cottage on Skye would be, it would be a hell of a flog getting to work each day – and not much fun in the rush hour trying to get back again at night - besides which, it would be too far away from her babies.

In the end we settled for thirteen-grand and a plastic box in Eastbourne.

17, Aisne Road went back to the army and we moved our goods and chattels into 6, Goldsmith Close, Eastbourne.

Committed as she was to her London job, Rachel moved into a flat in Town with a girlfriend during the week, and travelled home to Eastbourne at weekends.

I moved back into the Mess during the week, and drove down to Eastbourne each Friday.

We were able to watch the children's sports on Saturdays, attend their church services on Sundays, and have them home in the meantime to help them stick posters on the walls of their very own bedrooms.

One Saturday afternoon Alexis played his first away-game of rugger for Ascham, at a school called Newlands, over in nearby Seaford. His mother, sister and I duly went along to support him.

It was a filthy afternoon.

With my Barbour collar turned up and hands sunk deep in its pockets, I was sloshing about up to my ankles in mud watching my eleven-year old son and twenty-nine of his fellows play rugger while my wife and daughter sat parked in our car behind me, staring intently out through its rain-lashed windows.

Other stalwart, involved, character-conscious parents and dedicated masters ranged in galoshes round the touchline, spurring the little mud-pies on to even greater effort.

"Come *along* Newlands. Oh, do come along," shrieked one bellicose ex-colonel, ex-60s half-back, his mud-caked *veldscheon* slithering in imaginary pursuit of the ball as if he was following-up on his battalion chasing escaping enemy across a waterlogged sector of No-Man's-Land. "Follow it through, Newlands," he yelled apoplectically, tearing off and slapping his deer-stalker furiously against his calf and stamping up and down in a paddy, splattering the backs of his corduroys.

Just then, there came a gallant break-through from Ascham. 'Oh, *damn*,' blasted the colonel, taking it all terribly seriously as opposing parents on the far side of the field took up the yell for their own young champions.

Rachel, being Latin, was not quite *au fait* the rugger thing. This was the first time that she had ever seen her son at play.

"Oh, *God*," she wailed, clutching at her ample bosom on first catching sight of the forwards in their off-white scrum caps. "Those poor little boys have all got their heads bandaged and *still* they're being urged to play on. So young you train for war? How *can* you British be so cruel?"

It was difficult to differentiate between the teams by now, so covered were they in glorious mud. Short bony legs frantically scrabbled to acquire purchase for small studded boots on the annihilated greensward. Mild boyish expletives rent the air in piping soprano. "Watch it, Smith. Just you jolly well watch it, that's all." Then the whole pack went galloping off again like junior bison in a mêlée.

One young warrior, our son, Alexis, stood aloofly detached from combat. Proud, erect, still very clean and no doubt probably rather secretly pleased that his parents and sister had turned out to watch him, his cleanliness was not from any diffidence at play. He was dying for a piece of the action, but his team's forwards were so good that his lot that afternoon was quite a cushy one.

The rain eased momentarily and his mother emerged fussily from the car to stand beside me. "Why don't you shout?" she demanded. "I love to hear the fathers shouting. Why don't you shout, too?"

She tugged at my arm excitedly. "I'm going to shout," she decided.

Just then the whistle blew for half-time.

Undeterred, she deliriously commenced to support her offspring. "Come along, Alexis," she yelled, punching the air with inane encouragement where none was needed. "Show them how it is done, 'Lex," she shrilled.

While our Persil-white son tried not to bury himself with embarrassment, the other muddied twenty-nine surveyed him with horrified interest and pity through their squirting orange pips.

"Sock it to them, 'Lex," our tame loon persisted, punching the air again with her right fist and saluting with the left, totally unaware of the other parents' raised eyebrows, peer-grins and babble of amused mutterings from the far side of the field, remaining mindlessly oblivious to her son's chagrin.

"Darling, you must stop it," I hissed. "It's half-time, for God's sake."

"I do not know about that thing," she retorted, tugging my arm anew. "All I know is you encourage the boy, the boy responds. *Good old Alexis,*" she shouted again for good measure. "Don't you worry about half-time. You get in there and show them." Then as an inspired afterthought of maternally inflicted humiliation, our continental coot cooed out for the whole field to hear: *"Mummy loves you, darling."*

At least she wasn't wearing a hat!

At this stage Lex did the only thing any self-respecting male could do. He hurled his orange to the ground, turned his back on us . . . and sat down in the mud.

"Why'd he do that?" asked his puzzled mother, whipping her head round with a frown. I merely looked at her with squinting mouth. Still quite fondly though, I suppose.

When the ref blew his whistle for the second half, several of Lex's chums 'accidentally' managed to bump into him, and

446

contrived to tread on his face as they trotted out to resume their on-field positions.

"Oh, the beasts," his mother sobbed, chewing her knuckles with hurt bewilderment. "Now he's gone and got all muddy. He was managing to stay so lovely and clean before. Like a little white knight."

Although I knew where she was coming from, I had every sympathy for my son. Women who do not know the form and relegate the game to the level of the playpen should be . . . should be . . . they should be beaten to submission with a squash racquet.

But perhaps there *is* a perverse female logic after all. The score was nil-nil before our woman's beneficent if ill-timed intervention. Spurred by his mortification, with tears of frustration and anger splashing salt runners down his mud-flaked young cheeks, totally disregarding his position as full-back, Alexis suddenly leapt into the midst of the fray, retrieved the ball, and casting all-comers brutishly aside proceeded to carve a phenomenal swathe of amazed carnage up the pitch to score an awesome try.

The field erupted.

"Oh, bloody *good*; bloody well *done*, that man," the ex-colonel exploded, taken as much by surprise as the rest of us, his face recording a veritable coronary of delight as he turned to do two double-takes and then raised his deer-stalker to execute a stilted yet most heartfelt and courteous bow of respectful acknowledgement and appreciation to us.

My paternal pride, and through me at that moment the entire genealogical roll-call of all our male forebears, Lex's and mine, knew no bounds. Globally, graves stirred, their contents arched their tufts of mummified eyebrows above empty sockets, and sighing with dusty and contented fulfilment each old bloke turned over and snuggled in afresh, reassured by the knowledge that from this momentous day onwards the spawn of their loins, newly spurred Youngblood Hawk of that ilk, had justly won his right on the manly field of combat to hold and have his say in all future control of the family ball.

Ascham's young captain signalled Lex to convert his try, which, taking five years off my life while he did so, he did to perfection, and with a considerable degree of contrived, understated and dead cool aplomb.

For the rest of the game the score remained five-nil to us.

Alexis was fêted.

"There you are," beamed his mother with a vibrant flush, clapping both her hands, squealing, jumping up and down in the mud and jubilantly hugging me. "I told you he could show them how to do it; . . . er . . .

. . . what was it he *did* do exactly, by the way?"

THIRTY-SIX

THAT WAS THE YEAR we came into some money.

My late father's estate was finally wound up and we were able, briefly, to settle our debts and indulge ourselves a bit.

We forgot about budgeting to beat inflation for a while and played a new game, called What To Do With A Windfall. The lesson I quickly learned (never having had any practice before) was that it is as difficult to budget when you do have some loot, as when you don't.

What about those poor people who lose everything and find themselves down to their last million, eh? What sleepless nights they must endure: this having something to do with everything being relative.

With £75,000 and upwards (this was 1976) it might have been quite fun. With that kind of money we could have eased ourselves into a whole different ball park. Even £20,000 shouldn't really have been sneezed at either. That figure would have dictated that you stayed where you were, but moved up a house to do it from.

We got ten-grand.

Which would be about £75,000 today.

What would you do with that amount?

You'd scoff of course, and say there shouldn't be too much problem.

May I suggest you draw up a contingency plan now then, against the day it might happen, because if you don't you could very well find yourself frittering it all away in a mild panic.

Whilst being very nice to have, the rub was that £10,000 was not the panacea for all our financial woes. It temporarily eased the majority of them but couldn't be stretched to solve them all. We had to prioritise, to ensure this finite sum was used to maximum advantage. Yet despite our every firm resolve, when we got our hands on the cheque for the first time (taking a photocopy of it for posterity) we did not feel inclined to spend it all on debt settling. We were overcome by a feeling not unlike prickly heat, for which we felt the only cure would be to rush out and do something frivolous, like dine at *The Ritz,* just to prove that we could. It was like being king for a day. Did we review the troops after lunch – or before? Thank God I had some pre-listed options drawn up, otherwise I would have been in an indecisive tizzy for days. The possession of money requires executive decision making. Good decisions need to be planned. A new car? Or a holiday in Hawaii?

"Neither of those," my wife told me firmly. "First of all we pay off the mortgage, please."

"Don't be daft," I blustered. "Lose tax relief? Lose the long term effects of inflation reducing our payments to peanuts? You're mad, woman. Thank God this family has me at its helm. Trust a woman to make such an unreasoned suggestion."

She stood her ground.

"Paying off the mortgage would give us peace of mind," she said.

This was true of course; it would. There is no financial logic that can compete with a woman's. Trying to counter her argument was futile. We then only had £9,998 to discuss, two-quid having been blown on flowers so that negotiations could be resumed later.

As a sop to Rachel's peace of mind I did immediately repay our £3,000 bank overdraft. It saved the frightening interest we were paying each quarter, and released the £80 monthly repayments back into the family cash flow. This allowed Rachel's salary to be for frills now, instead of just essentials, like food.

I then gave her £1,000 to spend.

I felt this the least I could do, as I wanted to do likewise.

A couple of decent suits, shoes, shirts, a tie and a new pair of sunglasses saw off £500, the remainder being quickly filtered away on that term's school fees and other outstanding and assorted sundries.

The decks had now been swept clear for our first *big* decision.

I loved cars.

The Opel, that dear and faithful old family runaround of ours, had become very tired and mishapen by now all of a sudden, I managed to tell myself. A newer car would be a tremendous morale booster for the principal breadwinner, and if *his* morale was high (I reasoned) the whole family could bask in the glow of it.

No run of the mill production line job this time, dammit.

I only did shopping of this magnitude once in a decade.

My dream car had ceased production in 1971, but my love, loyalty, and longing for it had continued unabated. Now – I could either be sensible and stash the money in a building society, or I could live racily for a bit.

Could I be so frivolous, so foolhardy, so utterly irresponsible as to lay out a capital sum on such a depreciating asset as a motor car?

Bet your ass I could.

And did . . .

. . . and never, ever regretted it.

No one could ever have enjoyed anything half so much as I did, sitting behind the ivory wheel of my white leather upholstered, metallic blue Mercedes-Benz 280 SE 3.5 V8 Coupé, parked in the road outside our house: we tried garaging her but even by moving the lawn mower and rearranging the deck chair, it was impossible; the very least she needed was a carpeted hangar.

I bought her from a Persian businessman in London for £3,600: that would be £25,000 today, and if I had kept her, that is what this classic model would still be worth at today's prices, as well.

At 17 mpg we couldn't afford to drive her very far, but for eating our sandwiches in she was superb.

So regal was this George flagship that even the little tyke down the road refrained from dragging his initials across her bonnet with his sawn-off penknife.

She was an iconic and much sought after car.

Every man should be able to realise a dream at least once in his lifetime, even if he waits a lifetime to do so. There; I've convinced myself anew that it was a good move; oh, and it was; it was.

The acquisition of property seemed the next logical long term step for us to take, but we already had some of that and couldn't really afford more – so I settled for land instead.

Our house was the last in a row.

On the other side of our back garden fence was a twelve-foot by twelve-foot plot of seldom tended, coarsely grassed public ground, where two council saplings struggled vainly to survive. This had been classified an amenities area. In effect it served as a tip for rubbish, the home patch for our local eight-man football team, and teenage gang warfare.

A slim wooden fence separated it from our prize dahlias.

So I wrote to the council and asked if I could buy it.

They agreed in principle (it would save them mowing it) and referred me to the housing contractor who agreed in principle (the council was only maintaining the plot for him – not paying him for its use) and referred me to the local residents' association, who agreed.

It cost £200 for the land, and £200 to fence it.

This constituted my 'sensible' investment to offset Rachel's reservations about the car.

So much for port.

To starboard, the garden of our new house was separated from our neighbours' by a thirty-foot roll of waist high chicken wire, unfurled and staked into place by the builders. The fence erectors quoted me another £200 to erect a firm, six-foot timber construction to replace the chicken wire, which would withstand force eight gales, woodworm and local football teams till the year 2010. To make the garden look more attractive and afford Rachel the opportunity to sunbathe in (or out of) her G string in summer, we just had to build that fence. Previously we had not been able to afford it. Now we could. However –

. . . I decided to save myself £150 and buy my own DIY fence for £50, instead.

It arrived the day before Good Friday.

Next morning my young son, Lex, an ex 2 Para and later RAF Vulcan pilot, Ray Pearce, my opposite neighbour and I started to put it up.

Shirts off.

Get stuck in.

It was fun.

Men's work.

First, we had to dig six holes, each three-feet deep into which to sink and concrete the posts. No problem. Swing that pick. Feel the pioneering spirit burst through the blisters and aching shoulders.

"Daddy," one eager helper cried despairingly. "I can't get this pipe out."

"Put some muscle behind it, son," I encouraged."

To no avail.

Neither Lex nor I nor our combined efforts on the crowbar would shift that durned pipe.

So I sawed through it.

When the discarded section arced through the air to land with a thump on the rubbish tip, I noticed Ray Pearce's eyebrows arc along with it.

A thud of presentient apprehension hit my gut as briefly I caught the glimpse of coloured wires trailing from its severed ends.

At 8.00 o'clock we stood back and surveyed the fruits of our eight hours' manual handiwork. A heavy sea mist had started rolling in, but it had been a great day. So very satisfying. We cleaned the tools, Ray returned to his family across the road, and as the cement hardened round the six posts holding up our lovely new garden fence, I called out to Rachel to run the bath and slosh in plenty of bubbles.

453

It was at about 8.15 that one of the many little yellow Redifusion vans that had been zotting about the estate for the past hour, squealed up outside our house.

"You'll find him out there – lurking over in the far corner of the garden," Rachel told them, pointing through the rear of the garage towards me.

Shivering and petulant, clad in my dressing gown and slippers, I helped the two taciturn operatives scoop the semi hardened concrete out from the base of each post, prior to lowering the dismantled fence onto the lawn.

"Over eighty calls we've had," one of them told me. "Not a good thing for neighbourly relations, sawing through communal TV cable on a Good Friday. Lady at number eighteen wants to sue, I believe."

I remembered I still had her wheelbarrow to return.

"I live with these people," I croaked contritely. "What should we say to them?"

"Don't worry, mate. We'll tell 'em it was workmen; happens all the time."

After the estate's TV screens had flickered back to life, Rachel put our supper on hold while my daughter, Natalia, and I went out in the Merc for a quick and well deserved drink at the pub down the road.

When we came home twenty minutes later I gently reversed the magnificent beast, as was my wont, to park within three-feet of my neighbour Arthur's garage wall. Then, as had been my custom for many years with our manual Opel, I tapped my right foot to rev up once before switching off.

Silly old me.

One-and-a-half tons of inadvertently still automatically engaged 3.5 litre V8 with a chassis like a small tank, packs one hell of a punch when it hits British-built brickwork from a standing start; bit like an irate mule lashing at someone's ribcage.

Under the circumstances old Arthur was quite good about it really. He popped out to have a quick look, his bib still tucked into his beige cardie, mouth working hard while he continued masticating some gristle, holding his fork like a

454

The ill fated fence, a substantial portion of which had to be disassembled one hour after this photo was taken, because to sink one of its posts the author had cut through a Rediffusion cable.

Poor old Arthur's garage, which inadvertently got in the way of the author reversing his Merc that day . .

Author's long suffering, lovely wife Rachel, stoically hanging-on in there . . .!

trident while he clambered rummaging over the rubble like Churchill inspecting the East End in the Blitz.

Having heard the crash, Rachel now stood at our open front door in her pinny, arms folded, foot tapping. "I think I'd better just hold supper for the duration of all this stupidity that's going on, shall I - while you go out and accidentally kill somebody, or whatever it is you're planning to do next?"

A point well made.

It had been a bit of a funny day all round really.

But then, Life never was meant to be plain sailing.

THIRTY-SEVEN

ONE DAY MY HAPPILY TWINKLING little star came up against a malevolent rogue planet we found suddenly placed in our path, from where it persecuted me more than enough to make life an absolute misery for the next eighteen months.

I was about to enter a period dominated by a mammoth, inexplicable, and completely unwarranted personality clash, and some other unpleasant bits and pieces out of the same bag of bent nails.

There was no war on at the time, so wherever possible soldiering was meant to be fun, I thought.

Yet with the advent of this 'bad man', almost overnight the whole community around me seemed to be reshuffled to accommodate a host of funny people to whom one's every action and every riposte during every moment of each day was assumed to be serious or suspect.

Nobody could trust anybody anymore.

It became like working in Gestapo headquarters.

He was like Darth Vader to my Luke Skywalker.

I had known Jeffrey Norton, just to acknowledge, as a major working in some clerical capacity at HQ, and although he seemed a reasonable enough fellow, I thought him slightly charismatically challenged, a bit of an also-ran whose company I wouldn't have sought out at the bar, or in a trench.

Rather later in life than usual, he was then suddenly promoted to lieutenant-colonel, and given the appointment as my new commanding officer.

Along with everybody else, as was our military wont on such occasions, on the day of his promotion I took pleasure in cheerily congratulating him in the bar at lunchtime, and accepting a beer off him.

Over his ensuing first week in office he interviewed all his officers personally, and because by virtue of my circumstances I happened to be the most senior captain in the Corps at the time (if not the whole British army) I thought it a bit strange that came the Friday I still hadn't been summoned, but then that afternoon I was finally called for, last of all, even after the subalterns had been done.

I duly marched in, saluted, smiled pleasantly – and waited.

You can imagine my surprise when without even inviting me to stand easy or sit down, he then said: "You may as well know from the outset that I have never liked you very much. I consider you to be an arrogant person whose attitude I dislike. I shall be watching you very carefully indeed, every inch of the way. Now march out, please."

Jeez.

Sheeeeit.

Keeerist.

Where had *that* come from?

How to win friends and influence people – or what?

Well – at least he'd got it off his chest.

Some revolutionary sort of new management technique, was it - ? I thought to myself, still reeling; puzzled.

After that it was downhill all the way.

I never did get to the root of his antipathy, but this enmity, which can only have been based on personal chemistry, didn't ease up a jot for the rest of his tenure. For whatever reason, known only to himself, he was out to 'get me'. As the situation developed, and worsened, my only hope was that the efforts involved in him trying to achieve his psychologically disturbed and rather unpleasant aim, would give him a very painful ulcer. The expression on his face, and the twitching little Hitler-ite moustache whenever he saw me, certainly gave the impression that his stomach and I were successfully working to that end.

Unfortunately my discomfort was compounded by those who, perforce, were obliged to join ranks around him.

His second-in-command and his adjutant, both of whom were good guys and erstwhile chums of mine, soon got the drift.

They had their careers to think about.

The Colonel was the authority who wrote their confidential reports.

The word was out.

The new CO had let it clearly be known that I was now public enemy number one.

Hell – knowing how costly principles are, whose side would *you* be on?

The army had deprived me of my security clearance and thus rendered me less effective than a stingless jellyfish, and now - down at unit level - this jumped-up little squirt of a Johnny-come-lately half-colonel had decided to wade in and make my life an additional misery as well.

I had no friends at court.

I was to be ostracized.

I couldn't decide whether to slash his car tyres, or just stick my tongue out at him in the corridor.

Being a bit of a wordsmith. I can parry and thrust with a pen a little, but you can fell me completely with figures. Two-plus-two equals whatever you want it to be, and I can produce as many different answers as you like. To ask me to run an account would be like getting a blind man to walk through a tightly packed minefield.

Aware of this grey area of mine, and with many numerically competent officers at his disposal, one day our new CO decided it should be me who would take over the HQ Officers' Mess account.

Because of the size and importance of this account, I felt it would have been irresponsible of me to have accepted the appointment without first reapprising the CO of my position.

My acknowledged difficulty with figures was well documented on my records, and had never before attracted any adverse comment or discrimination, but when I brought it to the CO's attention it created much opportunist villification. Suddenly, any other prowess I enjoyed as an officer came

459

under his scrutiny also, and fell prey to scornful remarks about my 'all round ineptitude'.

"Colonel, despite any other shortcoming you feel I may or may not have, I am obliged to say that I know I wouldn't stand an earthly of being able to run this account to your, or anyone else's satisfaction," I said, trying to impress upon him, enduring great personal embarrassment in doing so, the 'meaning' of what I was saying. "May I suggest that someone else might be far better suited for it than me?"

A sensible person would have understood that this was a difficult admission for me to make, and taken me seriously.

Not this one.

He was delighted

He had me.

My genuine shortcoming had forced me to play right into his hands.

"In which case we'd better send you on a Service Funds Accounts Course then, hadn't we," he sneered, like Vincent Price.

The Service Funds Accounts Course was two weeks of double entry book-keeping, held at the Royal Army Pay Corps Training Centre at Worthy Down, in Hampshire.

Sergeants, corporals, and twenty-year old subalterns went on it, not senior captains in the evening of their service.

It was a nasty, vindictive, and in line with his emerging pattern of behaviour towards me a typically predictable thing for him to have done.

It was two weeks of sheer purgatory for me, sitting hunched at a school desk in a classroom from nine till five, scratching over incomprehensible figures which simply would not add up properly, subtract correctly, or do what they were meant to do.

One or two of the other students fretted if they were a farthing out in their calculations, whereas I emitted whoops of joy if I came within even a few grand of the right answer.

Predictably, it turned out that I was the first officer to fail the course since 1916.

My report read

We are loath to admit the existence of a blind spot in certain subjects, but if anything could convince us it would be a study of this report. It is recommended that under no circumstance should this officer ever be allowed to run a Mess account.

I was delighted.

Thus thwarted, the CO was not.

Naturally, he thought I had failed deliberately, in order to spite him, which was quite simply not true.

Five years later (after I had left the British army) I was a contract officer in the Sultan of Oman's Forces, in Muscat. There I was given the appointment of procurement officer where, ironically, I had an Indian L/Cpl (Moid Khan) with a pencil stub and brown envelope, and an annual budget of £55M with which to purchase all the vehicles for the Sultan's army, navy and airforce. I was Land Rover's third largest world customer . . . and there was nary a glitch.

Meanwhile, back at the funny farm, Colonel Nasty was really piling on the pressure, after a few more more weeks of which it was annual confidential report time once more.

Cackling with glee he drew his sword, dipped it in vitriol and gave vent in writing to his true feelings.

Let me share it share it with you.

Here it is

This officer lacks a sense of military purpose and has developed a cynical and careless attitude to his work which sets a bad example to other officers and soldiers. He has little ambition and little pride. This is evidenced by his apparent lack of ability in handling accounts and in general military expertise. The routine of military life is regarded as a chore to be dispensed with as quickly, and with as little effort, as possible.

He is an intelligent person, and when inclined can apply himself to tasks which he considers suitable. His efforts in the running of the Battalion Christmas Dance and other social functions were largely responsible for their success. If he were

461

to apply himself in similar fashion to his regular military duties, I would have no complaint.

He has been given a three month warning during the period of this report, and responded sufficiently to avoid any further action. Regrettably he is not prepared to extend himself in any way and needs to be subjected to constant and close supervision.

He attended a Regimental Accounts Course recently and obtained an E Grading. He does not apply himself in a mature or responsible fashion to any military activity. He appears to be incapable of writing in a military style and is regularly reprimanded for his appearance which at times is barely acceptable. When reprimanded he adopts a hurt, indignant posture and for a short time reacts by improving slightly before reverting to his normal state.

The real Lulu though, was his assessment grading:-

Characteristics	Excellent	V. Good	Good	Adequate	Weak
Zeal & Energy					x
Reliability					x
Commonsense				x	
Intelligence			x		
Leadership				x	
Initiative					x
Technical Ability				x	
Oral Expression			x		
Written Expression					x
Organising Ability				x	
Tact Cooperation					x

I stood before him and read the report, obliged to initial it, not to acknowledge that I agreed with its content, but that it had been read.

Immediately afterwards I went to my room in the Mess to start preparing my second in-depth Appeal to the Army Board of the Defence Council.

It was the *Weak* in the Written Expression box that had done it.

An appeal was the only recourse the system allowed me, and by letting himself go so OTT in venting his spleen he had at last given me justifiable cause to try to use the system to my advantage. Prior to this there was no way I could have formed up to the Brigadier, and said: "Please, sir – my CO's being beastly, and keeps picking on me."

When I submitted my appeal, it was not allowed to go beyond unit level, but at least it caused sufficient fluttering in the dovecote for the cocked eye of the local hierarchy to be raised. Someone must then have caused a soft word to be spoken in Jeff Norton's ear, such as "Now look here old boy, we think enough's enough, you know. You're grinding this poor chap into the ground, and it doesn't look good."

Shortly after this, the reign of tyranny finally came to a close.

He was posted to Germany.

My lasting regret is that when he toured the offices to say farewell, along with all the others, I shook his hand. I still don't know which of us found it the more hypocritically uncomfortable, or should have been the one to refrain.

Through an interesting turn of events, that will be revealed, shortly afterwards I was given access to the personal file he'd been keeping on me.

Wow!

The half-truths he had written about me, the pettiness and naked hatred were unbelievable.

He had even submitted to higher authority a letter requesting that under the terms of Queen's Regulations I should be dismissed from the service forthwith, my services no longer required. Pinned to the copy of this letter was a yellow post-it note in his own hand, upon which he had written *It is my avowed intention to get this officer drummed out of the army . . .*

He'd certainly had a pin (if not a bayonet) in my ju-ju, in a *very* big way.

At the time HQ had advised me that little satisfaction would be gained from pursuing my appeal against what the so-and-so had written about me, I was now pleased to see that the 'next higher authority' (the Brigadier) had to some extent overridden the derogatory confidential report. Appended to its file copy, he had written

I believe he merits an Adequate grading, although I have much sympathy with the CO in this situation. He cannot be promoted or posted from Deepcut. He has therefore been robbed of incentive. As he can now only be employed on mundane tasks he will seldom be able to draw much satisfaction from his employment. He does, on occasion, get near to meriting an Adverse Report without ever quite providing the substance for such action. It is a very unsatisfactory situation which will only be resolved when this officer reaches the end of his contract, and retires.

I have upgraded the report because I have never seen him other than very smart in his turnout. He also has the ability to write very well indeed and I think the CO has been somewhat harsh in this respect. If a review of his situation changes his present status and he can be given employment to suit his intelligence, I am sure we would see a very different officer indeed.

That was nice.

My waned confidence then got another little shot in the arm when elsewhere in the file I came across copies of some earlier reports that had been written about me, by previous officers under whom I had served.

Captain George has a good appearance and attractive manner. His deportment and dress have a certain elegance and distinction. He is popular with his soldiers. His fellow officers find him congenial company.

Golly: so I can't have been *all* that bad.

And when I was a youngster, running the Army Youth Team . . .

Lt George has been in charge of 31 AYT for the last six months. He has shown drive, initiative and enthusiasm in his approach to various duties. This young officer is full of self confidence, slightly flamboyant, and at times is inclined to allow his enthusiasm to influence his judgement. 31 AYT has developed a 'New Look' since the arrival of Lt George. The team is in more demand than ever, due in the main to Lt George's zeal and willingness. A very smart young officer. I hope the above will be enough to get George his promotion, which I consider he deserves.

That one was written by Colonel Desmond Shaw, previously Britain's Military Attaché in Nigeria.

So where had it all gone wrong?

How had it all turned so sour in so short a time?

I believe it was because since having lost my security clearance and been rendered 'virtually unemployable', I had found myself working under a succession of passed-over, narrow minded, and unimaginative small-time bosses. And under the rigorously observed military ethos, the superior officer is always right, the inferior officer wrong.

I had been grossly mismanaged, discarded, and thrown to the wolves.

Wolves?

For some reason I was reminded of the adage *How Can I Be Expected To Soar With Eagles, When I'm Stuck Down Here With The Turkeys?*

And it wasn't just me.

The army itself seemed to have become disillusioned.

The Falklands had yet to come. Gulf Wars I, II, and Iraq had yet to come. Kosovo had yet to come, and Al-Qaeda . . . as had Afghanistan. A newer, younger breed of general was also to emerge; the Mike Jacksons, Richard Dannatts and David Richards, heading up a different, faster form of warfare – but in 1977 expensively trained officers, NCOs and men, able men, family men, conscientious, reliable and responsible men were still being reluctantly obliged to leave the profession of their choice in disturbingly high numbers, for reasons that have been perennially well known in the army since long before Kipling ever wrote his Tommy Atkins: Insufficient pay; limited resources or career prospects; conditions, overstretch, and political abuse; lack of job satisfaction, and the seeming pointlessness of the whole thing. In between street fighting in Northern Ireland and attempting to meet its Nato commitment in Germany, the army was expected to empty dustbins in Glasgow, douse fires during *Op Burberry* (the firemen's strike), drive petrol tankers when their drivers went on strike a year later, and ambulances when their drivers went on strike in 1979. The public had understandably come to believe that the army was there on call to meet any national emergency, and that each time they came eagerly tumbling forth from their bunks like Battle of Britain pilots on a scramble.

And so we did.

Because we were told to.

Because we had to.

But it was at no small cost to our morale.

Contrary to what people thought, the army did not spend its life sitting on its backside waiting for the Government to find it extraneous jobs to do.

The army had plenty of work that the Government had given it to do already.

It was called Training for War, and Defence of The Realm, and the same as today, at the time of which I write there weren't enough soldiers, guns, tanks or ammunition to carry out either task properly.

Calls from the nation for the army to fall-in to clear snow in the middle of its annual training programme, because the grit drivers had gone on strike and local councils were not up to the task, were not greeted with cries of universal glee.

In a nutshell – if affairs of such import could be so whimsically compounded – it had become more than ever apparent that in the seemingly not altogether unlikely event of a ground forces confrontation between Nato and the Warsaw Pact countries, it might be a rather short-lived, messy, and humiliating affair - for us.

By 'us' I mean the good guys.

466

What we had left of the British army.

We would put up a few days token retaliation and endure much bloodshed and first degree burns, but Ivan would still have his tanks up The Mall before we could cry 'sickle'.

Or . . .

. . . it *might* be (we thought) that when the Redland Forces did finally mount their long awaited offensive on the west (although it should be noted that since the 1975 Helsinki Conference on European Security and Co-operation, they were now only allowed to be referred to - in our hypothetical battlefield scenarios - as Orange Forces, in order not to offend the 'real' people, to whom the terms Red and Orange euphemistically referred) – it might be that they would infiltrate insidiously. Rather than hordes of mechanised Cossacks clattering out of the Urals to carve a swathe of armoured destruction through Maidstone, there was the possibility that agents in London, Manchester, Edinburgh, and a few places like that, would simply pop chemical agents into our water supplies one night, and we would all wake up the following morning to find the Red Flag over Buck House and Reggie Bousanquet (the TV newscaster of his day) with a gun to his head reading out to us all how it was going to be from then on. You cannot till scorched earth or convert the dead, so rather than the south-east of England being reduced to a contaminated wasteland of charred and smouldering corpses, we thought the poisoned water idea, instead of a *blitzkrieg,* quite a preferable one for us to be thinking about.

But the general game plan still remained, that to stem the Russian hordes Nato and all us khaki-clad British dustmen and snow clearers, would deploy her ground and air forces in Central Europe, to halt the entire Red advance at the River Weser with our bullet.

One of the responsibilities of the army's Royal Pioneer Corps was to run labour forces and plot manning levels for various projects.

Out in Germany we'd had a RPC major in our Mess called Bert Cutbush, and between us in the bar one evening we all hatched up an alternative strategic plan to keep the Russians at bay.

"What we should do in reality," chortled one slightly inebriated officer, "is get old Bert here to nip up to Braunschweig, on the border, to stand atop some hastily constructed plinth in their path, fling both his threadbare arms asunder, and screech 'STOP' through an interpreter and a loud hailer – assuming we can muster either. 'STOP' he will cry again, rubbing his rheumy eyes in disbelief as he surveys a thousand receding kilometres of obese Russian armour, clanking and straining at its mechanised bit to smash its way unheeding through our barber's pole barrier. 'STOP' Bert will foolhardily persist, thinking of his medal and the power, told to him by his father, of the Raj, and the outstretched finger of British authority that for aeons has contained the ability to summon a gunboat round the headland in a flash. 'You can't come in here,' he'll cry. 'You're . . . you're . . . *surplus to establishment.'*

"'Very sorry, Sahib,' the Russian leader might reply, appalled at his presumptuousness in trying to break into Germany, and abashed by Bert Cutbush, our brave and noble Brit, prancing about atop his plinth, blowing the gasket of his finest hour for Queen and Country.'

"'I should jolly well think so too,'Bert will retort, pushing his luck a fraction. 'Now just you bloody well get your damn' chappies off out of it and back where you belong. *Capisce?* On yer bike, Ivan. Leg it. Go on. Shoo.'

"'Of course, sir,' the Russian leader will say contritely, apologising for the trouble he's caused and giving an about-face-and-back-to-Moscow-lads sign with his gauntlet."

As John Wayne would have said: "The-hell-he-would."

Although subsequently we learned that most of the Russian tanks would have broken down long before they ever reached the Weser, thank God none of these scenarios ever came to pass.

THIRTY-EIGHT

COCKTAIL PARTIES flourished, lavish regimental dinner nights took place, garden parties and parades continued to be held, and upon the unqualified success of each depended the future peacetime career of whichever luckless officer had been detailed to organise them.

I had known people reach the rank of brigadier on the strength of their social skills alone.

During my service I had been responsible at various times for athletics meetings, battalion dances and cricket matches, Corps swimming galas, setting up and running the last military marquee at Royal Ascot for three years in succession, weight training clubs, unarmed combat displays, collections, raffles, band concerts, guest nights, press receptions – name it and either I had done it or was doing it.

Each year the Director General of Ordnance Services (our overall boss, a major general) held a two-day study period, or conference, in the Tela Theatre at Blackdown Barracks, Deepcut. Those Corps officers who could be made available were required to attend and to feign attention to the largely uninspired, expurgated, over-censored, uncontentious, over rehearsed, rewritten, bland and usually boring presentations about certain aspects of the Corps' work, development, and future plans, put on by that year's co-opted batch of peers - have a cocktail party and buffet, two slap-up lunches, and then go home again. Attendance was usually compulsory, and excuses hard to come by. By the time he made DGOS, it seemed, each successive DGOS forgot what ball aching affairs his predecessors' annual conferences used to be, so sidles gleefully in on Day One with his select party of attendant staff officers and ascendant Corps personalities to sit in the plush for two days, lording it down at the front of the hall, perpetuating the tedium.

What of the admin required to launch the beast?

It was a military exercise, so had to go like clockwork.

Being held in December, planning had to commence in May. Clerks, typists, cooks, bottle washers and a small cadre of hard pressed staff officers started to put things together in April.

My task?

To arrange accommodation in the Aldershot area for 150 officers. A certain number of rooms were available in various army Messes, but another sixty still needed to be found on the civilian net.

Major Eric 'Womble' Adams, the GSOII, had been designated to run the admin side of things. Interestingly, he then went off to join the New Zealand army shortly afterwards; I can't think why.

Eric's team had already prepared a formidable but uninspiring list of likely hotels, B&Bs and dosseries in the area, and I was given the task of visiting them all to grade their suitability for a captain or a general (and everything else between) to sleep.

Eric handed me the list at 09.00 one Monday, with an accompanying list of all those to be accommodated, and gave me three weeks to complete the task of marrying everyone up with his appropriate level of bedroom in the area.

Taxing stuff.

Cramming both lists into my briefcase I went up to my room in the Mess to make myself a coffee, manicure a nail and plan my strategy.

Scanning Eric's lists it seemed strange to me that the Frimley Park Hotel did not appear on it, so quickly buffing my jodhpur boots down the back of my trousers, donning my saucy little side hat and stuffing a tenner in my pocket, I drove off for a pre-prandial snifter at the Frimley Park.

"Could you accommodate sixty men in khaki the first week in December?" I asked the manager, who'd joined me for a pink gin at the bar.

"I don't see why not," he said. "We've got nothing else pencilled in that week yet. Yes – we'd be delighted."

"Thank you," I said, downing my snifter. "You've just saved me three weeks work. Have another?"

"Eric," I said, back in his office that afternoon. "Rather than have all these chaps spread about all over Aldershot and its environs, with attendant transport problems bringing them in each morning, don't you think it might be better if we could get them all accommodated in one place?"

"Absolutely," he said. "But how can we possibly do that?"

"Well, it may be hidden away in the trees a bit, but I think I've found somewhere. The Frimley Park Hotel say they can accommodate the lot."

"You don't say. Can they really? They can't; can they? My God, Mike, you're a genius."

"I know. Can I go now, please?"

Come December I was naturally co-opted to be in attendance at the Frimley Park Hotel, to welcome the delegates as they arrived. This meant standing like a prune in Reception in my best bib and tucker (service dress and gleaming Sam Browne), ensuring that everything worked like clockwork. Naturally, there were only two arthritic septuagenarian porters available, the other two, younger, men being off sick and on holiday respectively.

It was 16.00.

People would start arriving soon.

"Hallo, Mike. What are *you* doing here?"

H-hour was upon me.

They were arriving already.

Convoys of cars came rolling in and drawing up outside, the chaps all piling in to the foyer from their respective units, and greeting each other as if they were returning to school after the hols.

With the rush intensifying I could see that the two septuagenarian porters were now fast approaching 80, as they struggled to heft the occasional suitcase to the lift, and of course I knew *exactly* what was going to happen next.

"I wonder if you would care to just help me up with these two bags of mine," a tin-legged old general asked me.

"Of course, sir."

What else could I do?

Nor could I complain.

Having staggered up three narrow flights of stairs and deposited his two cases on the floor of his room, one couldn't very well lurch against a general's washbasin, and gasp: "Christ, mate – 'd you bring all your spare parts with you, as well?"

Eight more times I lapped the hotel's two superannuated porters up the stairs to the top floor. If I'd been wearing a tracksuit and sweatshirt it would have been fine, a great workout, but my best service dress now had fungus spewing from its armpits.

One of the septuagenarians was shuffling across the foyer carpet towards me like a slow motion Chinese rickshaw boy, carrying a briefcase,.

"You might wanna know there's anuvver genl'man just arrived," he clacked, "waitin' outside wiv his stuff."

"Where's your hoppo?" I croaked. "Can't he do it?"

"No," I was informed, as he disappeared round a bannister. "'E's collapsed in the lift."

I knew who this last attendee would be. His was the only name still left unticked on my list. The highly decorated General Sir Simeon Beauclerk, late SAS, from the MoD, was the most senior guest speaker we had coming.

On gelatinous legs, I went out to the car park to meet this distinguished looking, iron-haired gentleman in his immaculate pinstripe suit, just locking the doors of a brand spanking new Ford Granada.

Good afternoon, sir," I said cheerily, trying to get some feeling back into my hands. "May I help you with your suitcases?"

"Thank you; that would be very nice indeed, if you wouldn't mind. I'd appreciate it enormously. But I must warn you, they're a bit heavy, I'm afraid."

They were, too. He had obviously brought along quite a lot of display material with him.

The lift was still full of one small old caved-in body, and this most senior officer's room was right on the top floor, at the far end of the west wing, so by the time we'd made it I was on my chinstrap.

"I'm really most impressed by the service you've laid on here," he said, as I lowered his gargantuan cases gently to the floor and eased myself erect again. "Would you be offended if I offered you a tip?"

"What's that, sir?" I asked, wondering what I had done wrong and what gratuitous advice my illustrious elder was about to give me.

"No – no," he laughed. "Good heavens, no – I meant a financial tip."

"On the horses, or on the market?" I enquired, still being dense.

"No – a couple of quid," he said.

A ghastly thought then entered my mind, so I quickly asked: "I wonder if I could just confirm your name please, sir?"

"Certainly; it's Colin Smith," he said, hefting one of his cases up onto the bed and flinging it open it to reveal layers of sales brochures.

"I'm the local rep for Birds Eye."

November 5th 1977 fell on a Saturday, and as general dogsbody it had befallen my lot to organise and run the Garrison Fireworks Display.

When the manufacturer's colourful brochure arrived I studied it carefully and then ordered an economy sized commercial pack of Golden Rains, Sky Rockets, and Salvos; Mortars and Fusillades; Marine Sirens, Spectaculars (assorted) and large Catherine Wheels.

They arrived mid-September, boxed and banded like an illicit arms shipment to an Indian reservation.

Painstakingly I unpacked them and checked each wick and taper before stacking them on the Quartermaster's shelf under lock and key.

In October I published a notice to inform the garrison at large of the forthcoming event, and suggested that anyone with combustible waste to dispose of should notify me, in order for its collection to be arranged.

The morning of Saturday 5 November dawned dark, dank and miserable.

With a work party of soldiers clinging to it like Asians on a bus, the unit's 4-ton tipper truck set out on its preplanned milk run of refuse collection.

By 11.00 a sizeable bonfire was steadily growing on the traditionally designated piece of waste ground in the valley behind the married soldiers quarters.

When I got there at 14.00 to supervise the final touches, it was to find that I was going to have to move it.

It was now 20-feet high and as broad again at the base, but in the wrong place.

Silver Rain Spectacular, our *pièce de résistance* of the whole display, required to be slung like a washing line of Semtex-packed socks 15-feet high across the open space between two conveniently situated oak trees, which had stoically endured having their nethers singed annually for decades.

In its present position, the bonfire was slap bang in the way.

It would have been more than my life was worth to have left it where it was, thereby having to dispense with the event's coruscating finale.

People came from miles around to see our Silver Rain Spectacular each year.

Dammit, men had moved armies before now.

Even our RSM had had a whole marquee moved once, because it was not quite in line with something it should have been.

Surely I should not have any qualms over messing a work party about, moving a mere bonfire?

It was my first decision in what was to become the very bitch of a day.

"You gotta be bloody jokin', sir," snorted the Provost Sergeant in charge of the ten-man work party. "Move the 'ole bleedin' bonfire? Really, sir? You're not serious, are you?" he asked, barely able to conceal his incredulity.

"Mmmmmm," I nodded, looking like Prince Philip conversing seriously with someone. "'Fraid so. You've put it bang in the centre of the only place we can string the main firework display, y'see."

Muttering hotly to himself, he shrugged his shoulders. Tossing his head like a gay waiter returning a rejected meal, he trudged off down into the valley below to relay my unsavoury order to the work party.

"YOU," he roared when he got there, stabbing the whole length of one arm at the smallest and frailest soldier of them all. "Move this fire, from . . . HERE, to . . . THERE. Come along now, close your mouth. Look lively now. *Chop-chop.*"

Everybody grinned.

In a parody of frenzied activity our chosen man commenced burrowing his way into the accumulated brambles and refuse, towards the centre of the pyre, as if to heave it onto his shoulders like Atlas humping the world.

Squaddies' humour having restored the situation, the rest of the team got off their butts and pitched in.

With the 4-ton tipper truck acting as a bulldozer, the fire was soon shifted and re-stacked in the correct place.

Next came the task of erecting the various pre-cut pickets, posts and palisades, that had to be sunk into the ground to support each different display.

The catalogue's complex illustration showing us how to lay out the preparatory props for this upcoming pyrotechnic phantasmagoria of ours, looked like the plan of a WWI minefield, randomly littered with wooden scaffolding resembling medieval ballistae.

I'd had the garrison chippy spend all week shaping and sharpening his own version of all this stuff, but now assembled before us *in situ,* the component parts didn't look strong enough to be able to sustain the dramatic effects we were envisaging.

I had always been quite a gentle officer. Butterflies and literature, classical music and fine porcelain lent themselves to me as being more enjoyable pursuits than car maintenance or DIY, so there was a myriad of things for which I would have been better suited, and enjoyed doing far more that damp, cold, grey Saturday afternoon in November than supervising the erection of a firework display.

Because of this you will more readily appreciate my pique (as events unfurled) that I did not receive at least a Mention in Dispatches at the end of the day, because what occurred was undoubtedly one of my finest hours.

The penny bangers, sky rockets and catherine wheels of my youth were small fry compared to the holocaust the team and I were preparing to unleash on an unsuspecting public at 19.00 hours that night.

The firework industry was well abreast of technology.

During a lull in the preparations I strolled into our site marquee and picked up one of the three dozen tightly packed compressed cardboard mortar-bombs from the six-foot table to look at.

It resembled a large and extraordinarily heavy onion, with an enormous and ominous fistula dangling from it.

Then I read the instructions.

A rush of blood surged up one calf.

No way was I sedately going to light the blue touch-paper of *this* baby and retire: it could prove to be permanent.

We could have waged a small war with these goodies we'd been sent; or sold them to a Third World nation as the real thing.

Each mortar-bomb had its own wooden-based launch-tube which had to be firmly buried at least two-feet into the ground. The implication was that it would be courteous to ring Canberra before lighting.

My game little work party had retrieved their shovels and were socking them into the turf, digging holes in the valley floor large enough to take the timber stanchion mainstays. The prospect of digging 36 two-foot holes along the valley floor to house these things was a daunting one. The physical effort required would be only slightly less than digging-in for real.

It was then that my superior intellect switched on.

There were six discarded tea-chests askew on the bonfire.

I ordered them to be removed and laid out in a row along the valley floor where we wanted the mortars sighted.

Then I got the work-party to fill each chest with soil and pack three mortar tubes in each.

That accommodated 18 of the 36 launch tubes.

So to let off all 36 of our bombs meant we would have to fire two from each tube, and if the tubes and tea-chests then blew themselves sky-high, I couldn't have cared less.

We banked earth round the chests, bedding them well in for additional stability (those mortars really did look lethal) and then walked back up the valley slope and stood on the road at the top, to survey our field of battle.

For two-hundred yards from left to right we had strung a heavy crowd-restraining rope barrier.

Fifty yards to the right of us there were two marquees, one erected to sell hot-dogs, soup and toffee-apples and the other containing our open crates of fireworks, which we had not purchased from the corner newsagent remember, but from an explosives factory in the Midlands.

Immediately to our fore there were three racks of rocket-stands pointing at the heavens like ICBMs in open silos.

At 7.00 p.m. precisely our rocket-man would ignite and release cluster after cluster of these to signal the commencement of our evening's pyrotechnic extravaganza, except that unlike the Big Boys, on Tower Bridge, for example, we had no computerised sequential electrical ignition device with which to do it.

Just matches and a couple of lighters.

Bizarrely arrayed up the far side of the valley, beyond the bonfire, in the middle-ground, stark and sinister timber pillars, beams and crudely nailed cross-members waited to have their sacrificial victims impaled, screwed and hammered onto them prior to lighting.

The heavy work was eventually done.

Phase one of our preparation was complete.

Unfortunately it had taken longer than planned. It was now four-o'clock and beginning to get dark. My intention had been to rehearse one or two dummy run-throughs, with each man standing at his appointed display and me shouting the ignition sequence to them as if I was Monty shelling El Alemain.

Ideally I should like to have synchronized it all to music, but this was a bit ambitious with my limited resources, which consisted of a loud hailer and a cassette tape of James Last.

It started to rain.

"Oh, bother," I said. "Hang on a moment, lads. We'll let this drizzle pass over first. Co'rl Smith, perhaps you'd like to get the Tilly-lamps in the marquee alight for us, will you?"

The rain was coming down quite hard now.

I trusted it was only going to be a short cloud-burst; God wouldn't be so mean as to piss on my parade like this, would he?

We all piled into the marquee.

By 5.30 p.m. the persistent downpour seemed to be setting in for the duration.

Even if a hot sun was suddenly to appear, which it wouldn't, the bonfire would still be too drenched to light.

My morale plummetted.

I resented the £1,000 worth of bangers laid-out like the start of a revolution on the six-foot tables behind me.

Nor could I see why hot-dogs, soup and toffee-apples by the hundred should be prepared for a 15-minute firework display. Couldn't the public even hang on that long without having to feed their fat faces?

It continued to pour.

There were twelve Tilly-lamps in the marquee and Corporal Smith hadn't yet been able to get even one of them to light.

It was 6.15 p.m.

Just three-quarters of an hour before the display was due to start.

What was I to do?

I had no authority to cancel it, but surely only a lunatic would turn out in conditions like these, just to see a few damp squibs go off?

If no-one turned up, then I could justifiably re-pack the fireworks and await further instructions.

But if just one snotty-nosed kid and his brother showed, I supposed I would be obliged to unleash a thousand-quid's worth of junk into the night sky.

It was 6.30 p.m.

In a dark recess of the marquee I caught sight of half-a-dozen dustbins, put there to collect the rubbish in afterwards.

"Sergeant Jones, I suppose what we ought to do is pack the fireworks into those dustbins. Two men at a time can then dash out when the time comes, like replenishing a gun emplacement under fire."

"What a very good idea that is, sir," said Jones, who was under consideration for promotion.

It was 6.45 pm.

"They still gonna 'ave the fireworks, Mister?"

They'd arrived. The snotty-nosed kid and his bruvver, plus their bedraggled terrier, stood streaming and expectant in their sopping trainers at the tent flap.

"Yeah," I said, realising that there *was* a reason for this madness after all. "Course we are, Sunshine." I ruffled his ringing wet hair and smiled at him engagingly, wondering if I'd be done for assault. Dragging the totally disinterested mongrel behind them they then squelched off to stand patiently beneath a dripping tree to wait.

It was now 6.55 p.m.

Five-minutes to 'Go', with still not a soul in sight except the two lads and their dog.

The rain was bucketing down.

"Sergeant Jones, we'd better make a move," I said. "Get your team together. Take three dustbins of those mortars down into the valley. You know where the tea-chests have been

479

sighted. After the rockets have gone up, you start letting off the mortars. When they've all been expended, double your team back here for the kero and we'll all converge on the bonfire for a concerted effort to get the blighter going, although I don't hold out much hope of success. Okay?"

"Right, sir" Like WWI troops bravely going over-the-top, Sergeant Jones and his team disappeared into the dark wall of machine-gunning water.

"Corporal Johnson," I yelled.

"Sah?"

"Rockets," I cried. "All yours. There's sixty seconds to go. Dash out there, stick 'em in their racks, light 'em and get 'em up to heaven as fast as you like. You will then have signalled the start of the display."

It was now 7p.m.

H-hour.

I stepped outside.

It was hissing down.

The attendant fire engine and ambulance that had arrived, were both up to their axles in mud.

Inside the marquee, Corporal Smith had finally got one of the Tilly-lamps alight.

It was almost thirty seconds past seven-o'clock and still nothing had happened yet.

"Corporal *Johnson*? Where are those *rockets?*" I bellowed.

"Here beside me, sir," he yelled back out of the stygian gloom. "Completely soaked. I can't get even one of them to light and I've only got two matches left."

"Oh, bother," I said. "Well, light your port-fires, for God's sake."

"Can't do that either, sir. Dropped them in a puddle."

"For heaven's sake, Corporal Johnson; look - go and bash on the door of one of those quarters over there. Get hold of some sort of light, somehow."

I think he mentioned something unpleasant about mother under his breath, but leaving his rockets sagging in their racks he dashed across the puddled road to the nearest quarter.

"Sir . . .?"

A plaintive cry wafted its anguished way up from the valley floor below, from Sergeant Jones and his mortar platoon.

"Not long now, Sergeant Jones,! I yelled back encouragingly. "We're just lighting the rockets and then you can let rip with your bombardment."

"Forget it, sir,' he wailed. 'The mortar tubes are full of rain, the tea-chests are floating away in a sea of mud and we're wallowing around waist-deep in water down here."

"Oh, drat,' I said. "Okay - hang on. I'm coming."

I leapt forward and started down the valley side.

As if torrential rain was not enough to contend with in my getting this show on the road, it had so swollen the water-table that an underground spring had been forcefully induced to rise and join in the fun as well.

Rushing determinedly into the valley it was this that had undermined the solidity of my earth-packed tea-chests.

But Sergeant Jones had exaggerated.

The water was only knee-deep.

I was now at the stage when the futility of the exercise had got to me. I should have aborted the whole thing long ago, and then we would all have been sitting round the television at home eating muffins instead of leaping about like rain-sodden idiots.

Then the sheer ridiculousness of the situation struck me and I began to giggle.

Sergeant Jones and his team looked apprehensively from one to the other for a moment and then they, too, grinned.

I laughed.

They laughed.

Just then we heard a foreshortened *whoosh*. Corporal Johnson, bless him, had finally managed to get one of his rockets off.

It had only gone 10-feet mind, hit the cloud base and spiralled crazily back down again, but it was medal-winning stuff - and a start.

There came a small cheer from the roadside.

I looked up and saw that there were one or two people standing there.

The fools.

Anyway - our £1,000 firework display had now officially commenced - even if only about a quid's worth of it had gone off so far. I made another decision.

"Sergeant Jones," I roared.

"Sah?"

"We've 'had' the fireworks. Forget it. Now get all the kero out of the marquee, gather up all the fireworks and let's get across to that bonfire. We're going to get it alight somehow if it kills us."

"It will, sir."

"I know that. No matter. All this is FUN. Now . . . *Move*."

I churned back up the slope.

"Bloody marvellous, Corporal Johnson. Brilliant. How did you do it?"

"With this, sir," he said, brandishing a blow-lamp he'd commandered from one of the quarters.

Like a half-crazed powder-monkey, some hastily recruited kid from the crowd was refilling the empty rocket racks with replacement projectiles from the box. Corporal Johnson was then nonchalantly spraying their soggy tails with his blow-lamp until each one forced itself to sit up and take notice, and launch itself off erratically in some direction or other to avoid having its piles further singed.

"Corporal Johnson, I say again - you're a very marvellous man. Well done. I shall need that blow-lamp, though. It's the only way I'm ever going to get that blasted bonfire even half way lit. How many rockets are left?"

"Just those, sir," he said, unthinkingly indicating them with his blow-lamp. "Oh dear," he said, giggling and covering his mouth with one hand. One of the rockets in the bin had been less soaked than the others. It caught, hissed and fizzed.

"I've always wanted to do something like that and get away with it," cackled Corporal Johnson hysterically as we dashed back down the slope to the bonfire together, leaving the ever-swelling crowd to laugh, duck and cheer as the contents of the dustbin erupted in front of them. So much for manufacturer's safety instructions!

Sergeant Jones was already standing on top of the bonfire sloshing kerosene all over it, with a small chain of helpers handing each of the six cans up to him.

"You've smothered yourself in that stuff, Sarge," one of the soldiers yelled. "Wanna fag?"

"Very funny," Jones shouted, emptying the final can, discarding it into the night and jumping down to land on top of the soldier.

"All stand back," I hollered, feeling a touch of the heroics coming on.

I grabbed the blow-lamp from Corporal Johnson, who possessively tried to yank it back from me.

It was his lamp.

He'd found it.

He wanted to do it.

There was no time to lose.

I scowled at him, sternly indicating my shoulder with my chin.

Grudgingly he deferred to the privilege bestowed by rank.

With bags of outward bravura but inwardly observing a modicum of care, I advanced purposefully towards the sorry pile of towering sludge which resembled more a rain-drenched barricade from *Les Miserables* than a Garrison bonfire.

Applying the blow-lamp's spluttering blue flame to a dripping baulk of protruding timber, I waited.

Nothing happened.

Next I pointed my flame thrower at a cardboard box I saw leering at me through its little slit eyes.

After a while that caught, charred, produced a few sparks, curled, retreated and died.

Useless box.

I was getting nowhere.

Why wouldn't the ******* fire light?

Come on, God.

Not twice in one day, pleeeease.

"Corporal Johnson, bring me one of those Marine Fusillade jobs, will you?"

That worthy stepped forward and handed me a lethal looking orange and purple thing the size and weight of a genuine Swing-Fire missile.

Like someone poking the grate at home I shoved and insinuated this as far into the fire as I could, and then applied the blow-lamp to its tail.

Thank God.

This time it worked.

There was a *whoosh* and a shower of sparks.

Something caught inside our reticent but potential inferno.

A flicker of flame. A glimmer of hope.

"That's it," I yelled. "Get all those fireworks over here, quickly now."

Willing hands fell-to beside me, ramming and shoving all the fireworks we could into the fire.

There were one or two isolated *pops* and the occasional spurt of annoyed sparks, but still no sudden and dramatic ignition of the loathsome kero and mass of waterlogged rubbish standing in all its mighty malevolence before us.

"Keep trying, Corporal Johnson," I instructed, thrusting the blow-lamp back into his hand. "I've got one last idea."

Rushing back up the hill to the marquee I whipped back the rain-sodden flap and stepped panting inside.

There was our still bone-dry, 20-foot, £100 *pièce de résistance* - Silver Rain Spectacular.

My secret weapon.

I gathered it up and bundled it as best I could inside my ringing wet combat jacket, making sure its precious fuse was tucked safely under my arm-pit out of harm's way.

"Here it is," I cried, back at the fireside where Corporal Johnson was still producing sparks but little else. "Let's unfurl it and wrap the whole lot round the base of the fire."

In seconds it was done.

"Corporal Johnson?"

"Sah?"

"All yours," I said, reverentially uncovering the fuse.

"Can't, I'm afraid sir," he said. "Blow-lamp's gone out."

"Oh . . . bother," I said, watching as the rain thudded relentlessly into Silver Rain Spectacular.

"There's a spark round this side, sir," someone yelled.

"Where, sir?' I cried. "Bring it here."

"I can't, sir. It's here."

"Oh ****," I cried, tugging the fuse and its disintegrating entrails off round to the far side of the fire where there was one expended rocket case still with a surprised cluster of soggy sparks huddled round its charred base.

Gingerly I touched Silver Rain Spectacular's precious blue fuse against them, and waited.

And prayed.

"Please little fuse, nice little fuse, dear little fuse; just do this one thing for me," I hummed.

And something started to happen.

The rain poured down my neck but something was definitely happening.

Silver Rain Spectacular was getting it on.

She was up for it.

 Her engine fired.

She writhed free of my hand and was away.

Sparks, crap and flaming magnesium leapt around the fire's base.

A great £100 concentration of intense heat gushed into its bowels.

A firework exploded.

Then another.

There was a violent *boom* as one of the onion-shaped mortar-bombs blew up and shot a wicker laundry basket forcefully 40-feet into the sodden night sky.

A wall of flame licked and spiralled its way up the outside of the fire.

A satanic orange pillar arose in the centre like Vesuvius erupting.

We cheered.

The by now swollen crowd of onlookers who had turned up on the roadside cheered and clapped.

485

I turned to look at them. There seemed to be thousands of them there now in the fire's glow.

I saluted and gave an exaggerated theatrical bow.

An appreciative ripple of laughter tumbled down to me.

A stray squib winnowed out of the fire and went up my trouser leg.

I clutched myself and leapt in the air.

An escaping rocket shot up the back of my jacket.

The crowd loved it.

After it was all over and the crowd had gone home I stood up on the roadside for a few minutes and surveyed the scene of battle. I was sodden, bruised, charred and filthy.

As soon as the last firework had gone off, it stopped raining, of course.

It occurred to me that I'd probably had an even worse time of it than Guy Fawkes.

THIRTY-NINE

LIKE A CLEANSING BREATH OF FRESH AIR there now entered my life and the lives of all of us serving in Deepcut at that time, an enlightened man of whom I shall speak with great affection.

Lt-Col Anthony Sharp flew in from Cyprus like a suntanned crusader, disarming everyone with his charm and flailing about himself with a stream of well enunciated Anglo Saxon expletives designed to dismiss cant, pettiness and bureaucracy; fools, hypocrites and any other of life's hangers on, whinge-ers and wankers who got in the way of his idea of how his new command, Training Battalion and Depot, and life in general should be run.

To say that I liked his style, would be an understatement.

We related instantly, and in every particular.

He was a parachutist, athlete, hockey player, piss artist and lunatic.

His personal life was a bit topsy-turvy, but his concern for the community at large and each individual's place within and contribution towards it – his own above all – was paramount.

He was dogged, tough and resilient.

He had suffered sufficient life's knocks of his own, but instead of succumbing had reeled a bit, staggered, and then returned with even greater zest and determination, compassion and justice for his fellow man.

The female hearts be must have broken just by charming their owners out of their pants, must have been legion.

He was hard as nails, soft as butter and one of life's gentlemen.

If the average Brit had as much about him as Tony possessed in his little finger, we could continue to rule not only the waves again, but most of Europe and a fair chunk of anything else that was going on as well.

I won't say more in case he's recognised, or I start to embarrass him.

Tony quickly identified my problem, picked me up, dusted me down, restored my self confidence (left shredded by the now departed, non lamented Jeffrey Norton) and insisted on me joining his staff.

The final twelve months of my service were now to become a dizzy delight.

I was asked to take the part of Algernon Moncrieff in the Blackdown Players' production of *The Importance Of Being Earnest* and found I had the time at last to indulge myself in such a frivolous extra mural activity for once.

Despite my father's theatrical proclivities and a tenuous blood connection with Ivor Novello and Ray Milland, distant cousins of his, I had not trod the boards since I was a 14-year old spear-carrier for Caesar in the school play.

How would I fare?

I had no idea.

A good friend of mine at the time, Jeremy Baines, was to play John Worthing, and the play was due to be performed in November.

With only a few months of service left I thought I would try to get away with and revel in allowing my hair to grow slightly longer than usual – to be more in keeping with the character of Algernon Moncrieff, doncha know.

Our Armistice Day Parade that year was to fall on 12 November. Because it would be my last parade in the army, I asked if I could take part.

It appeared that in order just to be allowed to stamp up and down I wouldn't need an awful lot of security clearance, so my request was acceded to with alacrity, my presence relieving somebody else who perhaps wasn't quite so keen on that occasion, as I was, to march round with the Band brandishing his sword in the air and saluting.

We had three parade rehearsals, and each time it was 'noted' by a rather shocked RSM that a certain maverick officer's hair was rather longer than the RSM 'liked' or could be expected to tolerate, so please might the officer be invited to get it 'seen to' in order to forestall unrest within the ranks.

The invitation was duly passed to said officer, but now in the evening of his service and soon to be a civilian, plus co-starring as one of the principal male leads in the garrison's upcoming theatrical extravaganza, said officer on this occasion flippantly decided to give two fingers and a raspberry.

The adjutant was beside himself with this latest management quandary.

As though he didn't have enough to worry about, here was bloody Mike George playing silly buggers again.

"Don't worry about it," he was told by Colonel Tony within my earshot. "Mike won't let you down. He'll play the game. Mike knows the form."

Well, I had to get my hair cut after that, didn't I!

My barber was on holiday, so for the first time in six years, there at the eleventh hour I had to pole up rather poe-faced to the camp barber's shack.

"Hallo, sir," said Ray the barber, grinning evilly as he shook out his sheet and pointedly began stropping a razor. "I don't think I've had the pleasure before, have I . . .?"

"Just a little light trim if you wouldn't mind please, Ray."

"Yes, of course, sir. Just a little light trim, you say . . ." and he started.

How does that funeral thing go? Man who is born of woman enters this world shorn and naked, and goes back out of it the same way, or something?

They'd given me a short back and sides when I'd joined: I supposed it was fitting that I should now receive a farewell shearing too.

When I marched round the Deepcut parade square with my soldiers next day, I'm sure the inspecting general didn't even notice the trouble I'd been to on his behalf.

Lt-Col Mike Day, the producer of the play did though.

"You c**t," he shrieked at me, hurling his script about in a simulated artistic tantrum. "What the hell did you go and do that for?" he demanded. "I mean, I know we're in the army, but this is ridiculous."

"Sorry, Colonel: conflict of interests," I told him. "I fought hard and resisted as long as I could, but there were too many of them and I had to concede."

Jo Rayne, my leading lady, who was playing Cecily, was a bit thrown as well. In every rehearsal so far she had knotted her fingers lovingly up the back of my neck, gazed wistfully at the back of the theatre and intoned the immortal words *"You dear, romantic boy, I hope your hair curls naturally - does it?"*

"Yes, darling," I'd always replied. *"With a little help from others."*

It was opening night.

Poor Jo nearly had heart failure.

"You dear, romantic boy," she crooned, concentrating on her lines, still blissfully unaware of the state of my sand-papered blue neck. *"I hope your hair curls . . . **Eeeeek**."*

She looked quickly down at me kneeling before her, as though she'd seen a mouse.

"Where's it gone?" she hissed, wondering whether I'd done it on purpose, to jinx her, or if it was something personal that I would rather not talk about up there on stage. Remembering where she was and what she was meant to be doing and that there was an expectant audience waiting out there, all of them assuming she'd fluffed her lines, she leapt back in and quickly had another go.

"You dear, romantic boy, I hope your hair curls naturally - does it?" she blurted.

"Yes, darling," I replied, before swivelling on my knee, grinning at our predominantly military audience, and pointedly changing one word . . . *"with **very** little help from others."*

It didn't bring down the house, but at least got a bit of a titter from those in the know.

As well as directing us thespians, Lt-Col Mike Day had been charged with running the Corps Ball that year, celebrating the Queen's silver jubilee.

He got me on his committee to do that as well: the theme was to be the splendour of the Roman Empire.

Where he'd dug up that idea was anybody's guess, but I was told to organise the décor for it.

Oh - what fun we had in those days.

It was more like a girls' high school than an army.

How the hell was I going to transform an Officers' Mess the size of an aircraft hangar, to represent the glory of ancient Rome?

Plinths and porticos, I thought.

I wasn't really sure I knew what a plinth or a portico was, but with the singlemindedness of the survivor I settled down with the Yellow Pages and the spare office phone to set about ringing up likely sounding people.

The Yvonne Arnaud and Redgrave Theatres at Guildford and Farnham seemed favourites to start with.

"Good morning. Don't suppose by any chance you've got any plinths or porticos lying around, have you?"

"No."

"How about garlands?"

"Tried a florist?"

"Any particular one you'd recommend?"

"Who *is* this?" they asked.

"The army," I said.

"Gawd, 'struth," and the phone went down.

After a week of this I was becoming cheesed off with the whole fruitless mission, but then I was given a dead cert lead in Harlesdon, so I rang them.

"'Allo, Marlene 'ere."

"Got any plinths and porticos, love?" I asked her.

"Yer what?"

"Plinths and porticos. Have you got any?"

"I don't fink so; what are they, then?" she giggled, obviously trying to visualise the nut down my end of the phone.

491

"Roman plinths and porticos," I explained. "Columns and busts . . ."

"*Ohh,*" she squealed. "This is one of them funny calls, innit?"

"Come on, love," I said. "Have you got any?"

"Nah, course we ain't," she said. "What we do's plastic parsley for the butchery trade," and hung up.

Two days later there was a progress meeting.

The members of the Ball Committee filed into the small ante room and sat down importantly.

Mike Day was in the chair, and declared the meeting open.

It lasted an hour.

He went round the table afterwards calling for a report on each activity.

Food was going to be okay apparently, and would rival that of the *Ritz*.

Music was already laid on and was apparently going to be a cross between Acker Bilk, and the Palm Court Orchestra.

The raffle had been arranged.

The menus, tickets, signs, and other bits and pieces had all been printed.

There was now only my décor to be discussed.

"Mike?" He turned his gaze fully upon me, which as he had a squint was a measure of his intent. "I understand you've been having a bit of difficulty getting hold of appropriate décor – is that right?"

"Not at all, Colonel," I replied, giving a questioning uplift of one eyebrow and a surprised little smile, as if hurt by his suggestion that I should *ever* experience any difficulty accomplishing *any*thing I had been tasked with doing.

"I must have been misinformed, then. You've got no problem?"

"None whatsoever, Colonel," I affirmed.

"The whole place is going to look like a splendid version of Rome on the night, is it?"

"Absolutely, Colonel," I agreed.

"And how exactly do you propose doing that?" he asked.

"Magnificently," I said.

"I'm sure we're all very pleased to hear it," he countered, "but what exactly are we going to be getting, with which to do it?"

"The film set of *I Claudius*," I said.

It was lovely.

The other committee members looked at each other and didn't say anything for a moment, but then all started to splutter together.

Mike Day drummed his fingers lightly on the table and pursed his lips musingly, smiled, drew back his chair and declared the meeting closed.

My persistence had paid off.

One lead, culled from all the telephone calls I'd made, had led me straight to the firm of Greenery at Hampton Court whose premises were stocked high with all the statues, urns, benches, busts and arches, plinths, porticos and the whole bit they'd made specially for the TV series *I Claudius*.

The day my convoy of four-tonners rolled up to collect it all, they even threw in some garlands of plastic flowers to be draped from the arches.

It was a job well done, but – God – I missed my rifle and bayonet.

It was definitely time for me to be moving on.

Before that, however . . .

FORTY

THROUGHOUT HIS CAREER the life and geographical location of an RAOC officer was governed by a department of the MoD called AG9.

Britain's security services over the years have been found wanting in certain areas, and been discredited for shoddy practices in others.

They certainly 'did' for me in a big way, when they'd withdrawn my security clearance for such a petty misdemeanour, in 1973 - presumably not only to be beastly, but *pour encourager les autres.*

Five long years had now elapsed since that event.

My telephone rang. It was Peter Foxton, the adjutant. "Mike, Colonel wants to see you; pop up, will you?"

"Oh, Gawd," I thought, programmed as I had become to reacting thus. But there was no need to worry – it was the jovial and ever popular Tony Sharpe I had been summoned to see.

"Mike," he bellowed, when I entered his office, saluted, and took the offered chair. "I've decided it's time someone did something about your situation, and as no one else seems prepared to stick their neck out, I've done it myself. Have a look at this. What do you think?"

He passed me a letter he had just written directly to AG9 at the MoD. In it he referred to various cruddy letters and documents about me which he'd dug out of my personal file, and I now read

I find it difficult to understand the reasoning of various of Captain George's former commanding officers. References state that Captain George gave no cause on security grounds for security status not to be reinstituted. A recommendation to this effect was not made because of Captain George's 'overall unsatisfactory performance' as an officer. I would regard Captain George's unsatisfactory performance as understandable, because lack of security clearance meant that his career would be restricted to sixteen years, a view which I feel is reinforced by one of the reference's statements that the lifting of vetting restrictions might improve Captain George's attitude and performance.

I have therefore reviewed Captain George's conduct.

There is currently no evidence of unreliability in his case. His personal habits remain moderate and his political views continue to give no cause for alarm. A competent and capable officer, he has overcome his resentment at his loss of security status and in routine and special employment I make no distinction between him and my other officers; indeed, he is currently a Company Commander awaiting call-out on fire fighting duties.

I can certify that the adverse information previously brought against Captain George has been outweighed by his conduct over the year which he has spent under my command. I therefore have no hesitation in recommending that Captain George be re-granted the security status of NV.

It did the trick.

Three months later my security clearance was reinstated.

A week after that Peter Foxton (who eventually went on to become a brigadier) was posted away on a long course, and Colonel Tony made me his adjutant.

One morning he popped into my office with a file, dumped it on my desk, and said "Mike, just out of interest you may want to read through that lot, before you burn it for me, please."

At the door he turned, and winked before leaving.

Colonel A.D. "Tony" Sharpe – the best o' the best; the author's last CO, mentor, confidant and close personal friend, who put his neck on the line to pull the author out of the mire

The Boss in retirement, resting from felling trees on his N. Devon estate – and this is the man who had the *gall* to tell the author to get his hair cut!

It was my Personal File, most of it consisting of the vitriolic ramblings of that odious little wart, Lt-Col Jeffrey Norton, which were referred to in a previous chapter.

A month later it was Annual Confidential Report time again . . .

. . . and it was with great delight that I was to discover I had become exonerated.

Soon after he qualified Colonel Tony wrote *and received recommendation for promotion in 1972, Captain George lost his security clearance and was notified that in February 1979 he would be retired in the rank of captain after 16 years reckonable service. A succession of reporting officers then had no option but to give him non-recommendation for promotion, and his employment was also limited to mundane posts. He has spent five years in his current appointment which requires no security clearance. His position here gives him no incentive or satisfaction and his relaxed performance of mundane duties created a reputation for casual disinterest, lack of zeal and even unreliability. I found this attitude understandable to some degree, in an officer who had been deprived of his prospects and career, but I made it clear that a change in approach was essential. However, I felt it necessary to broaden his appointment and level of responsibility and to give him a new interest and something to aim for, which would also enable me to assess his real ability.*

He has made a remarkable response to the new challenge, which gave him an expanded repertoire in his responsibilities and several major projects to oversee. He has served on the Mess Committee as Secretary and on the Mess Executive. He played an invaluable part on the 1977 DGOS Study Period by writing and directing a talented playlet which was the focal point of the presentation. His other special projects involve him in the management of the monthly pre-Regular Commissions Board interviews and liaison with 'O' type potential officer entry, as well as implementation within the Training Centre of the Fit To Fight programme. He is now acting as Training Battalion and Depot's adjutant, and doing it well. He is experienced and able and I have found him willing to seek both responsibility and a heavy workload of military and extra mural activity, all of which he performs with energetic precision as well as putting in a great deal of evening work.

He is a polished and articulate officer with a considerable degree of talent and a pleasant personality. When unchecked he occasionally allows himself to indulge in literary licence in his written work, which is otherwise impeccable, with an ability to convey main facts with an unusual clarity. He has worked very hard and sincerely and I am pleased that he has been able to reestablish and enhance his reputation throughout the Training Centre and the Corps.

On the performance he has shown this year, I believe he has well earned for himself a reprieve and that at the age of 40 justifies especial consideration to be offered late promotion to major, which I sincerely recommend.

And just look at the revised gradings I was given this time

Characteristics	Excellent	V. Good	Good	Adequate	Weak
Zeal & Energy		x			
Reliability		x			
Commonsense		x			
Intelligence		x			
Leadership		x			
Initiative		x			
Technical Ability					
Oral Expression	x				
Written Expression	x				
Organising Ability		x			
Tact Cooperation		x			

I was his man.

My compulsory 16-year-point retirement date was to be 27 February 1979.

Despite my magical CO's strong recommendation that the system should be bent a little in order to acquire a belated promotion for me, the MoD didn't feel they could quite run to that – too much trouble – yet after all the angst and misery they'd put me through, now that my security clearance had been reinstated they had no compunction in ringing me up one day to ask if I would care to consider extending my service for a few more years.

Que?

Moi?

Porque?

Simple . . .

. . . so many officers were leaving, that they were suffering a shortfall in qualified and capable captains.

Now that I'd been allowed back into the fold, to suit their convenience I could be useful to them again.

Cheeky buggers!

Nevertheless, I thought I'd go along with it up to a point, just to see what was being offered.

"It depends what's available, Mike," I said to Mike Roberts, the chap then occupying the chair up in AG9's ivory tower.

I had first met Mike from the railway station one Sunday night when he'd come to join my then unit on Salisbury Plain, his first posting on being commissioned as a 2/Lt from Sandhurst.

His task now was a thankless one.

For the duration of his tour he had to play chess with the lives and fortunes of all his brother officers, and as such found himself to be one of the most popular and feted officers in the Corps.

He was popular anyway, but still he had to work like a Trojan trying to please all the people all the time, while struggling to maintain the overall world-wide manning plot on as even a keel as possible against an ever shifting backcloth of deaths, retirements, resignations and dismissals on the one hand, and ever changing Corps requirements on the other.

In the past there was no way I could have asked AG9 what they had to offer.

In the grand order of things AG9's desk was situated just next to that of St Peter.

Now, however, I found myself in a position to be able to say "I am no longer just a number, I'm once more nearly a person. Tempt me."

"Come up here and see us," Mike said. "We'll have a natter."

It was worth a try, so donning suit, tie and black shoes, up to London I went.

Who knew – with this belated change in fortune of mine, the Rio de Janeiro attaché's job might be up for grabs at last.

"I'll extend on one condition," I told Mike.

"What's that?" He grinned, knowing he still held all the trumps.

"Borneo, Labuan, Hong Kong; Cyprus, secondment to the Sultan of Oman's forces, BATUS (British Army Training Unit, Suffield – a vast, tundra-like Salisbury Plain near Canada's Medicine Hat) – or – I'd even consider British Military Attaché to Rio de Janeiro."

"Military Attaché to Rio, eh?" He chuckled. "You'd need a set of red tabs for that as you know, and you're not *that* much back in favour."

I thought of the wasted hours I'd spent pining for it.

"As for the others, mate; I'm sorry," he said. "No chance, I'm afraid. I've got about one vacancy for each, and they're filled. The best I can do for you is back to Germany."

Germany!

I thought about it for a moment.

It was tempting.

I loved Germany.

Good, clean living for another couple of years.

Local Overseas Allowance.

Clear my overdraft and see some more of the continent . . . but then what?

No – I had made my decision.

It was time to go.

There was no point wriggling and trying to salvage something now, at the eleventh hour.

I thanked Mike for his offer, and declined.

No more shilly-shallying now.

The die was cast.

December was nearly half way through by now, and I realised I should start preparing something tangible for my February closure.

After four years of a very well ordered bachelor existence during the week, I packed up the trappings of my comfortable room in the Mess and got them ready for the haul down to Eastbourne.

The posters and pictures came down off the walls, and I wondered if Rachel would let me put them up in the drawing room at home.

It didn't seem likely.

Raquel Welch would have looked startling over the fireplace though, in her fur bikini.

I realised our home was going to be a tad small to have four years accumulation of masculine junk superimposed atop its existing ornaments and domestic chattels. No amount of artistic arrangement or feng-shui could triumph where space was at a premium. At weekends I banged either an arm or a leg, my elbow, or sustained a bruised buttock on something every time I moved across a room there. In my new life I was going to have to work really hard to buy a place that was large enough to accommodate all my stuff.

It was Thursday 14 December.

I brought the Merc round to the front of the Mess and started to load up for my departure. There was a formidable pile: two bulging metal Twinlock files, all my B&O stereo equipment, six suitcases crammed with every conceivable assortment of books and personal items, two grips of shoes and cleaning equipment, my portable typewriter, a small palm tree, an abdominal situp board, my guitar, squash racquet and sword, silver tankards and photographs, all my clothes – and a toothbrush. The Merc's rear suspension almost left a trail of sparks behind it as I surged off from Surrey to the south like a power launch attacking a gravel drive.

The weather was foul.

The children were already home for Christmas.

There was talk of a national TV blackout.

For the next four weeks we played Battleships, Backgammon, Monopoly and Scrabble together, while gorging ourselves on dates, chocolate cakes and puddings, and I slipped deeper and deeper into a slough of despond with Britain and with my lot.

My spirits were raised by Rachel on Christmas Day, though.

I had been hankering particularly after a pair of cut glass whisky tumblers I'd set my eye on earlier in the year, and had more than a sneaking suspicion that she'd managed to get them for me. Two identically wrapped packages of the correct shape and size had certainly appeared with my name on them beneath the tree. When we opened our presents, I deliberately left them till last. Finally unwrapping one of them my expression turned from one of momentary disappointment to surprised delight when I took out, not a whisky glass, but an exquisite pewter figurine of a Royal Sussex soldier in period costume with the old Roussillon plume cap badge emblazoned in miniature on its little felt bottomed pedestal. The pleasure hit me like a soft prong. Then I opened the sister box and took out another miniature. This was a modern Corps soldier, bearing the inscription

To A Successful New Life – 1979

In January I returned to Deepcut for a few days to complete my final documentation, to hand in my ID card, to sign the Official Secrets Act, and a certificate confirming that I hadn't retained any bullets or a gun (they were in short supply) – to have a pre-release medical . . . and then to be dined out. Oh, and I also had to read and sign my *final* army confidential report, written of course by none other than Tony Sharpe.

Captain George leaves the service having completed 16 years.

During his last year in the Battalion he has fulfilled a number of regimental functions, the most prominent as Adjutant. He has shown that he has a confirmed ability to hold down a demanding and diverse appointment with care, diligence and common sense, with a great deal of energy.

Always cheerful, helpful and co-operative, with a great flair for written work where he is able to put complicated factors into a concise paper. He has a sharp and witty brain and has been a pleasure to work with. He will be a loss to the Service and he retires with the best wishes of this Battalion.

Characteristics	Excellent	V. Good	Good	Adequate	Weak
Zeal & Energy		x			
Reliability		x			
Commonsense		x			
Intelligence	x				
Leadership		x			
Initiative	x				
Technical Ability					
Oral Expression	x				
Written Expression	x				
Organising Ability		x			
Tact Cooperation	x				

What a lovely man.

Why couldn't I have served with him sooner, and hitched my wagon to *his* star, instead of being dragged along and trampled on by all those other vindictive deadbeats?

Do you wonder, that after all this Tony Sharpe and I were to become dear lifelong friends?

Coincidentally he was leaving the unit at the same time as me - not to face the unknown rigours of civilian life, but to enter the better laced echelons of the General Staff.

503

He was going to the MoD on a well deserved promotion to full Colonel.

I was privileged in that he and the Depot arranged that we should both be dined out together.

It was a memorable occasion.

When the cigars were drawing fully and the port decanter being circulated like something round a well trained ouija board, the PMC banged his gavel and announced the Colonel.

Rising precariously on his long shanks, Tony launched on a touching eulogy about the departing Captain Mike George.

When he finished I then rose, just as precariously, and made my way carefully down the table to have him shake my hand and present me with a suitably engraved silver tankard *From The Officers.*

Grinning from ear to ear I assumed a stance back at my seat, placed my tankard down on the gleaming woodwork before me, where it became instantly lost against the glittering display of candlelit Corps silver, and surveyed my brother officers, resplendent in their scarlet and black mess kit, all sitting there with hushed and upturned faces awaiting my farewell speech.

It was a deeply moving, personal moment, considering the array of bemedalled life stories all relaxed warmly ensconced about me in that special camaraderie of men who have shared and lived a lifestyle together.

On the morrow, and God willing on many morrows after that, they and all others like them would be allowed to continue to live that life, while on the morrow I would be sloughing off my khaki mantel and most (but not all) of that which went with it, and I knew that I would rue doing so.

These were my last few hours as one of my Queen and country's commissioned officers.

Because of that ghastly and quite unnecessary security nonsense it might not have been a particularly auspicious or illustrious career, or the one I'd envisaged for myself, but – albeit a tarnished one – I was still privileged to have been a proud member of that sterling fraternity.

I tugged at my mess kit waistcoat for the last time, and cleared my throat.

"Colonel Tony; Gentlemen . . ."

It was only a three minute wonder, but I said what was required to be said, and said it with feeling. As had happened to me on such occasions in the past, it made my audience aware for a moment that they too would one day be standing as I was then, saying goodnight to the Club for the last time . . .

" . . . and so, Colonel Tony, Gentlemen, my brother officers . . . after twenty years service to Queen, Country and the Corps, may I now say Thank You, God Bless, Good Night, and . . . *au revoir*."

There was a pause before the applause, and then it seemed thunderous.

Next morning I drove away from my life in the British army.

EPILOGUE

I left the army in February 1979.

Twenty-one years later – in the year 2000 - the Freedom of Information Act was passed.

Out of interest I applied to the MoD for access to my case file of 27 years previously, not believing for a moment they would release it – but they did.

It was so thick that it arrived in two tightly packed brown foolscap envelopes, the contents of which took me two days to read and digest.

I was dumbstruck with the sheer conjecture, fantasy, supposition, surmise and pure fiction it contained.

My life-crushing case had been nothing more than a secret service 'exercise'.

MI6 having thus 'set me up', I'd had no idea at the time just how much my fate was being discussed in camera, by the military hierachy upon whose desk MI6 had dumped all the fall-out from their fun.

In order to half-way resolve the hiatus with which they'd been presented, The Army Board's recommendation at the time was that my appeal against the removal of my security clearance (naturally) should fail, and – even more dramatically – *that I should be called upon to resign my commission,* and that should I refuse or neglect to submit an application to resign within 14 days, steps would be taken to terminate my commission. The Vice Chief of the General Staff himself 'concurred' with this recommendation.

Completely unaware at the time that any of this was going on, supposing that the worst that could be done to me had been done, resigned to my lot and having bought a house and put both children into public school while happily going on to rehearse *The Importance Of Being Earnest* with the Blackdown Players, The Sword of Damocles had apparently been about to be dropped upon me from a great and unforeseen height – and I'd had no idea.

Worse - no understudy.

But then at the eleventh hour a rather clever Deputy Under Secretary of State, called Mr R.C. Kent, had interceded with a tightly typed two-page submission to the VCGS, presenting certain precedents and legal and moral complexities, which in his view precluded the promulgation of the Army Board's recommendation that I should be made to resign.

Upon reflection the VCGS (thank God) agreed with him, and reversed his original decision.

The final word came from the Adjutant General, who wrote to the Military Secretary and the VCGS: *'I do not believe that the withdrawal of NV clearance, coupled with a non-adverse report, provide sufficient grounds for requiring an officer to resign his commission. It is a different matter if the reasons for the withdrawal of NV Clearance are of such a nature that they themselves provide good and reasonable grounds. In this case they do not. I am aware that by continuing to employ Captain George we are creating a number of problems for ourselves, but this is something which we must accept'.*

And I'd had no idea that any of this was taking place.

As the Duke of Wellington said, after Waterloo, 'It was a damn' close run thing.'

I was so incensed now to discover that my army career and middle years had been ruined by so much fabrication, falsehoods and uncontestable high level argy-bargy, that I sought guidance.

Whilst I abhorred the litigious society we had become, I thought that if WRAC girls could attract awards of £½m compensation for being made to leave the army after becoming pregnant, then I, too, might have a case for consideration.

I showed my file to my one time commanding officer, Colonel Tony Sharpe, who twenty years before had put his neck on the block for me and helped tremendously at the time,

507

thereby having become a close personal friend ever since. 'By God,' he said when he'd read the file, 'we all know you were a silly boy, but did they ever set you up and hang you out to dry, old son! I think you should go for it, big time - and I'll support you completely.'

This is the letter he wrote, which accompanied my claim:

I understand that as a result of previous classified information about him recently having come to hand, Captain M. A. George is submitting a claim to the Ministry of Defence for compensation.

He has asked for my support in this matter since I was his Commanding Officer during the last two years of his service.

I was aware that in 1973 his NV clearance had been withdrawn, though naturally no record of the circumstances was available. Nor was there a record of any disciplinary action having been taken.

I took command of the Training Battalion & Depot RAOC in January 1977.

I found Captain George acting as 2i/c HQ Company on the held strength of the unit, pending retirement at the 16 year point. He had been given very little responsibility and had very little of any import to do. He had been at the unit in these circumstances, hemmed impotently in by bureaucratic rocks and sharp places, quietly vegetating, for four years.

At that time, as in any regimental depot, overstretch and understaffing were normal characteristics, coupled with 'Black Holes' in officer and senior rank levels. Additional demands beyond formal roles were constant features of our everyday life within the military.

Looking into the circumstances surrounding Captain George's situation, it was clear to me that he was damned by his lack of security clearance, which resulted in his being underemployed, mismanaged and leaderless. He had been in this state for four years, and it was very important that he should urgently be given gainful employment, and some direction and incentive for what remained of this officer's demolished army 'career'. There was a wide range of tasks which needed to be handled, and my complimentary confidential report about him at this time is included within his own resumé. He responded exceptionally well and took over as Adjutant for three months while the established incumbent was taken away to do the JDSC course. He did a splendid job, rising to the occasion brilliantly. I found that I could rely on him absolutely, and he was especially valuable during the Firemen's strike when my Battalion was stretched from East Sussex to South Wales!

Investigating his loss of NV status revealed little other than an indiscretion of a disciplinary nature. This misdemeanour must have been in contravention of military discipline, yet no record of summary jurisdiction or admonishment appeared to exist. Certainly he was not warned formally. Why was this? Some formal record should have existed so that at least he could have received some guidance in his future behaviour. I did not condone his previous misdemeanour in any way, but it was also clear that he had not been given any help, advice, leadership or direction, nor had he been formally disciplined for what was obviously a military offence contrary to good order and military discipline in the first place, prior to any action being taken regarding the 'security nature' of that 'offence'.

Prior to his leaving the Service, because of his military performance and the excellent way in which he had responded to responsibility, with some help from others I persuaded the authorities that his security status should be restored to him. But the damage had been done, over the preceding seven years, with the unavoidably automatic 'non-recommendation for promotion' which senior officers were obliged to give, because of the inescapable restriction imposed by his situation.

My attempts to get him belated retrospective promotion failed, but he was nevertheless offered a limited extension of service.

Some consolation?

Perhaps.

Exoneration from previous 'sins'?

Most certainly!

But as the oldest passed over Captain in the Army, probably not a great incentive - and he declined.

Recent revelations quite clearly disclose that senior Staff Managers, VCGS, DUS (Army) and the AG were nervous over the case, acknowledging that initiating officers could not support promotion whilst without NV, and that therefore Captain George would be destined to be unable to fill a proper post pending his compulsory retirement six years hence. It was even mooted that during the interim he would 'probably' do 'something which would require the raising of an Adverse Report against him', which would then allow the army expediently to dispense with his services more easily - but since he had not even ever been the subject of an Adverse Report in the first place, hardly surprisingly - this did not happen!

The facts of the matter are that although he never warranted an Unsatisfactory Report, his offence was deemed to be so 'serious' that they took away his security clearance, which rendered a professional regular officer unemployable. He was never charged or admonished for his 'offence'. No one saw fit to give him guidance, leadership or man-management. He was condemned to low standard non jobs, although he had done nothing wrong in terms of capability. No one gave him a chance to improve his performance in a decent job. His case was being discussed in high places covertly. He was consistently denied access to anyone who would explain anything to him. A service which prides itself on honesty, truthfulness and fair play, literally 'hung this man out to dry' - until they could get rid of him conveniently. There is evidence of spiteful vindictiveness in some of his confidential reports at this time too, keeping him down rather than giving him a chance, whereas I had proof that given just a bit of incentive and management, his response was remarkable.

At a crucial time in his life, and career, he was denied the fair treatment which he needed to consolidate his position and prepare for the future. Whilst his eventual exoneration was to be welcomed, there was no recompense.

His overall punishment was disproportionate to the insignificant gravity of his offence, for which, at the time, he had not even been 'admonished'.

I believe that he has a strong case for compensation, and I would be very pleased to give evidence to this effect in any investigation.

Having prepared my 20-page Claim For Compensation, to test the water I sent it first, with an enquiring covering letter, to The Royal British Legion's Head of Pensions Department, for their reaction.

Their respondent said that, in his opinion, I had 'described the position and presented the case with precision and clarity', but felt that (for various reasons) it was not one the Legion could support.

He went on: 'It has long been known that those responsible for personal security issues operate in a world separate from the mainstream of military life, and that they are virtually unanswerable. If you come to the attention of the vetting organisation 'adversely', it can prove fatal to a career, and it has done, in many cases.

Loss of NV status is always serious, and I am afraid that your actions were bound to place your NV clearance at risk. You make the point that there are two sides to every story, but not, I am afraid, where the security services are concerned.

I cannot say how the MoD will perceive your claim.

You will have to wait and see.'

I was amused by the irony of the fact that this letter had been written (yes, really) and signed by a gentleman called Bond; James Bond.

Rather like Mr Copper the policeman, in everyday life he must have enjoyed and/or endured much more amusement from his name even than I did, from my one-off encounter with him; but he'd written me a good and considered letter, for which I was greatly appreciative.

On 24 June 2002, I submitted my case and claim for £567,642 loss of potential earnings, from 1978, and subsequent adjusted pension level, to the MoD's Directorate of Claims and Legal Affairs.

A month later, on 25 July, I received a reply.

One Sarah Richards, writing from the MoD's Service Personnel Employer's Liability Group, informed me that prior to May 1987 Service personnel were prevented from pursuing claims for compensation from the MoD by Section 10 of the Crown Proceedings Act 1947. However, Section 10 was now repealed by the Crown Proceedings Act 1987 - but which was not made retrospective.

'As your service in HM Forces preceded the repeal of Section 10 therefore, I am legally prevented from paying you any compensation.'

That was it.

Job done.

Coffin lid now finally shut and firmly screwed.

Game, set and match.

They get you every which way.

My case was now irrevocably closed.

I had been brought up to respect my elders and superiors, but the older I became the harder I found this to do.

Why *should* the security forces have remained permanently unquestioned, unanswerable, unapproachable, non accountable; inviolate?

Then think on – to the June/July 2009 *Daily Telegraph's* highly acclaimed revelations about UK MPs' expenses abuses, brought to light by . . . an ex army officer – ? appropriately enough, SAS to be exact - one John Wick; bless him!

(What ever happened to *him*?)

And just before *that* long running major event, we had the Gurkhas scandal, so ably resolved by the bloody-minded determination of Joanna Lumley – a national treasure and iconic high born actress; bless her, too!

More of us need to stand up and be counted.

It's called Revolution.

Especially now that militant Islam is so successfully taking over the whole of Europe, the West, our Heritage, our Culture, our Religion – and soon, almost inevitably - our Politics and our Law . . .!

Then there was Henry Allingham (British *HISTORY*) - at 113 the oldest man in Britain, if not the whole world. He was born in the reign of Queen Victoria, was the oldest of the three sole remaining gentlemen who served in WWI, he was awarded the *Croix De Guerre* by the French, and yet despite much forceful representation by all and sundry, when he passed away on 19 July 2009 it was *sans* even having been granted so much as an MBE in the British Honours List.

What a measly-mouthed, crooked and inept bunch of A1, chateau-bottled, ocean-going, silver-plated dildos so many of our lousy leaders seem to be!

And what a note . . .

. . . upon which the 'rulers' of 'my country' . . .

. . . oblige me to close.

The trouble with Britain is that it takes such a long time, so much goading . . . and so much provocation, before the *Nice* people wise-up, get serious, and start to turn Nasty!

THE END

. . . of this part of the ongoing saga

Lightning Source UK Ltd.
Milton Keynes UK
11 November 2010

162720UK00001B/204/P